Highway to Heaven

GIANNA MARIA

Printed in the United States of America

Cover designed by Gianna Maria
Character art by Yadira Ortíz – yadi.oc@gmail.com
Editors: Tracy Roelle and Theresa Huber from Valkyrie Editing
Headshot photo by Ted Lee Photographer / ted@bizphotorapher.com

Paperback ISBN: 979-8-9907450-0-1
E-book ISBN: 979-8-9907450-1-8

CONTENTS

DISCLAIMER

This is a work of fiction. Every novel character is fictitious. Unless otherwise indicated, all names, characters, business, product, titles, places, events, and incidents in this book are either the product of the author's imagination or used in a fictitious manner for storytelling and entertainment purposes only, nothing more. Any resemblance to actual persons, living, dead, undead, or actual events, names, titles, business, products, places, on this planet, galaxy, or any alternative in the multiverse, events, or incidents is purely coincidental. No joke. I'm serious.

Even though I studied the K-pop industry for several months, I'm no expert but try my best to resemble how the K-pop music industry works. I took some liberties with some themes, since this is a work of fiction. This book is meant to entertain. Read it with an open mind. I promise you're in for an enjoyable ride that will entice your mind and senses. That's all that I want. This is not your usual love story.

Fly away with us, baby…

TRIGGER WARNINGS

EXPLICIT INTIMACY

SEXUAL THREAT

PHYSICAL ASSAULT

SHOOTING, BLOOD

ACKNOWLEDGMENT

First, *and most of all,* ***GOD****, without Him, nothing in my life could be possible.*

Second, ***Aurea Esther*** *and* ***Nelson Samuel****, you're the wind beneath my wings. Mom loves you to eternity and back. Even though we're miles apart, you're always with me.*

Third, *my brothers* ***Aurea Mercedes, Reinaldo***, ***and Haydee*** *for always being there for me. I couldn't make it without you. Thanks for all the encouraging words and support when I was down. I love you all to eternity and back.*

Fourth, ***Tania Gonzalez****, thanks for being there when I needed you the most. You're part of this process. You hold me up in my darkest moments, lifting me. I have a debt that I will never be able to repay you. Thank you.*

Fifth, ***Esq. Maria Jose Matta****, the word thank you doesn't cover my feelings. The way you encourage me to pursue my dream and pump me up is above and beyond. I'm so proud of who you are, and the future looks so bright for you. Dare to dream big. Remember the universe is the limit. May the force be with you, always.*

Sixth, ***Dr. Lauren Kim****, more than a doctor, you've became a true friend for me. Thanks for your hugs, your words of encouragement, and your time to check my Korean references* *are respectful and on point. I have learned so much from you. I'm forever in your debt.*

Seven, ***Earl Craig and Jessica Garcia****, for your encouragement to continue when I was down and ready to give up. You're my family, and I'm grateful to have you beside me through this journey, witnessing all the ups and downs this road has taken me. But the best is to see each other grow.*

Eight, *but not least, my "saviors"*
I was going to name them but, at the last moment, decided not to. One night, they entered my life without having been invited and saved me. The details of that night are mine to keep. They'll learn the details when ready. They teach me there's always another opportunity in life while I'm still breathing.

The freedom these gentlemen gifted me is unparalleled. I'll treasure their lesson until my last breath on this earth. Lessons sometimes come at unexpected times from the most unexpected persons.

I'm not afraid anymore of what the future holds for me.

There are a lot more people along the way who were key for this project to be born. Please forgive me for not mentioning you all; you know who you are. Thanks for holding me through this crazy, profound, painful learning experience.

To eternity, my heart will always belong to you all…
I honor you all with this book…

For Carlo Xavier

1992-2021

Nunca te olvidaré, hijo...

Chapter One

Gabriella

"Even before you touched me, I belonged to you;
all you had to do was to look at me..."
Louise Glück.

I'm certain the eyes are the windows of the soul. You can know how a person is by just looking into their eyes. *Eyes speak; they never lie.* When a person is true, pure, and honest, you notice it instantly just observing them; you feel it. They're clear and transparent. They show who they are inside without inconvenience. The eyes smile. On the contrary, if the person is untruthful, mean, or hiding something from you, they're foggy and clouded. Usually they avoid the stare to hide their true self. Knowing this has served me well to identify who I'm dealing with. I'm good at this. It takes me time to trust someone. But I always stare to get the initial glimpse of who they are. Eyes tell the story.

Why I'm like this? I've been hurt so many times, in so many ways, for trusting the wrong people. I've become cautious. I don't have many close friends. I know lots of people, but I only have a handful of friends.

I'm a loner and prefer to solve things myself rather than asking for help from anyone. This isn't healthy, I know. We should be surrounded by people who can cover our backs in times of need, people we can trust. But life's hardness has taught me to be this way, to survive on my own. I wish I could trust more easily, and also, maybe, love again.

Love… Another notion I'm positive I've never achieved in my life. Yeah, I thought I fell in love a couple of times in the past. Now I don't see it as a possibility for me in the future. I think it's too late and have accepted it's never going to happen. Truth is, my past failed relationships and marriage made me believe I'm unworthy of being loved. Sure it would be nice to be loved again, but I don't dare to hope, not anymore.

All these thoughts are rambling in my mind as I'm arriving at my apartment from a routine medical appointment. Dropping my purse on the bed, the doorbell rings. *Ug, who could it be now?*

"COMING."

Looking through the peephole, I see Saba, my next door neighbor. Saba is a sweet, old, Ethiopian lady who checks on me, even though I'm a fifty-two-year-old woman who doesn't need to be checked on. But I truly appreciate her kindness. We'd spoken last week about her moving to another state soon. I open the door to greet her.

"Saba, hi. How are you doing?"

"Hi, Gabriella. Just coming to say goodbye. We finished loading the last boxes in the truck, so we're leaving now."

"It's today? It's so soon. I haven't had a chance to cook for you before you leave." I see the mother's tenderness in her eyes.

"Don't worry, sweetie. Perhaps on another occasion. They've told me at the leasing office someone is moving in this Saturday. You won't be alone for long."

I don't want another neighbor. I'll miss Saba deeply. She's been a great company since Xavier moved to Arizona. He left barely six months ago to pursue his career as a computer engineer. These past six months, I've been battling Empty Nest Syndrome.

"I brought you this, dear."

She hands me a beautiful white and pink ceramic teapot I saw in her apartment one time.

"Why are you're giving this to me? I know this is precious to you."

"No, no. Take it." She pushes the teapot into my hands. "It's a farewell present so you remember me." She watches me with teary eyes.

I've been so emotional lately. I'm trying to avoid prolonging the drama. I take the teapot and give her my heartfelt answer.

"Even if you hadn't given me this, I'll always remember you, Saba. Thank you."

I kiss her cheek and put the teapot on the mud bench to hug her tightly. I'm kind of a hugger. It's in my blood as a proud Puerto Rican.

Releasing her, I put my hands on her shoulders—she seems so tiny, right now—reassuring her.

"Please keep me updated. Let me know when you arrive, deal?" I'm going to miss her dearly. Tears starts to cloud my eyes. Shit.

"You let me know how you're doing. You know, if there are any changes." Saba watches me, seriously concerned. I have to call Xavier and finally tell him. I'll deal with it later.

"Deal. Promise."

After our final hug and kisses, I stand at my doorway, observing her fragile figure walking slowly down the hallway to the parking lot entrance. I see myself reflected in her, thinking about my life. Is it my destiny to walk alone for the rest of my days? I watch her until she disappears from my view. A heaviness sinks in my chest. I'm alone now. I don't care who will move in next door. No one will replace Saba.

Closing the door again, I take the teapot, gazing closely at it. My mind is buzzing with thoughts on where my life is heading. No, I don't want to think. There's too much sorrow overflowing in my heart. I'm depressed. Involuntary tears stain my face, so I go to wash it. Splashing water, I look up, seeing my reflection in the mirror. I've never felt so old and alone as I do in this moment.

I observe myself closely. I've lost weight. As result of my meds, I eat less than I used to, almost recovering my younger body. I have received compliments that I look younger than my age, but I don't feel younger, right now. I don't feel pretty either.

Sad, broken-down, and lonely are the emotions swirling around in my brain, tormenting me. Dropping myself on my bed, I start crying. Ultimately I cry every night. Tonight I weep until I fall asleep. I'm definitely spiraling into my depression again. The sorrow overtakes me, and I can't control it.

The next few days, the only thing I do to ignore this engulfing sadness is occupying my mind with whatever distracts me. My book editing, gym workouts, and even inviting Lola to have lunch at my apartment this Sunday is part of it. Saturday morning arrives. I'm walking with my headphones on from my daily workout, seeing lots of moving trucks at the leasing office parking. I recall the new neighbor should arrive today.

I always take the freight elevator near the leasing parking lot because is the nearest to my apartment. I encounter the elevator is crowded as men in uniforms bring furniture up to our floor. Even being spacious, I don't want to be crammed in front with all those men. Pushing myself between them, receiving their uncomfortable stares, I stand at the back to avoid their comments. I'm humming Ednita Nazario's song *Metamorfosis* playing from my playlist. There isn't a Puerto Rican woman who doesn't embrace this anthem of empowerment every time is heard.

I get out at my floor's small lobby, to walk across to the entrance of the hallway. Several boxes are aligned on the floor. I'm stepping carefully to avoid tripping over one.

Glancing sideways, I see the moving guys carrying a big mattress, struggling to pass by me. I move to the right to give them space, colliding with someone I hadn't seen. Tripping on my feet, I almost fall on my face, but big, strong hands grab my arms, steadying me. Embarrassed and shaken for avoiding a major concussion, I stand up straight and turn to face my savior.

I'm dazzled by this young Asian man, over six feet tall—I'm 5'9" and have to look up—with assessing caramel eyes and dark brown, soft undercut hair, standing before me. He seems a couple of years older than Xavier. He's hot as hell; it's undeniable.

His skin is flawless. It's obvious he takes good care of himself. My eyes roam down to his soft, full, rosy peach lips and bright smile. Neatly dressed in dark blue jeans, his gray shirt, with sleeves rolled up to his elbows, hugs his muscles nicely.

For an instant, I'm spellbound. Could pass by one of those

Asian fashion magazine models. Shaking myself from my trance, full of shame, I apologize.

"I'm so sorry; it's my fault. I didn't realize someone was walking behind me. I only saw the movers. That's why I'd moved over, to give them space to pass." Blabbing quickly, I'm unable to unlock my eyes from him. He did something with the tip of his tongue, pressing it between his lips. Kind of like an involuntary tick, but flirty. The brightest smile welcomes me with an answer.

"No need to apologize." His voice is raspy, deep. "I'm glad I was able to catch you. Let's do this the right way. I'm Lukas, moving into 378. And you are?" He extends his hand to shake mine. *Lord, this kid looks so good it's disturbing.*

I shake my head before answering.

"Sorry. Gabriella, your next-door neighbor." I point to my door and shake his hand. Big hands, long sleek fingers, and several rings, none indicating he's married, just showing his taste for current fashion, nice. *God, Gabriella.* You have to overanalyze everyone.

"Nice to meet you, Gabriella." He squeezes my hand gently. A gentleman, double plus.

Another handsome young man approaches us, stopping where we are. He has black, short hair, but it's a little more rogue looking than Lukas's. Sharp cheekbones frame the newcomer's face with sunglasses resting on his nose, and he has the most adorable dimples, enhancing his already good looks. He's wearing ripped jeans, white sneakers, and a white t-shirt with a jacket. They must be college students from the Chapman University nearby, staying here for the upcoming semester, I assume. He turns to Lukas, smirking.

"Did you already begin flirting with the beautiful ones in the building?"

Turning to face me, he speaks, "Don't believe anything he's said. By the way, my name is Marc, nice to make your acquaintance." He smiles with another devastating smile, more wolf-like. Chuckling, I shake his hand. They both seem nice and are handsome as hell.

"Gabriella, your next-door neighbor."

"I wish. No, sadly this loser is your new neighbor. I'm just a passing-by friend who envies him for being so damn lucky to live next to a gorgeous woman." Punching playfully at Lukas's shoulder, he raises an eyebrow.

I couldn't avoid blushing at his remark. Lukas's face, upset and gaping at his friend, is hilarious. My laughter explodes. I'm sure he wants to strangle him. *Typical of younger men to be this playful and flirty.* I give them my best smile.

"Well, nice to meet you both. I'll leave you two to your moving in and get out of the way."

Inserting the key, there's this urge in my mind to turn back. Finding Lukas staring vehemently, I'm startled by the intensity of his gaze.

I nervously blurt, "I'll be here if you guys need anything. So again, welcome to the neighborhood."

"I apologize for Marc's behavior." Lukas gives him a deadly look. Marc lowers his face with a funny gesture, making me chuckle loud again. I already like him. He's won me over.

"That's my cue to leave. Nice meeting you, Gabriella. I look forward to seeing you again."

Lowering his shades to wink at me, he smiles. Lukas's infuriated face is comical.

"Again, please excuse my friend's conduct. He shouldn't be disrespectful to you. Sometimes he doesn't know how to behave or control his mouth."

"No need for apologies, no harm done. Besides he can pass as a Puerto Rican. Some Puerto Ricans behave the same way, so I'm used to it."

I talk too much when I'm nervous.

"You're from Puerto Rico?"

His eyes light up, and he sounds truly excited. I wasn't expecting this reaction.

"Yep."

"I would love to visit Puerto Rico. It's on my bucket list to visit in the future."

"Well, if you travel any day soon, I can give you some tips on good places to eat and visit."

We stand there, in this uncomfortable silence, gazing at each other. He seems eager to continue talking, but I don't know what to say. I break the silence.

"Well I'll be out of the way and let you finish. We'll see each other around. Bye, Lukas."

Closing the door behind me, I recline against it, jittery. Glancing through the peephole, he's still staring at my door. Nervously, I walk away to the bathroom.

Why am I suddenly so anxious? I'm behaving like a flustered high school girl. Internally it feels good, this tiny spark inside, but it's just an instant. I reprimand myself.

"Oh, girl, you're imagining things again. What the hell are you thinking? He's being polite, that's all. That kid could be your son. He should be around Xavier's age, no doubt. Sure, he's good looking…really good looking… Oh, stop it."

Shaking my head, I discard those thoughts. Taking off my gym clothes, I enter the shower, realizing I need to cool my thoughts urgently.

Lukas

Entering my apartment, I carry one of the boxes stacked outside in the hall, going straight to where Marc is unpacking one.

"What the hell, Marc? You just can't control yourself, huh? For you, it's like an itch to be like this."

"Chill, bro. She seems really cool and nice. I'm sure she didn't mind. Besides you got some sexy *ajumeoni* nearby. Damn fine, that one." He winks while grinning wickedly at me.

"Oh, my God. You're the one who needs to chill out. You need help with the overflow of hormones you have." I roll my eyes, snickering. We both laugh.

"Why didn't you stay in the apartment the record company offered you at the complex in LA? They're bigger, private, and the company will pay for it. You'd be near them."

"No. I convinced them I prefer an unknown place so that my creativity can flow freely, to be alone outside the media frenzy going on there. Like a normal person, to work without interruptions. These two productions are important for Ty's career and mine. Besides, I don't like LA. It's crowded and dirty. I need this time to decide what I'm doing next."

"Are you planning to retire?"

"You know this is my passion. Just figuring out if I stay with the record company after the album and tour is finished, or move on by myself. Okay? Can you get some food for us?"

"I can order some."

"Thanks. We still have a lot to do. My stomach is growling already."

Walking to my bedroom, I address one of the movers.

"Once you finish assembling the bed, just bring the rest of the boxes inside. We will finish unpacking what's left."

"Right away, Sir."

Overjoyed, I can hardly describe what my heart is experiencing right now. I finally negotiated a way to obtain my own space away from everyone. This time of solitude is so precious to me.

Time far from the madness back in Seoul with the music industry and fans. Away from the record company so I can breathe without the constant nagging or intrusion in my work.

I need this so badly to clear my mind and to decide the next step in my life and music career. I'm aware I'm more than lucky to obtain this. The record company and my manager, under normal circumstances, wouldn't allow it.

My thoughts trail off to Gabriella, the neighbor I'd just met. Even though she's an older woman, she's exquisite and uniquely breathtaking. She'd seemed so nervous when we'd bumped into each other. And Puerto Rican.. From the island of Ricky Martin, Bad Bunny, and other artists I admire. I've always had a thing for Latinas.

Gabriella. She's pretty damn fine, like Marc said. Tan, golden skin, plump, rosy lips. Hypnotic dark eyes and a delightful smile showing a pair of dimples make her stunning and youthful. Almost my height, great body. Those hips and curves, *Jesus.* She takes good care of herself.

I'd watched her from inside the elevator. Her headphones had her murmuring some Spanish song, swaying her hips to the beat. She was clueless I was standing behind her, hidden by some furniture in the back. I followed her, walking closely behind. Her black gym clothes hugged her curves so deliciously.

That body is asking to be taken care of. The tightening in my groin tells me so. Her black pixie haircut frames her charming face perfectly. I hadn't seen a ring on her finger, so maybe she's not married. *Come on, Lukas. Stop it.* She could be your mom. The truth is, *she isn't.* I chuckle wickedly. She could be an enticing adventure to add to my long list of conquests.

"Do you want me to order pizza or fried chicken?" Marc queried.

"You know I can always go for fried chicken," I reply, smiling satisfied.

Gabriella

Well, I did it. The truth is, I was avoiding telling him, because I know he can get out of control. I can't deal with drama right now.

Yep, I called Xavier on the phone. He's doing great in Arizona, and business is blossoming there. I'm relieved I'm able to open up. He finally knows what's going on with my health. He kind of freaked out at first, like I'd predicted, but calmed with the truth. I'm taking care of myself, and as of now, everything is under control, thank God. He babbles some nonsense about jumping on a plane to be with me, but I forbid it. I promised him if anything changes, he'll be the first one to know.

I finish applying my facial creams. I plan to do some work on my laptop before going to sleep. Observing the clock on my bedside table, it is 12:30 am. Nope, no work at this hour.

Shit, it's late, I'm not sleepy, and Lola is coming tomorrow. I put on my satin bathrobe and go to the kitchen to prepare some chamomile tea to help me sleep. With my hot mug, I head straight to my balcony to sit down and just sip it and relax.

My mind goes to my new neighbor, Lukas. There's something about him I can't put my finger on. He's unusually handsome, truly a gentleman. Not common in young people these days. He seems so mature in the way he expresses himself. It makes me wonder what has happened in his life that's made him have to mature so quickly. To be so formal.

Finishing my tea, I put the mug on the chair to stand at the rail, watching nature at night. An ambulance siren sounds in the distance, while I stand there enjoying the cold breeze blowing and the peaceful night silence in the building. I love the view of the gardens below from my balcony. They are breathtaking.

There are a lot of trees and flowers, and the sunsets here are picturesque. The sweet smell of jasmine bushes rising from the gardens is soothing. It's a beautiful night with stars filling the sky. Usually I can't see them, and tonight there's a full moon that looks bewitching.

"You too, huh?" asks a deep, raspy voice, scaring the hell out of me.

Startled, I look around to see where it came from. Glancing to my left, I discover Lukas on his balcony, half naked, torso over the rail. It took me several seconds to realize it's him. *Wow, those muscles are impressive.*

"Shit, Jesus Christ. You scared me. I wasn't expecting anyone to be out here at this hour." With my heart in my throat and my hand on my chest, I'm breathing heavily.

Letting out a soft laugh, observing my face, he shows his

bright, gorgeous smile. Yep, he does that thing again, biting the tip of his tongue. I'm beginning to like it.

I notice he has a tattoo on the right side of his torso. The head of an African lion with blue eyes painted so lifelike it seems like the lion is watching you. It's beautifully drawn.

"Sorry, didn't mean to scare you. I couldn't sleep either. It's my first night away from my family. It still feels weird. And Marc's snoring doesn't help." He looks straight to the stars.

"I like Marc," I confess, casually grinning, lowering my eyes.

"You like him?"

I hear a tone of disappointment. Immediately I clarify.

"Don't misunderstand me. I like his personality; he seems funny. A free spirit, big heart, that's it."

"I see…"

"I like you too, Lukas."

Raising his eyes to meet mine, the initial spark I saw earlier has returned to his eyes.

"I like you too, Gabriella."

It surprises me until he adds, nervously, "I would like very much for us to be friends. If it's okay with you, of course." He lowers his eyes in a sign of embarrassment.

I giggle sympathetically. "Of course, I'd love to be friends with you guys. It's hard to move alone to a place where no one knows who you are and with no friends or family nearby, I suppose."

"My family is in Seoul. I came here for business purposes. I'll be here for about a year."

Business. I'm the one feeling disappointed somehow. Just a year until I'll go through the process of losing another neighbor.

"Don't get me wrong, I'm here to fulfill a contract but haven't decided if I'll return to Seoul or stay working here." Did he read my mind or maybe my facial expression?

A cool breeze blows, disheveling his soft hair. The moonlight paints a perfect picture on him, his ripped muscles marked by the soft light. The veins in his arms making him seem much older and his fair skin glowing under the light.

He must exercise a lot to be this fit. Lord, some place, there are girls dreaming and drooling about this guy. The woman who wins his heart is going to be a lucky one.

He oozes a sensuality through his pores without even realizing how powerful it is. It gives him this air of maturity. He seems older, grown-up, even more than Xavier. He doesn't just enter a room with his presence; he stands out in it. Shit. That tongue-biting he does makes me fluster.

"It's ok. It's your life, your choice. You have plenty of time to decide."

"True."

"My best advice is to always choose where your passion lies, what makes you feel accomplished. Do whatever makes you happy, Lukas. It's what life is about, that simple. People usually complicate things with rules and other nonsense."

I fix my gaze on him. Another awkward quietness fills the space between us as we stare at each other. His eyes darken dangerously. I'm somehow uncomfortable with the way he's gazing at me. I break the silence.

"Well, I'll retire now, need to sleep. You should get some rest too."

"Sleep well, Gabriella." Curious eyes observe me.

"You, too." With one last stare over my shoulder, I go inside. Closing the sliding door, I put the mug in the sink before entering my room to take my satin robe off and slip under the covers.

Turning the lights off, I think of him. He seems to be a gentle soul on a soul searching journey. I'm positive he's on the right track. Where he's supposed to be.

Hello future...

Lukas

Still surveilling Gabriella's balcony, she's left me mesmerized. Damn, what a fascinating woman she is. Stunning, different, centered, sexy as hell, and aged to perfection.

She'd glowed under the moonlight, her skin, the contrast of her lavender satin nightgown she was wearing. So damn sexy. Her supple breasts had risen and fallen with each breath. The way she had watched me, I know I've affected her too. The breeze had blown her scent, and I inhaled it. Sweet gardenia, so sensuous. She has a certain calmness, security in who she is. The craving at the end of my fingertips prickles with curiosity to touch her. Feel the softness of her skin. Fuck. I'm struck by her. To tease my mind the way she does, that's powerful in a woman.

Yep, I prefer older women. I've had my fair share of hormonal, dumb-witted girls and women around my age. I'm attracted to a woman who can give you a good, intelligent conversation, along with her good looks.

Obviously her *experience* is a plus. She must know some impressive hip moves. I grin wickedly to myself. But I've never been with a woman this much older. I presume she should be pretty close to my mom's age. An intriguing woman indeed. There's something I can't put my finger on. I see her as she is. She doesn't seem to hide anything. Inside of me, a little obsession with her is starting.

Closing the sliding door, I glance where Marc is sleeping on the sofa bed, soundly and snoring funny. I couldn't avoid chuckling.

I walk in to my room and slide under my covers, thinking of her. She sounds like a wise woman who could teach me, lead me. Who knows? With luck, she can make up for my flaws. Either way, I'm going to enjoy it.

You're my missing puzzle piece... Finally it fits...

Chapter Two

Gabriella

The doorbell rings, and I hurry up to open it after closing the lid of my rice pot. There's Lola, all smiles and cheering.

"Gabriella, *Bonita* you look amazing. How are you doing, girl?" she greets and hugs me.

I know she loves this sleeveless, yellow, cotton knee-length dress. She's mentioned it before. It feels comfortable hugging my curves. The temperature is particularly warm today, so it's perfect to wear.

"Lolita, so nice to see you. Thanks for the compliment. Lunch is almost ready, so make yourself at home." I step aside to let her in.

At the office, Lola is the most cheerful of us all. She's twenty-nine years old, almost my height, awesome body, beautiful face, and long, wavy, brunette hair. Her big, joyful, green eyes are stunning. She can give any man *the look*, and he'll madly fall right at her feet. Born in Mexico, she's lived all her life in the States. She's my assistant at the publishing company where I work as the lead associated editor.

Being one of the top editors in California gains me respect among my peers. I will maintain my reputation among publishing companies in the state with a recent book I'd worked on. It is another sure hit on the shelves. My line of work and position allows me the advantage to work from home whenever I want to.

I've bonded with Lola because we both come from hard backgrounds. Life wasn't easy for either of us, though it was harder for her. She came through with a noble, kind heart I adore and respect so much. Even though she's young, she's wise beyond her age. I adore her spontaneity, her joyful character. In simple words, we understand each other's craziness.

"Smells so good." Lola bends to stare inside the oven. "Is that roast pork?"

"*Pernil, querida.*" I reply with my *Puerto Rican* accent. We laugh.

"Do you want a michelada before eating?" I ask as I pull the glasses from the cabinet.

"You know I do. With lots of tajin and lime, please."

I'm about to prepare the micheladas when the doorbell rings.

"You're expecting someone else?" Lola asks puzzled.

"Nope."

I look through the peephole, finding Lukas standing at my front door. He's dressed in a Lakers' T-shirt showing his well-built arm muscles, jeans, gold earrings, and a scared expression. I open the door immediately, and wide eyes stare at me from head to toes.

"Lukas, hi. Everything ok?"

"Eh… Sorry to bother you. I was hoping you may have a

small flathead screwdriver I can use. We're assembling a desk, and we don't have one. Please, say you do."

I giggle to his playful, pleading face.

"I have a toolbox with several screwdrivers, even an electrical one. Let me get them. Come on in while I fetch it."

"Thanks. You're a lifesaver. Saves me a trip to the store."

Turning to Lola, I introduce Lukas.

"Lola, I'd like you to meet my new next-door neighbor, Lukas. Lukas, this is Lola, my assistant and friend."

Walking to my coat closet to get the toolbox, I catch him staring around at my apartment, fixed on my movie poster wall.

Lola's eyes widen seeing him. A big smile surfaces to greet him, extending her hand.

"The pleasure is all mine."

I observe the eye trick she does when flirting. For the first time, I'm uneasy watching her flirt. He's clueless, unaware of her tease.

"I apologize for the interruption. Lola, nice meeting you."

"Do I know you from somewhere? Your face looks familiar to me."

Grabbing his hand to shake it, Lola can't hide her fascination with the handsome man Lukas is.

"No, don't think so. I'm from South Korea. We arrived yesterday."

Why am I uncomfortable seeing her flirt? I shouldn't feel like this; it's not ok. He's perfect for Lola. I think they're around the same age. Understanding this doesn't help the way I feel.

"Here you go." I hand my toolbox to him. Lukas takes it quickly.

Glancing directly at me, he blurts, "Nice dress."

"Thanks."

After a brief pause, I feel the impulse to invite him to eat with us.

"I just finished making lunch. There's plenty of food. I usually cook enough for an army. Do you guys want to eat or have you eaten already?"

His expressive eyes brighten up, like he had been hoping to hear what I just said.

"Yes." Lola jumps to answer.

I'm perplexed and surprised by her outburst.

"You should have lunch with us."

I stand near Lukas, watching him intently. I hold my laugh at her reaction.

"No, we haven't eaten yet. And it smells delicious in here."

I'm aware he smiles with his eyes, making his face glow more.

"It sure does." Lola blurts, still flirting.

His face turns serious, realizing she's hitting on him. The situation becomes awkward. He starts to walk backward.

"I'll go now. I'll talk to Marc, and we'll come back as soon we finish. Nice meeting you, Lola." We exchange looks between us.

Both grabbing the doorknob at the same time, I accidentally caress his hand, pulling back quickly. I swear I feel some kind of electricity. Maybe it's static.

"Sorry." I apologize, flustered.

"Don't be…"

Raising an eyebrow, he's smirking at me. My cheeks heat to red. Grinning with a satisfied attitude, he walks out. Closing the door behind him, I'm flushed and disturbed.

I turn to find Lola watching me with an amused face, grinning wickedly.

"*Nena*, that Asian god is so hot. And you standing there next that hunk of a man, come on, Gaby. That piece of meat is Grade A choice. And to have a "plumbing service" this good next door is a major plus. Impressive body, tall, hotter than the sun… You can't deny it."

"Yeah, sure. For you," I argue nervously. "He could be my son. That's a big *No* for me."

"But he's not Xavier, sweetie." She grins mischievously.

I raise my hand, signaling for her to stop it.

"No, no, no. Don't you even think about it. I don't want anyone calling me a cougar or some shit like that. No way in a million years."

I'm pissed off. The truth is, I'm not only upset by Lola's remark but by Lukas's *Don't be…* Sounded like he's sure he can have his way with me. Who does he think I am? An easy target? The lonely, mature lady needs companionship; maybe she's eager for some attention. Surely he's accustomed to women falling for his looks, but he must know not everyone falls for it. I'm upset he thinks I am so easily obtained.

"Why? You're still a beautiful woman. You're single, without commitments. Sure, he's young, but who cares? Don't go all Handmaid's Tale on me. I know you. Maybe happiness is just next door." She's winking at me.

I respect Lola's wisdom immensely, which is always on point. Even being younger than me, she's wise beyond her years. I understand it's my Puerto Rican culture getting in my head and holding me back. In Puerto Rico, I'd be ostracized for dating a younger man. They're so judgmental about these things. So my upbringing is a powerful mixture, preventing any possibility of anything happening between us.

"Let me serve those micheladas. Extra tajin and lime for

both of us."

"Now you're talking. I'm thirsty after all that hotness around here," Lola replies, slapping her hand on the kitchen countertop, laughing.

Lukas

Walking with the toolbox in hand, I'm grinning to myself. *I really like this woman.* She's ravishing in that yellow dress. The contrast of her tan skin against the yellow fabric is simply exquisite. There are some sparks there. I sense it. The electricity was palpable when she touched my hand. She was on edge. So bewitching. She's messing up my mind. It's not her looks; it's the confidence and sensuality she exudes. Her sultriness is stuck in my head. A woman who knows what she wants and is secure in herself. For me, that's potent stuff. A dangerous and tempting mixture.

"Does Gabriella have any screwdrivers?" Marc asks the moment he sees me. I lift my hand to show him the toolbox I'm carrying.

"Sweet. A handywoman too. Man, you definitely hit the jackpot there." He chuckles.

"I'm beginning to think you're right. By the way, Gabriella has a guest and invited us to have lunch with them. Please, behave and don't embarrass me again. Okay?"

"Homemade food? I'm in. Let's finish this quickly. I'll be polite; at least I'll try." Marc extends his hand to grab the toolbox.

My cellphone rings. Our manager, Baek Jong, is calling. I

answer, speaking in Korean.

"*Annyeong*, Jong. I wasn't expecting your call so soon."

"*Annyeong*, Lukas. Relax, I'm just making sure you're getting settled ok. Is everything as you expected?"

"Oh, it's better than I could have imagined." My answer is heartfelt, but I'm thinking of Gabriella.

"That's good to know. Just to remind you, the presentation by Marc and Ty in LA is in three weeks. I need you to be present. If everything goes according to plan, we'll be arriving next week. That way, we can coordinate a meeting in person before the presentation."

"Sounds good. I already have the last four songs of Ty's album, although they are missing some minor adjustments on the sheet music. I also have two more songs finished for mine."

"That's awesome, Lukas. You're a talented, hard worker. That record is going to be a sure hit once the public hears it. See you around in one week. *Sugo-hae. Hwaiting.*"

"I'll work hard. See you there, Jong." He ends the call.

"Jong checking on you?"

"Obviously he's gonna check on me. He's the one who made this possible." I point around the apartment.

"You're so lucky they allowed you this. We all think so. The company doesn't do things like this. Make us proud, man."

I'm grateful Marc's here to share this moment. He's been by my side since the beginning of our journey in the music business as trainees, friends, and brothers.

We're singers in a male group from South Korea called SMX18. Each of us are on a hiatus from the group activities while four of us developed our own solo careers. The other three are fulfilling their conscription military service. I had decided to do mine earlier to be done with it. I've been the front face of the group with Marc from the start.

Marc was the first to launch his solo career, turning out to be a complete success with his rap-urban style music back in Asia, which he's now bringing to the States. One of our bandmates, Kim, had his own debut after Marc, featuring an upbeat, sultry style of music that fans back home love. It went number one on the charts in no time. Now it's Ty's turn. His music has a metal-vibe, which aligns more with the American taste. I don't have any doubt it's going to be another success. The first single and arrangement I made for him released in Seoul a couple of weeks ago. Fans love it, making it climbing to the top of the charts too. It's time to make the American public fall in love with our music, to open doors for us.

Because of my involvement on those projects, executives have noticed my input benefits the company in many ways, including increasing profits. When my recommendations are taken into consideration, the singles turn into hits, which equals a higher income for them.

They'd once called me the *Golden Child*, a term used when a singer not only has a great voice but also can adjust to any type of music style, is a leader, a talented songwriter, plus a superb dancer. There's a burden on my shoulders to be better because of this.

They're conscious my contract ends soon, and I'm aware their agreeable behavior is to butter me up. Their constant praise shows they see a great future in the business for me. I'm smart enough to see their actions as exactly what they are. I'll deal with things my way. That's how I got to live a year alone in exchange for Ty's record and mine with them. After this, I'll be free to do as I please. I can sign with another company or create my own with the backup of investors on the projects

I wish to develop. That's why all the connections I've acquired during my time in LA will help me launch my career further.

"I will; you'll see. Let's finish this."

Gabriella

Lukas helps me collect the dishes and puts them in the sink after we finish our lunch. It's been quite a while since I've had so much fun and laughed so often. These guys are hilarious, especially Marc. We had a fun conversation during lunch, getting to know a little bit more of each other. They both seems so amenable, sharing stories, knowing each other, giggling.

Marc stares at the ceiling, eyes half closed. "My God, Gabriella, that was so good. I've never tasted pork with these spices. That's how you do it in PR?" He rubs his belly and lets out a chuckle.

"Yes. I can teach you how to cook it. It's not difficult."

"Don't teach me. Teach Lukas. He's a master chef himself."

Glancing at him, he's observing me, amused.

"You cook?"

"Yeah, but not as good as this."

Laughing mischievously, Lola adds, "You should exchange recipes and cook for us. We'll sacrifice to taste them. Even if we die of food poisoning." She's exchanging flirty looks with Marc, who's chuckling.

Grinning suspiciously, I know what she's trying to pull.

"It would be nice to exchange recipes."

"Sure. Next time it's my turn to cook for you." *God, he's doing that thing with the tip of his tongue again that makes me a puddle.*

Lola and Marc exchange looks, smirking. I'm watching Lola with wide eyes, trying to tell her to control herself.

Marc asks her, "Lola, what do you think about meeting up again? Maybe going out on Saturday night? We discovered this club in downtown LA that we want to try. People say it's the place to go. Would you be interested?"

The chemistry between these two is fast tracked. Lola did the damage intended with her eyes. Lukas's shocked stare speaks louder than words. I chuckle.

"Well...only if the four of us go together," Lola responds, glancing at us.

My smile dies. She has my full attention. We're both watching them in disbelief.

She's still smirking. "What do you think, Gabriella?"

Her undertone of fake sweetness mocks me.

"Oh, no, no. Count me out. Dancing clubs are for you, young people. I'd be out of my league there."

Lukas faces me, upset.

"You don't like clubs? Clubs are for everyone who wants to enjoy dancing or have a good time. It has nothing to do with *age*."

He seems offended. Why? I'm puzzled by this reaction, but it feels like it's personal to him.

"I love to dance. When I was young, I frequented clubs, but now, most clubs are for young people, like yourself. I'm not that young anymore, and I'll look like I'm chaperoning," I explain.

"And who cares what others think, Gabriella? The idea is

to have fun. You're allowed to, you know, or don't you want to go out with us?"

He perplexes me, and I don't understand why he's reacting like this. First, he's upset by Marc's suggestion, now with my response. I want to say something, but I don't have a logical response, so I shut my mouth. Raising my hands in surrender, I concede.

"Okay. Okay. You three win. I'll go. I don't wanna hear any of you complain when you get bored of me, though." I'm pointing my finger at all of them.

"I don't think I'll ever get bored with you, Gabriella," is the sultry confession I get as dark caramel eyes scrutinize me.

Silence descends over the room.

The boldness of Lukas's response astonishes me, my mouth falling open. Lola and Marc gaze in shock too. Glancing at Marc with the embarrassment I feel, I plead for help with my eyes. Marc, thankfully, understands and speaks up to save the situation.

"Well then, it's settled. The four of us will go out Saturday night to have a good time. We'll pick you girls up around nine."

Turning to Lola, Marc takes her hand and kisses her knuckles.

"It was nice meeting you, gorgeous. Looking forward to seeing you again on Saturday."

"Likewise," Lola responds, all skittish.

Walking to Lukas, Marc touches his shoulder, speaking in a whisper, but I can hear them.

"Hey, man. We still have several pieces of furniture to assemble before nightfall." Then, he winks at me.

"The lunch was superb, Gabriella. Thanks for inviting us."

There's some shame reflected in Lukas's face.

"Thanks for the lunch, Gabriella. I'd love to cook dinner

for you, as soon I buy groceries."

He's walking backward while Marc pulls him by the arm out my door.

"See you, Lola."

Closing the door, I'm already expecting Lola's outburst and jokes.

"Girl, what the hell was that all about? He definitely has the hots for you."

She's teasing me, shaking my arms. I don't know why I'm ashamed of it.

"I can't. I can't encourage this, Lola. It's not right. I'll talk to him later and excuse myself from going on Saturday. Call one of your girlfriends to accompany you instead."

"Oh, no, no. You're not getting off that easy. Oh, come on, Gaby. Today was fun; don't deny it. Those guys seem so nice, and both are damn hot. You complain all the time you're locked up in here. Well, this is your chance to go out and to do something different. I really liked Marc, but I won't go if you don't go, period."

I inhale sharply. She's right. I'm trapped in this. I don't see a way to escape, so I might as well embrace it.

Oh, tell me... Do you want to make that big mistake...

It's late at night. Walking across my living room, I can't turn the light on. It's utterly dark. Maybe there's a damaged fuse or something. Hearing a loud knock at the door, I open it without looking to see who it is. Lukas stands there, naked torso, wearing black, satin pajama pants over his hips. The eyes of his lion tattoo are glowing bright blue, like they're alive. He looks like a Korean warrior god should look with his dark brown hair and impressive body.

"Lukas, are you okay? Why are you up so late?"

"I can't hold it in anymore."

Pouncing, he encloses me in his arms, crushing me against him while kissing me passionately. His lighting-fast motion takes me by surprise. The warm skin of his naked chest on my hands is real. He's making me dizzy, breathless. His kiss speaks eloquently as to how turned on he is. I start to drown in him, beginning to feel faint. For a split second, I realize what's going on.

I shout, "No."

Jumping to sit up, sweating profusely, I pull myself from under the covers. *A fucking dream.* It had felt so real. Jesus Christ. Sitting on the edge of my bed, I cover my face with my hands, my heart thumping rapidly. *Damn it, Gabriella. What the fuck is wrong with you? Are you mental? Now you're going to have sexual fantasies about this boy? Control your mind and yourself.*

I'm conflicted by this unending debate in my mind. He's not a boy. He's a grown man, a hot one indeed. But this is so fucking wrong on so many levels.

Getting out of bed, I head straight to my bathroom, needing to splash water on my face to cool off. I raise my eyes, watching myself in the mirror. I reprimand my reflection aloud, sounding like *Boricuas* do when they talk to each other. "Gabriella Morales, *tu sabes.* This cannot happen in any way possible, okay? You're the mature adult here. You have to control yourself and be firm for both of you. You're in charge of drawing the line and establishing limits. Do you hear me?"

Angrily, I pull the towel from the bar with such force I almost drop it to the floor. After drying my face and hands, I return to my bed, hoping to get some normal, PG rated, peaceful sleep.

I know you wanna ride with the kid... You wanna say hi with a kiss...

Chapter Three

Gabriella

My headache is getting worse. Maybe it's because I haven't slept well these past few nights. Or maybe it's Harrison, my boss, pressuring me to quickly finish the final revision for the new author the company is so enamored with.

The day is a bit cold, so I meet Harrison at my apartment. Those chilly days sometimes amplify my headaches, so I prefer to stay home. Even indoors, I'm wearing my black jeans with knee-high, flat, black, leather boots, a white and black striped long-sleeve shirt with a black sweater on top of it.

Harrison acts like an old man, but he's ten years younger than me. A brilliant editor in chief and a workaholic, he believes everyone should work as much as he does. Every conversation turns to work, no matter where you are. He's good looking in an average way. He's the same height as me with strawberry-blond undercut hair and honest blue eyes. He always dresses in pastel-colored jackets with jeans or white pants. Lola and I joke that he's stuck in the Miami Vice era, all because someone told him he looked like Don Johnson once.

Harrison has been a good friend, allowing me to work from home as often as I want due to my health. He respects and endorses my opinions in terms of corrections, editing, and copywriting of the books the company acquires.

"Harrison, I told you I'm taking the necessary time for the book to be flawless. On Monday, I said approximately a week. Today is Wednesday, ok? It will be done on time. You know me. This is not the type of work I rush. It never ends well, and you know it. Or you've already forgotten the fiasco with the daughter of the owner? I will not jeopardize my reputation doing a sloppy job." I'm standing in my living room, hands on my hips, watching him seriously.

"Okay, okay, I know."

He stands from the sofa, waving his hand, while putting the invoices I approved in his briefcase.

"I'm only the messenger. I'm well aware you're doing a marvelous job with this book. I'm not complaining. The guys upstairs are nagging about it, that's all. As always, I'll cover your back and take the heat for you."

"I won't fail you, I promise. Sure you don't want some coffee or juice before going?"

"No, I just passed by to check on you and get these invoices signed. I have a lunch meeting with Mackenzie in"—he stops to look at his watch—"half an hour. I'm late."

Heading to the door, I follow him.

"Keep me posted on everything, including your health, ok?"

Smiling tenderly, I assent. In the end, he's only concerned about me. We hug each other, and he kisses my cheek, then walks away toward the garage entrance.

I'm about to go back into my apartment when suddenly the skin on my neck prickles with the sensation that someone's watching me. Turning, I find Lukas standing in his doorway, observing me. With a raised brow, he seems uncomfortable and upset. He's dressed in ripped black jeans, a black polo, loafers, a brown suede jacket, and gold earrings. My sight rests on the ripped part of the jeans showing his flesh. *Fucking long legs.* I'm hoping my eyes don't betray my thoughts.

"How you're doing, Lukas?"

"Is he your boyfriend?"

He's assuming. He and his youthful impulsiveness. Somehow I'm exasperated to explain myself.

"No, Harrison is my boss and friend. Why? Is there a problem?"

I face him with my *Puerto Rican* attitude. It's time to establish some boundaries, but I wasn't prepared for his reaction.

Face turning pale, his annoyed expression changes to shame, his lips pressed tightly.

"No, it's none of my business. I apologize for my inappropriate question." Bowing before me, he starts to walk in direction of the parking garage.

Jesus. These Koreans guys are so damned formal. His reaction somehow hurts me as he strides by me without looking, clearly troubled. As an impulse, I grab his hand to stop him.

"Lukas, wait just a moment, please…" I plead, softening my voice.

He stops, looking hurt. I calm myself, conscious of my harsh reaction. I have to be the mature adult in all of this. *Dios mio, que rico huele. He truly smells good.* Control…

"I apologize for my response. It was rude, and you didn't deserve it. Please, don't be upset with me. I want us to be friends. I understand you like me. I like you too, but as a friend. You barely know me, Lukas. We just meet a couple of days ago. We should start getting to know each other first, don't you think?" I suggest heartily.

I disarm him. He exhales sharply, complying.

"You're right. Okay, deal."

"Great." I let go of his hand, delighted.

He steps forward to chatter quickly. "Would you like to have dinner with me this evening? I'll cook and teach you one of my recipes, as you requested."

And the thing with the tongue, fuck. Now he disarms me. "Okay, deal." Chuckling at his enthusiasm. "I'll be over around six pm. I still have some papers to send. See you then."

His bright smile widens. He won this battle, but not the war. Waving goodbye, I turn to my apartment to continue working.

After sending the last corrections and revisions through email, I check my watch. It's 6:15. *Lukas's invitation to dinner.* Shit, I almost forgot with all the paperwork I've done. I wash my face and put on pressed powder and lip-gloss, nothing more. I spray my gardenia splash with one final look at myself in the mirror.

I notice how much weight I've lost over the past few months. With these black clothes, it's even more obvious. Although it seems I look great, younger, I don't feel like it. Too much insecurity still torments me, but these past couple of days, knowing a handsome, young man might be interested in me—I've felt kind of cheered up. It's more like the reflection I see, and I can't deny it.

Walking up to his door, I press the doorbell. In a couple of seconds, the door opens with Lukas greeting me. He's taken off his jacket, wearing only his black jeans and a long sleeve black polo.

"Finally. I thought you forgot. Welcome."

"I'm sorry for the delay. I lost track of time. Let's see if what Marc says about you is true." With a quick glance around the apartment, I don't see Marc.

"Marc's not here?"

"No, tonight he's in LA, but I promise I'll be on my best behavior. Please, come in."

"Okay."

Passing beside me, I follow him straight to the kitchen.

"Would you like a glass of white wine? I've got some cold Chardonnay."

"Sure, of course." I stand next to him in the kitchen, not knowing what to do.

While he pours the wine in crystal glasses, I inspect his apartment. Some soft jazz music sways in the air, setting the mood. How different it looks from how Saba had it. Now the decorations are kind of minimalist rather than the explosion of colors and ethnic tapestries on the walls she had. The predominant colors are now black, white, gray, and red. I see several paintings and movie posters, similar to my apartment. I've been a *Star Wars* fan all my life, so my apartment's walls are covered with all the movie posters from the franchise.

"Here." He hands me the wine glass, clicking it with his. "To a wonderful and long friendship." I really like his confidence.

"Cheers to that." I take a sip.

Browsing around, I've discover a keyboard in the corner of the living room and a guitar in a stand beside it.

"You play piano?"

"Yes, I work in the music industry, composing and producing music. That's why I'm here."

Puzzled eyes examine my face, like it should be obvious to me he's a musician or composer.

"I didn't know you worked on music."

His eyes grow wide and a friendly smile replaces the puzzled look on his face. He's relieved for some reason, although I can't imagine why.

"Well, now you know."

I'm shyly grinning, confused and curious about his reaction. Taking a big gulp of wine to ease my nerves, I change the subject.

"What are you teaching me to cook?" I observe the counter where the ingredients are displayed: noodles, chicken, a variety of vegetables, and Korean condiment flasks I don't recognize.

"This is one of my favorite dishes I make at home called *Dak Kalguksu.* Is a hand-cut noodle soup with chicken. Today's been chilly, and this soup is perfect for cold weather. I like mine extra spicy. So I bought spicy kimchi for you to try. I bought everything from a Korean grocery store nearby. The noodles are usually homemade, but it would take us around an hour to make them, so I bought them for today. Someday I'll teach you how to make them from scratch." His voice is cheerful.

"Well, tell me how I can help." I put my wine glass on the counter and roll up my sleeves. He brings me a cutting board and a chef knife with a dish full of vegetables.

"You can start slicing these."

I mince four garlic cloves and ginger. Glancing over my shoulder, I see him putting a pot of water on the stove, adding what looks like dried kelp.

"I'm making a kelp stock, the base of the soup." Lukas informs me like he's reading my mind.

I grin amused with myself. Peeling the carrots, I ask, with my back to him, "How do you want me to slice the carrots and zucchinis? Strips, or diced?"

Approaching to stand behind me, his body touches mine. He grabs the knife and carrot from my hands. I freeze. His body is flush to mine, disturbingly cozy. Staring at his arms touching mine, my skin is darker than his. He has strong, magnificent hands. He should be a great pianist. *Or good at fondling things.* His proximity is triggering every nerve in my body.

A husky tone blown in my ear wakes me up from my trance.

"Cut them julienne style, like this," he says as he starts to cut, showing me how he wants them.

My heart pounds, adrenaline rushing through my veins. His hot breath in my ear is too much. I'm hit by a whiff of his cologne mixed with his manly scent. *God, he smells so good.* All of this is making me lightheaded. Closing my eyes, swallowing hard, I try to break his sorcery. Opening my eyes, I find he has stopped cutting the carrot.

Slowly I gaze at his perfect skin up close. Gawking down at me, his hungry eyes darken, making me tense. This closeness, this proximity is too intimate. My inner goddess stirs inside of me, aware of this. I must stop this, think straight.

Shaking my head, I peer down unlocking our eyes. I grab the knife back, nervously pushing him away with my elbows.

"Got it. I'll continue slicing them while you continue to do your stock over there." I point at the stove, trying not to sound nervous.

Snickering sensuously at my reaction, he backs up, hands raised in surrender.

"Okay. As you wish."

He turns to the stove, putting on another pot with water to boil. Exhaling, relieved, I roll my eyes and continue my chore. God. This dinner is going to be difficult with him behaving like this.

We finish preparing our superb dinner. He's outdone himself. He brings two steamy bowls of soup to the table, with other side dishes he places before us. There's kimchi, fish cakes, slice cucumber salad, and some spices to sprinkle on the soup. We eat while we talk.

This is delicious. I must copy this recipe with the fish cakes and everything. I've also learned how *Kimchi* tastes. Lukas truly impresses me with his cooking knowledge in addition to being a gracious, *sexy* host. And I think I impressed him with my knowledge of using chopsticks to eat soup.

Our dinner is surprisingly entertaining and educational. Between slurps of hot broth we talk about family, and I touch lightly on my failed marriage. Our talk is mostly work related. He's a music composer producing music, a record for some famous Korean singer I know nothing about. Right now, there's an exchange contract between two record companies, one in Seoul and other here in LA. He belongs to the one in Seoul.

He gets up, taking our plates with him.

"Want more wine? I've saved the best for last."

Putting the bowls in the sink, he takes a bakery box out of the fridge. Placing it on the small dining table, Lukas opens it.

"This is one of my favorite desserts. I'd like you to try it. Strawberry macarons, freshly baked."

I beam at his efforts to impress me.

"I love macarons. It's one of my favorites too."

Lukas pours more wine in our glasses while I take a first bite. They're exquisite. I roll my eyes, enjoying the taste.

"This tastes so good."

Staring, he points his finger at my face.

"You have some cream over..."

His finger picks a tiny piece of macaroon filling at the corner of my lips, caressing me to scrape it off. He sucks the cream from his finger slowly, with the tip of the tongue licking the tip of his finger. My mouth goes dry seeing this. Famished eyes tell me what he won't say aloud.

"You're right. Tastes good."

I have a brief *what the fuck?* moment hearing him. His feral-cat stare intimidates me, and my heart skips a beat. *Okay, the wine is talking here*. With a big gulp, I empty my glass as I process everything. This my cue to leave. Rising from the chair, I excuse myself nervously.

"Well, it's late. We work tomorrow, and I'm tired. Thanks for this delightful dinner, Lukas. I'm truly impressed. Tell Marc he was right."

Forcing a smile, I walk fast to the door. I sense him following me, both trying to grab the doorknob at the same time. I let him grasp it. We're both silent as I wait for him to open it.

On edge, I carefully raise my sight to encounter full lips partially open, eyes pleading at me. Tension crawls up my spine to be alone with him like this. Maybe it's the wine making me uneasy. My chest rises and falls with each rapid breath. He must notice my panicky state and opens the door for me.

"Rest well, Gabriella. Thanks for coming by. We're still going out on Saturday night, right?" He's making sure I'm not freaking out. Heat rush to my cheeks.

"Sure, Sure. We're still on for Saturday. I already promised you three I'll go."

All I want is to walk out of his door. Stepping outside, he grabs my hand the same way I did earlier. I gasp, surprised.

"I know you like me, Gabriella. The same way I like you. Let's not fool ourselves. I saw it tonight in your eyes. I'll win you over, you'll see." He's brutally honest.

Lifting my hand to his lips, he gently kisses my knuckles. Warm lips burn my flesh. The heat of that kiss echoes in the center of my belly. He speaks the truth; *I like him*. There's no point denying it. Reason and reality hit me like lighting, hurting me.

"Lukas, this thing between us…can't happen. It's not possible, okay?" I blurt sadly.

I don't wait for a response, just walk quickly to my apartment's door, opening and closing it behind me. My back is against the door, and I draw in a sharp breath. This is getting out of control. He's making me lose it.

Before I breathe even once... You've captivated me too fast...

Lukas

I close the door, frustrated, furious with myself. *Damn, this woman is driving me crazy.* Why is she resisting? This is new for me. Hearing a woman rejecting me like this. Both back in Asia and here in the States, women of all ages practically throw themselves at me. But she's different.

I'm conscious our age difference may be the main reason she's resisting, plus I'm well aware some people will not agree with a relationship between two people so far apart in age. Right now, I don't care about anyone's opinion. I only see this bewitching woman I desire to be with. I'm pissed off with myself for scaring her. I want to understand where this fascination with her comes from.

Sometimes you can't explain what you see in a person. It's just the way they take you to a place or make you feel in a manner no one else can. She's doing it to me. I'm at ease with her in a way I never knew was possible. What's clear in my mind is from the moment I laid eyes on her, she's enchanted me. I've been lost in my thoughts about her since then. Something is brewing inside me.

Taking off my shirt, I stare at myself in the bathroom mirror, upset. Glancing at my lion tattoo while my fingers touch it. It's my reminder to pursue, relentlessly, every goal I've set my mind on. My dad taught me this lesson, and I'm grateful for it. I strive to achieve perfection in everything, but tonight, I didn't.

I was too forward. The mutual spark is there, but her mindset doesn't leave her open to experience a relationship with me. It sounds so much like my culture back in Seoul when we talk about it. Deep inside, I hate the control society imposes on me and everything I do. I'm comfortable being myself the moment she's near. It's as if a single glance from her breaks down the exterior the rest of the world sees, and she sees me for exactly who I am.

I've learned a lot about her tonight, and I'm glad she was comfortable enough to open up to me. She's mentioned her ex-husband, who left her for a younger woman. She's been divorced for eleven years and in no relationship right now.

The last part pleases me, but she'd been deeply hurt in the process. I never thought I would desire to strangle another human being as much as I do now for causing her so much pain and misery. What a coward.

She doesn't trust easily but still believes there's good in every person. I've learned she has a son the same age as me, twenty-eight. I'm certain this is the main reason she rejects me.

My mindset is different. After everything I've lived and seen in this business, I know it's rare to find someone who likes you for who you are, not what you represent. She hadn't even known I'm a singer, nothing about who I am back in Asia. That's so precious and valuable to me. Most people usually think they know Lukas Lee, the K-pop idol, but that's not me. She seems to be attracted for who I truly am. I'd like to maintain that while I can.

Unbuttoning my jeans and turning on the shower, I ponder. *I have to be extra careful with her.*

Let's see if I can break the barrier she insists on raising between us. Now I see her more as a challenge I want to accomplish, another goal set. That's something I know how to handle. Overcoming every challenge life has guided me since I'd started in the music business. That's how I'd grown and learned. She will be another delightful challenge.

Touch me, tease me, feel me up...

Chapter Four

Gabriella

My walk-in closet looks like a war zone, clothes scattered everywhere. I'm searching for something appropriate to wear tonight, and my foul mood isn't helping this morning.

Since our dinner, I haven't seen Lukas nor he has stopped running around in my mind. I somehow feel guilty for rejecting him, but it's best he understands we can't be together now rather than later. We're going to the club tonight, and I can't ignore the knot in my stomach. If I could, I would cancel everything. The idea did cross my mind. I'd even thought of calling Lola to tell her I'm sick, but I don't want to lie, and I had promised to go.

"I don't know what to wear." I shout, frustrated. Anxiety is eating me up.

I suddenly remember a dress I love that's folded in a box. Since I've lost weight, it might fit. Searching the top rack of my closet, I find the box. I pull out the dress folded in tissue paper.

It's a burgundy red, cotton spandex, knee-length dress with short sleeves and a plunging V neckline. It's a simple dress, but it's still elegant and flirty. Quickly I remove my t-shirt and leggings to hold the dress up to me, looking at it in the mirror. *Wow*. It looks new. I hope it fits. Trying it on, I inspect my reflection.

I don't recognize myself. It fits perfectly. And the neckline. *Jesus.* My breasts peek out in a way that's so sexy. It hugs my curves like it was specifically made for my body. Still, my mind plays tricks on me, making me insecure.

Lola always says I should embrace my age with confidence. But my own mind sabotages me constantly. I feel like a fraud, pretending to be something I'm not. Picking up my cellphone, I call Lola.

"Hi. Lola? Yes, it's me. Can you come over, please? I'm trying on a dress, and I'm not so sure it's appropriate for tonight. I just want your opinion. If not, I'll go buy something. You can? Wonderful. See you in half an hour."

A half-hour later, Lola arrives as promised.

"Thanks for coming. Let's go to my bedroom. I'll show you."

I put on the dress for her. She opens her eyes, observing me with a pleased grin.

"What do you think?"

"Oh, my God, Gaby. You look so beautiful and sexy as hell. Lukas is going to flip out when he sees you."

That's exactly what I didn't want to hear.

"That's not the reaction I want. I'm so frustrated. I don't know what to wear." I sit down beside her, hiding my head between my hands.

"This dress is perfect. You're attractive and have a great body. Stop this self-loathing, for the love of God. Why are you so hard on yourself? Being an older woman doesn't mean life is over," Lola scolds, staring me down.

I exhale, resigned. She's right. I've been undermining myself lately. Besides I control what I allow or don't. My dress has nothing to do with it.

"I brought my bag with everything. I'll do your makeup tonight. We're gonna do a spa day today. You're going to look amazing."

She goes for her bag. I smile for the first time today. I just want to look good and feel confident. More for me than him.

Bullshit, Gaby. Who are you kidding? Deep inside, you want to impress him. For him to appreciate you for who you are, not only on how you look. This night promises to be intense.

After a day of pampering and getting ready, the doorbell rings at 9:10 pm while I'm tying my stiletto sandals.

"Lola, please open the door. Give me one minute to tie my shoes."

The knot in my stomach is tightening. This is my first night out in a year. My social anxiety is flaring again. *Breathe, girl.*

"Sure."

I hear their voices greeting each other. Marc is whistling at Lola, commenting how breathtaking she looks in her turquoise, mini, strapless dress. Her laugh and Lukas's voice asking for me could be heard. She's telling them I'm just about ready.

Giving myself one last look at my mirror, I'm proud of what I see. The dress and the burgundy high heel sandals match perfectly. Diamonds stud earrings a final touch. Lola did my makeup simple. Smoky eyes and red matte lips. *Wow, Girl. You look good.* I smile to myself.

Opening the bedroom door, I meet them talking to Lola in

the living room. They stop their chatter to stare at me. Their faces are speaking loud and clear. Marc is the first to say aloud, "Damn, Gabriella. You look…" His hand covers his mouth.

I laugh at his outburst, turning around, playfully showing myself off.

I'm tense, anticipating Lukas's reaction. I can't help stare at him in wonder. He looks impressive all dressed in black. His open collar shows silver chains. He wears a black suede jacket with leather sleeves and his hair combed to the side, with a lock of hair falling casually over his forehead. Silver earrings complete the look. I admit he is to die for. He could be mistaken as a big black panther about to jump with that feral look. For me, his reaction is priceless.

"You look stunning, Gabriella." Lukas breathes out in a whisper, raising his eyebrow while doing his tongue-biting thing.

Marc and Lola exchange looks between them, grinning in complicity.

"Thanks. You look good yourself."

Marc looks spectacular in his black suit, white shirt, and diamonds earrings.

"You look nice too, Marc."

"Oh, so I look *nice,* and this dude looks good?" Marc replies jokingly, playing offended by my comment. I laugh.

He turns to Lola, who's giggling with us.

"You see, sweetheart? This is what I have to deal everyday with this dude. Girls always go for him."

Lukas gives Marc a deadly glare.

"Marc, you look handsome too." I wink at him, beaming.

"Shall we go?" Lukas seems desperate to change the subject.

"Yes." I walk to grab his arm gently.

Surprised by my gesture, he grins like he just won the lottery. His devastating smile is my reward.

"Let's have a good time."

They take us to a club called *Elevate Lounge* located in the middle of Downtown LA. The club is on the 21st floor, and the view from it is breathtaking. You can see LA from every angle. I've heard gossip about this club being exclusive. My employer's PR department has tried to book this place before and has been denied, though we're allowed access thanks to Lukas and Marc's connection with the record company.

Marc is walking in front of us, holding Lola's waist. I'm aware of men staring at me hungrily. I grin, pleased. I'm just holding Lukas's arm. He stares at me with a proud gaze. They're playing a dance version of *Levels* by *Nick Jonas.* A host of the club leads us to a VIP booth. I confess, I'm impressed. Lola drops her purse on the table, taking hold of Marc's hand.

"We came here to dance, so let's dance."

That's my girl, go get him.

Marc chuckles.

"Lead the way, baby girl. I'm all yours."

While sitting down, a bar attendant comes to ask Lukas, "Would you like something to drink, sir?"

"Bring us one bottle of Bollinger and four glasses. Also a McCallan for me."

He glances at me asking, "Would you prefer something else?"

"No, that's fine with me."

Turning to watch Marc and Lola dancing, the sultriness of his hips moving cause me to blush. He moves so well leading Lola. It seems he's trained to dance. Well they work for the industry. It is logical they'd see and learn from choreographers and artists dancing.

The waiter returns with the McCallan on the rocks, champagne in an ice bucket, and four glass flutes. After opening the bottle, he addresses Lukas.

"Do you want me to pour it now, sir?"

"No, it's ok. I'll do it myself."

Pouring one flute, he inclines to speak in my ear, clinking his glass with mine.

"Hope you truly enjoy yourself tonight. That's why we're here."

His hot breath in my ear makes my heart skip a beat, giving me goosebumps. He's aware of my reaction, smirking seductively. I'm trying to behave respectfully, but he's messing with me. These insinuations have the sole purpose of making me uncomfortable or pushing my boundaries, so it's time I teach him a lesson. I drink my champagne in one gulp.

Surprised eyes watching me, he chuckles.

"Thirsty? Want more?"

I don't answer. Snatching the bottle from his hand, I'm gazing into his eyes. Pouring myself another glass, I drink it again in one gulp. My nerves need to be eased so I can find my courage.

Now he looks worried.

"Woo, Gabriella. Go easy on it."

I stared defiantly at him. *Okay, lesson starts now.* I stand up with a pissed off attitude.

"Let's go dance. That's what we came for. Or not?" I'm showing my *Boricua* attitude.

I offer my hand to him. His astonished eyes watch me sensuously. I've caught him off guard. Drinking his whiskey in one gulp, he jolts up. Lukas grabs my hand to lead me to dance floor. The flash of electricity through our entwined fingers is rattling my inner core. They're playing *Raining Again* by *Betoko.*

On the dance floor, he pulls me to the center among the people. Standing in front of him, I lazily stare at his eyes. The champagne has the desired effect. My hands slowly caress his arms to hold them. To his surprise, I push my leg between his, feeling the hardness of his thigh between mine. He adjusts his hand, placing it on my lower back. I'm behaving so naughty. Pressing my breasts against his chest, while biting my lips, I eye him, breathless. He pants sharply, as if in shock. He didn't expect this behavior. I chuckle at his surprised face. Smirking seductively, I order him in a sultry voice, "Come on, Lukas. Lead me, sweetie."

Eyes darkening dangerously, his wicked smile widens. I've challenged him, and he's accepted without thinking. This is going to be so much fucking fun. Dropping his hand to the top of my buttocks, he presses me against him. We start swaying our hips to the rhythm of the music, sensually.

I've failed to remember how much I enjoy dancing at clubs. This instant with him in my arms is igniting a fire long forgotten. Sparks reignite the dormant, passionate woman who has been restrained under my skin. I feel so young and alive again.

My ex-husband didn't dance. It's been too long since I've enjoyed this. I'm reveling in reconnecting to this freedom dancing gives me. I love music, and I'm dancing with this handsome young man who likes me. My inner goddess is stretching her arms, awakening from her slumber. She jolts up, standing proud, murmuring… *Show him… Show him what you got.* He's making me feel sexy and beautiful as hell. I didn't realize how much I'd miss this—being desired and wanted. *Well you haven't lost your touch, Gabriella.* I sway my hips, turning all around him the way only Latinas can do. I'm sure I'd make Shakira very proud.

Lukas dances so well. I'm mesmerized by the way he moves that tight ass. Turning my back to him, pressing myself against the hardness of his body, I raise my hands to wrap them around his neck. Swaying my hips to the beat of the song, I'm grinding against him. I sense a hardness starting to pulse.

Big hands grab my hips firmly, stopping me. His warm breath in my ear sounds surprised, but his sultry words amuse me more.

"Okay. You win. You've made your point. Take it easy on me, Gabriella. A bit more and I won't be able to leave the dance floor without you covering me."

I laughed aloud. That's what I wanted to hear. *Learn your lesson, pretty Korean boy. Don't mess with a Latina, particularly a Boricua. If you play with fire, you'll get burned pretty bad, guaranteed.*

"Okay, let's return to the table. I'll give you time to recover from your…predicament."

I wink at him. He bursts out laughing, throwing his head back, shaking it in disbelief.

"You're truly full of surprises, Gaby."

It's the first time he's called me *Gaby*. I like it. Gently squeezing my hand, Lukas leads me to our booth.

The music lowers for the DJ to announce through the speakers. "We have a request from fans of some special guests tonight. My men Lukas and Marc, SMX18 in da house."

His excited announcement is followed by a roaring crowd clapping excitedly. Some stare at our table, gasping in surprise. Others point at us excitedly. I'm confused. A song starts to play I've never heard before called *Making my Wish True*.

Did I hear right? Did he say *fans of my men Lukas and Marc?* What is SMX18? The record company? Turn to watch the color as his face drains, frightened eyes stare at me.

Marc and Lola arrive when the DJ makes the announcement. His color also fades, looking scared too. Both have the same reaction, exchanging looks between them.

Lola watches, puzzled. Turning to me, she speaks with her eyes.

What the hell is going on?

Something is awfully wrong.

Confirming my suspicion, two gorgeous, young Asian women approach our booth. They seem nervous, speaking to the guys, ignoring us.

"Hi. Sorry to interrupt, but would it be possible to get your autographs? It would mean the world to us. Meeting two of the hottest singers in Asia is insane, an honor."

She's so giddy and excited. The other girl immediately extends her hand with a napkin and pen, handing it to Lukas.

"Please. Make it out in my name—Ji-Ho."

Lukas's lips are almost white. Something is definitely off here. I feel like I'm in a *Twilight Zone* episode, kind of an altered reality I'm not familiar with. Did she say hottest singers? No, they're confusing them with someone else. I must clarify this right now. So sure I'm speaking the truth.

"Sorry, maybe your mistaken, but they're not singers."

Lukas tries to intervene to avoid the impending catastrophe but is interrupted by the girl who had spoken first. Addressing me in an upset tone, she seems offended by my clarification.

"Do you even know who you're sitting next to? He's Lukas Lee, lead singer of SMX18, number one K-pop group in South Korea and all Eastern Asia. Everyone here knows it.

And you danced with him and didn't know? It figures."

Her disdainful face observes me from head to toes. She stares at me with distaste, a mocking expression, almost laughing.

My skin prickles like a bucket of ice water has been dropped over the top of my head with their mockery. My chest tightens. A dangerous mix of rage, shame, and hurt grows inside me. My insecurities are rising fast. I'm disappointed, understanding why he's in a panic. He hid the truth from me. He lied.

Why? I told him I don't trust people easily. He knows I was hurt by lies. I don't tolerate lies. Why the hell would he conceal he's a famous Korean singer? Why hide it from me? I'm enraged at him right now. Does he think I'm so dumb I'd never find out? I'm so stupid and naïve for thinking this could work. *I shouldn't be here.*

Inhaling in short breaths while hiding my face, I compose myself. Glancing emotionless at him, I pull my shoulders back and raise my face haughtily.

"Well Lukas, go on. Remember, it's important to please the fans. Don't disappoint them."

Turning to the girls who still stare, puzzled at our exchange, I respond to them.

"My sincere apologies. No, I didn't know. I've just learned it. Sadly, I don't follow any Korean or Asian music as obsessively as you both do, it seems."

Both gape, shocked at my polite insult. Lola watches with empathetic eyes, knowing how upset I am. I look over at Marc who lowers his head, seemingly ashamed too. I act as if nothing has happened.

"I need to go to the bathroom. Take your time, don't mind me."

Picking up my purse, I stand up. He watches with a mixture of shame and sadness. Pleading eyes, he grabs my hand.

"Gabriella, I…"

Rotating my wrist to release myself from his grip, I grin, sounding cheerfully cynical.

"It's ok. Relax. Just giving you time to attend to your fans with the respect they deserve."

Turning my back to them, I stride fast to the entrance where the bathrooms are. I'm so humiliated. I shouldn't have come.

"Gaby, wait for me." Lola shouts behind me.

The squeaky sound of her heels walking fast to catch up follows me.

I don't go to the bathrooms. I head straight to the elevators, pressing the down button. Lola grabs my arm, in a panic.

"Gaby, stop. What the hell are you doing?"

"What the hell am I'm doing? Going home. The night is over for me. Or didn't you hear what just happened?"

"Gaby, please. Take a deep breath. Don't overreact."

Never tell a Boricua woman she's overreacting when she's mad. Chaos sure follows.

"Oh, *perdona mi ignorancia—pardon my ignorance.* So now I'm overreacting?" I shout sarcastically.

People stare at us.

"If you want to stay with them, feel free to do so. I'm taking a bus or cab or whatever appears first. I'm out."

The doors open, and I wait for the people to come out. I walk inside, followed by Lola.

"Don't be mad at me. I'll go with you."

Another couple enters the elevator, kissing each other, without noticing we're there. Maybe they don't care. The doors start to close. Raising my head, I recognize Lukas and

Marc walking toward us. Lukas notices I'm inside the elevator. In disbelief, he starts to run, shouting my name. I don't move or stop it, my sight fixed on him, showing the disappointment he's caused me. They couldn't reach it in time, and the doors finally close with me inside, disenchanted and hurt.

Stride the first step... Moonwalk...

Around two am, I arrive at the leasing office in the cab we took to Lola's house after leaving the club. She'd insisted on it. At her home, I finally cried out my disappointment. Lola suggested I stay with her, but I just wanted to go home and crawl under my comforter to do my usual pity party.

Learning he's a famous singer changes everything. The first issue is that he hasn't been honest about himself. My distrust is messing with my mind, thinking about what other things he's hiding that I still don't know. Second, his fame. Relationships with famous people always ends up in a mess. I know. I've collaborated with artists and singers in the advertising industry in Puerto Rico. I know how it goes.

My mind is running a thousand miles per hour in different directions. The headache comes back like lightning. I sit down on the sidewalk for a moment, putting my face between my hands, hoping the pain will ease a little. It's cold tonight, and I start to shiver. I hear footsteps approaching. I raise my face to see who it is, watching him stop and stand beside me.

"Please go away. I don't want to deal with you right now, ok?"

Lukas gazes down seriously while taking off his jacket. He wraps my shoulders with it. The warmth of the fabric on my skin burns me, enough to jump, standing up. Taking it off, I hand it to him.

"No, thanks. I'll retire now."

As I'm walking away, he grabs my arm, halting me.

"Gabriella, I'm so sorry…"

I yank my arm from his grasp without letting him finish.

"Don't touch me." Teary eyes gape at him.

I spew out my rage, "You lied to me. We're supposed to be honest with each other to build a true friendship. Friends don't lie or hide secrets from each other. I don't tolerate lies, Lukas. Did you think I'd never find out about this? Now I don't know if I can trust you. Is there something else you haven't told me? Like a girlfriend or wife back in South Korea?" I'm glancing away, sounding like the hurt girlfriend.

"Gabriella, I didn't lie to you. I'm here as a music producer, not a singer. My career as a singer is on hold right now. I was going to tell you eventually. It's not supposed to be like this. The last thing I want is to upset you."

"And that explanation is supposed to make me feel better?" The sarcasm trails my voice, my back to him.

"I know right now you're disappoint—"

I don't let him finish. My Boricua nature is on full display.

"Oh, no. Disappointment is an understatement. I'm deeply hurt AND disappointed by you. I'd looked like a fool tonight in front of those girls. They'd disrespected me."

Turning around to continue my rant, I shut my mouth. His face melts my rage. He's sad and upset. His eyes, they don't lie. Maybe I'm overreacting. Nothing has happened between us. I don't understand why I'm so emotional. It confuses me. This has nothing to do with being the mature adult. This flirting game has to end.

"Lukas, honestly…I can't compete with this lifestyle of yours. You're a famous singer back in Asia and maybe here. I don't know. I'm not a fan or one of those groupies who follows you. I hadn't even known what the hell K-pop music is until tonight. Do the math here. I'm an older woman, twenty-four years older than you, and you're a young man. Our worlds are so different. We're from two very diverse cultures. Besides this isn't right or proper. You are the same age as my son, Xavier…"

Now he's the one raising his voice, pissed off.

"I'm not your son, Gabriella. Don't compare me to him. Stop bringing this damn excuse up. Really, I'm sick and tired of hearing it. I'm a grown man. Maybe not your age, but old enough to know what I want and make the choices I desire. I don't need anyone telling me what's correct and what's not. I let the age excuse go, why won't you?"

One step forward, he stands before me, truly upset.

"The reason I didn't tell you I'm a singer is because I'm tired of people using me for my fame. Or for what I represent to them, not who I am inside. Why do you think I'm living here? To not be recognized, to be like everybody else. Being in this business is a lonely life, Gaby. You must be flawless. There's no space for mistakes. You build this personality for fans and the world to see, but inside, you feel like the prisoner of a lie. It's an armor to protect yourself from further hurt. Sometimes it pains or chokes you, but you must wear it. We have lots of enemies who want us to trip and fail. You can be surrounded by thousands of people yet feel so utterly alone. Who can we trust?"

Strong, gentle hands take mine in his, stroking them. His kind voice soothes my troubled soul.

"I came here for an opportunity to taste life outside the madness I've been surrounded with for the past seventeen years and I was lucky to meet you. A gorgeous, kindhearted, beautiful woman who sees and treats me differently. You see me as I am. I don't have to pretend to be someone I'm not. I'm at ease around you. The truth? It's a blessing you didn't know who I was. You've shown me your true self. I did the same for you."

I'm speechless. What he's implying is understandable. No one has talked to me the way he did. I whisper, ashamed by my overreaction, "I don't know what to say."

Stepping forward, he wraps me in his jacket while holding the lapels beaming at me, relaxed.

"You don't have to do or say anything. I propose this: let's get know each other for who we are, as you suggested. No more age or any other excuses. Please, get to know me for who I am, Gabriella. I promise no more secrets or hiding anything. Deal?"

Slowly, I nod in agreement. We're gazing at each other differently. Mesmerized by smoldering eyes, I've realized the attraction is mutual. Pulling me by the lapels of his jacket, he lowers his mouth to take mine. The force of my wanting surprises me. I'm trying to keep it under control. Closing my eyes while surrendering, my heart races rapidly, *so curious.*

Lucious lips touch mine tenderly. Such gentleness. God, it feels so much better than I imagined. My hands crawl up his chest. My fingertips touch the hardness of his muscles, exploring the heat of his body, palpable through the fabric of his shirt. Parting my lips, I let his greedy tongue search for mine. Dizzy from his kiss, I crush the fabric of his shirt in my hands for balance, and a low groan of pleasure leaves his lips.

His guttural groan makes me realize where we're standing, the hour, and what's going on. Pulling back from his spell, I break the kiss.

"Lukas… *I can't.* We can't… Too soon… Not now… Please…give me time."

That's all I can say to him. I'm agitated and release my grip from his shirt. His gaze betrays his desire, his guilt. Breathless he's ogling me. He can't seem to help it. Drawing in his breath, he nods in understanding. Lukas wraps me gently in his arms, kissing my forehead.

"It's okay, Gaby. We'll take it slow. I know. You don't have to explain."

His arm is wrapped around my shoulders. He grins at me, adding in a happier tone, "I'll escort you to your door."

Oh, I'm so curious... Yeah...

Chapter Five

Gabriella

"HE DID WHAT?" Lola shouts. "He kissed you? And you were fine with it?"

The realization of what I've just confided makes her explode in laughter, throwing her head back.

"Yeah, I know. Everything happened so fast and unexpectedly."

Lola came to pick up the bags she'd left yesterday. I've just told her everything that happened last night while I was outside with Lukas.

"Is he a good kisser? I want to know if these Korean guys, you know…take care of their business as impressively as they say." She pushes my arm, chuckling.

I nod in affirmation, shutting my eyes, without uttering a word, grinning stupidly.

"Oh, shit, way to go, girl. So, Stella got her groove back. Go J-Lo all the way on him, girl. Obviously, J-Lo before this baseball guy she's dating now. You know, those younger ones she dated before. It's about time; you deserve it."

I'm laughing loudly at her words.

"Last night, I asked him to take it slow."

"Poor Lukas. With his hormones raging wild inside him, he must be suffering. I can imagine him last night, looking at your fine booty and thinking: Shit, that could be mine. Let me work that out."

We both shake with laughter.

"Let's see how long he's the proper gentleman without succumbing to your charms." Standing up, she grabs her bag, ready to leave.

"Well, *Bonita*, I have to go. If you see that delectable morsel of Marc, please apologize on my behalf for leaving the way we did. At least from my part. And getting his cellphone number for me would be a plus. You owe me that." She winks at me. At the door, I hug her.

"Thanks for being there for me. I'm sorry for my outburst last night."

"It's ok, girl. That's what friends are for. To do stupid shit together and get away with it."

With a final wink and peck on my cheek, she walks to the parking lot entrance.

Closing the door, my curiosity takes over. I've decided to learn who Lukas really is. Sitting down with my laptop while drinking my ginger tea, I start to research, as I do with all my clients. I'm not mentally prepared for what I discover.

Indeed, Lukas Lee is the lead singer of a male group in South Korea called SMX18. Several of his songs are hits back in South Korea, and he's considered an icon in Seoul.

I'm watching video after video, interviews, all the internet can provide me. I've observed him dancing sensuously, crotch grabbing, and executing carnal choreographies. My heart races, seeing him dancing so provocatively. His whole musical performance oozes sexuality. He can sing in Korean, Chinese, English, and Japanese. I don't understand anything he sings sometimes, but I don't need to. The way he sings, dances, and performs is intoxicating and addictive enough to get stuck in your head. It's simply a brilliant formula.

Fans gave him the nickname of *gwiyeoun agma* (*Cute Devil*). As an advertising expert, I can say Lukas is what we in the business call the whole package. I know in my gut how profitable he likely is for the company he's working for.

When we had dinner in his apartment, he'd spoken about his parents briefly. Today I'd learned he has an older sister who's married, and his family lives in Seocho-gu District in Seoul.

His supremacy in the K-pop movement is undisputed. His personality, magnetism, and talent are without precedence. He can transform into anything, absolutely anything the record company asks, pulling it off without any problem, turning him in a megastar there.

Each member belongs to a different famous group in South Korea. The synchrony and musical registry of their voices is impressive, complimenting each other perfectly, with no one overpowering the others. This group has been carefully crafted and is a perfect puzzle, musically speaking, that would be impossible to reproduce with a different piece.

The training rehearsals and preparations I'm witnessing are demanding, relentless. Exhaustive videos, filming repetitions, TV shows, concerts, and sideline gigs are non-stop. They have to compete to earn first place on the charts, leaving it all on the stage during their performances so fans pick them by vote. Sometimes the fatigue is obvious, reflected in their eyes. The pain of pushing themselves to the limit evident as I've witnessed tears of emotional exhaustion on occasions, Lukas included.

I discover some pretty things about this life but also some ugly truths. It's like Lukas told me; he must be flawless, no room for mistakes. What I witness is brutal and draining, in my opinion. My heart constricts during one particular video when I see people carrying Lukas off the stage at a concert. His face was contorted due to pain in his lower back, so severe he couldn't walk properly. He'd performed with that level of pain until the end of the concert. Tears fill my eyes seeing this, thinking how he must have felt.

I also discover a compassionate Lukas I didn't know about. Caring for his bandmates, he seems overly protective of them, earning his nickname, *Bossy*. I chuckle reading it. They consider him the responsible one, the one who looks after everyone, gives advice, and often admonishes them. I notice how close they are, like family. I can only imagine how hard it must be, being apart from their families and friends at such a young age. My heart swells with an overwhelming sense of compassion toward them.

Reaching an emotional point, I couldn't watch anymore. I close my laptop. Sighing I try to release the oppression of everything I just watched and read. My chest is so tight. He's telling the truth. What a nightmare of a life, in my opinion. He has to love music so much to immerse himself in this world.

I go to the kitchen to the fridge to take out an open bottle of Moscato. After pouring a glass, I take a big gulp to release the knot in my throat, processing all I've learned. It's slowly sinking in. He's sacrificed a lot while away from the ones who love and protect him.

Now it makes sense when he'd mentioned taking advantage of an opportunity to taste life outside the madness he's lived for so many years. I would want it too. My heart swells with tenderness for Lukas and Marc. They've had it rough, relinquishing a lot and working non-stop to be where they are. I'm compelled to do something nice for them. My mind starts scheming.

After a shower, I dress casually in white jeans, a pale blue shirt, and sneakers. Grabbing my purse, I walk to Lukas's apartment. The sound of the keyboard can be heard, so he's working. I ring the doorbell. Lukas opens the door with a sexy smile that could brighten even the darkest of days.

"Gabriella, so great to see you. Care to come in?"

Dressed in a white sweatshirt, some ripped jeans, and white sneakers, you wouldn't know you're standing in front of a famous celebrity. Marc is peeking over Lukas's shoulder, with curious stare.

"No, actually I'm here to invite you both to grab some burgers. The best burgers here in California are at *In & Out*. If you haven't tried them, you don't know what you're missing." I give attitude while smiling. Their faces, etched with worry, now beam at my suggestion.

Marc jumps to answer, "I'm in. Let me grab my jacket." He turns inside.

"Let me get my keys…"

I interrupt him. "We'll go in my car. Meet you both in the parking garage. It's my treat."

Arriving at my car, I immediately lower the rooftop of the convertible. With gaping mouths, the guys walk to where I'm standing. It moves my heart to see their reactions. *Boys and their love for toys.*

"So, you're the owner of this piece of art we've been admiring all this week?" Marc shouts, excited as a schoolboy.

"Yep. Ford Mustang '65 convertible, my pride and joy. I'd

always wanted one, so I got it as soon I came here. California can fulfill your wildest dreams," I reply, caressing my blood-red convertible baby, folding my arm across my chest, and reclining against the door.

"It sure does fulfill your dreams." Lukas beams, amazed, from the car to me. I blush.

"Ok, hop in, let's get those burgers. Afterward a movie night at my apartment, no more work for today. This is time out. It's Sunday, for Christ's sake." They chuckle.

I want them to shed some of the weight of responsibility they've carried for so long, maybe years. Make up for those precious moments stolen from them. Faces of pure joy confirm my suspicions. Lukas sits beside me, and Marc jumps in the back seat.

"This ride is so sweet, Gabriella. When I can drive it?"

"When I am dead. Nobody touches my baby but me." Lukas chuckles.

We buy the burgers and shakes in the drive-thru, heading home to eat while we start a movie. They love *In & Out* burgers, and I've manipulated my way in to watching my favorite movies, the first three episodes of *Star Wars*. We sit down on my living room, watching. I've made some popcorn, and we each drink a couple of beers. I explain I'd watched the originals in the theater when they'd come out. They ask lots of questions about it. I'm more than happy to answer all. Well, maybe I'm a little bit too enthusiastic.

"You're a Star Wars know-it-all," Marc acknowledges.

"Since '77, honey."

Marc mocks me with a look of shock like it's so long ago, we laugh. I turn to find Lukas staring at me with admiration. I'm intrigued by his vehemence as he observes me.

"If you could acquire any of those props from those movies, what would it be?"

What an odd question.

"Well, my dream is obtaining the Windu light saber. The purple one we saw in this last movie. I've been told it's childish and stupid, but I don't care. I want it. They recently opened a new section called Galaxy Edge at Disneyland last May, where they sell replicas. I need to make time to go but just haven't had a chance yet." Disneyland is only around five blocks away from our building, so there's really no excuse. Marc stands up, stretching and interrupting our conversation.

"Well people, it's been amazing, but it's late, and I'm driving all the way to LA. Tomorrow is my photo shoot for the presentation, so I don't want bags under my beautiful eyes for those photos." He moves his hands with a *Diva*-like mannerism.

I giggle. I adore Marc, always making me laugh. Without talking, we understand each other perfectly. For him, life is as it's supposed to be: happy, not taken seriously, and fun.

"Jong and Ty arrive tomorrow. Remember he wants to meet us Tuesday, 10 am sharp."

Extending his hand, helping me get up, he hugs me tightly. I have this urge to tease him.

"Today I learned I'm friends with Ironman, correct?" Raising one eyebrow, my expression jokingly serious.

I saw a video where his bandmates had played jokes on him dressed in an Ironman costume. Everyone had teased him.

They both let out a roar of laughter, throwing their heads back.

"Who told you?"

Blowing my nails and rubbing them against my shirt, I respond, "Got my sources."

Chuckling again, he embraces me and kisses my cheek.

“Thanks for this afternoon. We needed it. And I apologize for last night. We didn’t mean to upset you. You’ve been a true friend since day one. Is there anything I can do to make it up to you?”

I’m touched by Marc’s words. Smiling devilishly, I make my request. “Give me your cellphone, unlocked of course.” I extend my hand.

Both look at me, puzzled. He complies. Wow. He really trusts me. I enter Lola’s and my contact info into to his phone.

“I’m writing Lola’s cell number and mine. Just call her and apologize like you did with me. She’s expecting your call. It’s all I’m asking.”

The biggest smile greets me while handing his cellphone back.

“Thanks, Gaby. You’re truly special. Good night, Master Jedi.”

“Good night, my Padawan.”

I like how Gaby sounds in Marc’s voice too.

“See you tomorrow, man.”

“Rest well. I’ll be there after eleven.”

Marc walks outside, closing the door behind him. I turn to find Lukas standing behind me.

“I have to go too. Tomorrow I’m doing some last minute touches to the tracks I’ve recorded. Thanks for this evening, Gaby. We had a wonderful time. The truth is we both needed this respite from work.”

“That’s my goal, glad you both joined me.”

He bends down to kiss my cheek. The warmth of his lips on my skin triggers me, and I’m instantly flustered. Aware of my reaction, I peer back with the desire he’s projecting. A door opens in his eyes. I see him. Staring at his silky lips parted, I’m sensing the same.

Grabbing my face with both hands, he pulls me in to kiss me, a soft, sensuous kiss. His lingering obliviates my resistance. Is he trying to see how far he can go? His big hands move to my back and press me against him. I raise mine to his soft hair, running my fingers through it, caressing him. I adore how he feels, everything about him. This feels so right. *I don't want to think... This is wrong... I shouldn't... I don't want to think...*

His tongue probes inside my mouth, deepening the kiss. A moan inflamed by his lips escapes. I'm losing it. I don't care about anything, just him. I'm starving to be kiss liked this, to feel desired, alive. I'm starting to be dangerously turned on. I hum in surrender. But to my own surprise, he steps back, panting for air.

"Gaby, I gave you my word... To take it slow and I will... Even right now, I'm dying inside because all I want is do more than kiss you. You're special to me, and I don't want to ruin it."

We're both struggling to regain control of ourselves.

My wake-up call. I lower my hands to his chest, simmering myself down. Stepping back from his embrace, I nod in agreement.

"You're right. We better slow down, getting to know each other more. I'm so sorry, Lukas," I answer, utterly ashamed.

Ogling, he shakes his head, grinning.

"You're driving me crazy with the mixed signals you send, woman."

Pulling my neck with his hand, he smooches my forehead. I chuckle with him, understanding. I'm not easy. I'm confusing sometimes. *I know...*

Vroom... Like a Black Car...

Lukas

Closing the door, exhaling in frustration, I wipe my face, annoyed with myself. Damn it, I was so close to making her mine. If I'd pushed it a little, I'd probably be in her bedroom, undressing her, fulfilling the fantasy tormenting me since day one.

But I didn't. What's wrong with me? In the past, with other women, I would have gone for it without thinking. But with her, it's different. She's new and uncharted territory for me. I want more than her body. My desire is for her to surrender completely to me. This is no ordinary woman. And this is no ordinary infatuation.

Like a mysterious adventure that presents itself, she's addictive and tempting. The only way I can describe what I'm experiencing is that there's an invisible connection pulling us together. This is some other level shit. I like this version of me when I'm with her. I don't quite grasp it, but somehow it feels *clean* to do the right thing. She makes me want to do good. I have to do the right thing with her, no skipping steps or pressing fast forward. She's a classic lady and should be treated as such. It's going to be another night involving cold showers.

Oh baby, it's you... Baby, I don't want nobody but you...

Gabriella

Closing my door, I lean against it, my hand covering my eyes in shame. What have I done? If it wasn't for him stopping us, we would be having sex right now. *Gabriella, eres una hipocrita.*

I asked him to take it slow, and when the guy complies, you lose it. What does he think of me? The embarrassment is overwhelming. I say one thing, but my behavior shows something completely different.

You're driving me crazy with the mixed signals you send, woman.

What's changed in my head? Realizing he's not a boy, that's what changed. I'm now aware of the desirable man in front of me. Inside lives an older soul, in some ways more experienced than men my age. A soul so weary, waiting for someone to understand him, and no one has. I've arrived to fulfill his wish.

He's gained my trust with his actions tonight. But my long history of pain and betrayal still holds me back. I'm scared to trust again. Besides I think it would be unjust to feed his hopes of a relationship destined to failure. Our age difference will catch up with us eventually. This thought fills me with despair and pain. I enjoy his attention. I can even admit I'm beginning to have feelings for him.

My headache returns like lighting, shooting pains more intense than last time, forcing me to bow my head and shut my eyes. I stand there until it subsides. I'm worried now. This isn't normal. I'll call my doctor first thing tomorrow to inform him about this. A cold shower doesn't seem a bad idea now.

Like helium got my lungs like...

Chapter Six

Gabriella

"You can relax. Everything seems fine, Ms. Morales. Since last labs, no changes have occurred. If you continue taking the meds as prescribed, you should be okay. Sometimes these occasional pain flares occur as side effects related to it. In the event those pain flares become too intense or continuous, we will run more tests to make sure nothing has progressed. I'll prescribe something to help you relieve them. Is that okay with you?"

"Of course, Rene."

Maybe these last days with Lukas has altered my state temporarily. I remind myself to take things slow and don't overreact all the time.

"Thanks for seeing me on so short notice. You're my angel." I said, giving him a heartfelt hug.

Dr. Rene Davis is like a father figure to me. He's been in charge of my health since I came to live in California. We'd developed a strong bond since day one, and I consider him my true best friend here.

"Gabriella, you know I'm more than your doctor. Anything that goes on with you, I consider family business, so always feel free to call me. Any questions you have, it doesn't bother me nor is it a nuisance."

My heart overflows with love for this man.

"Linda asked when you're coming to dinner. She hasn't seen you since you came with Xavier before leaving."

I exhaled. "Tell her I'll let you know. Soon, I promise. Right now, my job is crazy with the convention, the pending launches…" I let the conversation trail off. Maybe he can put my mind at ease or tell me I'm making a huge mistake. I need to talk through my inner turmoil.

"Rene, you know I don't have friends around here my age. The closest ones are you and Linda, Lola, and my boss. I need to share something very intimate and personal. Do you have time to spare?"

"Of course. You're my last patient. Tell me what's troubling you."

I sit down to share what's going on between Lukas and me. The nature of our relationship, my worries, and everything that has happened since day one. His expression is unreadable, fixed on what I'm saying. Once I'm finished, I observe him, waiting for his response.

"Well? What do you think?"

"What is the question you want to ask, Gabriella? Ask directly. Don't dance around it."

I'm mortified how easily he reads me. I draw in a deep breath and pour out my heart.

"I have feelings for him. Inside I know it's wrong to have them, because of the age difference. I'm old enough to be his mother. He's Xavier's age, for Christ's sake. I'm disgusted with myself for this. I wish I could make these feelings go away, but it's beyond my control now. I don't want to send him away either. I want him near me. He has turned to be air for my lungs, and I can't get enough of him. I haven't felt this alive, this happy, for a very long time. And yes, it scares the hell out of me to feel this way." Tears start to fill my eyes.

"When I first saw him, something dark inside lit up, and he hadn't even done anything. I had been dead inside, and he's brought me back to life, rescued me. I love how I feel when he's around me. The way he gazes at me makes me feel beautiful, valued. What do you think I should do? I'm confused."

He's so calm and sure in his response.

"I don't see any confusion, Gabriella. Do you hear yourself? You're clear on what you think, what you're feeling. I'll be very blunt and direct. Life is a tiny speck in time. Humanity believes we're going to live forever. That's why death hits us hard when we encounter it so unexpectedly. Life is now, Gabriella. Yesterday is gone; you can't change it. But you can learn from it and make it better next time. Tomorrow is not guaranteed. What you have is today, now, this moment, but we keep making up for each moment as it passes. In simple words, my child, grab happiness tightly when you see it, and don't let it go, no matter where it comes from. Even if he stays with you one night, a year, or the rest of your days, take those moments life gives you and treasure them. Believe me, it would be more than enough. If he decides to leave or you both part ways, it will be enough. Finding someone who makes you feel the way you describe is rare and precious. Life is about taking risks. Don't deprive yourself of happiness because of the fear of the opinions of others. Enjoy it while it lasts," he concludes by putting his hand on top of mine.

How can this man hold so much wisdom inside?

"Thanks, Rene." I lean down to kiss his cheek.

"If anyone deserves to be happy, it's you, Gabriella. You have been through so much. It's about time, *Mujer.* Go and be happy."

Don't slow me down when I wanna speed up...

Lukas

Putting on my gray jacket, I walk fast through the corridor to arrive at the meeting on time. I stride quickly to the meeting room, excited to see Ty. I've missed him. We're like brothers or close to it. Taking the stairs, I run up, knocking on the door.

"Come in," Jong's voice answers.

Opening the door, I'm pleasantly surprised to see Kim sitting next to Ty, talking with Marc.

"Kim, wasn't expecting you to come to LA," I shout, truly happy, walking over to hug him tightly.

"Good to see you."

"Hey, man. You look good. Life here suits you."

I see Ty standing behind Kim.

"Hey, Ty. I've missed you too." We hug each other with a slap on the back.

"It's great to see you."

I move to pass them to greet Jong, bowing before him first, then giving our customary hug.

"Glad you could make it here safely."

"It's good to see you doing well, Lukas. You look re-charged. This change of scenery has been good for you." Jong puts his hand on my shoulder, and I grin back.

"Well gentlemen, let's get down to business. We have to discuss the American presentation of Marc, Ty, and now Kim to make a real statement with this opportunity. Let's sit down." Extending his arm, he points for us to sit.

The meeting takes several hours. We discuss all the details already in plan for the night of the presentation. All press communications packages have already been sent, and confirmations have begun to be received. Dancers, stage, lights, projection screens, media packets, everything is meticulously coordinated. I'd given my input on some ideas to improve what's already outlined.

Once the meeting is over, I invite them to my apartment for the four of us to hang out. Jong declines, allowing the others to go with the promise to return them to LA by nightfall. He doesn't want them wandering outside the record apartments tonight.

Immediately we take off, chatting non-stop during the drive, catching up on everything that has happened since we split apart. Kim has recently spoken with Kei. He's doing well in the military and misses us all. Ty talked to Liu and Jung-woo, who both send their best wishes on our solo debut. I've informed them about Gabriella, not the details, only the attraction transpiring between us and how special she is.

Arriving at the building's parking garage, we get out, laughing, pushing each other playfully, and making jokes. Once in the hallway, I see her at her door about to enter. That woman has a powerful spell over me I can't escape, even if I wanted to. Her stunning silhouette is hugged by those tight jeans, gray knee-high boots, and a baby blue and gray sweater so nicely. She has to be mine. I know it.

"Gabriella, wait."

Gabriella

Hearing Lukas's voice pulls me from my thoughts. I turn to see him walking in my direction. There are two new Asian guys walking beside Marc, and my mind is trying to recognize their familiar faces. That's when realized these are his bandmates from his videos. I'm panic-stricken.

"Lukas…"

Arriving by my side, he puts his arm around my shoulder. His face lights up, showing me off to them.

"Ty, Kim, this is Gabriella, the special lady I've talked about. Gabriella, this is Ty and Kim, my bandmates and practically my brothers."

I observe them bashfully. Ty is as tall as Lukas with a handsome, long, oval face. All these guys look extremely good. Not to say hot as hell. His skin is a lighter amber color than the others. His dark hair is the same as Lukas's, combed sideways, showing his golden earrings. He's dressed in a pale blue shirt with the sleeves rolled up, jeans, and boots.

Now I'm eyeing Kim. He's handsome in an unconventional way. Any girl could easily fall for him with one stare. He oozes a powerful sensuality, same as Lukas. His hair is dyed gray in color, cut short in a way that looks perfect on him. Full, deep rose lips and gray eyes make him an instant heartthrob. Dressed in a long sleeve, printed shirt, black pants, and dress shoes, his entire assemble screams "I'm a celebrity". My face turns red-hot as I extend my hand first to Ty.

"Nice meeting you. I don't know what he's told you, but I hope it wasn't anything embarrassing." I turned to watch Lukas with questioning eyes.

"Pleasure to meet you. He's said nothing bad, be at peace. He just keeps talking about how wonderful you are. Now I understand why…" he adds, shaking my hand.

I blush. Kim is watching me intensely. It confuses me, the way he gazes at me, almost in the same way Lukas had done the day we'd met. I extend my hand to him.

"And you must be Kim. Nice meeting you too."

Instead of shaking it, he raises it to lightly brush his lips on my knuckles. I part my lips in surprise.

"*Dangsin-eul mannaseo yeong-gwang-igo bangawoyo.*" I think he's greeting me.

I notice the same spark Lukas had shown me the first time I met him, but Kim's is a sinful stare. A darker version of Lukas. He releases my hand, caressing it. The gesture feels overly intimate, but I ignore it. Lukas watches him seriously and appears upset. Marc's concerned eyes tell me this can go either way.

The atmosphere is tense all of a sudden. To help break the tension, I walk to Marc and hug him.

"Marc, long time no see."

He's confused by my greeting.

"Wow, Gaby. We just saw each other on Sunday."

I open my eyes wide to get him to follow my lead. He seems to understand.

"Oh, yes. Yes, I've missed you too." He hugs me back.

We both turn to find Lukas still staring at Kim, pissed off, while Kim gawks at me. I'm compelled to do something to end this possible feud brewing in the air.

My crazy mind emboldened, I walk straight to Lukas, grab his shirt, pulling it down to kiss him in front of everyone. My unexpected maneuver stunned him, but immediately, he's grabbing my neck, responding to my kiss.

I don't mind this kissing in front of everyone. This feels so good right now. Caressing his cheek softly, we part lips, getting lost into each other's eyes. He smiles looking down at me. Thank God. Crisis averted.

"I've missed you too, sweetie," I whisper, breathless.

Their reactions are unique. Marc covers his mouth, holding his laugh. Ty's astounded face is hilarious, his jaw dropped in disbelief.

But Kim… Kim still studies me differently. Wet his lips, while his dark gray eyes are fixed with fascination and desire. I'm sure he knows I kissed Lukas on purpose. I'm uncomfortable with the way he's trying to pierce my soul. I excuse myself.

"Well I'll leave you all to your afternoon together, since I presume I interrupted it," I address them, ready to leave.

I turn to Lukas to add, "I still have work to do. We'll see each other later."

Kim interrupts us.

"You invited Gabriella to our presentation, right? She should assist. To see and hear our music, don't you think?"

His tone of voice gives me the impression he's implying something else.

"Yes, she's coming with me." He puts his hand on my waist.

Watching their exchange in disbelief, I don't recall being invited to this presentation, but I go with it.

"Yes, I'll be there, you can count on it."

"Looking forward to it. It was enlightening, meeting you. *Annyeong*." He bows before me, raising his head with a wicked smile on his face.

"It was a pleasure to meet you, Gabriella. Looking forward to seeing you at our presentation. You seem truly as special as

Lukas told us," Ty adds, bowing before me, grinning.

"Thanks."

Marc… Oh, Marc. I can't help biting my lips, holding my laughter, observing his face. His twisted lips are holding on painfully so as not to explode in laughter, understanding what I did. His amused expression says it all.

"Bye, Marc."

"See you later, Gaby. Master Jedi…"

Lukas searches his pocket, pulling his keys to throw them to Marc.

"Go ahead, I'll catch up shortly. I need to say something to Gaby."

Darkened eyes speak tons without saying a word. I'm learning to read them. My own hunger flames my insides, seeing the way I affect him. Entering my apartment, I grab his arm to pull him inside, closing the door for privacy.

Lukas doesn't give me time to react, pinning me against the wall. Holding my hands above my head, the hardness of his body pressed against mine ignites my own fire. His kiss shows me the raw passion erupting between us.

Releasing my hands to hold my face, he ravishes me with his mouth. I'm lost. Clawing my fingers in his back, he lets out a moan of pleasure. His ardent mouth trails down to my neck, gnawing lust devouring me. A very fine thread of reason appears before my eyes.

"Jesus, Gabriella. I want you now."

"Lukas… Oh my God, Lukas. We've got to stop. You have guests." I gasp aloud, panting for air.

He stops. Shutting his eyes, frustrated, he slaps the wall behind us upset. I jump, not expecting this. He growls like a lion that caught his paw in a trap, furious. Looking up, I hear him exhaling his frustration.

"Sorry for the inappropriate language I'm going to use, but you're fucking driving me crazy, Gabriella. I don't know how the fuck to behave with you. First, you entice me, and now you stop me. I'm a gentleman but also a man. I'm barely holding it together. Can you understand how hard it is? Please, don't temp me anymore."

I try to explain what I'd done was to avoid a confrontation. He doesn't hear me. He's turning his back, opening the door, striding outside, and ignoring my pleas to stop and listen. *Shit, I fucked up.*

Baby we can stay up... Throw you at me...

Chapter Seven

Gabriella

I haven't seen or heard from Lukas since our last awkward encounter. I keep my distance. My guilt keeps me away. Maybe he finally understands I'm not one of those girls he's used to dealing with, and he's disillusioned.

Today I leave the protection of my cave to attend a meeting at the publishing company. Those are the only moments I visit the office. We'll discuss my trip to Las Vegas next week for the annual book convention taking place at *The Bellagio.* It's been requested by the CEO that I attend, representing the company. The CEO himself is attending this meeting. So I decided to try the classic approach, you know, dress *classic.* I'm wearing a black skirt suit with black pumps and ruby square rhinestone earrings. A very 50s look.

Juggling a cup of coffee, my purse, and laptop, I walk to my car. A hand grabs my arm. I spin, scared, encountering the face I've missed so much.

"Lukas."

Famished eyes devour me, revealing how much he seems to have missed me too, drinking me in with them.

"Sorry to scare you. Give me five minutes of your time before you go." Oh, God, he's a sight for sore eyes.

"Sure."

With a heated gaze, I'm eating up this hunk of a man. He must be arriving from one those meetings, dressed in a dark gray suit with a black tie and a diamond earring that can't be missed. The hunger and longing reflected in his face equals mine.

"Do you have plans tomorrow morning?"

"No, nothing right now. Why?"

"I booked a surprise for you, but it's a short distance, around five or ten minutes from here. Please say yes. Just trust me." *How can I not trust you?*

"What time?"

"Around eight thirty, nine maybe. Are you up for it?" The bite of his lower lip enchants me.

I can't help but laugh. "Yes."

"Dress comfortably, jeans and sneakers." He walks backward toward our building. He's piqued my curiosity, but first, I need to apologize.

"Lukas, I want to say I'm truly sorry for last time I saw you. I got carried away, and I hadn't intended to upset you."

Striding forward, he grabs my face, with both hands, to kiss me in desperation. How I miss those aphrodisiac lips. Responding shyly, I try to control myself, closing my fists to avoid touching him. Slowly he steps back.

"You don't need to apologize. The desire we have for each other is strong. The right moment will come for us to share our intimacy without forcing it. In the meantime, for now..." He raises the back of my hand to kiss it gently. "See you tomorrow morning at 8:30."

He continues walking backward, smiling, turning to our hallway. Funny how life answers your most intimate, burning desires.

Make a wish...

Eight-thirty am. Earlier I put on my dark blue jeans, gray-blue sneakers, and my baseball shirt the LA Dodgers, number 14, shortstop, Enrique *Kike* Hernandez gifted me at one of the off-season games I got the privilege to meet him.

Lukas has been in my head since yesterday. The battle is there, but Rene's words resonate inside me, giving me strength. Whatever happiness he can give, I'll take it. I recognize this is insane. I'm taking a big risk here. It's possible after he satiates his raging desire, he won't want to be with me or may disappear, ghosting me. I have to be prepared for it.

But the woman in me comes alive in his arms. Why should I deny myself this happiness? Before him, I'd had nothing. This is better than nothing.

My doorbell rings. I open it to encounter Lukas's stunning smile. Dressed in a white hoodie, blue jeans, black sneakers, and baseball cap, it seems I'm dating a college student. I adore the way he drinks me with his eyes thirstily.

"Ready to go?"

"Yes."

Holding my hand tenderly, he walks me to his car. We exit our garage, turning left toward Katella Avenue, then going straight. I realize where he's taking me.

"We're going to Disneyland?" I ask excitedly, like a little schoolgirl.

Watching the road, with a satisfied expression, he just blurts, "Yep."

Letting out a small shriek of joy, wrapping my arms around his neck, I peck his cheek multiple times. He chuckles aloud at my reaction.

Once in the parking lot, he wears big dark sunglasses that almost cover his face while he hides his hair under the baseball cap. Seeing my puzzled stare, he explains.

"Fans are in the park, Gaby. I don't want anyone recognizing me and stopping us."

I completely forgot about this little detail.

He holds my hand, glancing at me every time he has the chance. We walk behind Cinderella's castle, passing the Frontier Land until I see flags and symbols I recognize very well. I stop, beaming straight at his face.

"You're taking me to Galaxy Edge?"

His smile shows me he's moved by my reaction. Nodding, he pulls me to follow him. Turning the curve, the first thing I see is the *Millennium Falcon* in full scale. The fan girl in me loses it.

Screeching, star struck, I run off to see it up close. He follows like a dad running after his little girl. Taking out my cellphone, I hand it to him excitedly.

"Please, please. Take my photo with the Millennium. This is insane. Arrgghh!"

Laughing out loud, observing me, Lukas takes the picture. Then he takes out his phone to capture another picture of me.

"This one's for me. I want to remember how you look right now. Believe me, you're breathtaking."

I'm speechless. Those are the most romantic words anyone has said to me in a long time. The way he lovingly stares at me shakes my very core. All those butterflies flying around in my stomach for him, for this, and immediately, the panic alarm in my head rings the usual warning. I'm scared to let go and dive into this feeling. I don't want my heart broken again. I will not survive another heartbreak.

Once I open my heart, there's no turning back. I know perfectly well what comes after. But Rene had advised me to grab happiness and don't let it pass. Don't let fear stop me. *Life is now, Gabriella.*

Lukas is so thoughtful, kind, and gentle. This gesture, bringing me here, shows me how much he cares and wants to please me. He wouldn't go all this way just for a moment of pleasure with me. Why go to this extra effort? He seems to want more than my body. I want to believe there's more for us, this thing between us could possibly work. I want to believe again.

"I made an appointment for your surprise, let's go. It's time."

Walking toward a building, similar to a workshop, with a sign, reading *Savi Shop*, I see flags, with various symbols, outside the store. People are waiting in a courtyard in pairs. He's purchased us two medallions we wear on our shirts. Still I'm clueless to what's going on.

"I chose this one for you. It's supposed to represent peace and justice. That's how I see you. You became the peace I needed that I didn't know existed. You completed that missing part of my life."

His words touch my soul powerfully. He's opening his heart, taking the risk at being rejected, just like me. I raise my hand to caress his face reassuringly.

"Believe me when I tell you I'll be your peace as long as you need me. That's my promise to you." I wink at him.

We're called to enter the shop. I'd thought this is one of the new Disneyland rides, but I'm in for a bigger surprise.

There's a big round cantina. Everyone is standing in front,

all-around the working area. The host informs us we're in a workshop to build our own lightsaber. *Did I hear right*? Turning to stare wide eyed at Lukas, I'm grinning ear to ear. We're building our own lightsabers. Covering my mouth in disbelief, emotion overtakes me.

He had taken time to plan this, understanding how much it would mean to me. Overflowing with emotions, I can't help crying, touched by this detail. It's been so long since someone has taken the time to do something nice for me. His arms offer me solace to my overflowing emotions.

"The idea was to make you happy, not cry." He chuckles in my ear, kissing my forehead. Wiping my eyes, I stare at him in adoration.

"You made me very happy, Lukas. Thanks for this." I wipe my nose.

The host presents us with the kyber crystals. Obviously I go for the purple. Lukas picks a blue one. It's fun and kind of special assembling it by yourself. We glance at each other occasionally instructing the other how to do it. The peak moment is when we light it up. Seeing the lightsaber I've only ever dreamed about light up in my hand makes me feel so empowered. I catch Lukas taking another photo.

"Sorry, had to take this one. You look so stunning." And he proceeds to show me.

I don't recall a time I've seen myself smiling as I am in this photo. My face glows. It's my eighteen-year-old self living inside me. He brings out this part of me I didn't know still existed, and I'm able to see myself the way he sees me. The revelation smacks me in the face, and I'm delighted all over.

"Nothing can top this, Lukas. Thank you."

Grabbing his sweatshirt, I pull him to brush my lips tenderly on his. Opening my eyes, I encounter the most mesmerizing smile gracing me. Doing his tongue pressing, smirking wickedly, raising an eyebrow. He descends to my ear to whisper, "I can think of several other things I can do *to you* to top this. And I'm pretty sure you're going to enjoy them even more."

I blush, deciding to shut my mouth. Watching me, he chuckles.

"Well, this is a first with you. Cat got your tongue?"

With his finger, he moves a strand of hair from my forehead.

"Gaby, even though I'm dying to spend the rest of the day with you, I have to go. I have another meeting in LA this afternoon. We can get together later or tomorrow, if you wish."

My body language speaks volumes in protest. I'm enjoying his company so much. But I understand he has his duties to fulfill. I suggest without thinking, (I swear to God) on what I'm proposing.

"Let's meet tomorrow morning. I'll make breakfast for us. You can even come in your PJs, nothing fancy."

His widened eyes darken instantly, eyebrows raised. A devilishly smirk appears, making me realize what I just proposed to him.

"I'll be looking forward to that. At what time do you *want me*?" he asks, gazing seductively.

"Eight..." I babble breathlessly, knowing what would probably happen in the morning.

"Eight sharp, I'll be there," Lukas replies, seemingly satisfied, kissing my hand, leading us to the park exit.

Hitchhiking, Baby...

Lukas

As the meeting ends, Marc pulls me aside to ask how it went with Gabriella today. Ty and Kim are talking amongst themselves. Jong is entangled in a discussion with two other executives from the company on details of the upcoming presentation.

I'm all smiles, recounting the details. I even show him Gaby's photos. Her happy face shakes my soul so unexpectedly. I need to be the reason for that smile always.

"She was moved beyond tears. I can say I scored big time with her. Seeing her reaction, today, Marc… It was beyond words. She's so amazing."

Marc's astounded face watches me, startled hearing me talk this way.

"Oh, buddy, you got it bad. I've never heard you speak like this. I think you're falling for her, even if you don't see it."

The doors of the meeting room open without a knock. All eyes go to the person entering in such a manner. Standing there, while glancing seriously at everyone, is a breathtaking woman with copper-red, wavy, long hair. She looks impeccable in a green apple, hugs-her-curves dress with a black jacket and black stiletto pumps. Marc's the first to recognize her.

"Oh shit, Lukas. *Vivian…*"

I spin to encounter her eyes gazing at me with her usual seductress smile. Jong is the first to address her.

"Miss Orly, so nice to see you well. I'm sorry to hear about your car accident on your way here. Mr. Pierce told us all that the part of public relations is done and set."

She glanced to Jong and the executives, bowing before him.

"*Annyeong*, Mr. Jong. I truly apologize for my delay; there's no excuse. I was desperate to be part of this meeting. But rest assured, as Mr. Pierce told you, public relations is ready for the presentation. All the responses from the media packets have been received."

"I'm glad everything is going according to schedule." Jong responds, bowing before her.

This is going to be a problem. I know it. Kim stands to greet her as Jong exits the meeting room, speaking with the other executives on their way out.

"Vivian, I swear you look more beautiful every time I see you. It's always a pleasure to encounter such beauty." Putting his hand on her waist, Kim kisses both her cheeks gently.

"Kim, nice to see you too. Always so gallant."

I'm uneasy with the way she keeps staring at me.

Ty is next to greet Vivian Orly, public relations executive for the record company.

"Nice seeing you again, Vivian. Sorry for your car accident, hope you're okay." He shyly hugs her.

"Nice seeing you, Ty. Thanks for your concern. I'm okay. The media is already loving you. We're going to score big time. I've been receiving feedback, and the reviews rolling in say everything is going to be beyond our expectations."

Smiling sweetly, she walks slowly to where Marc and I are standing, stopping in front of us.

"Well? Aren't you both going to say hi to me?"

"I'm glad you're ok," Marc responds coldly, shaking her hand, his face somber.

"Wow. That's cold. After all the history, *Marky*?" Smirking, she stares toward me.

Her presence causes me so much irritation. I was hoping there was someone else in charge now, not her.

"Vivian…" is my only reply, immutable.

"No hugs for me? Like last time?" She's biting her lips.

"What happened last time is not going to repeat itself. You can be sure of that." I'm determined not to let her intimidate me anymore.

"What happened last time?" Kim asks curiously. Ty put his hand on his shoulder, shaking his head, not to ask.

"That's none of your business," I say aloud.

Kim backs down in silence, raising his hands in surrender. But she has to talk.

"We know each other a little more *intimately*. At the end, Lukas was unhappy, learning the relationship wasn't exclusive."

She's doing this with all the intention of creating gossip between us. I watch this foul woman, enraged. She's startled by it. *Good…*

Chuckling at her comment, I show her how unimportant she is.

"Well that's ancient history. There are things far more important in my life now that take my full attention."

There's some rage in her words.

"The past can repeat itself, Lukas. Never say never."

"I don't think so. Normal people usually learn from their mistakes and don't repeat them. I'm one of them."

She doesn't deserve any of my time and effort. Turning to Marc, I ignore her.

"Let's go, we have work in the studio, finish those arrangements…"

We walk past her, touching Ty's shoulder to instruct him to follow us.

"Come on, Ty. We still have work to do."

The three of us walk out of the meeting room, leaving Kim and Vivian alone.

Ty grabs my arm, seemingly puzzled, asking what he'd just witnessed.

"Lukas, what was that all about? Did you sleep with her too, like Kei?"

Marc's the one to answer.

"Ty, she's a dangerous, unstable, manipulative woman, okay? Be on your guard. And yes, so you finally know, she slept with all of us. We're not so sure about Liu but the rest of us, yes. Even Jungwoo. We thought you already knew."

"What the hell? All of you? I didn't know. I only knew about Kei. Also that Lukas was upset about something she did in the past, but I didn't know the details."

Mark stares at Ty, serious. "She's a seductress. Like morons, we all fell for her sultry talk and tempting tricks. The *fuck her* part isn't the problem. It's her twisted mind. She craves control. Manipulating people is a drug for her. Kind of a psychotic game. She tried to blackmail some of us, just for fun. The job isn't the problem either. In Public Relations, she's brilliant, one of the best, and she knows it.

Stopping our walk in the hallway, I stare at Ty's face, concerned, to add to Marc's words.

"Beware of her. If you can avoid being alone with her, do it. She knows how to seduce a man and give a good fuck. So good she'll have you eating from her hand, at a big cost. She studies you, learning your weakness, what you like and don't. It's a hunting game for her. She's treacherous. By her behavior today, we know you'll be her next target so be on guard. I recommend you limit your contact with her to purely business." He's shocked by our revelations, Marc's and mine.

What truly worries me is this amicable behavior from Kim with her today, knowing how manipulative and menacing she is. Being familiar with how competitive Kim is, this change of behavior is worrisome. We all know he already slept with her and is another victim of her games.

I'm hoping he's not stupid enough to plan alliances with the enemy to start a new conquest game. I've already spoken to him, telling him those competitions are over. We should grow and move on. But I suspect he hasn't internalized the message, starting a new one between us for a certain woman we both know and lives next to me.

Chapter Eight

Gabriella

The cramps in my stomach have been torturing me since seven am, expecting him. Walking in the kitchen a hundred times, seeing everything is set perfectly. My heart is thundering fiercely in my chest. I put coffee on to brew and a pot of green tea, as Saba instructed me how it should be done. I lay a plate with some fresh fruits, a pint of vanilla yogurt, a package of granola, honey, and nuts with dried fruits on the kitchen counter.

I'm well aware anything can happen. I've thought about it. I'm still gaining my courage to let go of my fear, to open myself up. And honestly, I don't know what I will do.

The doorbell rings, waking me from my thoughts. One last look in the mirror to see myself. Like I told him, I'm still in my knee-high satin purple nightgown with a bathrobe. Yeah, I look okay.

Opening the door, I encounter Lukas in his PJs. Wearing black satin with a bathrobe of the same fabric, like the Korean warrior I've seen in my dream. He's holding what seems to be a bag of freshly baked croissants by the smell invading my apartment. Admiring me from head to toe, smiles adoringly.

"Good morning. If this is how you look every morning, I should visit more often, to be greeted by such beauty." I flush.

"Please…" I invite him to enter.

He puts the bag of croissants on my kitchen counter. I try to pass by him to the coffee maker.

"Do you want some coffee or green tea? Both are freshly brewed…"

Doesn't let me finish. Grabbing my waist with his big hands, he pins me against the refrigerator door, staring down. Caressing my torso up and down, the heat of his hands through the satin fabric is inflaming me. Every nerve in my body is screaming *let me live.* He's so close I can hear the hammering of his heart. Ogling, he wets his lips, whispering, heaving.

"I'm so hungry and starving right now, but food isn't what I'm craving, Gabriella."

Everything in me is throbbing with arousal for this man. The heat of his hands burns my skin through fabric of my nightgown.

"Right now, I can't think of anything but you. You're stuck in my head in a manner I can't comprehend. I've never felt or behaved the way I am with you. It's new and confusing for me. I don't know how to act that doesn't make you uncomfortable, but I can't contain this suffocating desire to have you, body and mind."

There is this agonizing silence between us. I'm lost for words. I'm terrified to let go.

"Please, Gaby, say something. Tell me your suffering is the same. That this is mutual. If you want me to stop right now, I will, just say so. Tell me, Gaby… Do you want me to stop?"

His dark brown eyes pierced the very center of my core. I couldn't lie any more. Breathless to his confession, my defenses fall. We feel the same, this raging fire burning out of control. He just took the words right out of my mouth.

"No, Lukas. Please, don't stop."

That's all I could say, surrendering myself to him.

Jumping at each other with all the passion unbound, it takes control of us. Our kiss is desperate. I let all my inhibitions go for this man stealing my heart, without me realizing it. Or maybe I do.

This isn't just physical. There's something more. He pushes us to the bedroom door, devouring my mouth. Walking backward, I raise my hand to caress his hair. Our moans are loud, desperate. We're gasping for air between kisses, hungry for each other. Holding his shoulders for balance, lips locked, we begin softly nibbling each other's lips in desperation.

He picks a condom from his pocket and tossed it on the bed. I undo his bathrobe, pulling it back from his shoulders to drop it on the floor, savoring every tiny detail. My hands go under his PJ shirt, caressing his rock-hard abs. Closing his eyes, he groans at my touch. Pulling off his shirt, he drops it on top of his robe.

He's undoing my bathrobe slowly, like opening a gift. Kneeling before me, he puts his hands around my thighs. I let out a small gasp of pleasure, feeling his hands on my skin. He continues to caress up my thighs. Finally he grabs the hem of my nightgown, standing to take it off, leaving me mostly naked, only wearing my underwear.

His eyes have a burning look in them. His famished stare makes me feel so cherished and beautiful. I know this is more than lust.

Raising his hands to gently cups my breasts, he sends pleasure blasting through me. I close my eyes, my moan responding to his loving touch awakening every inch of my skin. His long, sleek fingers crawl up, sensuously stroking my neck and face. My skin tingles with the sensations he's arousing in me.

His fingers drag down my belly, to encounter the waist of my panties. Curious fingertips swipe inside to find my swollen bud wet for him, circling it. A heated moan leaves my lips, feeling him.

"God, Gabriella. I dream of touching you like this so many times. I'm fucking trembling like a school boy. What have you done to me?"

My arms wrap around his neck, while his fingers do their magic, making me weak. His touch is light and slowly teasing. I'm almost dizzy from this heated foreplay, gasping for air. His bare chest against my naked breasts, his frantic fingers rubbing me back and forth is enough to make me lose control. I'm famished, tugging him closer, walking backward, entangled in hungry kisses. We trip, falling on my bed. Flustered caramel eyes gaze at me. We're both panting for air. *That's it.* I plead with everything my heart is feeling and desiring.

"Make love to me…now. Take me now."

"Gabriella."

That's all he could say, letting out a sound of agony. Covering my mouth with his, he quenches his thirst for me. Curious hands slide down caressing my hips and legs. Trembling fingers search the waist of my panties, pulling them down my legs. Once discarded, he kneels in front of me. Gazing down, inflamed, while lowering his PJ's pants pulling them down, he locks eyes on me. He reaches for the condom, rip the foil with his teeth while I hungrily watched rolling unto him.

Reason left the room, desire is overpowering. Bending down with one swift move, he thrusts his thick, hard arousal inside, stretching me out. We gasp, observing each other, love drugged, and moaning loudly. I can't believe this is finally happening.

It's much sweeter than what I imagined it would be. His slow movements torture me. He knows how to make the core of a woman glow brightly with unrestrained arousal. We're gasping and moaning.

Holy shit, he feels so good. Driving me into madness, my gasps are louder. I'm mindless with lust. He's skillful and knows it. But at the same time, he's gentle and caring. Moving his mouth to my cheek and neck, I'm beyond reason at this point. This is everything I need and more.

"Tell me what you want." Dragging his mouth on my cheek.

"Please, baby, don't stop," I plead in agony.

Chuckling at my neck, he increases the pace of his thrusting. Closing his eyes, he gasps in sweet misery.

"Gaby, oh God… Don't hold back, baby. I want to see you come… You feel so good around me. You fit so perfectly. Come on, surrender to me." Lukas groans, while increasing the speed of his thrusts.

Pinning my hands down on the bed, he dips his mouth to my neck, licking and kissing. His heated breath burns everything inside me, down to my very soul. I belong only to him. My soul is shouting yes to all of him. He releases my hands. I caress his back, crushing him into me. Falling into the abyss of his eyes, my release is coming like a tornado out of control, I wiggle against him. He quickens his thrusts until I start spasming in his arms.

"Yes, that's it. Let it go, baby. Feel me deep in you."

In a blissful second, our eyes meet, and the world freezes around us. I've surrendered my soul to him without realizing it. My body shudders with the jolt of my orgasm, screaming his name.

"Lukas!"

I arch against his chest while shaking with tremors against his hips, screaming the release rippling through me, gasping for air. It's so intense my eyes roll back.

It's the cue he needs. Tormented eyes stare back, tensing while gasping my name, shivering on top of me.

"Oh, God. Gabriellaaa!"

Pushing deep inside, he tilts his head back, squeezing his eyes shut while he finds his release. While he gasps for air, I place feathery kisses on his closed eyelids, nose, and lips, still panting for air. He responds to my kisses, slowly catching his breath. I'm short-winded, drunk on love, and satisfied. We fall asleep cuddling each other lovingly. Surrendering to the powerful bliss we've encountered in this moment of our lives, dare I say, it was meant to be.

Like a bursting Volcano...

I wake with a pressure on my chest. Turning slowly to observe Lukas's arm above my bare breasts. That's when memories of what had happened earlier pops in my mind. I watch the clock on my night table. It's almost 10:30 am. Glancing again at him, he sleeps peacefully. My fingers slowly pull some strands of hair off his forehead. He looks so gorgeous sleeping.

My heart overflows with indescribable joy. This has finally happened. I'm alive again. Why wouldn't I want this? I deserve to feel this giddy. We're incredibly and wonderfully made for each other, even years apart. His fire matches mine, and honestly I hadn't imagined he would be this passionate and fierce in bed.

Grabbing his wrist carefully, I move it to be free of his embrace. Stirring a tiny bit, he turns sideways and continues sleeping. I grin lovingly, observing him.

Sitting on the bed, covering my nakedness with the comforter, I look for my nightgown in the scattered clothes on the floor. I can't find it. Maybe it fell under the bed. I grab Lukas's shirt, standing to dress in it. Looking over my shoulder in the mirror, I see my ass cheeks peeking out at the hem of his PJ shirt. I tip toe to the door, when a raspy voice I adore from behind stops me.

"If I knew that PJ shirt was going to look so good on you... *Mmmm.*"

Words don't do justice to the scene I'm witnessing. He's gawking at me, arms clasped at the back of his head, eyes full of renewed desire. The comforter barely covers his hips, his hard arousal jumping eagerly. Seeing this naked man in my bed, I can't help but think how favored I am. I'm mesmerized by the magnificent view he's showing me.

"Good morning. I thought you might still need to recover."

He chuckles, amused by my comment. Lifting the sheet with one hand, he simply orders, "Come back to bed Gabriella. We still have unfinished business to take care of. I promise you I'll top yesterday's gift. Let me show you how."

Grinning seductively at his invitation, how can I refuse? I walk back to the bed, smiling, curious to know how.

We made love once more that morning. He's intoxicated all my senses. Lukas knows how to make a woman go wild with passion. Each time, he makes it better and more intense. His lips know the right places to kiss, his hands the right part to touch, caress, or tease. Triggering every nerve in my body, he awakens the goddess within. He's my drug. I'm hooked on him with no hope of recovering nor do I want to.

I've gifted him all of me. My kisses, my passion, my very self. Every cell in my body craves and screams desperation for him. The passion is so overwhelming it worries me, but I don't want to think about it now.

We stay in bed, chatting, caressing, and playfully teasing each other. His cellphone rings. He jumps out of the bed, looking around.

"I don't remember where I dropped it."

Picking up his PJ pants, I throw them to him.

"I think is in the pocket."

"Thanks." Pulling the phone from his pocket, he quickly answers it.

"*Anneyong*, Jong…"

I leave him in my bedroom to talk while I take a shower to clean up. Going under the hot water, I close my eyes, feeling so relaxed and carefree. My body aches, the kind of sore from an intense body workout. I chuckle to myself. The water runs down my naked body, washing away the wonderful soreness, from our intense lovemaking, between my legs.

The shower curtain opens, and Lukas enters. Grabbing my waist to press his body against me, he starts to complain.

"Why didn't you wait for me?"

My God, he's insatiable. His gaze full of renewed desire and his body *showing* it. The stone hardness of his arousal is nested in my buttocks.

"Lukas, do you plan to kill me with orgasms? Because if that's so, I'm willing to die that way." Laughing I turning to hold his waist, pulling him under the water. He cackles out loud.

"Well, it's not my plan, I assure you. But with you, right

now, I can't help how much you turn me on. I'm still hungry for you."

The sweetness of his lips possess mine, obliviating my mind. Wrapping my arms around his neck, intensifying our kiss, my hands caress his wet hair. Water drips from our mouths as we kiss hungrily. Grabbing my knee, pulling it up, positioning himself, he holds his arms firmly bracketing my head, while his arousal slides deep, filling me completely. Gasping in delight, we make love, standing under the shower. He's thrusting steadily, in no rush. My heat increases while he satisfies me in every way. I'm in heaven and don't want this to end.

After our steamy shower, we eat a midafternoon brunch with all I'd set out for breakfast. I've brewed a new pot of green tea, and we sit down in the floor of the living room, feeding each other like it's a picnic. He seems relaxed, at ease with me. Watching him, I'm fascinated by how fortunate I've been to capture his attention.

But the little voice inside my head starts to torture me. Insecurities come back, and I question my decisions. I've let this happen, and I'm having doubts. I don't want to be a stone in his path or career either. For now, I'm content with this. So why is my heart so troubled, anguished?

He's talking, but I don't hear his words. I'm mesmerized, observing his handsome face, hypnotized by every expression he's making. He's pure art developing in front of me. It's like I'm watching him through a dream.

I'm starting to feel weird, not myself. Reality strikes with a brutal lighting headache making me flinch, shutting my eyes tightly. Grabbing my head, I curl in to myself. Distantly I hear Lukas calling my name. *Oh, God ease this pain. These fucking side effects.* Slowly the pain decreases. Lukas's desperate voice is calling me. He grabs my shoulders.

"Gaby… Hey, Gaby, don't scare me. Do you hear me? Gabriella?"

Regaining consciousness, gazing at him, I'm ashamed he's witnessed this. Inhaling deeply, Lukas appears frightened and hugs me tightly to his chest.

"Don't scare me like that. What the hell happened?" He's holding my face with his two hands.

"It's some meds I take. Sometimes they cause these headaches."

"Like the one you had in the leasing office parking lot. I was watching you."

"Yes." No point denying it. "The only problem is they're getting more intense each time." I sit up straight.

"And have you seen a doctor for this?"

"Yes, I'm seeing one. As recently as this last Tuesday, and everything is okay. He'd warned me about the effects of the meds and pain flares. I was returning from the doctor when you all intercepted me, remember?" I stand up, already feeling ok.

"How can I forget?" Rolling his eyes, he raises an eyebrow. "By the way, why did you kiss me in front of the guys?"

I watch him in disbelief.

"Really, Lukas? You want to bring that up? Okay, I'll explain. Kim was openly flirting with me in your face, challenging you. It was obvious to all of us you were upset. So I decided to let him know in a particular way that I'm with you, hoping to avoid a confrontation between you two."

He hadn't realized, understanding now. "Why do you think he was flirting? Because he kissed your hand and saluted you in Korean?"

My response lets him know I'm aware he knows.

"No, it wasn't because spoke in Korean and kissed my hand. I'm not gullible. I saw in Kim's eyes the same flaming desire your eyes had shown me the day we met. It's like you both crave and desire the same thing, like a competition between you two. I'm almost certain you know what I'm talking about."

His awkward expression shows me I'm right. *Got you, babe.* A mischievous grin appears on his face. "You're a treasure, Gabriella. Smart, beautiful, honest. I don't need or want anything more than we have." That ends the subject.

The rest of the day we'd shared each other, making love, talking until we'd finally been spent. Lukas stays the night with me, and we pass out cold early.

Around two am, I wake to watch him sleep soundly beside me. My arm rests on his chest while his hand holds it. Pulling slowly from his grip, his face distorts. He's speaking, visibly disturbed in his sleep.

"No, no. Please no."

Sounding panicked, scaring me with his rambling, I shake him gently to wake him. Desperately I grab his face with my hands, whispering softly to avoid scaring him more.

"Lukas, sweetie? Wake up. It's a dream. Wake up."

Opening his eyes, he seems disoriented and scared as hell, covered in sweat.

"Gabriella?"

He's looking at me as if it's the first time he's seen me.

"Yes, it's me. I'm here. You were having a nightmare." My hand caresses his face, wiping his sweat.

Embracing me, he crawls on top, kissing me with a desperation that troubles me. When I finally gasp for air, I ask, "Lukas, what's going on? Why are you behaving like this? What did you dream about?"

His anguished expression is unsettling, but I can't decipher it. There's some pain in his eyes.

"You... I dreamed about you. It was disturbing, that's all. I'm okay now."

"Want to talk about it?"

Shakes his head. "No. I'm all right. It was just a bad dream."

Gazing at me with adoring eyes, his lips slowly and tenderly take mine. Once those lips have touched mine, I melt in his embrace. His famished mouth trails my skin, worshiping me, my face, ears, jawline. Tracing down my body with his mouth, creating a sultry map along my skin, he's driving me crazy with his lovemaking. Our moans start to fill the room.

Again, I become one with him. Staring into his eyes, hearing his moans with each plunge, he's about to reach his release. I hold his face in my hands, love drugged, my hips matching his thrusts.

Between panting and breaths, I order him, "Open your eyes for me... Look at me while you're coming, baby. I want to see your eyes while you come... Don't close them."

Almost closing them, he complies, watching me, panting for air. He's surrendering his soul for me to see, discovering a magnificent lion staring back at me, how he really is.

I'm staying up... I don't wanna come down from your love...

My cellphone rings. I hurry to grab it from the night table. 7:30 Sunday morning, Marc's number flashes on the screen. I answer sleepily.

"Hello... mm... Marc... sweetie, what happened?"

"Gaby, I'm so sorry to wake you up so early, but by any chance, do you have info of Lukas's whereabouts? I've been trying to contact him since yesterday. I think he ran out of battery. His phone goes directly to his voice mail. I'm here at the apartment, and he's not here. We're really worried. Ty is with me."

"Oh, yeah. Sure, give me just a moment."

I pass my phone to Lukas while cuddling up on his chest, eyes closing. He grabs the phone to answer, still groggy from sleep.

"Hum… Hello… Marc? Morning. I ran out of battery late afternoon, sorry." He hugs me with his free arm, pecking my forehead.

"Bro, what the fuck is wrong with you?" Marcs shouts so furious and loud I hear him. Believe me, you don't want to mess with a mad Marc. He sounds scary and funny as hell. I chuckle to myself.

"You know, every night, we must report to Jong, every fucking night, you know it. Do you have any idea the stress you put me through last night? Jong asked for you yesterday, and I had to cover you, asshole. We called more than twenty times, twenty voice messages, and you didn't answer. We were worried sick about… Wait, wait a minute… Why… Why you are with Gabriella at this early hour? Did you… Did you sleep there last night?"

"Yes," we both answered, chuckling. Hearing his laughter on the phone, giggling too.

"Oh, wow. Okay…good for you both."

I hear Ty's voice interrupting, asking something in Korean. Marc explains to him, I suppose. Ty laughs aloud hysterically. I wonder what the heck Marc told him. Lukas is snickering too.

"As soon as you have time, call me back. Kim informed of a meeting with Vivian tomorrow to go over the presentation for next Saturday."

"Meet with Vivian? Why do I have to be there? The presentation is for you three. I'm only the composer in all of this."

He sounds upset. I open my eyes to observe him.

"I don't know, man. This is Jong and Vivian's idea. Jong approved and requested it."

"At what time am I'm supposed to be there?"

He sits up straight, his expression irritated.

"Eleven am."

"Okay, I'll be there. Call you later."

Once he hangs up and hands me my phone, he glances at me lovingly, exhaling. His face lights up, beaming again.

"Good morning. Sleep well?"

That mischievous grin has moisture flooding between my legs already. Answering playfully, "Yeah. A young, hot Korean guy I encountered yesterday exhausted me, so I slept soundly."

Laying on my back, I stretch my arms sensuously. He jumps on top, kissing my cheek and my neck, laughing.

Giggling while he mumbles in my ear, "Can you take one more exhaustion? I promise just one more…for the road."

With his knee pushing to spread my legs, positioning between them, I smile joyously, letting him take me where he's taken me for the past 24 hours: to heaven itself.

By noon, we decide to eat outside. He'd gone to his apartment to shower and change clothes. After an hour, the doorbell rings, open it to find Lukas.

"Ready to eat?"

"Yep, I'm famished. Where are you taking me?"

"Another surprise."

Lukas drives all the way to Los Angeles, taking an exit I know well. I imagine he learned how much I love this place. I know that Lola and Marc are seeing each other, maybe she said something.

"How did you know I love Santa Monica Pier? Who told you?"

Embracing his neck, I kiss his cheek, moved by it. He observes me, appearing dumbfounded and laughing.

"Well, this is a plus. Yes, we're going to Santa Monica but not for the usual places you think."

He keeps impressing me. We arrive at Santa Monica Pier, finding a parking lot about one block away. It's a busy Sunday afternoon. Lots of people walking through the park in front of the sea, others riding bikes. A handful of couples are having their own picnics in the grass or scattered across a pair of nearby benches. I've always loved Santa Monica's beach front. It's one of the most breathtaking sights to see.

Covering his hair with a black baseball cap, his sunglasses practically hiding his face, he takes my hand, guiding me. We stroll along the sidewalk bordering the beach in the direction of the pier. It's a beautiful afternoon, and the wind is blowing like a caress to the skin. It brings memories of the beaches back in Puerto Rico. We have the most beautiful beaches in the world, and that's not up for discussion. Closing my eyes just to smell the sea salt in the air is enough to transport me back there, and I feel nostalgic. Lukas pulls my hand, making me open my eyes.

"Here's the place. We've arrived."

In front of us, there's a food truck with Puerto Rican and Dominican Republic flags all over. A big sign says *Puerto Rican Food.* I cover my mouth in amazement.

"I found it about a week ago. Marc and I came for lunch, and we've returned two more times. I recommend the *moufoungleeta.* I think that's how is pronounced. The pork is really good."

I laugh, amazed, grabbing his face and smooching him quickly.

"It's pronounced *mofongleta*, but it's close enough. I'm impressed, Lukas. Thank you. This is really thoughtful. Pork sounds great."

We order our lunch and go searching for a bench in front of the bay, near the pier. *The mofongleta* is delicious. It brings back memories of the flavors of my island. I couldn't eat it all, so I saved half for later. Lukas ate his completely. What an appetite. *His stamina must be the reason.* He surely burns a lot of calories. That's why he's so fit. I titter to myself.

The bench we sit at is near the boardwalk, facing the sea. Putting his arm around my shoulders, he explains about this presentation for the guys and what it means to him. He informs me, after this presentation, there's a media tour for TV and radio programs in several states. Once concluded, he starts recording his own album. The plans are to present it first in South Korea. I've already learned he has completed seven of the ten songs the album will include. I love the fact he's so comfortable with me, talking about his dreams, goals, feelings in general.

We both watch the sun go down in one of the most breathtaking California sunsets. Walking back to the car, there's a group of small children running in a playground near the parking lot. Holding hands while passing by, one of the children sitting with his mom points at us, asking aloud, "Why is his mommy hold his hand? He can't walk by himself?"

The mom's face drains of color, watching us, instantly reprimanding the child. We both hear it but act like we don't. I receive a slash to my ego, affected by his words. It's a slap to my self-esteem. My mood suddenly changes. Lowering my eyes in shame, I quietly keep walking. Lukas observes me.

Inside the car, he takes off his sunglasses, almost reprimanding me.

"Gaby, don't pay attention to a child's words. They're nonsense." I'm upset and vulnerable right now.

"No, they aren't. Children don't lie like adults do. They say it like it is, like they see it. This is a reality we must live and accept, Lukas. If we decided to continue this, there will be lots of judgment from people we know closely when they find out. The world is cruel, brutal. I know this cruelty personally. Are you ready to face it? To be humiliated because of me?"

I stop talking. I'm choked up. *Why does my heart hurt so much?*

"Please, take me back home."

Grabbing my chin, he turns me tenderly to look at him.

"Gabriella, I don't care about the opinions of others. Neither should you. I only care what you and I have to say in this matter. This is about us. No one else should decide or give an opinion of what we should or shouldn't do. Everybody has their own idea what life should be. We're two grown adults. We make our own choices. Can you please finally understand that?"

I observe him with teary eyes. He's wise and mature beyond his years, but still… His thumb wipes the tear that's about to fall from my eye.

"The only thing I know and I'm sure of is I don't want to get over you. You came in to my life in a moment I needed a person to give me focus and teach me to be a better, more centered man. You're doing it. Because of you, I want to be better. I'm behaving better and, for the first time, like the man I'm turning out to be."

Bending over, he gives me feathery kisses on my lips until

he makes me grin.

"Now, that's my girl."

I open my eyes to find him looking at me seriously, caressing my face.

"I'll take you home."

Smiling, he pulls the car out of the parking lot to head back home.

If I let go of your hand, you'll fly away
and break...
I'm scared of that...

Chapter Nine

Gabriella

Shit. I'm late. The meeting starts in half an hour, and I'm still getting dressed. Pulling up my boots, I'm in a hurry to pick the media packets and be done with this last meeting with Harrison before my trip tomorrow to Las Vegas, when my cellphone rings. It's Lola.

"*Hola, Bonita.* How are you doing?" She sounds worried.

"I'm good, Lola. Getting dressed. I'm on my way there to pick up the material. What happened?"

"Had to call you. Harrison gave me the schedule for the press interviews at the convention. I discovered Shayan Anderson is on the list of press journalists who are going to interview you. I thought you should know about it ahead of time."

I sit straight up, my mood changing instantly. She has my full attention.

"Shayan is gonna be there? *Sea la madre.*"

"Yep, it's a bummer. But you know him better than anyone, so you can handle him like last time."

How can I forget? Shayan and I had an intense romance more than a year and half ago. We'd met at a media book launch the publishing company did in LA three years ago. Shayan is fifty-four and a descendant of the Navajo Indians. Extremely handsome with tan skin, he has soft, jet black hair he usually wears down to his shoulders or tied in ponytail. With a hard jawline and great body. He'd gotten too possessive and controlling with me, so I broke up with him. He didn't take it too well.

"Thanks for the heads up. I know how to handle him. Be there in a half hour, okay? Lukas and I overslept…"

"WHAT?" Her shout through the phone makes me aware she doesn't know.

"Oh, my God. I haven't told you…"

Now I have to fill her in. She will not give it a rest until I spill everything that has happened.

"Well, Lukas and I…have been seeing each other. And this Saturday… well… we finally *did it.* That's it."

This isn't over.

"Oh, no girl. Spill it out. You know that's half the information I need to know, so…talk," she commands, laughing.

I'm annoyed. I'm eating my own words, and she's enjoying this.

"We were supposed to have breakfast together. I suggested for us to stay in our PJs in my apartment. Lukas came in PJs, all right. We saw each other, one thing led to another, and we couldn't take our hands off each other. So we got naked and…we made love. That's all."

My face is so hot. Talking about this, my tone of voice reveals my shame. I recall his hands touching me *so intimately.*

"Okay, you're already embarrassed enough. For now, only one question remains for friendship's sake. How does it feel after a long drought of not getting laid?" Lola now laughs openly.

I giggle, thinking about him and answer honestly, "With him, it's pure heaven. He satisfied me into a sore and sweet oblivion. It was that intense."

"It sounds like you're falling for him."

My mood changes instantly. Her comment makes me uncomfortable. I'm still not ready to accept it.

"Of course that's not happening. I'm merely describing the level of *endurance* these guys have. Well, Lukas's at least. They're hardworking dancers. Just watch one video and you'll understand."

She chuckles. "Sure, hardworking dancers. Bet he danced a *hard* number into you."

"Lola," I exclaim, shocked.

"C'mon, Gaby. I'm not judging. On the contrary, I'm happy you finally allowed yourself some blissfulness. Bet his stamina matches yours."

"I'd compare him to the battery ad. The one with the pink bunny…it keeps going and going and going."

We both shake with laughter.

"How are things going with Marc?"

She inhaled, a resigned tone in her voice, timidly grinning, "We're in what I called the Trial Zone. He's testing the ground, and that tells me there's still no confidence yet. I don't feel bad. It's something he has to grow, learn, and overcome for himself."

So maybe Marc is having his reservations too, seeing what's going on between Lukas and me. I change the subject.

"Did the print material arrive? It has to be packed by now."

"Yes. Everything is packed in boxes and ready for you when you arrive. Harrison coordinated a chauffeur to pick you up tomorrow at one pm. Your flight leaves from LAX."

"Ok. Tell Harrison the chauffer should be earlier than that in order to make sure I arrive on time. Traffic is unpredictable at that hour."

"Got it. See you in thirty." I hang up.

I have to deal with Shayan again. Even just thinking about it exhausts me. I've handled him in the past, so I'm sure can do it again. Shayan can be so persistently annoying. I finish putting on my brown suede jacket. Opening my front door, I find Lukas standing about to ring the doorbell.

"Hey, you're going out?"

"Yes."

Sweetie, you look and smell divine. I could eat you up. Oh, crap… I realize I forgot to tell Lukas about tomorrow's trip to Vegas. My free hand grabs his neck to pull him down for a kiss to cool the blow. Grabbing my waist, he tugs me in to deepen the kiss. I step back.

"Lukas, tomorrow I fly to Vegas."

His face turns instantly serious, surprised.

"What? Why did you wait to tell me this now?" He holds my waist, confused. I close my eyes, feeling awful.

"I completely forgot. We've been so caught up with ourselves that I didn't think about it. It's a book convention that takes place every year. The company I work for is sending me to be their representative for several interviews taking place there. It'll be streamed so you can watch it if you want. I'll be back on Friday before the presentation."

"What time do you leave tomorrow? Do you want me to take you to the airport?" He looks gloomy.

"Thanks, but it's not necessary. The company is sending a

chauffeur to pick me up."

He exhales, resigned. A wicked smile grows on his lips, before whispering. "Do you have time for a *quick bite*?" he asks in a husky tone, biting his tongue.

Lowering my laptop bag to the floor, I caress him lovingly. I slowly open the top button of his shirt, putting my hand inside to touch his bare chest. My fingertips are cold, and he flinches at my touch, inhaling sharply. Chuckling at his reaction, I ask teasingly, "*Papi*, you're so warm. Can I get a rain check? They're waiting for me at the office right now. I'm already late. But I can meet after 6 pm for dinner."

Closing the button, I gaze at him adoringly.

"I'll have a *hearty meat* for you. Six pm at my apartment."

His lips softly trail the skin of my cheek.

"I can't hardly wait." I smirk while my lips hungrily find his to kiss them before leaving.

Lukas

It's a waste of my time. I know Vivian, and this is likely another one of her tricks to manipulate things. But Jong had requested my presence, so I'm complying. As I enter the meeting room, I find Marc sitting beside Ty, talking. In the far corner of the conference table, Kim and Vivian speak privately, and I become aware it's only the five of us. I'd expected to see other executives here, but there's no one else. Vivian's eyes widen, a panther watching her prey, when she sees me enter the room. Observing her in disdain, I sit with Marc and Ty.

"Well, what's so important I have to be here?"

With a sarcastic grin, she answers. "Wow, aggressive so early. I think you're actually going to like what we have planned, so let me tell you all about it."

The meeting is surprisingly productive. The executives' and Jong's suggestions in their last meeting to included me, not only as composer but as a solo singer, in the presentation on Saturday as a last-minute surprise, just one song, is genius. Now it's a presentation of four members of SMX18.

One tiny detail: I have to stay in LA the next few days to work on image, photo shoots, and wardrobe, all in a short period of time. I should be thrilled. This is what I've wanted. My solo career will be promoted before it even starts. But I can't help this weird feeling I'm being played. Vivian's made all the arrangements with the executives' and Jong's approvals. She doesn't do things from the goodness of her heart. She'll probably want to collect something in exchange.

Once the meeting ends, I try to leave quickly, putting away my laptop when she approaches.

"Well, what do you think? Still mad at me? This is a big step for the career you've always wanted. I know how talented you are. This is going to be a sure hit with you, and doors will finally open in the American market."

Her index finger caressed my hand. I flinch at her touch, upset, pulling away. Raising my eyes to meet hers, I can't hold my tongue any longer.

"I'll comply with the suggestions made here today. Like you said, it's a very smart career move. But let me make something very clear to you, Vivian. What happened between us was a huge, huge mistake. An unwise decision on my part. I already told you I've learned from my mistakes, and I am not going to repeat them. Do you understand? Let's keep it professional between us, for the business's sake, but I will give you nothing more than that."

My response seems to take her by surprise. She's uncomposed, reflecting the shock on her face. I stand and pass by, ignoring her.

God, it feels so good to let her know she doesn't control me anymore. I've really changed. She'd thought I would lower my defenses with this turn of events, manipulating me as always. It hasn't gone the way she'd planned, so I will have to be on guard with her this week. She's made it clear she wants to collect and gain control of me again. *You can't tempt me anymore, Vivian.* My new temptation is far more satisfying and wondrous than you'll ever be.

Obsession...

Gabriella

Once the meeting is over, I return to my apartment late afternoon. My carry-on has everything for two days of interviews, conferences, and meetings. I'm uneasy knowing Shayan is going to be there. I'm hoping we can be cordial with each other again.

I've picked up a couple bottles of strawberry Soju on my way home to try to understand why Koreans like it so much. I want to learn more about my man's culture. I chuckle to myself. My man. *He doesn't belong to you, Gabriella.* That damned tiny voice in my head, tormenting me. I shut it down instantly.

Serving myself one glass of Soju, I take a gulp to silence

my mind. This shit tastes good, like juice. Well, to be honest, this is my fifth glass of Soju, and I'm starting to feel the effects of the strong alcohol.

I think of Lukas all afternoon, creating a playlist for the plane. I've picked several songs Lukas sings in his videos, and I'm trying to find this particular song I saw him dancing to sensuously. Finding the English version, I gulp the last of the Soju in my glass, sit on my bed, close my eyes while listening to the lyrics, and imagine Lukas in front of me singing it.

...Everything changes when you enter my life,
I'm not the same man I was
My world now is revolving around you...

Sweet Jesus. It sounds like he's singing about me, us. I don't know if it's the Soju affecting me, the lyrics of the song, or realizing he's been residing in my very soul, haunting me since the we met. I'm grasping the hurt that's been in my heart these past days.

I'm in love with him. Lola's right. I've fallen in love without realizing it. It's too soon; this isn't right. How have I let this happen? This isn't what this is supposed to be. My heart hurts.

I'm dumbfounded at this realization. Like a ghost shouting in the distance, the words from Rene creep back in my mind.

In simple words, my child, grab happiness tightly with both hands, and don't let it go, no matter where it comes from. Don't let happiness pass you by.

It's only 5, but I've decided to head to Lukas's early to get all this off my chest. Striding to his apartment, I ring the bell, knocking on the door with my fist at the same time.

"Lukas, open up."

The door opens, showing a shocked Lukas, only dressed in

his jeans with his chest bare. *Fuck,* why must he look so freaking hot right now? I want to lick that damned lion looking back at me.

I hold the door frame to regain my composure. Really my balance, if I'm honest. I'm shit-faced drunk.

"I came here to tell you… I've fallen, fallen in love with you, which I understand is totally wrong… but I'm go-gonna do like Rene told me and grab happiness while it lasts."

I stop slurring my words, dizzy. Pointing my finger at him, I babble on.

"I kno… I know this isn't going to last. Eventually you're going to leave me, but I don't care."

I'm not making any sense.

"Have you been drinking?"

He's upset. Grabbing my arm, he pulls me inside his apartment to avoid our other neighbors seeing me in this state.

"Why are you drunk like this?"

Reclining on the entrance wall, I stare at him with sad eyes.

"I only drank a couple of glasses of Soju. I'm not that drunk. *No me regañes.*"

Tears flowing, I let my feelings out.

"I tried not to fall in love with you, Lukas. With God as my witness, I did try not to. But you…you've upended my life completely. Since day one, you've penetrated my mind and my heart. You're a disease inside me. Do you understand how wrong this is? I can't… I can't… I can't think straight anymore. Now I can't get you out of here." I point with my finger to my heart and then my head.

He exhales and rolls his eyes while wrapping me in his embrace, comforting me. The warmth of his bare chest on my cheek feels so exquisite. A sense of belonging overwhelms me. This is where my face should rest, always.

"What if I tell you I've fallen for you too? That I feel the same way you're feeling right now? You've occupied my very soul, tormenting me since I met you. I can't think of anyone else but you. You've made me realize I don't want any other woman beside me. I only want you. I love you too, Gabriella."

"This is not supposed to happen."

"I know. Maybe you didn't want it to happen, but it did. Sometimes you don't get to plan or choose these things; they just happen. And it's happened to us. I agree with you that this is crazy, unexpected, and sudden. But I also know this is rare, not everyone experiences this. I don't care if the whole world thinks this is wrong or twisted. For me, it feels so right and perfect."

My mouth falls open in disbelief, processing his words. *He loves me back.* He feels the same way I feel for him. When the right person comes along, you don't have to speak elaborate words or explain yourself to feel happy. It happens effortlessly. With him, it's easy to be myself, to trust and feel again.

Raising my hand to slip my fingers through his hair and pull him down, our lips touch. It feels like home. I don't care about anything but him. He deepens the kiss, while his skillful hands roam down my body, to grab my hips and grind himself on me. I'm unbuttoning my own shirt, wanting to feel my bare breasts against the skin of his chest. His desperate hands help me take it off, discarding it on the floor as he leads me to his bedroom. All of my senses are engulfed by him. I'm alive, in a way I haven't dared to hope before, getting to experience this exhilaration again. I'm grateful to heaven and life to be granted these feelings once more.

Sitting me on his bed, he takes off my boots, to pull down my pants while his warm lips trail kisses, along the skin of my legs, upward. Lukas stands back up, effortlessly pulling me with him. But instead, turns me around to face away, taking off my brassiere while planting tiny, hungry kisses on my shoulder. My head reclines on his shoulder, consumed by all of this. I close my eyes, letting this forbidden ecstasy spread inside of me. A moan escapes my lips as I sense his hands touching my skin.

We kiss with all the love pouring free, sweet and tender. He's doing something for me I couldn't do for myself. He's loving me for who I am. No demands to be someone else. We're perfect for each other. This thing between us has become so profound, so quickly that is impossible to ignore it. Eyes still closed, I connect with his soul. That's how I know it's meant to be.

I face him, to desperately unbutton his jeans. My greedy fingers caress the rim of his underwear. I touched the hair line below his belly button and goes all the way down. He gasps in delight, then moans, feeling my greedy fingers exploring those hard abs. I push him to sit on the bed. He watches me in shock, kneeling before him. I remove his pants with his underwear, leaving him naked, his marble-like arousal free. Standing, I slowly remove my panties for him.

The uncontrollable hunger flaming inside makes him wet his lower lip. The way he's watching me get undressed turns me on unmeasurably. Holding myself up by his shoulders, the lust in his eyes makes me frantic. I straddle him, lowering myself as he sheaths himself in me.

"Baby…"

His loud gasp of delight rings in my core. He leans down to kiss my breasts with tantalizing possessiveness, moving up to kiss my neck, embracing me tightly.

"Gaby… Oh, baby, I adore you." Exhales in my neck, in a

sex-love drugged frenzy. The fire of his passion meets my desperate thrusts with his. His arms wrap around me clingingly, while his hips pound me with desperation. I can't think anymore, only feel.

"Lukas… I'm yours. I'm all yours." I lovingly hug his head against me.

He gasps, while his mouth murmurs against my skin.

"Fuck, Gabriella, I'm insane for you. You feel so fucking good."

Grabbing his shoulders to steady myself, I plead breathlessly. "This feels so right. Please, don't leave. Don't push me away."

God, this moment feels so intense, so shattering, as I ride the wave of pleasure, that I want to cry.

"I'm not going to leave you. I belong to you…" Staring straight at me with his eyes full of promise, he slams into me faster.

"That's it, baby. That's it. Arghh!"

Raising his right hand to hold my head, he pulls me down for a kiss, wetting my lips with the tip of his tongue. I want to burn bright for him, to blind him with this fire inside. This spellbound intensity is new to me, not even with Xavier's dad had I felt like this. Is this how true love feels? Right now, it makes me want to live. Not survive, not merely exist. *Live.* The first waves of my release are hitting me.

"Lukas, this is so intense, baby." I'm gasping in a whirlwind of emotions engulfing me, my whole body throbbing to the ripples.

He captures my buttocks to quicken his pace. I can't hold back any more as I'm ogling into his eyes. Every cell in my body shatters. At the same time, I confess.

"I love you, baby…" I continue my scream of pleasure.

The orgasm goes on and on.

Tears rolls down my cheeks, matching the intensity of my pleasure. Never in my life have I experienced what I have with him. Ripples and ripples of energy flow through me as I'm shaking violently.

He's panting aloud, and lets out a half screamed, "*I love you.*". Lukas closes his eyes, finding his own release, branding me with his warm seed. He's crushing me in his embrace, while deliciously riding out our orgasms. We hold onto each other, understanding this love is meant to be, and we were meant to encounter each other. In this age and mindset, it is our time.

You'll always be my favorite...

Stop that hammering sound. This pain is horrible. I wake up to the most disgusting headache ever and nauseous. Trying to open my eyes, a ray of light comes from the window hurting them. I shut them again quickly, bringing my hands to my head.

"Oh, God. I'm not drinking Soju again. *Sea la madre.* My head is going to explode."

I hear his loud chuckle.

"Good Morning, Gaby. Last night was amazing."

I half open my eyes to see Lukas standing beside the bed, dressed in black pants and a white long sleeve shirt, which is still open while he fastens the buttons at the cuff.

"What time is it?" I sit up, covering my breasts with the comforter.

"It's 10:15 am. There's still plenty of time for your flight. Here..." He points to the nightstand.

"There's some orange juice, freshly squeezed and aspirin. I'm quite sure it's a hell of a headache you have."

"No shit."

He lets out another chuckle.

"Why are you dressed? Do you have a meeting now?" I hadn't considered he may be required to be somewhere else. He sits down on the bed beside me, gazing adoringly while caressing my face.

"I have to be in LA by noon and stay there. There's been a change in plans. I'm actually going to be presenting as solo singer with the guys. It's a smart career move to perform one song, so I'm doing photo sessions, wardrobe, you know, everything for promotion in a short period." He walks away, buttoning his shirt.

Crap. This is the part I don't like, the fame and what comes with it.

"Here's a note for the address of where the presentation is being held. Your name is on the VIP list. I'll be waiting for you."

I pick up the aspirin and the juice to wash down the pain reliever.

"Where are my clothes?"

"Here."

He brings them, folded. I pull up my underwear and jeans. He stops what he's doing to watch me get dressed.

"Are you gawking at me again?" I raise my eyebrow and smirk.

He grins, biting his tongue. "Yes. With you, always."

"I need to use the bathroom." I pass him with my shirt in my hand, closing the door behind me.

When I return, he's fully dressed in a black suit with a dark blue tie hanging around his neck.

"Can I do your tie? I used to do it for my ex. I'd love to do it for you."

His fingers signal for me to approach. I stroll slowly to stand in front of him. I tie the knot, adoringly watching this marvelous man life granted me to love so dearly.

"Now you look perfect."

Seeing his small carry-on luggage beside the door, I put my boots on and stand up.

"Well, I'll be going now. I need to shower and make several calls before noon."

Grabbing my waist, he kisses my neck. I can't get enough of how good he smells.

"You smell so good, and I must smell like drunkenness."

Letting out an honest laugh, he embraces me tighter. He bites his tongue, leans toward me, and speaks in my ear.

"Yeah, but you also smell like gardenia mixed with the passion we shared last night. It brings warm memories I wish we had time to repeat now." He kisses my cheek and lips. I blush.

Exhaling while gazing into my eyes, he confess. "It's going to be torture, waiting till Saturday to see you."

He gifts me one of his dangerous smiles. My mind shifts, momentarily thinking about the potential problem waiting for me in Las Vegas. Ugh, I don't want to deal with it.

I finally add to his heartfelt comment, "You have no idea how much I'm going to miss you."

Baby we can stay up... to the deepest point fall in love...

Chapter Ten

Gabriella

The check-in line at the Bellagio is longer this year than in previous years. I didn't expect so many people to be attending. The lobby is packed with representatives of various publishing companies here for the book convention. I meet with the employees of my company to deliver the materials I brought for the booths, making the final arrangements for the exhibitions.

I could match the decorations in the hotel lobby. There are Chinese castles and bridges everywhere, and the entire lobby is decorated in red, gold, and black. Something about the year of the pig. There are even cute pigs made of flowers all around. My black leather pants, black velvet thigh-high flat boots, and a red long-sleeve tunic match my surroundings perfectly.

Lukas texts. He misses me and wishes we could be in bed right now. Grinning like an infatuated school girl, I'm about to respond when I hear a familiar voice.

"Gabriella, what a wonderful surprise to see you again. I wish I knew who or what makes you smile like that. Your face is glowing in a way I've never seen before."

Shayan stands in front of me. He hasn't changed much and seems to have been taking proper care of himself. His jet-black hair is tied in a ponytail, a hint of gray in his sideburns. I'm pretty sure he was searching for me, knowing how he behaves.

I swallow hard, seeing him.

"Shayan, it's been so long. It's good to see you looking well."

He kisses my cheek, casually putting his hand on my waist. I shift back to drop it off my waist. He notices it.

"Still upset with me?"

"I'm not upset with you, Shayan. I truly wish you understood I have a life away from you. It's been more than a year, you know… And I've met *someone*."

His face turned in earnest.

"I see. You're still with the same publishing company?"

"Yes, that's why I'm here. I noticed on my schedule you're going to interview me tomorrow," I reply, smiling politely.

"At what time? I have several interviews to do throughout the day." He's trying to act uninterested, but he knows.

"I think 11 am."

"Afterward, do you have anything scheduled? Let's get lunch together to talk about old times. I promise I'll be on my best behavior." I knew it.

"Shayan, I don't know if that's a good idea."

"Just talk and lunch, Gaby, nothing more."

He's starting to toy with my emotions, knowing I will not be impolite.

"Okay. Just lunch. Afterward, I have other interviews." I can't hide my uncomfortable tone.

"Great. I'll let you settle in. See you tomorrow."

Winking at me, he walks away. I have to stay on high alert with him.

Going to the elevators, I catch sight of this beautiful dress in the window of a boutique. I haven't even thought of a dress to wear for the presentation on Saturday. It's a cocktail dress, with a heart-shaped neckline, in a sultry, see-through black lace, with bare back to the waist. The sleeves are long, and the hem of the skirt hits above the knee. I buy it without hesitation, adding a pair of dangling rhinestone earrings to match. Walking giddily with my purchase, my cellphone rings. It's him.

"Lukas, sweetie? Are you okay?"

"You didn't respond my message. I got worried." His voice sounds like music to my ears.

"I saw it. I wanted to be alone in my room to answer."

"I shouldn't be calling or interrupting. It's… I can't stop thinking about you. I need your naked body under me. Love you, Gaby."

With an audible sigh, my heart melts at his words.

"Love you too. I truly wish we could be together now. A couple more days," I reply, heartfelt, entering the elevator.

I want you to love me now… Love me, Love me now…

Lukas

I barely recognize myself. When has a simple call brought me so much joy? I watch myself grinning like an idiot, in the dresser mirror, just by hearing her voice. Is this what being in love feels like?

I'm putting my clothes in the drawers and closet of the record company's apartments, where I'll be staying for these next few days. There's a knock at the door.

"Come in."

Jong enters, his expression more serious than usual. I narrow my eyes, puzzled, bowing before him.

"*Joheun jeonyeok*, Jong."

"Lukas, my boy, we need to talk. Do you have time now?"

"Of course. Please come in."

I'm uneasy as I step aside to let him in. He enters and sits on the sofa.

"Lukas, I'll be direct. I'm worried. Kim came to me concerned, informing me that you're in a relationship with an older woman. And when I mean older, I mean older than you should be with. Ty confirms it. Even if your contract doesn't stipulate you can't date, this can harm you. If news of this gets out to the press, you know the possible damage it could do to your career here, not to mention back in Seoul. You've witnessed it happen to others. Did you stop to think about it?"

I feel exposed and dumbfounded. Kim must have fallen for Gabriella too. It's the only logical explanation for this.

The fucking competition. We've kept each other's secrets in the past. I've told him this rivalry is over, but I know him so well that I should have seen this coming. Damn it, Kim.

"Jong, my relationship is strictly private, away from the media. We both agreed to keep it like this."

"Well, your bandmates informed me she's invited to the event this Saturday. Please correct me if I'm mistaken."

"Why are we talking about this?"

I'm getting pissed off. I already know where this conversation is going.

"Lukas, I'm going to explain this as your manager, not as a friend. You're here in the States, *allowed* to live here, because the company deems it profitable. You don't realize it, but you're the crown jewel of years of efforts to produce a complete idol. You're about to become the ultimate one; everyone knows it. The next D-Dragon. That's why you're here. If not, you'd probably be back in Seoul. Many people around you respect you, but others hate you. They are envious, willing to do whatever it takes to make you trip and fall, for you to fail to get you out of their way in their path to success." He seems uncomfortable to be talking about this.

"I'm here not only as your friend but as the company representative. In this instance, my main responsibility is to protect our investment in you. That's why on Saturday, as your manager, I forbid any interaction with this woman. Is that understood? I can't control what you do in private. That's your business. But if you fail to comply with this, your privileges and working visa will be revoked immediately. Do I make myself clear?" Commanding eyes dart toward me.

My chest tightens in anger, and I inhale sharply, clutching my fists tightly, the rage boiling inside, "Yes, crystal clear."

"That's one thing I admire about you. You're one smart businessman and always do the right thing. Take care of the situation."

Putting his hand on my shoulder, he grips it lightly. Exiting, he leaves me to process what we just talked about. I'm annoyed, enraged, and frustrated.

Now I need to figure out how to explain this to her. It may cause her to back away from me again, and we'll lose all we've gained in these past few days.

Putting my hands on my head, I'm without answers. I don't know how to deal with this. I need to steady my heart and head, balancing both, and speak with Gabriella. I hope this doesn't end in a dumpster fire.

Simon Says...

Gabriella

Gazing at myself in the mirror, making sure the white *palazzo* pant suit looks okay, I see no panty lines. I add white high heel sandals, a gold choker, and gold earrings. I look like a fucking CEO. I'm giggling to myself cheerfully. I'm obligated to look my best today.

Since the interviews are streamed live on the internet, people I admire will be watching. My assignment today is to acquire contacts and achieve arrangements to expand the company to other countries, especially eastern Asian, if possible. If I obtain some partnerships, my financial future will be secure; that's the promise I received from Mr. Mackenzie.

I go down to the publishing company booth, meeting with my staff who are already waiting for me. Everyone's already drinking coffee or tea, chatting bubbly among themselves. Someone hands me my Puerto Rican coffee. They all know nothing else will do. This is non-negotiable.

"People, let's get busy. Let's make a statement."

Everyone clapped to my words, moving to their assigned places. Two of the members come to me to put a small microphone on the lapel of my jacket along with a small square transmitter on the back of my pants.

"You're truly made for this. It's in your blood, and you look amazing. I've always wondered why you haven't pursued journalism with your advertisement expertise." Shayan's voice sounds behind me. I face him.

"I never liked snooping around other people's business. It's not me. Why are you here? You're not my first interview."

"No, I'm next. But I wanted to tell you I'm looking forward to our lunch date afterward."

"I can imagine."

The guys finish setting up my microphone, and Shayan approaches, standing much too close to me. He lowers his face nearer to talk quietly.

"I'm not the same man you met several years ago. I've changed. I'm just asking for the opportunity to show you, that's all."

He leaves me rattled with his confession. I stare down, pissed off with myself for being this affected.

"See you later, Gabriella." He turns to walk away toward another booth.

When facing the camera, I see the green light lit. It's turned on.

"Is this live right now?"

His response is a normal *Yes*. My heart sinks in my chest, hoping no one has seen it, someone being Lukas.

Lukas

"Lukas, you're next."

Getting up from the makeup chair, I pull the tissues from the collar of my shirt while I make my way to the photo shoot. Today I've searched for news about her, anything mentioning her name. I've read the entertainment news on the internet and seen a picture of Gabriella at the Bellagio lobby, taken from a distance. She looks magnificent in those leather pants, boots, and red tunic. *Shit.* Now I'm craving her.

I'm walking through the hallway, accompanied by a team of assistants assigned to make this all happen before Saturday. My life has always been this frenzied with the expectation to do things in a short time.

I'm trying to connect to the convention's online transmission to see if I can get a glimpse of her today. The link is active before time. I see her standing sideways while one guy puts a microphone on her lapel and another puts the transmitter in her pant waist. She looks irresistible. I'm craving her right now. The microphone turns on.

"You're not my first interview."

"No, I'm next," a male voice speaks to her. It sounds like they know each other. "But I wanted to tell you I'm looking forward to our lunch date afterward."

I stop walking, my full attention on the video.

"I can imagine."

She sounds uninterested, but still… *Chill, Lukas.* Maybe it's a business contact, a lunch meeting. I see him standing close, lowering his head, obviously to whisper to her, with lustful eyes.

"I'm not the same man you met several years ago. I've changed. I'm just asking for the opportunity to show you, that's all."

A cold sensation in my chest spreads to rage inside me. *I'm jealous.* I've just realized never felt this intense discomfort in the past. This is new for me. Knowing she's miles away with this dude hitting on her has my blood boiling.

"See you later, Gabriella."

So they're meeting for a lunch date. I have to stop torturing myself. A voice in my head is screaming… *I don't want him near her, and I can't avoid it.*

"Is this live right now?"

That's it for me. I turn it off, not wanting to hear or see more. Something is going on there, and I'm concerned. I text her, maybe making a mistake. *We need to talk.*

Gabriella

I receive a text from Lukas. *We need to talk.*

Shit. He probably saw us and must be confused. I have to explain Shayan to him to avoid any misunderstandings. Not right now though. I decide to call him later to let things cool down a little bit before talking.

Good morning. Getting ready for my first interview. As soon as I have time, I'll call you. Love you.

Since then, everything has been trouble-free. My first interview goes great, and the interview with Shayan goes more smoothly than I anticipated, thank God. He only asks pertinent questions about the books we're presenting. But at the end, something he says makes me edgy.

"Gabriella, you're one of the top ten editor-slash-copywriters here in California. We know many writers who would love your input for their books. Have you received an invitation to the next book convention in Seoul, South Korea?"

I try to control my facial expression. Panic crawls up my spine hearing his question. *Seoul...* How does he know? Has he found out about Lukas and me?

"No, I don't know what you're talking about."

He must notice my uneasiness and clarifies it for me.

"One of the biggest book conventions is taking place in Seoul, South Korea in one month to bring together a huge merge of world writers and people from the industry. It's a unique gathering to exchange ideas and connect to the readers on the other side of the world. Surely you are invited."

"Sadly, no. I haven't received any invitations that I'm aware of."

"I'm sure you'll receive it shortly. No convention is complete without you."

Giving me an intense look as if suspecting something, Shayan wraps it up.

"Well, thanks for your time. We're looking forward to seeing more of Longest Quill Editorial and these new books coming out next quarter. Thanks to the viewers tuning in, until next time, read your way to smartness."

We wait for the cameraman to say, "Cut."

"You've never heard about the biggest yearly convention that takes place in Seoul, Gaby? How's that possible?"

"I don't know about every convention or conference going on, Shayan. If the company receives the invitation and deems it pertinent for me to attend, they inform me. They haven't mentioned anything, so I presume there's no invitation yet."

"Okay. Don't get all piss about it. I'm sure before this day ends, you're going to get that invitation; you'll see. Ready to go to lunch?" he asks, raising an eyebrow.

"Yeah, sure. Let's go. My next interview is at 2:30, so I have to be back before then. Where are we going?"

"Just around the corner to *Noodles*, the Asian restaurant here in the hotel."

What a joke today. Everything is revolving around Asians. As if I don't have enough with the Asian guy back home, driving me crazy.

I inform my co-workers where I will be, and we walk to the restaurant while he talks about his TV segment.

"Anderson, table for two."

We sit down, and he orders the drinks.

"I would like some scotch, soda with lime, and the lady still likes a dry martini, James Bond style?"

"Martini, not too dry, shaken, twist of lemon zest, two olives, please."

Our conversation turns cordial. I'm grateful for it. Usually when we talk, it's uncomfortable. Conversation always leads to him attempting to make me come back. Today seems different. We talk about business and future projects. Eventually the conversation leads to the part he's most interested in: my love life. I knew eventually we'd get here.

"So… Who's the new guy who has gotten your attention?"

"That's my private life, Shayan. The only thing you're allowed to know is that he's Asian."

"Asian guy? From which country?" He tries to pressure me.

"That's none of your business. We keep it private, so I'm not telling you anything."

His expression turns serious, upset. He isn't accomplishing what he wants.

"You know I can find out anyway if I want to." He utter those words, staring at me intensely.

I freeze. My chest turns cold. It's a threatening remark, and my mood turns defensive.

"Is that a threat? I hope not. You better leave us in peace. Don't mess with me; it's not going to end well for you."

I stand indignant, ready to leave him there. If someone tries to damage Lukas in any way, I'll eat them alive. Never mess with a Boricua and her man. He tries to mend his words.

"I apologize for my last comment, please don't go. You're right. It's none of my business, and I've overstepped. Forgive me."

Signaling with his hand, he invites me to sit back down. I stare at him with rage bubbling inside me, trying to cool down.

Sitting slowly, I want to hear what his next move will be so I can protect Lukas. He can send his investigators, and in less than two days, he would know Lukas is the one I'm sleeping with. They're really that good. I'm aware how devastating this could be for Lukas if the press finds out he's sleeping with a woman old enough to be his mom. I can't allow it. So I have to be more clever and wiser.

"Assuming by your protective reaction, the guy must be in the business, entertainment maybe."

I don't blink, my expression unreadable.

"I already told you that's none of your business. That's my private life. It feels like you're stalking me again. Why?"

I lean in so only he can hear me.

"Why do you insist on this behavior, Shayan? Why can't you understand what I felt for you is gone? You personally drove it away, and you know it. These are the consequences of your actions; understand that."

Standing up to leave, I've decided I don't want to put up with him anymore.

"You know what? This is the very reason I left. The stalking, the constant harassment, the lack of trust on your part, you never let me breathe. I can't deal with you right now, okay? You had plenty of time to figure it out. I'm not going to fall for your game of guilt trips. So I'll ask you to leave me alone and don't approach me again, understood?"

"Why don't you let me show you I've changed, Gaby?"

He keeps trying to use the manipulation card on me. Well it won't go as he's planned.

"In what way have you changed, Shayan? Threatening to stalk me again is an improvement to you?"

My Puerto Rican rage is blown out of proportion. I point my finger in his face.

"Let me make myself clear. If you ever in any way attempt to harm me or anyone dear to me because of your stupid, sick obsession, I'm going to search for you. I'll find you, I'll rip your head off and eat it like candy. Is that understood, Shayan? *No jodas conmigo.*"

His face falls like I've slapped him. People at nearby tables watch us when I raise my voice. I'm so enraged at him for threatening Lukas without even knowing him. His reaction is fearful. He knows in my rage I'm able to do what I just said.

Walking out of the restaurant to the publishing booth, I quicken my pace, still fuming. I'm pissed with myself for thinking he could change. Strutting furiously, I turn a corner without looking, and I collide with a group of Asian gentlemen in dark suits, bumping into the oldest one. I'm appalled and ashamed of my carelessness.

"Oh, my God, I'm so sorry. It's my fault. I wasn't looking

where I was going." When the old guy I collide looks at me, he smiles like he's glad to see me.

"No need to apologize, Ms. Morales. It's just a harmless accident. We were in a hurry to catch up with you. Your staff told us where you were having lunch. So we also apologize."

Every single gentleman in the group bows before me in a sign of reverence. I feel my cheeks burning. I'm blushing terribly at this.

"Please, don't... Wait. *What?* How...how do you know my last name? Why...why were you looking for me?"

Today a mixture of Asian situations surround me. It's getting scary.

"We learned you're one of the top ten editors-slash-copywriters in California, but from a reliable source, we also learned you're actually one of the top five in your line of work. We would like to extend an invitation to the Seoul International Writers Festival taking place a month from now as one of our foreign guests. As our guest, your expenses will be covered. We apologize deeply for offering this invitation on such short notice, but we would consider you a valuable asset for our Festival"

I'm speechless, processing his words. As if it's a matter for me to say no. This is the opportunity of a lifetime and to be invited personally is the cherry on top.

"Yes, of course. It's an honor and a privilege. A dream come true, believe me. Thank you." This has turned out pretty swell.

Way to go for a jibarita from Caguas, Puerto Rico.

"Our assistant will contact your team to make all the necessary arrangements. It's a huge honor for us to have such a distinguished guest. We will see you soon."

Again, they all bow before me. I turn around to see if anyone else is witnessing this. My whole team observes with wide eyes and mouths open. Staff members, from other publishing companies' booths, nearby gaze dumbfounded at the display before me. Still bowing, they're waiting for me to reciprocate. I return the bow. They straighten up, smile, and walk away.

I raise my hands in the air, dancing and swaying my hips in a victory signal. We're cheering and clapping for this major win for my team, the company, and myself.

Can't stop me... Can't stop me. I'm going far away...

Chapter Eleven

Lukas

After long hours of rehearsals and photo shoots, I'm desperate to be alone. Walking past the common area where several of the dancers are sitting and talking with the guys, I notice Kim and Vivian sitting in a far corner, chatting in whispers. They stop to watch me passing by. I'm so pissed off at him this very moment. I turn away, avoiding their glance, not wanting to intrude or know what the heck they're scheming about.

Marc approaches, all smiles, his hand going to my shoulder.

"Ty and I are going to eat at a restaurant nearby and maybe have a few drinks. Come with us. Today was hard on you with all those rehearsals. You need the break."

"Thanks for the offer, but I just want to take a hot shower and lay down. Perhaps some other time. I'm in a sour mood. You know me. I'm not fun to be around when I'm like this. I need some rest."

His curious stare says he knows there's something bothering me.

"You wanna talk about it?"

"Nah, it's nothing. Nothing you can help me with anyway. Don't worry about me, I'll be fine once I rest." He pats my shoulder in agreement and walks away.

I'm still upset about what I saw this morning. I haven't heard from her all day long. I'm restless like a lion locked up in a cage, knowing someone's trying to conquer her while she's so far from me. Insecurities I didn't know existed are playing tricks with my mind. The guy must be around Gabriella's age. He's more up to her alley. And he's going for her.

Entering the bathroom, I take off my clothes and step into the shower to cool down my mood. Standing there under the running water for some minutes, I think of her, wondering what she's doing now. I have to calm my thoughts. I trust her. But the knot in my chest won't go away.

Coming out of the shower, I wrap a towel around my waist and dry my hair with another, my mind is divagating. Her image, naked and laying sensuously on the bed, is haunting me. That view should be mine only. My thoughts are interrupted abruptly. I'm now upset to find Vivian waiting for me, reclining on the sofa.

"Surprise."

Sudden anger lights my eyes, seeing her take the liberty of entering my room without invitation. The nerve of this woman.

"What are you doing here? I don't recall asking you to my room." With my hands on my hips and droplets of water still falling from my hair, I'm annoyed to see her.

I knew it was just a matter of time before she tried something. Her mere presence irritates me now.

"I'm in no mood to deal with you, Vivian. Please leave my room."

Walking to the door, I open it for her to leave. Standing up, she closes the door with one hand, facing me. She slowly starts to unbutton her blouse, revealing her breasts. It's one of her old seduction tricks. This woman is unreal. I'd learned this seduction script of hers so well that it's not fun anymore. How did I fall for this in the past? I didn't know what I wanted back then; that's for sure.

"I'm not going anywhere, Lukas. I just want to talk, sort things out. You know, solve our differences like we have done in the past, that's all. It's always been so easy. The truth? In the end, it will be you, darling. No man can satisfy me the way you do. I need to feel your body on me again."

Speaking with her sultry snake-like voice, she caresses my wet chest with her hands, raising them around my neck. Her lips trail kisses down my neck, going back up. Taking her hands from me and lowering them, I step back. She's disconcerted by my action.

"There's nothing to be resolved here. Why don't you understand I don't want anything to do with you? I thought made myself clear."

She's trying to force a grin again, ignoring me, her face indignant and obstinate. She keeps talking like everything is fine between us. I don't understand.

"C'mon, Lukas. What's going on? You've never rejected me before. Last time, we argued pretty rough. Maybe I said things that hurt your ego, but you know I'm impulsive sometimes, and you like me like this. I admit our relationship is unusual, but you've never objected in the past. It's worked out for us without problem. What's different now?"

She approaches again to put her hands on my chest, caressing it. "I'm hungry for you. You know how to give a woman so much pleasure, ravishing me. And you know I can melt this tension you're experiencing with my mouth around your cock. Don't you want it?"

A couple of months ago, I would have dropped my towel and made her kneel to fulfill her offer. But she's right that something has change in me. Something is different now.

"Please, Vivian, get out of my room. I need to get dressed."

"We have seen each other naked before, and you've never asked me to leave. What's going on with you?" Gazing lustfully at my abs, she caresses them as her fingers trail down to take my towel off. I grab her wrist to stop her.

"Vivian, don't. My patience is thinning. I'm in a bad mood today, so don't try me. Get out."

My cellphone rings. Releasing her, I walk to the night table to pick it. It's Gabriella calling. *Shit.* What a bad time to call. With Vivian here, I can't answer. She'll surely do something stupid to compromise me.

"Well? Aren't you going to answer? Unless...your new plaything is calling you," she concludes, smirking.

That's the cue I need to lose it.

"Okay, that's it. Get out, Vivian. Now."

Rushing to her, I hold her firmly by the arm, open the door, and push her outside. She trips on her feet against the doorframe. With her red hair disheveled and her blouse still open, she straightens herself, watching me, full of rage.

"This isn't over, Lukas. You'll regret turning me down."

She stomps past me to the elevator. I gaze to the other end of the hallway to find Kim standing there observing us. He stands there a minute and walks slowly in opposite direction. What the hell is he up to with Vivian? I watch him, upset, not feeling the necessity to explain myself nor the interest to do so. So I turn around, enter my room, and close the door behind me.

Jealousy, baby, jealousy...

Gabriella

Lukas has called me several minutes since I'd hung up. My disposition is so cheerful I can't hide it.

"Lukas, sweetie, are you okay? Did I interrupt something with my call?"

I hear him exhale sharply, as if hearing my voice relaxes him.

"No, I was taking a shower when you called. Are you okay? I've been worried about you all day," he confesses to me.

"Why? You know I'm perfectly fine. What's troubling you now? Tell me."

He pauses as he's looking for the right words, making for an awkward silence.

"I think I sense what's troubling you. You saw the initial morning transmission when the crew was setting up the cameras. You overheard my conversation with Shayan; am I correct?"

Now he knows I know.

"Yes..." is his heartfelt answer, ashamed to admit it.

"Shayan was my fiancé a couple of years ago. I broke up with him when he became too controlling with me, to a point I felt constricted. He's still having a difficult time understanding it. But don't worry, it's already taken care of. I made it clear he should leave me alone. He shouldn't bother any more."

"I'm sorry. It's not like me to behave this way. My world has turned upside down since you came in to it, Gaby. I can't bear the thought that someone else is pursuing you. I've never felt this way before," he confesses. "It's new for me."

His words moves my heart. A love that's pure and genuine. I change the subject to improve the mood of the conversation.

"I have some good news to share with you. One of the biggest publishing companies in Seoul has personally invited me to the Annual Seoul International Writers' Festival as a guest of honor in a month. I'm visiting your country for the first time. It's a big step in my career and the company, so I'm ecstatic."

"That's great news, Gaby. I'm so proud of you. You're an amazing, talented woman. There's so much you can accomplished there. You said it's going to be held when?"

"A month from now."

"I'll be here with Ty, but Kim and Marc will be in Seoul by then. They have several presentations there, I think."

He seems lost for words. I sense a certain sadness in his voice.

"What's going on, Lukas? I can tell there's something you want to tell me, and you're holding back. What is it?"

He inhales nervously. "Gaby, I want you to understand this wasn't my idea. I'm not happy either. Please, don't be mad at me."

He's alarming me with this line of words.

"Lukas, please just tell me. You're scaring me, and I don't like to feel like this."

"My manager came to my room last night. He knows

about us. The guys told him they met you and confirmed the *nature* of our relationship. He made it clear we cannot be seen together at the event."

A cold shiver creeps up my back hearing those words. I'm kind of freaking out. Not for me, for him. I'm aware what a bad blow to his career it would be if news we're together got out to the public back in Asia.

In that part of the world, fans are so judgmental about everything. The way you dress, the color of your skin, your race, even who you date is reason enough for gossip and bullying. I saw it. The backslash could destroy his career, without considering the wreckage they leave behind by their actions. They extend the same foul behavior to family members. My chest compresses, and headache flares start to pulse.

"Lukas, I know you want me to come, and I promised your bandmates I'd be there. But it's better for you and everyone else if I don't come at all."

"No. Don't suggest it. I want you there, even if it's just to see you from a distance and stare at your eyes. You're my peace, remember? I need you with me that night."

To reveal this part, this hidden vulnerability deflates me. I understand for him being in love is more intense. I have the calm mind of years of experience. For him, it's something completely newfound, strong, and confusing. I must honor and respect his openness and trust.

"Okay, okay. Calm down. I'll be there for you. I promise. I'll stay far away, like I don't know you. No worries, Lukas."

Letting out an audible sigh, he sounds relieved by my answer.

"I don't deserve you, Gaby. I'm the luckiest man in the world to have you in my life. Being with you makes me believe in a joy I never knew existed. I confess, as the years have passed by, my heart has hardened to protect myself from getting hurt by others. I'd become numb to emotions, and I'd about lost hope of ever feeling anything again. The truth is I've never understood what it means to be in love. I'd believed infatuation and some unhealthy attachments had been love. The idea of real love had been a fake one, only in pretty lyrics to sell to fans. But with you, everything is so intense and unexpected."

I'm all teary, hearing his confession. I'm unworthy of gaining this fresh, new love when I hadn't hoped for it. God, I know it's wrong, but I deeply love this man. I don't see a boy. I see a man. I see his soul, and now he shows me his heart. I'm overwhelmed.

The tireless debate of what's wrong and what's not starts in my mind. Why am I feeling guilty for loving him? Why should I have to deprive myself of this love? The time the heavens grant me with him, I'll take it, no complaints or questions. I sniff my running nose caused by my tears and try to sound more cheerful.

"I'll be there for you, sweetie. Look for the *Boricua* in a black lace dress; she'll be there, watching from a distance."

Chapter Twelve

Gabriella

Opening my eyes lazily, I wake up and stare at the dress I'm going to wear tonight hanging from the door. I'll finally see him today. His absence now leaves a void in my heart only his presence can fill. It feels unusual, craving his company like this. I get up and go to the kitchen to brew coffee when my cellphone rings.

"Lukas, sweetie, how are you doing?"

"Hi, Gaby. Still in bed. Doing fine, a little anxious. It's always like this for me every time there's a first presentation. Are you okay?"

He's speaking so fast and sounds overly keyed up.

"I'm okay. You're the one sounding worried. Hey, hey. Take a deep breath. Everything is going to be okay, baby. It's going to be spectacular tonight, you'll see. You've nothing to worry about. You have already told me all of you are a hit back in Seoul. I'm sure all four singles are going to be a hit here too. Easily."

He sighs audibly. He's anxious or wants something.

"Woke up thinking about you. Need you right now in my arms, in my bed, naked, to help me relax." Slowly he exhales, his voice sultry. I let out a chuckle.

"I bet you do. Sadly, I'm almost an hour and a half away from you. There are traffic jams at this hour, and I know your day is going to be hectic. I think we have to wait till later tonight. Your apartment or mine?"

He laughs, knowing I'm the only one who can match his hunger.

"I don't care which one, as long as you're in it and ready for me." A vaguely sensuous tone surrounds his words.

My body aches for his touch, so I don't deny it. "I'm ready for you, Lukas. Just several more hours."

Grunting in agony, almost chuckling, he complains, "That's not fair, Gabriella. Hearing those words, my morning *wood* hurts now."

I laugh. "I'll make it up to you, for your suffering, later on. See you tonight."

Think you're ready for the monster...

I'm mortified beyond belief. I'm almost an hour and a half late. This traffic jam to LA tonight is impossible.

"Traffic is going nowhere. What's going on in LA tonight?"

The Uber driver watches me through the rearview mirror to answer. "I think there's a Lakers semifinal at the Staples plus a concert at the Hollywood Bowl. Several things going on tonight. Once I take the next exit for a shortcut, we will arrive at your destination quickly. I apologize for this."

"It's not your fault. I should have known and made plans ahead of time."

Staring at my cellphone, there are no messages from Lukas. I decide to write to let him know.

I'm on my way. There's a traffic jam to LA, many events going on, should be there in next fifteen minutes or so.

The driver arrives twenty-five minutes later. I'm upset and pissed off at myself for arriving so late. I walk directly to the entrance and identify myself with two hosts.

"Morales, Gabriella, from Longest Quill Editorial, should be on the list."

One of the hosts verifies and smiles.

"Yes, Ms. Morales, your table is 2A in the VIP section, Harold is going to take you there. Enjoy the presentation."

Following the host, we enter a huge, impressive salon. Most of the tables are set around a massive stage for people to have the best view. From the roof hangs four monumental banners, each with a photo of one of them. They look like wizard houses representative in those famous books. Marc is blue; Ty is yellow. Kim is all green, and Lukas is red. I can't hold a smirk at the similarity.

People are shouting and clapping. Everything is dark. I assume one of them had just finished singing. A small group of fans had won tickets through a radio contest to get a glimpse of the new material. It seems like a concert vibe is going on, and the energy from the people here is contagious. That's great news for the guys.

Walking to the table, I'm aware several eyes are staring at me, murmuring, trying to figure out who I am to be walking to the VIP section. My host shows me to my table. I'll be sitting beside all the press. *Fuck.*

"The waiter will be with you shortly. Enjoy your evening." The gracious host smiles, bowing candidly. This whole assembly speaks money. I'm almost certain they're wearing

Ellie Saab couture, maybe some PR exchanges through partnerships. Even the waiters are sharply dressed and seem to being accustomed to attending to celebrities at these type of events. He steps away, walking with such confidence while I observe him.

Shortly after, an elegant dressed waiter arrives. His friendly face greets me. "Good evening, madame. What will the lady be drinking tonight?"

"Martini, not too dry, twist of lemon peel, shaken, two olives, please."

A familiar voice speaks near my ear.

"There's only one woman I know who orders that drink. Believe me, I'm not following you; I swear. It's interesting you're here, when you don't have any reason to be. So maybe *he* will be around here."

Shayan's voice scares the hell out of me. The lioness in me jumps out, on guard.

Lowering my voice for only him to hear, I whisper, "What the fuck are you doing here?"

"Think I should be asking you that, Gaby. I'm entertainment press; it's my job to be here. But you...you have to have been invited to be here."

I'm tense. Shayan is a clever man, and he can deduce why I'm here. He's making clear he knows I shouldn't be here. He suspects but is not positive why, which gives me an advantage. All I need to do is mislead him.

"You and your imagination. You will never change. The nagging, the stalking, your need for control. I'm representing my company here tonight. We're planning a photo book of the K-pop industry and artist's history, nothing more."

I lie unashamedly to cover myself. I go with this story so Lukas isn't connected to me. In truth, it's a great idea. Maybe

I can make it possible and profitable, especially with the Seoul International Writers Festival next month.

Lights over the stage turn on, and I watch all four of them receive standing ovations. I spot Lukas dressed in a black velvet suit with a black see-through shirt with tiny rhinestones, showing his naked chest. His black hair has some red streaks in it.

I observe him searching for me, and I panic. I don't want anyone to connect us. Finally he sees me, his eyes wide open, staring back. He must notice my scared expression and Shayan standing beside me. He opens his mouth, seemingly worried. I shake my head quickly for him to do nothing. He switches his focus to the fans screaming and clapping for them. The waiter arrives shortly with my drink.

"Your Martini, Madame…"

"Thanks." Grabbing it from his hands, I drink a big gulp.

"Please, bring another. This one is almost empty," I tell the waiter, who watches me, astonished.

"Okay." Wide-eyed, staring back before he turns to walk away. Shayan's intense gaze studies me.

"I think I hit a nerve for you to be this thirsty."

Let me stop him right there.

"Okay, Shayan, enough. Is this how you think you'll win me? You're going the opposite direction, behaving like this. Haven't you learned your lesson? Why do you keep making the same mistakes? It's tiresome with you. All I want is to be far away from you right now. That's how uncomfortable you make me feel."

His face falls. Something finally may have clicked in his brain, and my words seem to get through his thick head. He must realize his behavior pushes me further away by his ashamed face. It has taken me reprimanding him like a little boy to react, lowering his eyes, heavy with the realization. His tone was apologetic.

"I was out of line again, I'm sorry. I want you for myself again, and don't know how to make that happen. What we had was so special, Gaby. I miss it... You're right. This isn't the way, so I'll keep my distance for now." He walks backward, expression ashamed, his humiliation obvious.

"Shayan. Wait."

Shit, mi corazon blandito—my soft heart. He keeps his distance, lowering his eyes.

"You have great qualities, but you still have to work on this distrustful behavior of yours, and you know it. The last thing I want is to be enemies with you. It's not who I am. So, please let me be. Let's do the friendship card again, okay? Deal?"

He raises his eyes and half smiles.

"Okay, deal."

Picking up my hand slowly, he kisses it and walks away.

Exhaling with relief, I glance at the stage. Lukas concerningly stares at me. With my lips, I confess, *It's okay. I love you.*

He gazes adoringly at me with a timid smile, followed by his mimicking lips answering*: Love you too.*

Lukas

Lights ignite, I fix my sight to where Gabriella should be sitting. I see her and the Shayan guy, from the video, standing at her side, talking to her. She seems scared. I have this urge to run across the stage to protect her. She shakes her head quickly to stop me. She's trying to be casual so no one suspects us. I switch my attention to the fans, saluting them, smiling.

Turning to see her, she's arguing with him. My chest feels tight, not knowing how to act. Returning my eyesight to the fans and hiding my emotions, I control my turmoil. I can't concentrate and watch her. He's kissing her hand before walking away, looking forlorn. It boiled my blood that he touched and kissed her hand. I want to be the only one to touch her skin.

She looks ravishing tonight. Just observing her, I'm at ease. How can I be so lucky this magnificent woman allows me in her life? She moves her lips… *It's okay. I love you.*

I'm the king of the world right now, got it all. I don't care if someone watches me. I mouth, *Love you too.*

I'm the last to perform. Tonight I'd decided to release the song I'd composed barely three days ago. It had been easy to write this song, just thinking about her. It's the first time, in all my years as a composer, a song ever made so much sense. Thinking about how everything has changed since she bumped into my life, I want her to listen to how she makes me feel. And the best way I can express it is through my music.

I'm happy she's here to hear *her song*. I've asked for a spectacular grand piano to perform it acoustically. Turning my earpiece on to speak, a string quartet sit on chairs beside the piano.

"For those who don't know me, I'm Lukas Lee."

The usual screams silence me.

"I know for some this is unexpected. This is a last-minute arrangement I want to share from my first solo album, which I am currently working on. I hope you like this particular one;

it's my favorite. I've had recent inspiration for it, so here it is. For your approval, *I Surrender My All.*"

While I sit at the piano, Marc, Kim, and Ty walk off the stage. All the lights dim except for two spotlights over me. I play the overture of the song, looking up to stare in her direction briefly, just to say aloud.

"This one is for you."

All fans present started screaming and clapping at my words.

Gabriella

I inhale, overwhelmed by hearing his introduction, gazing back at him. My chest bubbles with overflowing emotion. It's so difficult to pretend we don't know each other. But right now, I don't care. Even though we're not alone, it feels like there's no one else here. In my mind, we're the only ones in a huge auditorium while he sits at his piano, ready to start singing. And then he sings for me.

In the eye of the storm
I was lost, all alone
Masked faces, hearts unknown
Feeling hollow inside, nowhere to go.

Then like lightning, you came along
My world awakened
Shaking me to the core
My mind was blown
Now I want you for my own.

Life is just a moment
A tiny spec that can go away
I don't want to postpone it
Please, I want you to stay.

I surrender my all to you
Even if it means for a short time
Even if they believe loving you is a crime
I surrender my all to you
You're the part of my life that is sublime.

I don't care what the world may think of you
With you I found my strength, my way
You're my everything, I cannot repay
The love and happiness I always prayed

I surrender my all to you
Even if it means for a short time
Even if they believe loving you is a crime
I surrender my all to you
You're the part of my life that is sublime.

I don't want to postpone it
Please, I want you to stay...

Hearing those lyrics fills me with tears I've tried to suppress. Everyone gets up giving Lukas a standing ovation. I stand, overcome by emotion, clapping with everyone. It's a breathtaking piano arrangement, full of emotion. Everyone knows it came from his heart, and his voice sounded impressive. It's a relief seeing so many teary eyes in the room. I'm not the only one. I've never in my life felt the intensity he's gifted me in this moment. It's so hard to not run and kiss him with all the love overflowing in my heart.

Standing from the piano, he signals the musicians to stand and take a bow with him. People are still clapping, screaming his name with his performance. The signal every industry executive knows they've got a sure hit in their hands.

And then he looks at me, smiling, more relaxed. I'm clapping and staring teary-eyed. No words, no lip movement, we have our own language. We've just discovered it. He knows what I feel and is happy about it.

After the presentation, there's a meet-and-greet session with fans and press. Some fans and press photographers are taking photos of everything going on here. I've decided to take advantage of a line of people to greet and take pictures with each one. It's the closest I can get to them.

My first turn is to greet Marc, and I didn't expect his reaction. The truth, I didn't know whether he would react at all. His smile widens. He embraces me, spinning me around, honestly happy. The press takes photos, flashes blinding us. I glance at him in panic. He presents me formally.

"Ms. Morales is a dear friend from the Longest Quill Editorial doing a book on K-pop history."

I gaze at him in amazement at coming up with the same explanation I had told Shayan. *I adore you, Marc.* Standing, more relieved, I chuckle. Whispering in his ear, "Owe you one, sweetie. You're a life saver. Ask me later."

Winking at me, he knows he's saved the day for me. *He really is my young padawan, and the force is with us.*

Next, I candidly embrace Ty. Thank God he is less effusive.

"Thanks for being here. To all of us it's a beautiful gesture. By the way, you look breathtaking, with all due respect." I'm flattered by his words. He's always so proper.

"Thanks. I'm happy everything has turned out successfully for all of you. I know how hard you work for it. I'm proud of you." We bow to each other, grinning.

I find Kim observing me hungrily. I'm not eager to be close to him. He makes me uncomfortable.

Pulling my hand, he holds my waist in an intimate gesture. The press starts to take photos, flashes blinding me again.

"Ms. Morales is a *very* dear friend working with us. She has been so welcoming, especially with me. Isn't that right, Gabriella?"

His gaze darkens like there's a secret between us, waiting for my reaction. I'm astounded by his audacity. Lukas stares, clearly upset.

My awkward smile tries to hide the uneasiness he causes me before I address the press. "Yes, our company is working in partnership with them." I inform the press, without any fuss.

Shayan watches us suspiciously. I meet Kim's eyes, letting him know I'm upset by his insinuations. Walking away from him, I move to where Lukas is.

Ravenous eyes watch as I approach. He's been waiting all night for this, to be close to me. The prolonged anticipation to touch him is unbearable. Standing beside him for the press to take photos of us, his bewitching male scent fills my nostrils, making my heart jolt. But I have to be proper as if I don't know him intimately. I'm part of the news now. Mentally thinking of Harrison's speech, he's going to flip out on me when he learns about this book project through the press.

Putting his arm on my waist, he caresses my bare back with the tip of his fingers, giving me goosebumps. Inhaling, I try to control my expression while this sexual tension sizzles between us. Leaning to my ear, he whispers sensuously.

"You look ravishing. Resisting the urge to be inside you is

a delicious challenge to endure until later. I'm so ready for you right now. Please, let me take this dress off you when we're home. I need to do it myself."

Those words melt my insides like molten lava. He turns casually to the press like nothing has happened, smiling and waving after telling me those steamy words. Inclining again to add,

"I bet you're soaking wet right now. I'm dying to feel how much."

I'm breathing unsteadily. His fingers crawl up and down my back. I'm so turned on I can barely think straight.

The overwhelming stress pushes me to walk away, taking him by surprise. A quick peek over my shoulder, I discover his crestfallen face observing me walking away. I hadn't been able to stand there any longer.

Grabbing the martini to take a sip from it, I turn around to find this redhead staring straight at me, walking in my direction. She could pass for a model with her great body. I'd noticed her standing behind Kim and Lukas on the stage. She's glaring, pissed off. Maybe she's press or public relations. She halts in front of me.

"So… You're the famous Gabriella, right?" Asking without saying hello and with this bitch attitude, her behavior puts me on guard.

"Who wants to know?" I already don't like her.

She laughs sarcastically, like a bimbo. "Vivian Orly, CEO of public relations of this record company. You're feisty for an old woman. If I were your *age*, I think I'd be the same."

Oh, no she didn't. She's mocking me, being disrespectful. My *Boricua* girl is dying to come outside and give this bitch *su merecido.*

"What's your problem, Little Mermaid?" I stand up in

defiance to show her I'm not intimidated.

"My problem is you're intruding in my relationship with Lukas. I'm aware he's always had these *playthings* to keep him amused. But with you...he seems more distracted than usual. He discards them at the end. You're not the first one, you know, nor will you be the last."

It feels like she pushes me without touching me. I stare at her with the fury unleashed inside. *Let me put this bitch in her place.* My wicked smile widens, and I just stare at her. A stunned face tells me she hadn't been expecting it.

"Well I must be doing something extremely well and satisfying to him, if he prefers me over you, don't you think? Refined tastes know when a wine is aged just right. It's sweeter and tastier. It's not my problem your performance doesn't impress him or measure up to his expectations, you know...if he has to constantly seek someone else for it. So sad and pitiful."

My triumphant devilishly smile says it all. That's a big, fat slap to her face without putting a finger on her. It's my turn to see her rueful at my words.

Now I'm seeing something that is not right, scary, *crazy.* Her upper lip trembles while she speaks. She can barely control her anger.

"I'm going to give you some advice to avoid pain. Leave Lukas alone, stay away from him. You're collateral damage, and you know it. What would happen if the press knows who you are? If they get a hold of you, find out the truth? I'm sure you do. It could destroy him. Is this what you want? To damage his future career? Would you go to this length to prove how good you are? Don't think so. I suggest you get out and disappear from his life this instant."

Even though I hate everything she's saying, it's true. Her

glower shows me she's capable of crazy stuff, and I'm not going to refute it or try to find out. She seems off, obsessed with him.

I glance at Marc, who's watching me, concerned. Our eye connection is at work. He reads me. Moving behind Ty and Kim, he touches Lukas's arm, signaling discreetly in our direction. He sees her standing in front of me.

Her threat is explicit.

"Don't worry, Miss Orly. I'll never hurt him or make him do something against his will. That doesn't end well. I'll leave peacefully for him, not you. I'll let him deal with you. Believe me, I guarantee you he'll be beyond furious."

Picking up my purse, I give her one last disdainful glance. I don't believe her story of a relationship between them for one second. She smiles triumphantly. Turning my back to her, I walk to the entrance.

With one final glance over my shoulder, I see Lukas's concerned expression as he watches me leave. He starts to walk off the stage when Kim grabs his arm, stopping him. That's the last I see of them. I catch my breath outside, tears of rage choking my throat. I want to strangle someone. I take the first cab I find to go back home, furious and defeated.

You became my Trauma...

Chapter Thirteen

Gabriella

Swallowing my whiskey in one gulp, letting the amber liquid burn my rage, I sit on the sofa, thinking about Vivian Orly's threat. There's no way out right now. I'm positive she'll be monitoring Lukas. I know well this crazy type. I've encountered them before. She's the type of woman who will do anything to get what she wants. Right now, she's fixated on Lukas.

Her hateful look really scared me tonight. I'm sure she's deranged. It makes her a dangerous person. He made it clear where his feelings are. I will prevail and be smart to protect him.

Searching on my laptop for one-way flights to San Juan, I scroll down selecting the quickest one. It'll be good to be away a couple of weeks before the Book Festival in Seoul, to cool things down between us. It's my way of helping him ease the burden for both of us.

I've booked the ticket to fly back to my home island tomorrow morning. I write Harrison, informing him I'm taking two weeks' vacation to rest before my trip to Seoul. I also write my brother Rey, letting him know I'll be staying with him. He'll be happy to spend those days together. Besides it will help me recharge my batteries and think through things clearly. Pulling my carry-on luggage out of the closet, I open it on my bed.

I'm about to finish packing when my doorbell rings. I ignore it. There's a second ring with a knock on the door. I hear his voice loud and clear.

"Gaby, open up. I know you're in there. I see the light on through the balcony from downstairs. Please, open up."

I stay silent. Maybe he'll think I've fallen asleep. But his voice gets louder.

"Gabriella, open this door, or I swear to you I'll start shouting until the neighbors call the cops on us, and my career will be ruined anyway. Open up." He's almost shouting, so I open it.

His hand is holding the doorframe. He's still dressed in his concert clothes, pissed-off.

One of the neighbors opens the door, staring at us, asking in disbelief, "Is everything okay?"

I smile amicably.

"Sorry for the noise, Fabricio. Nothing is going on. We're okay, thanks." Then I glare at Lukas.

"Enter, now."

Once I close the door, I encounter his annoyed expression watching back at me. I'm puzzled why he seems so upset with me.

"Gaby, I don't know what the hell Vivian told you, but what happened between us is in the past. She's a mistake I'm not going to repeat. We don't have any personal relationship whatsoever. You must know that."

Exhaling deeply, I realize he doesn't understand the gravity of the situation. I'm going to be the wise one for what I'm about to do. He'll understand, but it's going to hurt him.

"Lukas, listen to me and don't interrupt, please. I don't have any doubt, whatsoever, you love me as much as I love you, *papi*. Nobody can change it in my mind, not even crazy Vivian. Having said that, it's the very reason we have to take some time away from each other."

He tries to interrupt me, but I shush him.

"Just for a couple of weeks, to let everything cool down until we figure out how to handle her, making sure she doesn't damage or jeopardize your career. She's made a threat against you and your career tonight. Made it clear what she's going to do if I you don't cast me aside. This type of person is unstable, without boundaries. She's not thinking clearly. In a moment of rage, she could damage your career, baby. She's obsessed with you."

Disheartened, Lukas shakes his head in denial. He understands my words, but his eyes say he doesn't want them to be true. I grab his face with my hands, finally informing him.

"I booked my flight to Puerto Rico for tomorrow morning and plan to stay for a couple of weeks…"

He doesn't let me finish. Arms wrapping around me in desperation, he pulls me closer. With his warm breath on my forehead, he opposes my leaving.

"No. You can't leave now."

A misleading lull sounds in my voice.

"Lukas, sweetie, calm down and listen, please. It will be as if I'm here. You informed me with this change of plans you'll be with the guys on that media tour for the next couple of weeks. We won't be able to see each other anyway. You're schedule is going to be frantic. Eventually I have to prepare for my conference at the book festival in Seoul. Let's lay low until things cool down, then decide where to go from there. It's a smart move. We'll overcome this together. Please, understand I'm protecting you the same way you would for me."

Exhaling in surrender, he nods in silence. Stepping away from his embrace, I'm immersed in my thoughts.

"This is hard for me too, but I can't think of anything else to do to resolve this."

"So we have to be apart for a while."

Strolling to where I am, he pulls me in, caressing my bare back softly. Observing my face adoringly, he shakes his head in denial, still unable to accept it.

"This is nonsense. I'm so fed up with people interfering with my personal life, with us."

I caress his face empathetically, understanding his turmoil, while he holds me so lovingly.

"Lukas, my love... Remember even though we love each other, this type of love between us isn't common. People will have their own opinions about us. It's the truth. Some will judge us. And people like your fans or your company will always want to threaten what we have. We have to make wise decisions that don't harm what you have worked so hard for. I don't want to be the downfall of your career."

He kisses my forehead, hugging me tightly, and exhales his heartbreak. With his lips still on my forehead, he murmurs, "So you're saying I have to be the bigger man here. Comply with everyone, even you, on this. For our sake?"

"Yes."

We stand there, just looking at each other. The back of his hand caresses my cheek gently. Closing my eyes, I enjoy the warmth of his skin against mine, and my heart hammers in my ears in anticipation. A delightful shiver of wanting ripples through my body with awakening hunger.

He bends down slowly to claim my lips in a soft kiss, savoring me. I move closer, impelled by my own passion, enraptured at being adored and worshiped by this man, who I'm learning to love so much.

The tips of his fingers grab the lace neckline of my dress and pull it down the front, taking the delicate lace sleeves with it. The dress drops to my waist, exposing my breasts. The sight of them makes him catch his breath. The flame of longing burns bright in his gaze, tearing off his jacket and see-through shirt and discarding them on the floor. His big hand grabs my head to kiss me again, ravishing me. It's an emotional moment. We understand it's going to be quite a while until we will feel each other like this again.

With his hands on my shoulders, he turns me around. Gasping between tremors of delight, he opens the small zipper at the top of my buttocks. The dress falls to my feet in a pool of black lace, leaving me only in my matching panties and my stilettos.

His desperation increases, inflames. Facing the kitchen counter, he stands behind me, pulling down my panties. I look down to see the tip of his shiny shoes pushing my feet apart opening my legs. I hear the sinful sound of his zipper opening. His hard arousal glides deliciously in with a quick, deep thrust, crushing me in his embrace. A guttural groan of pleasure escapes his lips. My palms are pressed on the kitchen counter while his hands grab my hips firmly. His thrusting is frantic. We've waited too long for this.

"Fuck, Gabriella. We belong together."

Fondling my breasts softly, taunting my sensitive nipples

with his fingers, moans of passion fill my apartment. We're trying not to be loud, but it's almost impossible. Pounding steadily, he circles his hips while his tongue licks my neck, murmuring agitated, "I can't get enough feeling you like this, baby. You're my new kind of high."

"Oh, God *papi,* I love you. I'm yours." I almost howl in agony.

I'm lost in this fierce scorching fire wrapping around us. I'm not myself anymore. I'm his. My chest is heaving.

He continues to thrust until waves of ecstasy throb through us, pushing me to the edge.

"Fuck, Lukas. You fit me so good."

Slamming my hips in desperation, his breathless voice commands me, "Come for me, baby. Squeeze me. Need to feel you..."

His ragged breath in my ear pleads in agony. The desire is too much. Bending down on the counter, I bite my fist, my scream of pleasure unleashing my release. A moment later, he leans on me, pushing his release, jerking profoundly inside me, letting out his scream of satisfaction on my neck, convulsing.

"Fuck, woman."

When we finally regain some speech, he blurts out first, "I don't know how to be apart from you, Gaby. I don't want to."

I understand his feelings. It's the same for me.

"I know...I know, babe. We'll learn."

We make sweet love again a couple of times this evening, feeding adoration to each other until there's no space for more. We're showing how lost we are for the other. Morning comes, and it's time for me to leave for the airport.

It took some effort on my part, but finally he agrees with me, not without complaint. No phone calls, texts, social media, or emails, neither from ourselves or through our friends. I'm disappearing for two weeks so everyone thinks I've fled the scene.

I don't give him my brother's address either. Knowing how strongly he feels, he might do something stupid like show up on his doorstep.

We walk down the stairs in silence, holding hands, caressing our fingers. Life has granted me an opportunity to love again, but at what cost? I shouldn't get my hopes high this will last. Lukas is the sweetest miracle to help me regain my confidence and move forward, but I can't allow him to put his life on hold for me. It's unfair to him. Well for both of us.

The cab is waiting downstairs, and the driver opens the trunk when he sees me approaching. Lukas puts my bag inside, closing it. We gaze at each other with the saddest eyes.

"This is going to be hell for me. Just when I've found you, I have to let you go."

"We will see each other again soon, Lukas; you'll see. We will not be apart, even if thousands of miles are between us. My heart is with you, always."

Placing my briefcase on the trunk, I press my body in to brush my lips on his, hiding my dismay. Our passionate embrace feels like clinging to a last thread of hope.

Breaking the kiss, he moves his lips to my ear to whisper full of emotion.

"You're a part of me, Gaby. I love you."

"I know."

With one final kiss, I pick up my briefcase, entering the cab. Daring to take a last glimpse of his face, my heart breaks into millions of pieces, seeing his sadness.

Tears roll down my cheeks. The cab starts to pull slowly from the parking lot while I watch him. My heart had decided to stay in that parking lot with him rather than coming with me.

I'll make it up... I'll make it up to you...

The blood orange color of the hibiscus flowers on the bushes at the entrance seems brighter than usual, surreal. They are also a lot more plentiful than the last time. While my brother's home hasn't changed much since my last visit, there are some changes in the garden. He's already waiting for me on the front porch, and he calls to me as I exit the cab.

"*Bienvenida a casa.* I was surprisingly pleased to receive your message yesterday. You look amazing. How was your trip?"

"A little bumpy at the end, but in general, it was fine."

I drop my bags to the floor, opening my arms to hug Rey, my only sibling. Rey is six years younger than me and also divorced. He's a renowned biotechnical engineer in Puerto Rico.

"Thanks for having me on such short notice. I understand how busy you are. Your big sis got an invitation to the largest book convention in Seoul, so I just needed to take some time off to rest."

"Gaby, I know you. You don't need to pretend with me. Something major has happened for you to be here."

Putting his arm over my shoulder, he picks up my bags to walk inside the house.

"Let's talk over dinner and the bottle of Shiraz you like so much."

How I've missed real *Puerto Rican* cuisine. Rey had cooked a superb rice with beans, fried pork chops, salad, and *tostones* with garlic. Nothing like home-cooked food to help lift your spirits. After dinner, we sit down on the front porch to talk.

"Is everything all right with Xavier? Or are you still struggling with Empty Nest Syndrome?"

"Well, not exactly. Xavier is fine. It's something a little more delicate, personal. Please don't judge."

I retell Rey everything going on my life with this adventure called Lukas Lee, ending with what's transpired these past few days.

"Woo, you've been busy." Rey lets out a chuckle.

I couldn't avoid chuckling too. It has been a fast paced time with Lukas; I have to admit.

"Is so unfair, Rey. Finally a chance at happiness, and I've had to go away because of Vivian, a.k.a. psycho bitch-The Little Mermaid, who's infatuated with him doesn't accept what we have."

"That's a threat. Did you file a report?"

"I can't. An investigation would be devastating for his career. She made it clear she would use any means necessary to keep us apart, even causing damage to his career."

"So that's why you're here. Hiding is so unlike you. Have you considered what you're going to do if things never cool down for her?"

He's caught me off guard. Honestly I hadn't thought about that woman, Vivian, not eventually letting her threat go. He interrupts my thoughts.

"I think she's playing you both. She's not going to do anything against him. It's not logical. If the guy doesn't want anything with her and she's one of the music company's executives, she's not going to jeopardize her job for this. Don't you think?"

"If I report her for her threat, she will lose her job. Lukas would be the one who suffers most. In Asian culture, our type of relationship is ill seen. She will expose us to society, and his career could be jeopardized where the majority of his market is. She's not in her right mind I can assure you."

"Then don't expose her. There are other ways. You're a smart woman, Gaby. I know you'll figure it out. Finding love is rare. You're probably mortified by the age gap but don't let this chance pass you by because of something as silly as an age. These things are once-in-a-lifetime and especially uncommon when it repeats itself. As you've informed me, he truly loves you, and it's his first time to fall so deep. We're not getting any younger, Gabriella. This could be your last chance to enjoy happiness. If I were you, I would live and enjoy this while it lasts, Sis."

Tears fills my eyes, hearing his words. I'm grateful for his support.

"Xavier knows about him? You know how protective he can be with you. He's going to ask what you're doing in Puerto Rico."

"No, he doesn't. If he asks, I'll tell him it's a mini vacation. We haven't talked about Lukas. It's an intimate matter I want to discuss in person, but I understand what you're saying. When the time comes, I'll tell him."

"Okay. Don't let time pass by."

"I won't."

My cellphone rings. It's Lola calling.

"This call is from work. I have to answer."

"I'll be sending some emails."

Once he walks away, I answer quickly.

"Lola?"

"Gaby? Are you okay? Why are you in Puerto Rico so suddenly? What happened? Your photos are all over the entertainment news today. Harrison has informed us by text you left for vacation and not to bother you. Don't try to deny anything happened. I spoke with Marc this morning, and he told me about last night. Some woman executive at the presentation upset you? Also he told me he's never seen Lukas so devastated." Hearing those last words constrict my heart.

I tell her about last night and the reason I had taken a plane so suddenly. She's outraged.

"That bitch. Can she cause damage to Marc too?"

"No, don't worry about Marc. He's fine. Her infatuation is with Lukas. Last night, he expressed his love for me in a subtle way for everyone to hear. I think it triggered her. After the show, she came to make the threat."

"How long are you going to stay there? An invitation arrived for you last Friday. A book convention in Seoul, that's major stuff, Gaby. Everyone's commenting about the news you got some deal for a book on the history of the K-pop movement in Asia. I don't have to tell you every one of the bosses here are beyond themselves. So congrats. You're the flavor of the month now."

Oh, God. *The book.* Well I can make it happen. I have the connections.

"I'll be here around two weeks. How's Marc?"

"He's okay but concerned for both of you, especially Lukas. He's mentioned he's never seen him affected by someone like he is with you. By the way, I saw in the news a glimpse of the song Lukas sang to you. I knew it. Everyone there was blown away by the song. That's so romantic."

Yes, it is. Sadness is trying to creep back in my heart, but I don't allow it.

"It was beautiful. Let's not talk about it, please."

"Of course, sorry Gabriella. Please, remember I'm here for you if you need someone to talk to. You're my best friend, and I love and miss you so much, *Bonita.* Don't be sad; everything will turn out fine, you'll see. Enjoy this time off."

"Thanks, Lolita. Love you too, girl. Miss our time together. Everything's going to be fine; that's my hope," I assure her before hanging up.

Lukas

My eyes are fixed on Vivian. We're at the meeting, discussing results of the presentation and media coverage. I'm barely paying attention to what's been discussed, more focus on watching her like a lion about to pounce. I want desperately for this to end and calculating in my mind the right moment to approach her.

When the meeting finally ends, I stay seated, glowering. One by one, everyone starts to exit the meeting room, while she's picking up files and her laptop. When she starts to walk out, I stand quickly to grab her arm, pulling her inside, and in a menacing voice, whispering, "We need to talk. Now."

Closing the door, I face her, trying to keep my rage under control.

"I already gave you a piece of my mind for approaching Gabriella at the presentation. What I didn't know was what you said to her. How you disrespected her."

She grins at me, amused.

"The old lady went to gossip about me?"

Now I'm incensed.

"Don't insult her in my presence. She's more woman than you ever were or will be. She's better in every way. You know why? She makes me a better man, satisfies me in every way, and I've fall for her. Yes, she's the one I love. Do you hear me, Vivian? I love her. Neither you nor anyone in this world can change it, no matter how much you try. You're a sick, twisted, pitiful woman who thinks she can control everyone's life. Gaby left California because of your threats," I bark at her.

She laughs at my words. This is a joke to her. I step back, astounded by her smug reaction.

"I already know she left. I have eyes on you 24/7. Seems she's the smart one for leaving. That's why I'm beginning to like her."

Her mocking attitude fuels my anger even more. She doesn't seem to care a bit, running her fingers through her copper hair, and I can't help but react.

Losing my composure, I approach her menacingly. I'm so infuriated I'm easily capable of harming her. Backing up, her frightened gaze proves she's never seen me like this.

"I'm going to make something very clear so it finally enters that thick skull of yours. Maybe you can keep us apart, for now. I know her, and she's going to stay away to protect me. But I'll never have anything to do with you. You disgust me, Vivian."

Wide eyes stare in disbelief at my words. I've never spoken to her this way. Not even in my angriest moments have I used such harsh words with her.

She's realizing it's really over, and I'll never go back to her. Pain and jealousy reflect on her face, and something in her mind seems to crumble, revealing a darker version of her. I don't back down.

"I'll never touch you. Not even with a ten-foot pole. I'm done. I will request a change of PR with Jong. I no longer need your services, nor do I want them. Change to PR in Seoul or ask for another person to be assigned to. This was the final straw, Vivian. You've crossed the line."

The rage is flaring up in her. The true Vivian is surfacing, transforming into something quite alarming. Raising her head haughtily, with intense eyes, she spills her true self.

"Wow, that was harsh. So you're disgusted by me now, Lukas? I'm not your burning desire anymore? Your sex goddess as you so often whispered in my ear when you conveniently fucked me? Okay, fine. Do what you want, but hear me out, Lukas Lee. These words are going to cost you. If I learn you're seeing each other, and believe me I will, I'll personally expose your relationship to the press in the most embarrassing and messy way. You know I'm capable. And that's my promise to you."

Turning her back to me, she furiously storms out of the meeting room, leaving me standing there alone. This revelation of who she really is, is disturbing indeed. I'm comprehending what Gabriella had told me the night before she left. This is another level of insanity. She is really off, obsessed with me.

Chapter Fourteen

Lukas

It's been a painfully long, difficult two weeks since Gabriella had left. We haven't called or texted each other as agreed in case Vivian is tracking us. Vivian has shown me she's clever. She has the means, drive, and connections to fulfill her threat. I've witnessed her falsely damaging reputations to gain her advantage or the company's before. I'm sure she would follow through.

With each passing day, I miss Gabriella more and more. Walking the hallway in the building, I occasionally gaze at her door. Knowing she isn't there is strangling my chest. The desperation to have her in my arms, in my life, is torturing me. My whole body is screaming for her to come back. I'm not thinking straight anymore. In a last-minute decision, I temporarily move to the apartments with my bandmates. The truth is, I can't tolerate being without her anymore.

We've commenced our media tour at radio stations and TV programs to promote our new releases along the West

Coast. I requested that Jong remove Vivian from my team, expressing business differences without commenting much, and Jong agreed to it.

They've agreed to everything I've asked for, thanks to the success of the single "I Surrender My All". Social media and press are talking about my interpretation as the song born from the heart, moving everyone. Entertainment headlines talk of a new Asian music sensation taking the nation by storm. The same question repeats in every interview I've had: *Who's the lucky lady who has inspired this song?* The same answer comes out, as instructed by the record company: There's no one special, no girlfriend, of course I'm single. This is pure writing talent.

We'll be in New York with representatives of the company to continue the media tour for radio and TV in a week. Marc and Kim will return to Seoul with Jong for booked presentations.

My song had been recorded live during the presentation and is now being played on radio stations all over the country, moving up the charts.

Even with this success, I don't feel cheerful about it. Jong watches me suspiciously, seeming to notice the change in my behavior. I don't hide my sadness any more. I can't help it. Inside me, it feels a light has turned off. Most of the time, I'm serious, gloomy, and tired. Obviously Jong starts to ask, worried. I dismiss his worries as fatigue.

On Wednesday evening, Jong walks into the common room of the company apartments to find Marc and me watching TV. He approaches us with caution.

"Lukas, can we talk for a few minutes? It's important."

"Sure, Jong. Do you want us to talk in my room?" I stand, confused.

Marc interrupts, "If you want me to leave, I can go."

"Thinking on it now, I prefer you stay, Marc. Maybe you can help me out with what I'm about to say."

We observe each other, intrigued. The three of us sit down.

"Lukas, I'm concerned about you. I'm not denying your hard work is paying off. Your single is rising on the charts fast, and it means more invitations to perform it. Numbers are going up for you with one song. You should be thrilled, ecstatic about it. I'm seeing the opposite, watching sadness swallow you. Your soul is dimming a little bit each day. Do you want to talk about it? I want to help you. Remember I'm here for you, as we've discussed in the past."

Overwhelmed by this sudden intervention, I avoid the subject.

"The truth is I prefer not to talk about it. I'm dealing with the situation, don't worry. It takes time, but I'm working it out."

Marc's face twists, clearly upset, glancing at me. I think he's fed up with being quiet.

"That's a lie. Sorry, but I can't stay silent anymore. You're my brother, and it hurts me to see you like this. Since Gabriella left, you're not the same. You act like a ghost, floating around here."

Marc turns to Jong, feeling free to vent the frustration he's been hiding, watching me be depressed.

"He's not himself because he's suffering. He's in love."

"Shut up, Marc. Don't talk on my behalf."

Jong watches our exchange, the argument unfolding between us.

"Oh, perfect. This is how you're going to react? Denying the truth? Come on, Lukas. It's time Jong finally knows what happened."

"I said shut up, Marc, stop it. I don't want to talk about this. Why can't you respect my wishes?"

I'm staring and acting like a wounded lion in a cage, being poked through the bars. Marc stands to face me.

"You've been my brother for more than seventeen years. We grew up together in this business. We know each other's secrets and how the other thinks. What happens to you obviously affects me. I thought that's how friends…no, brothers are. Please, let Jong know what's going on so he can help you. It breaks my heart, seeing you like this. Never in our lives together have I seen you this affected by someone. You're not giving your best in your performance, and that's not like you, Lukas."

I'm aghast, unable to answer. Exhaling in surrender, the sorrow swallows me.

"I can't. She'll destroy us, destroy me, everything I've worked for."

Jong stands, alarmed with my words.

"Someone is threatening you? I told you that your involvement with this woman could bring trouble. Is she the one harassing you?"

"No, she hasn't done anything. This isn't her fault."

"So, speak up. This is a serious matter, Lukas. Why didn't you tell me this before? Are we not friends?"

Marc adds, "Come on, Lukas. Either you tell him, or I will, your choice. This ends now."

Both gape at me closely, awaiting my answer. Dropping myself onto the sofa, I'm done. I'm weary from being strong for so long. My inner self screams with the pain of her absence strangling me. *That's it.*

I don't recognize my voice sounding hollow and frightened.

"Vivian Orly threatened to expose my relationship with Gabriella to the press in a messy way if we didn't stop seeing each other. She has this…sick obsession with me because…" I pause, ashamed. "Because I slept with her a couple of times in the past. It was a mistake on my part, I know. I regret every single second. Gabriella left California to protect me. She threatened her also."

I'm miserable, not caring about anything anymore. Jong sits down beside me, concerned, putting his hand on my shoulder gently.

"Lukas, you should have brought this to me earlier. Of course there's a solution, and your career doesn't need to be damaged. Do you know where your lady, Gabriella, went?"

I raise my head, tearful. Is he giving me a small spark of hope?

"She's in Puerto Rico. She's staying with her brother, but I don't know exactly where she is. I don't have the address. Vivian hired people to track us, everyone around us too. She will not answer my number. I know; I already tried."

Marc blurts, "I know who can find us the address. Lola. I'll call and ask her."

Jong stares at Marc in disbelief.

"Who's Lola? Don't tell me you also have a girlfriend?"

"Yes… Yes, I do. She'll find us the address."

Hope is crawling back into my heart. Could it be possible? Jong stands to address both of us.

"Let me take care of the situation concerning Miss Orly for you. She won't bother you nor will her threat be real. I'm going to regret what I'm about to say, but in this instance, I'm first your friend and then your manager. This situation will be dealt with in a legal manner. It will be strictly between the three of us, understood? I'm booking you a flight to Puerto

Rico tomorrow morning. You'll return Saturday night. No one will know where you are. Do you understand me? I need you to be your best for New York, Lukas. Go, find her, and spend these days together or bring her back, whatever you decide. Regain and recover your drive, your fire."

He turns to Marc. "Find him that address now. We will talk about Lola later, you and me."

Marc beams, grabbing his cellphone to make the call.

That's all I need to hear for my faith to be restored. I don't have to endure this any longer. Standing up, I hug Jong with tears in my eyes.

"Thank you, Baek. This means more than you can imagine. Thanks for this."

He's taken aback, surprised by my reaction. Rarely do I call him by his first name nor am I this affectionate with him. The occasions I've called him by his first name are the times we're the closest. He's not the type to be sentimental or expressive either. Tonight he hugs me tightly, like a father with his son. He knows I've gone through so much and survived. Sacrificed so much. He understands me.

"Go and recover your happiness, Lukas. You been a good boy and have your whole career ahead of you. You deserve to be happy."

Gabriella

I push my chair back, proud of my work. Typing the final details for the proposal on the book is done. It turned out to be far more interesting than I'd expected it. Now it's a matter of selecting the right photos to be used in it. Obviously I'm going for the best photographers in East Asia. Learning from all the marketing research I've done these past couple of weeks, this will surely be a hit. It's the right time in the market, now that the K-pop industry is starting to invade the States by force.

Listening to the internet radio start to play "I Surrender My All", I sit up straight, lost in emotions, hearing Lukas's voice singing through the speakers. Closing my eyes and suppressing the sorrow, I remember that night and the way he sang it for me. I'm missing him so badly. I've realized how cruel life has been to me. Just when I've finally found love, the world says I can't have him. The reminder alarm beeps on my phone, pulling me out of my sorrow. I have to book the flight back home today. I stand, wiping my tears, to get a glass of water. Rey enters the kitchen, grinning weirdly at me.

"Gaby, I was sitting out front and someone arrived, asking for you. It's a young Asian guy, didn't tell me his name."

My eyes widen in shock. My heart sings with delight. I start to tremble.

"You're joking, right?"

"Nope. Go."

Placing the glass on the counter, I run to the front door to see. I'm standing on the front porch, Lukas is staring at me, his gorgeous smile illuminating my day.

He sees me as if it's the first time. Relief on his face, his honest smile and teary eyes tell me he's missed me too. A hopeful glint is behind those caramel eyes.

"Told you I wanted to visit Puerto Rico, and you promised to recommend some good places to eat. So I came to collect on your promise."

I'm overwhelmed seeing him. He's real, and he's here. A small cry of joy escapes my lips, jumping into his embrace. I cry out loud, unable to contain myself.

"Lukas, oh, my God, Lukas, you're here. I can't believe you're here. You shouldn't be...she'll know..."

I stand before him, caressing his hair, his face, unable to grasp the fact that he's here in my arms. He grabs my face lovingly.

"Everything is okay. She can't harm us, love."

Reclaiming my lips, he crushes me to him. I can't hold it in either. We embrace desperately, his tongue sending shivers of desire through my body, not caring if anyone is watching us. He kisses my face, my cheek, my nose, my forehead. I laugh, overcome with happiness to be in his arms again.

"Oh, God. How much I've missed you, Gaby. I was dying without you."

"I was in agony too, sweetie. These past weeks have been torture, not being able to call or write to you. But you're here. I can't believe you're here."

My hands caress his chest, making sure he's really there. It isn't a dream. He chuckles, seeing my reaction. Encircling me in his embrace, he kisses my forehead.

"I'm here, Gaby. I've come for you. I love you with every fiber of my heart. You're my force, my strength, my everything."

He bends down with aching need to kiss me tenderly, caressing my back. I don't need anything more at this moment. He's all I need.

We finally step away from our heated embrace. I find Rey standing at the door, arms crossed, smiling at us. I'm grinning, embarrassed he's witnessed our intimate outburst.

"Lukas, I'd like you to meet my younger brother, Rey. Rey, this is the man I've been telling you about, Lukas."

I'm still wiping my tears with the back of my hand.

Lukas walks forward, extending his hand.

"It's an honor and a pleasure to meet you."

"I figured out who you were. She's spoken nonstop about you. It's a pleasure to meet the man responsible for that glow on my sister's face. Thanks for coming for her and making her happy. She's not going to tell you, but she has been miserable since she arrived here."

He grins at my brother's comment, while adoring eyes gaze at me. His famished stare speaks before his lips blurt to inform me.

"I came to take you with me."

He isn't asking; he's telling me. I understand instantly what he wants. It's the same as I want. Simple and so complex.

"Rey, I'll grab my purse and come back tomorrow, okay?"

We leave Rey's home and head to Lukas's hotel in San Juan. He opens the door of his room, moving aside for me to enter. As soon the door closes, raw passion explodes between us, uncontrolled. Dropping my bag on the floor, I jump on him, kissing him in desperation. My hands grab the front of his shirt to rip it open, buttons flying in all directions. I don't recognize myself being this unrestrained.

"How I missed you like this. Eager, are you?" He groans needily, seeing me this ravenous.

"You have no idea." He pulls my shirt up, unclasping my brassiere. Panting anxiously while undressing each other, we're naked in less a minute. He sweeps me off my feet to gently drop me onto the bed.

Lukas stands at the foot, staring at me with a primal longing. He crawls slowly on top of me, gazing at my face, biting his tongue with his lips. I feel the tip of his hard arousal trailing my thigh as he moves upward, making me tremble with anticipation.

His warm whisper in my ear speaks of how libidinous he is.

"I'm going to make sweet love to you, Gaby, but not now. Right now I need to let out this fire consuming me. I'm burning out of control for you. It's going to be rough."

"I want you to do whatever you want to me." I hum in response.

I shiver with his promise, his fire matching my own every time. Yes, I want him to take me rough. I crave this ravenous form of him. Lowering his mouth, he presses his lips against mine in a fiery kiss full of desperation. Positioning between my legs, the tip of his arousal glides easily to thrust deep while his mouth drinks my gasp of pleasure. *Oh, baby you don't know how much I desire you.*

He's thrusting fast, frantic, hard. Moaning in agony, trying to hold himself back, he's watching my face. The sound of his hips slamming into mine echoes across the room. His thumb traces across my lips, full of raw desire, and I suck it greedily, swirling my tongue around it. Lukas is breathing heavily, watching my hungry sucking.

"Fuck, woman. I'm going to come if you keep doing that."

Fire stares at fire. Hunger equals hunger.

"*Papi*, make me come with you."

His ardent slamming is winning. The intense hunger we have for each other is too unrestrained to be contained any longer. It doesn't take long for both of us to get our releases, screaming at the same time. He collapses on top of me, his labored breathing in my ear.

"Gaby… Oh, my God, baby. How fucking good you feel…"

We're panting frantically to catch our breath, eyes half

closed. I can't utter a word. I'm floating down after this shattering orgasm he just gave me. Opening my eyes, I encounter his overflowing with love, watching me back.

"I love you, Lukas. With everything. I love you."

"You're mine, Gabriella. Meeting you was fate. Knowing you was my choice. But falling in love with you is beyond my control. I'm yours wholly and completely, baby."

A soft kiss seals those words. Sensuous slow kisses cover my lips drinking from them. Caressing his soft hair, I remember the nights I cried, longing to do this. His hand caresses the skin of my face tenderly.

Warm fingers trail down my neck all the way to fondle my breasts. Lowering himself, he starts to suck them. I moan, feeling him, our passion reignited. He pushes his hard arousal inside, filling me again. My body is so keyed up I'm still slick and ready to go again.

Right then, he does as he promised he would. He makes sweet, slow, satisfying, beautiful love until we both are sated and exhausted. Falling asleep, we embrace each other. Happy, complete, satisfied.

I like it better after midnight...

Lukas

Rays of sunshine beam through the open curtains of the windows, prickling my eyes. Through the window, I see the beach and the palm trees bending under the wind. It takes me several seconds to realize where I am. I turn to find Gabriella sleeping soundly beside me.

I'm in Puerto Rico with her. I can't believe it. I beam with love and joy overflowing in my heart to finally have her beside me. I never thought I'd fulfill my dream of visiting Puerto Rico. Thanks to Jong and her, I have. Watching her while she sleeps, so peaceful and glowing, makes me feel like the luckiest man in the world. With my finger I gently caress the frame of her face. Feeling my touch, she stirs slowly, batting her eyelashes.

"Mmmmm. Good morning."

She gifts me with her beautiful smile, showing her dimples I adore.

Pulling her into my embrace, her face rests on my chest, and I seal a kiss on her forehead. Shut my eyes briefly to inhale her scent and mumble low against her skin.

"Morning, love. Can I tell you how happy I am right now? I wish we could stay like this forever."

She lets out a small chuckle.

"Me too. But we both have responsibilities to fulfill. I have several things to do. One is to book my flight back. When are you returning? What happened with the media tour? I saw your interview at San Francisco two days ago."

She knows I shouldn't be in Puerto Rico.

"Finished in LA. Ty and I continue next Monday in New York. So Jong gave me this time with you. I'll return tomorrow night. Why don't you go back with me? I'll buy it so we return together, don't worry."

Hearing Jong's name has her sitting up in the bed with a scared expression.

"Jong knows you're here?"

I let out a chuckle, seeing her face.

"He's the one who booked the flight for me to come. He learned about Vivian's threats. I finally told him."

Now she's in a full-blown panic.

"Lukas, why did you tell him? That woman is mental. Don't you get it? She can demolish your career. She's so obsessed with you and with revenge."

Her voice sounds really frightened.

"Because I was dying without you, Gaby. Everyone around me noticed it. I couldn't give my best. Jong confronted me about how down I had been, and I admitted it. He's the one who took care of Vivian. They called her into a board meeting yesterday morning while I was flying here and confronted her about the threats she made toward us. At the end, they made her sign a non-disclosure agreement. If anything, even a tiny detail gets out to the press, she'll be deemed responsible for it. Not only will she get sued but she'll be fired as well. Her choices were to sign it or get fired and sued instantly. Obviously she's been removed from her position with us and moved to another department as well. Vivian may hate us, but she loves the influence she's gained through the record company more. She won't bother us anymore."

"My God, Lukas. I hear you, but I can't believe it. This is surreal. I don't think this is the last we're going to hear from her."

Embracing Gaby, I reassuringly kiss her cheek and pull her head to rest on my chest.

"If she tries anything, she'll lose everything. Don't worry anymore. Okay?"

I gaze at her face in adoration. Smiling seductively, she moves under the covers to straddle my lap, facing me. Feeling her naked on me, my arousal jumps eagerly for her.

"Gabriella…"

Caressing my chest, she's eyeing me with desire.

"I need to pack my luggage. I'll return with you. But before we go, I'll show you a good place to eat like I promised. Are you hungry?"

She grinds herself against the hardness of my arousal. I gasp, adoring her naughtiness. It ignites my blood instantly.

"It's not evident?" I grab her hips, rubbing her wetness against me. She moans softly, smirking wickedly, enjoying this little game. Raising herself to accommodate my length inside her. I'm the one gasping for air by this unexpected onslaught. She knows how to make me lose it.

"Let's take a quick bite now, then eat later." I couldn't agree more.

I stir up a hurricane...

Gabriella

After breakfast, we walked along the seashore near the hotel, holding hands. I show him where the kite-surfers gather to practice in a place called Ocean Park. He hears our vibrant Caribbean music as we pass by a group of people playing congas. He's curious about the rhythm, suggesting he can integrate some of those sounds in his future songs. I tried to show him some of my *Salsa* moves, swaying my hips around him like I did on our first date. He matches me sensuously, surprising me. What was I thinking? He's trained to dance, for God's sake.

He asks me about other beaches around the island. I mention there are other more breathtaking than the one we're seeing.

We dip in the sea, playful with each other, laughing a lot.

He's holding me in his arms, kissing me so lovingly and unabashedly. We are carefree, not minding anyone. We have the advantage that K-pop isn't known yet in Puerto Rico, so we're able to pass as a couple of tourists, minding our own business. I wish we could be like this everywhere we go, hoping people understand the way we love each other is pure and real.

We return to the hotel to take a bath and dress for lunch. I take Lukas to one of the best places to eat Puerto Rican cuisine, a neighborhood located in the mountains called *Guavate*, in the city of Cayey. We arrive at one of the restaurants in the area, sitting to order.

Because it's Friday, the place isn't crowded like it usually is on the weekends. His face beams like a child discovering a new world. I'm flattered he's so pleased with my island. He's looking everywhere in amazement, absorbing everything. Trying to learn all he can about my culture, he's asking lots of questions, and I'm more than happy to answer them.

A sweet, young girl approaches our table to greet us in Spanish. "Good afternoon. My name is Alannys, and I'm your waitress for this afternoon. What would you like to order?"

He stares at me wide eyed, laughing with shame.

"Please, pick for me. I still have to learn more Spanish, and the truth is I don't know what to select anyway. I trust whatever you order for us."

He looks apologetically to the girl. I let out a chuckle.

I place our order in Spanish. "Please bring us two orders of roast pork, rice with green pigeon peas, and an order of yucca with two water bottles. Thanks."

"I'll bring your order in a moment." She finishes writing and leaves.

"So, tell me. How do you like the island so far?"

"Honestly everything is far better than I could have imagined. I love the beach. We have to return and tour the island together when we have more time. Maybe try the sturdiness of the beds in all the hotels." He raises an eyebrow sinfully.

"Lukas," I admonish his wickedness. He grins, amused.

"When do you leave for Seoul?"

"A week from now. Next Friday. It's my first time in Seoul. I don't know anything about your country. I wish you could be there to guide me." I raise my fingers to comb through his hair.

"How long is the flight?"

He inhales, almost laughing.

"It could take anywhere from ten to fifteen hours from LA, depending on the airline. And the weather."

I must have made a funny, awkward expression because he dissolves into laughter.

The food arrives, and we eat hungrily. He enjoys it, the flavors and spices. He asks me if I can cook the same meal for him in LA. I explain that we can try, but it will not taste as good as this. Here the food is cooked with wood and charcoal, so flavors are better.

We leave the restaurant to walk around, checking the artwork on display in the stores nearby. We visit one of the *kioskos,* observing several paintings and serigraphy. He's mesmerized by one. It's a painting of the countryside with a red *flamboyan* tree at the center. He's in love with the intensity of the blood-red color of the flowers.

"This would look perfect in my bedroom," was his excuse for buying it.

Walking back to the car, at the distance, I spot my ex-husband William with his wife, about to enter the same restaurant we had just eaten at. I freeze, and I tighten my hold on Lukas's hand. He turns to look at me with puzzled expression.

"What's wrong, Gaby?"

"Xavier's dad," is the only thing I say.

I'm nervous and uncomfortable seeing him. The traumatizing memories are resurfacing, triggering my panic. My stomach hurts.

Lukas watches him. William turns to notice us, wide eyed wearing a shocked expression. He looks much older than I remember. Life hasn't been good to him.

Lukas sees the judging way he stares at us. Immediately he puts his hand around my waist, standing tall and strong like the Korean warrior he is to me. He raises my hand to his lips, brushing them reassuringly.

"Let's go, Gaby. You're not alone anymore; you've got me."

I exhale, relaxed, gazing at him. I'm secure, protected, and so proud to be by his side. I'm not scared anymore of what other people may think. After he kisses my forehead, we walk to the car, our chins raised. His wife stares dumbstruck at us from the entrance of the restaurant.

Showing off his gentlemanly gestures, he opens the door for me. His gaze is fixed on William the whole time. Once inside the car, he does the unexpected. He pulls my head to him, kissing me so lustfully I blush from it. I'm aware it's for their benefit.

Backing slowly from the kiss, we beam at each other. That's when I realize there's nothing for me here.

"Take me back, Lukas. Let's go back to California."

Ready, set, yeah... Kick Back.

Chapter Fifteen

Lukas

"Would you care for another glass of champagne, sir?" the stewardess's voice pulls me from my thoughts.

"No, thanks. We're all right."

We're sitting together in first class on the late-night flight back home. *Home…* Home is wherever she's with me. How has this happened? Glancing at her, I'm overwhelmed. Gabriella sleeps peacefully reclined on my shoulder. The most unexpected love in the most unexpected woman.

She's the storm who entered my life and changed me. It's not only her ripe beauty, it's her soul understanding mine. Seeing my true self, with the ugly parts, and still loving me for who I am. She connects with what I feel.

Going back with her by my side fills me with a joy I can't describe. Kissing her hand lovingly, she pulls it from mine, stirring in protest for disturbing her rest. I grin, gazing at her. Taking out a notebook and pen from my briefcase, I'm inspired by this. I start to write the words of a song that has been crawling around in my mind since we boarded the plane.

Took a flight to the cloud nine…

I stop writing, sensing her stirring uncomfortably. Opening her eyes, she shuts them tightly, grabbing her head with her hands. *The headaches.* I drop the notebook in my briefcase to embrace her.

"Gaby… Gaby. Tell me what I can do to make it better."

Holding her head gently against my chest, hoping I can take her pain away. It hurts me seeing those pain flares on her.

Lowering her hands, she opens her eyes lazily, facing me.

"There's nothing you can do. This is part of what I have to endure for the rest of my life."

"Can you please explain to me what's going on with your health? Why do you have to take those meds that cause you these headaches?"

I'm apprehensive about the answer. But I'm not going to let this one pass.

"We promised to tell each other everything, no secrets. And you always avoid explaining the details of this situation to me. Come on, Gaby."

Her trouble eyes tell me she doesn't want to spill the beans, but we agreed on this by her own request.

"Lukas, this health situation started several years ago without me knowing it. Please, please don't panic, everything is under control now, okay? Here it goes… I have a very small…*mass* in my brain. It's benign, okay? Because it had grown for so long without detection, when they finally discovered it, they'd found it's inoperable. It has roots in my brain. I take these meds to shrink it so it doesn't affect motor functions. To live a normal life like I do. It usually works perfectly, until recently. The only bad thing are the pain flares that come and go as a side effect. Please, please don't be concerned about it. Don't let it be a burden for you."

My chest constricts, learning she's been suffering this condition in silence.

"You'll never be a burden for me. Why didn't you tell me this before? Have you consulted other doctors for possible solutions?"

"You think I haven't? I've consulted all of the top specialists in this field, and the answer's always the same, inoperable. So it's something I've learned to live with. I do labs and tests every four months to make sure everything is okay."

My expression betrays me. She admonishes me.

"See? This is the reason I didn't wanted to tell you. You're worried. That's precisely what I don't want."

Grabbing my hand to caress her cheek softly, she kisses it.

"Please, sweetie, I'm okay, really."

I exhale, deeply concerned. It doesn't sound okay, and I wasn't prepared to hear this. Surrounding her shoulders, pulling her close to me, I kiss her temple.

"I'm here for you, Gabriella. Like I told you back in Puerto Rico, you're not alone. You've got me. We will figure this out."

Gabriella

We arrive at three am, deciding to stay at my apartment. He'll be returning to the company apartments tomorrow, so we take this time to enjoy ourselves before splitting again.

Something has changed in him since the news of my health on our flight. He's more tender and caring. Making sweet, slow love to me in a way every woman should experience in her life. His warm lips over my skin worship every inch of my body with his love, nourishing me. His soft touch jolts every nerve on my skin. Why? Why have I found this kind of love now? I want this every day. I want him with me forever.

We take a shower together before departing. Playing and laughing under the water, we hear the doorbell ring. We shut up. Grinning with my finger on my lips shushing him.

"Let it ring. Whoever it is has to wait." Wrapping my arms around his neck, I kiss him hungrily.

The doorbell rings again, now I hear the voice of my son, Xavier, calling in Spanish.

"*Mami, soy yo, Xavier.* Open the door. I know you're there. I called Uncle Rey, and he told me you flew back here yesterday."

My eyes widen in panic.

"It's Xavier."

Opening the shower curtain and grabbing a towel, I turn to Lukas to order him, "Please, get dressed quickly." He's surprised by my reaction.

"Gaby, we're not doing anything wrong. We're two grown adults…"

"He doesn't know about us. He's going to freak out, I know." I respond while putting on my white terrycloth bathrobe.

Drying my hair with the towel, I hurry to the door and open it. Standing there is my son, Xavier. All my motherly love overflows seeing him. He's grown a beard. He seems so grown-up, or maybe I'm just now noticing. I have mixed emotions, seeing him after six months, happiness and apprehension at the same time.

"Xavier, baby, *Dios te bendiga.* This is an unexpected surprise. I was taking a shower. What are you doing here?"

"Can I come in at least?" he asks sarcastically, appearing to be upset.

I realize I'm blocking him from entering and quickly move aside.

"Sure, Sure."

Entering my apartment, scrutinizing everywhere, he's searching for something.

"Why are you here, Xavier? What's going on?"

His displeasure is evident.

"*Papi* called me yesterday to tell me he saw you in Puerto Rico with a younger guy, kissing each other in public. An Asian guy my age. That you made a spectacle of yourself in front of everyone there. Is that true? I'd like to think this is a fucking joke or lie. I've come personally, because I know if I called, you'd avoid telling the truth."

To make things worse, Lukas decides to come out of my room, wearing his jeans while pulling a T-shirt over his head, wet hair like mine. He walks toward Xavier, and his face is calm, as if everything is fine. I cover my face with one hand in surrender, knowing what's going to happen next.

"Yes, your mom and I are together. Hi, my name is Lukas…" He extends his hand to Xavier.

They're seeing each other for the first time. Xavier's eyes widen in disbelief and disgust, completely ignoring his handshake, instead turning his rage to me.

"*Mami*, what the fuck? What the hell are you thinking? He could be your son. He's my age. Do you see how ridiculous you seem, believing this could work?"

The rage of his insult grows inside me, making me raise my voice.

"*No me faltes el respeto, Xavier.* I'm a grown woman and make my own decisions. I'm not an ignorant girl. Neither your dad nor you have any authorization whatsoever to discuss who I'm with."

Lukas tries to intervene. "Please, don't argue by—"

Xavier interrupts, speaking furiously, pointing his finger at his face.

"You stay out of this. This is between my mom and me."

He turns to address me again. "I wanted to believe this is another of Dad's sick lies to hurt your reputation. But I see this one is true. Do you realize how wrong this is? It isn't going to work or last, Mom. He'll take advantage of you, and as soon a younger woman appears, moving her ass better than yours, you're history." He's almost shouting, pointing his finger at the floor.

Now an upset Lukas interrupts us.

"Stop this. Don't disrespect your mother. That's not true. I love her. Why won't you be happy for her instead of criticizing her?"

"Yeah. Sure you do."

Xavier raises his hand to wipe his face in frustration.

"You know what? Do whatever you want, Mom. It's your life, your reputation at stake here. You'll see in the end I'm right."

He turns to walk out the door. I grab his arm to stop him.

"Xavier, please. Don't go. Don't be mad at me. It's been so long since we saw each other, *mijo.* Don't go like this. Please, please understand I'm happy. We both love each other. I know it doesn't look right, but it feels right in my heart. This is real, my love. Why can't you be happy for me?"

He looks back at me hurt, scared. I've seen the same eyes on multiple occasions, pulling me out from my depressive outbreaks. He reminds me of the time he'd suffered, seeing me at my lowest.

"This is an illusion, Mom, a fantasy. This isn't going to end well. I know who he is. I saw you both in the news several weeks ago. I know he's famous, and he's going to hurt you. It pains me so much when you're hurt. Remember? I was there with you. I'm the one who'd pulled you out of your darkest days, and I've cried with you. Don't you recall those times? It was so hard seeing you like that. And you know what? I'm not going to stay here to see it again."

He yanks his arm from my grip, raising his hands in surrender, nodding his head. Opening the front door, he walks away without looking back. I call out to him, teary-eyed.

"Xavier, don't go." But he's already gone.

Slowly closing the door, I'm devastated by his reaction. I put my forehead against it, exhaling, deeply heartbroken.

I'm so fucking tired. I'm tired of justifying myself. Tired of explaining to everyone why I do the things I do. Tired of society dictating what's acceptable and what's not. I'm really fed up.

Lukas's hands gently squeeze my shoulders, turning me to face him, me weeping in his chest, weary and overwhelmed. He's caressing my hair, consoling me.

"Shhh… I know. It's okay. Calm down, love."

Stepping back, I compose myself to gaze at him. He's aware the sadness Xavier's reaction has caused me. His fingers wipe my tear-streak face tenderly, his expression sad.

"I'm so sorry to be the cause of this argument between you two, Gabriella. It's not fair he doesn't understand. I thought he would be happy for you." Kissing my forehead, he wraps me in his arms.

"He's always been so protective of me. There was a time I

believe I failed as a mother. My emotions were so crippled I was unable to support him in the many trials we faced together. He witnessed how devastated I was by his dad's behavior. Even though I taught him to respect and love his father no matter what, he saw and knew the truth of what was going on. He watched me live the hell of my depression, my sadness. Xavier helped me cope with my pain, distracting me. His aid pulled me out of it."

I should have followed Rey's advice and talked to him sooner. *Damn William, you're still an asshole.* This is going to take me time, to make him understand this isn't a mistake, that it's real and I want to be loved. I deserved to be loved again.

Wiping my cheeks with the back of my hand, I stop crying, straightening my shoulders. This pity party ends now.

"I'll deal with him, explain my reasons. He's a bright man. He'll understand me. If not… I'm fed up, Lukas. I'm happy with you and don't care what the world thinks about me. I'm exhausted from complying with other's wishes, making everyone happy but me. I'll be beside you until you tell me to go or you go away. I don't care anymore. Maybe this makes me a lesser person, but I want the happiness you can give me, even if for a short time. I'll treasure these moments we spend together forever. My life was nothing before you, nothing." I hold back a sob.

Awestruck by my confession, he stares at me with pride. I've bared my heart for him to see. No shame, no regrets, no secrets…just plain truth.

"I don't care what the world thinks either. I'm happy with you, Gaby. I'm aware others think I'm making a huge mistake with you, saying this is a sick infatuation, not love. I only know this feels so right in my heart. Like you said, I want to share my happiness with you, even if it's for a short time. I'll be beside you until you tell me to go or you go away."

We stand in front of each other, and I'm overcome by emotions. His hand caresses my face lovingly.

"I can easily love you till the end of time." I responded a low, matter-of-factly tone.

A shy grin appears on his lips, and I smile at him too. We just made our vows to each other, and we know it. Our simple yet powerful promise of love is what we've needed. This isn't a foolish obsession. Our souls have joined because it is meant to be. This is real.

Yeah, you. If it's not you, it's not anyone... Not anyone.

Chapter Sixteen

Gabriella

Times flies so fast when your mind is occupied and now I'm realizing it. I can't believe it's been a week since I've seen Lukas. I miss him terribly.

I'm on my way to the other side of the world, ironically his hometown. The thirteen-hour flight is exhausting. My legs are stiff and my headache pounds for several hours, causing me to feel nauseous.

At Incheon International Airport, the people from the festival are waiting for me with a sign with my name outside the first gate. After walking what seems a mile to get to customs and picking up my luggage, I'm bone-weary. My escort guides me outside where a driver waits to take me to my hotel.

Even after a hot bath, I still feel awful. I order room service and stay in for an early sleep. Around four am, my cellphone rings. It's him.

"Hey gorgeous. Sorry to wake you this early. It's the only free time I have to call you."

"Hi, sweetie. I haven't felt good since yesterday. I've been nauseous with headaches and went to bed at seven last night. I'd been hoping to feel better, but right now, my stomach is still a little upset."

His voice changes to a concerned, happier tone.

"Gaby, when is your period due?"

"My period?"

Takes me several seconds to understand his question. We never discussed this, either. *Oh, God.* It moves my heart that he doesn't see a problem if he gets me pregnant. He asks so casually, even sounding happy.

I had never given much thought about this. We've made love without any protection after the first time, and he hasn't question me. Maybe he wants kids. And I'll never be able to give him that. My heart constricts in a painful way.

"I'm sorry to disappoint you, but I'm unable to have babies anymore." His oddly cheerful tone changed, seems to hide something.

"I'm not disappointed, Gabriella. I'm just trying to identify what could cause your symptoms. You can ask for a doctor to check on you. The people in charge of the festival can provide it."

"It's not necessary. I'll be fine. It's probably jet lag from the long flight, that's all."

I decide to change the subject. "How are you guys doing in New York?"

"I just finished our last interview a couple of hours ago. We're on our way to the airport, going back to LA. Ty is staying with me couple of days before returning to Seoul. I'll start the recording, finally."

"I am glad you're finally doing what you love, recording your music."

"I love you more, and I'd rather be doing you right now."

I grin, blushing, thinking of his naked body.

"Love you too and miss you terribly. We'll see each other in a week."

Lukas

Ty and I decide to sit at the back of the plane. The record company representatives are discussing subjects we don't quite understand amongst themselves, ignoring us. I'm lost in thought when Ty pulls me out of them.

"I heard Gabriella got invited to a book festival in Seoul."

"How did you learn about it?"

"Kim told me because he's performing there. By the way, he insists I inform you. He didn't tell you? This is one of his presentations. At this festival, they do mirror performances in different art forms—music, dance, theater. He's been assigned one of the books she edited to perform a song in her honor. He's planning to surprise her. He told me he made a reservation for a dinner at *Jihwayaha*, you know, to make her feel welcome."

I glare at him in disbelief. Sometimes Ty can be so naïve. I know Kim's intentions well. He's going for Gabriella, no doubt in my mind. He's taking advantage of the fact that she's alone and far from me. By the time we arrive to LA, it will be too late to contact her. She'll already be attending the festival. My anxiety blows out of proportion.

"Did I say something wrong, Lukas? You seem off all of a sudden."

"Kim is going for Gabriella, Ty. The same fucking competition as he's done in the past. He's going to try to win by sleeping with her. You know damned well he'll go to any length to achieve his goal. Gabriella could be in harm's way. Sometimes he's not aware he takes things too far. We have to let her know, but we cannot communicate with her until we land. Now do you understand?"

He knows how intense Kim is and how he acts without first thinking about the consequences of his actions on most occasions. Not only if he does any harm to her, I'll rip his head off. But also he could lose the music career he's passionately built. He would be charged criminally for his actions if he forces her to do anything. Ty widens his eyes, making the realization.

"We can call Marc. He's near and can assist her," Ty nervously suggests, trying to figure out how to help.

"As soon we land, I'll call Gabriella. Call Marc, and let him know Kim's plans. This is a twisted game for him. That's why he instructed you to tell me. I hope we can avoid a disaster for both of them."

Several years back, Kim and I started this stupid competition with older women on who could conquer the lady and keep her at the end. Over the years, he's become more competitive, driven. He's hurt feelings or sometimes resorted to *tricks* to accomplish his goals, upsetting some of ladies. It's all about competition for him, winning over me in a cunning or masterful way, trying to steal thunder to prove he's better than me. I know for sure Gabriella will not have sex with him willingly, and that scares the hell out of me right now.

Gabriella

I've been to enough book festivals and conventions, in twelve different countries, but this one is on a whole new level. It's a real opportunity to interact with writers, editors, and copywriters from around the world. The extent of people in the industry present that can help authors improve their work is impressive. This blows my mind completely. I'm learning so much and getting lots of ideas for future projects.

Before we started, they asked to turn our cellphones off to avoid unnecessary interruptions. After today's conference, the organizers inform me I'm in for a real treat this afternoon. The moderator asks the audience to maintain our cellphones off during the *Mirror Performance* we're going to witness, because no recording was allowed.

We sit at tables around a stage where they're going to hold the show. Our festival host explains it's a type of performance that imitates or reflects something written in a book—the theme, the title, the main character, the plot, anything that brings the art outside of the artist who interpreted the book.

I've never seen this type of performance at any other festival or convention. I'm going to witness something unique and from the heart. It's designed so the author or creator can see their work as any other member of the audience. There are several books on the center of each table, so we don't know who'll be picked for tonight's performance. The host explained is kind of a pleasant surprise. The book that lights up will be the one selected for the performance.

We're served a superb dinner and exquisite wine, which I enjoy very much. I've tried to make amenable conversation, but my dinner companions speak mostly amongst themselves. Maybe they're bored by me or my lack of basic Korean language. Ignoring them, I stare amicably at everyone, in silence, drinking the wine I repeatedly ask to be refilled.

All of the lights dim, and one of the books of my table lights up. I recognize the book I've worked on, called *Loving You Is a Crime.* I'm eager to see what type of presentation will be given for this romance novel. The stage is revealed, looking like a cave with blue lava coming up through some crack in the floor. Everything looks so real. It's truly mesmerizing.

A huge throne appears at the end of the stage. It's moving toward the audience with the backseat facing us. Smoke and fire flares all along the stage, an impressive show of lights, plus this sultry music. The throne turns around slowly. I'm in shock when I see Kim sitting there. Dressed in a black suit and black tie, he looks to die for. No one in the room can take their eyes off of him, me included. When the audience sees him, they start to clap in awe, starstruck, shouting his name.

Smoke billows from inside his suit to give the illusion he's burning. Both wrists are clasped in golden handcuffs that have a long, thin, golden chain hanging from the middle.

If I'm being honest, if he intended to look desirable, he's succeeded admirably. There's a tall table that lights up the moment he stands to grab a single red rose from a vase upon it. He starts to sing in English:

Once you taste me, you'll be thirsting more...

He sings and sways his hips sensuously, moving in my direction. It's a sensual choreography with all the intention to entice the senses. His sexual energy is impregnated in every aspect of his performance. A brief shiver ripples through me while I stare at him. Pure sensuality in motion. My pulse quickens with the view before me.

He's disturbingly hot. The way he moves those hips makes me think naughty things like being taken in naughty positions. It's futile to not be affected by him. Fuck, I feel feverish all over.

There is forbidden desire tempting you...

He stops in front of me. The lyrics, the sultry music, and his movements are so intimate I blush deeply. All eyes are on us. I'm petrified, perturbed. The raw passion his darkened gray eyes show me is predatory. I lick my dry lips nervously.

My God, he's trying to imitate Lukas. No doubt they both crave and desire the same thing. Lowering his hands, he offers me the long chain for me to hold, like surrendering to me. *What the hell is happening here*? My face burns hot with embarrassment. He grins wickedly.

But you'll be wanting more, craving for more...

Giving me the rose, he takes my hands to close them. I'm holding the rose with the long chain. The warmth of his hands on my skin agitates me. Gazing sensuously, lips parted, he's smirking.

Bastard. He knows exactly the turmoil of this seduction performance is causing. Without warning, he yanks his hands backward. Both hands slide out of the golden handcuffs which fall to the floor. I'm holding the chain with the rose.

You will fall in the twister of my passion...

This is his foreplay, nothing more. Kneeling before me, he pulls slowly the long chain until all I have is the rose in my hands. Taking one of my hands in his, he finishes singing.

Once you taste me, you'll be back for more...

This guy is a menace, and he knows it. What a fucking jaw-dropping performance. It's left me speechless, and my heart is still racing fast. I'm aware of what he wants to achieve with this. He almost did. A couple more glasses of wine in my blood plus the sensuality of this performance is enough to make my knees weak for a second.

I'm sure he's provoked lust in most of the women present, based on their reactions. I recognize he's powerful, cunning, and aware of it. It gives an air of security surrounding him. I have to be on guard at all times. He's trying to imitate Lukas.

Everyone gives him a standing ovation, which he deserved. The essence of the book was in his performance. The symbolism of the seductive nature of the main characters and their forbidden love, the mystery around his intentions, the tormented obsession of the lovers was portrait in every aspect of his presentation. My input is in there; he got it. He's talented, no doubt whatsoever.

After one more presentation, I spot him walking to my table. He looks impeccable, staring straight at me. Even the way he struts mimics Lukas. I can't help to compare these two. Lukas is the lion, and Kim is the cougar.

Women are gaping, some almost drooling, as he passes by while not taking his eyes off me. He walks past, proud and aware of the commotion he's causing. He doesn't stop until he is standing right in front of me.

"Gabriella, you look stunning tonight. I hope you liked the surprise. Tell me, did you enjoy my presentation based on your work? I'd be grateful for your honest opinion. I made this performance exclusively for you."

I smile at his certainty.

"It was a work of art, Kim. Really, I was blown away by it.

I think everyone believes the same with that standing ovation you got. But I'm sure you are already well aware."

I'm letting him know I'm way passed his seduction game.

"You're a delightful enigma, Gabriella. I understand perfectly why Lukas is so besotted with you. Your uniqueness is intoxicating, and you don't even realize it."

Oh, he knows his way with words. *Well played, Kim.* His smile widens.

"I came to make an invitation. Accompany me for a late dinner in one of the best restaurants near the heart of Seoul, called *Jihwayaha.* I've reserved a dinner table to make you feel welcome. It would be an honor if you accept to taste some authentic Korean food and talk. What do you say? Lukas wouldn't forgive me if I didn't show you this courtesy."

Well, he knows about my relationship with Lukas. I've made perfectly clear we're together when Lukas and I kissed in front of them. There's no harm to be done by simply going to dinner with him.

"Ok, Kim, just dinner and talk."

His smile grows, curling up.

"Wonderful. Shall we go, then?"

Lukas

I've been calling Gabriella's cellphone non-stop since we landed. It has been going directly to her voicemail. Desperation starts to eat at me. Anything could be happening right now, and I've already left her five messages. She probably turned off her cellphone for the festival or is without battery. I crane my head outside of the airplane door to where Ty is standing, calling Marc's cellphone.

"Any luck with Marc?"

"No, goes to voicemail too. I've left him four messages already. He told me he's free today, so maybe he's sleeping or visiting Jungwoo, who's on military vacation. Let's text Jungwoo as well. Maybe he'll read it."

We text Marc, Jungwoo, and Gabriella about Kim's schemes and where he's planning to take her. Now starts the tortuous waiting game to see who's the first one to read or hear those messages and reply to us.

I'm really worried about her. And Kim too.

Gabriella

The restaurant is a beautiful three-story building, very chic and modern. Is a mix of contemporary architecture with hints of traditional lines in it. Walking inside, people stare at us, and some take photos with their cellphones as we pass by. I hope this doesn't get me in trouble with Lukas when my face is plastered all over the social media beside Kim's. Our host leads us to a *private* dining room on the second floor. I'm a little alarmed, having thought we would sit with everyone else. I wasn't expecting to be in private with him.

My discomfort is evident. Noticing, he tries to calm me.

"It's okay, Gabriella. Remember, we can't expose ourselves because fans can be very passionate here. It's for our protection."

Even though I don't like this, I understand. We enter a

booth with a long seat surrounding the table, all in red leather. The walls are covered with rectangular mirrors all around the room. Dim Asian lamps hang from the ceiling, giving the room an eerie atmosphere. The long seat resembles a leather stretcher. The vibe I'm getting from this room creeps me out.

Kim sits beside me, and our host takes our order. I let Kim order for me because I don't understand the menu. He also orders some rice wine, sake for me and an absurdly expensive cocktail for him. They bring us the food and drinks in a short time, and everything looks exquisite.

Our conversation is amenable, Kim telling me about the time they'd come together as SMX18. The bond they share is so strong they're like a family. I'm more relaxed hearing him talk about the whole group rather than the focus being on either of us.

Kim keeps staring at me lustfully, fixing his sight on my lips. He's truly handsome, but for me, no one compares to Lukas. The magnetism Lukas exudes is spellbinding. He's not only incredibly handsome, but his beauty comes from within his precious heart.

I ask Kim for a bathroom, and he explains where they are located. Returning to the private room, I almost bump into a waiter who is leaving the room in a hurry, gazing with scared eyes. The hair on the back of my neck starts to rise. Kim smiles seductively when he sees me.

"Let's take this last toast before we leave," he suggests, offering me my glass of wine.

"Thanks, Kim, for this wonderful dinner. I truly appreciate it. Cheers." Clicking his glass, I take a big gulp while I sit down.

Seeing my purse, I remember my cellphone is off. I turn it on in case Lukas has called or texted me. I'm tipsy, assuming it's the wine. My phone buzzes, restarting. Text after text from Lukas start to pop up. When I read them, panic rises in my throat. My head is spinning, and my eyelids are heavy. Everything around me looks weird. *This is not okay.* He must have drugged me. The cellphone falls from my hand, unable to hold it any longer.

"Kim…What did…what did you do to me? What…you put in my…drink?"

Losing all strength to stand straight, I fall onto his shoulder, eyes half-closed, limp but still conscious.

His hand caresses my face. Kim is grinning. His touch feels perverted, emotionless. Putting his arm around me, he pulls me closer to him, his evil chuckle terrorizing me.

"I knew you wouldn't comply willingly. Like most of the clueless women, you fall at first for him. Not seeing the best is nearby. I gave you something *extra* to put you in the right mood so we can enjoy ourselves here, Gabriella. Once you know me intimately, taste me inside, you'll turn down Lukas for good. I can satisfy you in ways you can't even imagine."

His hand moves down my neck to my breasts, caressing them slowly, licking disgustingly at his lips. I'm horrified but unable to do anything. He kisses my cheek slowly, sensuously while his fingers fondle my breast through the fabric.

"You desire me. I saw it tonight while you watched me perform for you."

His hand goes down to caress my thigh, moving up between my legs. His lustful words blowing in my ears.

"It's there. I'm going to bring it out, the fire I saw clearly in your eyes while I touched you. That look boiled my blood… You'll enjoy this. I'm going to give you so much pleasure, you'll see."

His mouth trails my skin going for my lips while his other

hand touches me under my skirt, almost reaching my panties. I can't move to defend myself. I'm at his mercy. Whatever he wants to do, he can. Terror drowns me. I can't even scream.

The door of the dining room suddenly swings open. A young Asian man with military-cut black hair enters, followed by Marc. Even in my drugged state, I'm overjoyed to see Marc. I try to speak with my eyes in the silent language we both understand. Marc stares at me and instantly recognizes what's happening. They glare furiously at Kim. The rage in their faces is fearsome. Kim is frightened. He's been caught red-handed. Marc addresses Kim in a menacing tone.

"If there's a single person you shouldn't messed with, it's her. You've crossed the line here. Not to mention, you'll have to deal with Lukas yourself once he sees you. She was never a competition, stupid asshole. They love each other, and if you weren't so fixated on winning, you would see it. She not only has Lukas to look after her, she has me."

He takes my hand, pulling me toward him. My head hits his chest. I'm moving like a rag doll, and he has to adjust quickly to support my weight. He realizes in horror I'm paralyzed.

"Gaby, why can't you move? Talk to me."

Facing Kim, he shouts in a full-blown rage.

"What the hell did you do, Kim? What did you give her?"

Holding me in his arms, Marc looks down at me with a concerned stare. I fixate my eyes on his, pleading with them, conveying.

Help me.

Finally succumbing to panic, I faint.

Chapter Seventeen

Gabriella

My eyelids are heavy. Where am I? I don't recognize this room. My head pounds painfully, and the taste in my mouth is awful, like some type of anesthetic. I'm wearing the same clothes from yesterday. Forcing my mind to remember, memories slowly come back of what went on with Kim and seeing Marc rescuing me.

Black, white, and silver set the atmosphere of this room, very masculine and minimal, similar to Lukas's apartment back home. I know it's an apartment located on a high floor because through a huge glass wall. I see the city of Seoul. The view is impressive. Sitting up straight, I look around to find something that might give me a clue who this room belongs to. The door opens, and Marc enters, carrying a steamy cup in his hands.

"Good morning, Gaby. How are you feeling? Doctor said you'll be fine."

Seeing my confused stare, he adds, "Company doctor is

available for us at any hour."

Extending his arm, he hands me the cup.

"It's hot green tea. Lukas told me you like it."

He walks around to sit on the edge of the bed, watching me.

I touch my temple. "My head hurts. Where am I?"

"This is Lukas's bedroom. You're in our apartment here in Seoul. We're roommates. I didn't know where your hotel is, and you were knocked out. I couldn't leave you alone like that."

Staring gratefully, not only for saving me but taking care of me, I impulsively grab his neck to hug him tightly. He jumps, startled.

"Thanks, Marc. Thanks for saving me. I was so scared. So scared. Thank you."

He lowers his eyes bashfully.

"I'll never let anything bad happen to you, Gaby. You're my friend, my brother's girlfriend, and I protect my friends. Lukas was calling you and me yesterday to warn us. I came with Jungwoo. There isn't any damage to your reputation. We pulled you both out through the back door. How's the tea? I don't know how you like it."

I take a sip. The hot brew revives me. It's perfect.

"Thanks, Marc. It's amazing. Precisely what I needed." I answer, grinning and caressing his face with tenderness. His face blushes. That's a first with him.

"What Kim did is dishonorable, a dirty move. He sees you as another prize or trophy to collect but failed to see what you and Lukas feel for each other. His blind ambition to win didn't let him see he was about to commit a crime. He went too far this time, acting stupid, and there are consequences. The company has been informed of what he did. His career is over.

He can face justice. If you want to, you can press charges against him."

My eyes widen in disbelief. It hasn't crossed my mind to press charges against Kim, even if it's the right course of action. Knowing how severe the laws and punishments are in this country, I understand what this situation implies for all of them. I would have to explain myself and details of my relationship with all of them—Lukas, Marc, Kim—to the police. I don't want to add more trouble to what they already have.

"No. I'm not going to press charges. But I don't want him near me ever again. I understand he acted irrationally for that moronic competition. Whatever you guys or the company decides to do with him, that's your business. But if he ever dares to even look at me again, I'll present charges, understood?"

There's some admiration in Marc's eyes.

"Every moment I learn to be a better person by hearing and watching you. I understand what Lukas means when he says you make him aspire to be a better man. It's what Lukas and I want, to be better."

I blush at his words, beaming back with gratefulness to have encountered him in my life. Even at his young age, his perception of the world is so close to mine. It's truly remarkable, this deep friendship we have even though we haven't known each other for very long.

My heart is at peace when he's near, and I don't need to explain myself further. I can count on Marc for anything, and he knows he can count on me whenever he needs me. It's a relief; goodness still prevails today, and Marc gives me hope for humanity. We develop a strong bond. I trust and love him.

My cellphone rings in my purse. Picking it up, I look at the caller ID.

"It's Lukas calling."

"Say hi for me. We'll talk later. I'll take you to your hotel once you finished."

He leaves the room, closing the door behind him.

"Lukas, sweetie?"

"Gaby? Thank God you're up. How you're feeling? Are you okay?"

"I'm fine. A mild headache, but I'm fine now."

There's a silence. I start to cry, deeply disturbed by last night's events. I need him at my side, comforting me.

"He scared me. I thought he was going to rape me. I was unable to do anything. I was dumb, careless. I should've foreseen he would plan something like this."

"This is not your fault, Gabriella. How the hell would you know he'd go to this length with you? He crossed a hard line, and there are consequences. Everything he worked for is lost now because of his overgrown ego and stupidity."

"I'm not going to press charges. Not because he doesn't deserve it. For me, he should pay the consequences and be locked away. But if I do it, I have to tell the whole truth, and that would mean reveal the nature of our relationship. You and I will be exposed to the public scrutiny. I prefer not to disclose this to the police and affect your career. My peace and you are my main concern right now, Lukas. I already told Marc I don't want Kim near me ever again. I hope this brings an end to this stupid, dangerous competition. Whatever the company decides, it's your business."

I hear an audible sigh.

"You amaze me, Gaby. I must have done something right to win over a woman such as yourself. I'm truly lucky. I adore you, woman."

"Love you too, sweetie." And just like that, the sound of his voice soothes my troubled spirit, reassuring me I'm doing the right thing.

The rest of the week passes smoothly, without any more incidents. I learn from Marc that Kim has been removed from every presentation contracted by the record company. All of his artistic appointments have been canceled.

The press release says he's pondering the possibility of beginning his conscription military service earlier. The record company has released a press statement, along with social media, informing the public that Kim has decided to take a hiatus for a while, pondering options for his future. He asks for privacy and respect while he decides on the correct course of action. This is typical company PR damage-control action when they see a possible huge lawsuit on the horizon and start to cut ties with the problem.

To forget this ordeal, I keep my mind occupied on the book festival and the contacts I'm acquiring for the publishing company in hopes of expanding our business in Eastern Asia. I've made agreements with several new authors for their book launches through our company back in the States. Of course, with coordinated distribution in East Asia through some promising, emerging wholesale distributors, the publishing company can contract later on.

I wake at 4:00 am to speak with Lukas, the only time available we have between his recordings and my attendance at the festival. He explains his album recording is going fast, like is usually done in the Korean music industry.

Marc turns into kind of a bodyguard/tour guy, checking on me annoyingly often. We've gone to dinner every evening, and he's shown me several places around the city. He's promised me that on Friday he's going to take me to see the best sight in Seoul.

When I speak with Lukas about my plans to meet Marc for dinner and visit the Namsan Tower after, I ask him to tell me about it. He tells me it's the highest point of the city with a view of Seoul all around, and it's breathtaking. There's a story about a bridge and a love promise. Or more a legend. It tells about two lovers who had decided to make a pact with a love padlock. Now people hang their padlocks on a wooden deck connected to the tower. He says it's a beautiful sight, and I will love it.

Another worry is how much weight I'm going to gain with all the delicious food I've being eating, thanks to Marc. He's been taking me to this common marketplace with hundreds of tiny food vendors coexisting beside each other, so marvelously in harmony.

It's been an extraordinary bonding experience for me and Marc between the exquisite aromas of street food. These couple of days have been outstanding, a learning experience, knowing each other more profoundly. My respect and admiration for Marc has grown hearing him. He's an extraordinary man, even if he tries to be a joker about it. We developed a relationship like he's another Li'l Bro' who knows the real me. And I understand him.

After tonight's superb dinner, we joke about this, talking during the drive to the Namsan Tower.

It's a beautiful, clear, starry night, and I see a couple of shooting stars flying by. There's a new moon, giving the night an air of mystique and magic. The wind blowing, it's a bit chilly.

We arrive on the lower deck at the base of the tower, and I'm awestruck, seeing thousands and thousands of padlocks of all different shapes, sizes, and colors hung along the fence. It reminds me of the bridge crossing the Seine River in Paris. It moves my heart, seeing thousands of love promises. I can't help but think to myself... *Love is the most powerful force in the universe.*

I notice even though it's early in the night, there aren't a lot of people around us. It should be more crowded at this hour. Besides a couple near us with their backs turned, the deck is empty.

We walk to stand in front of the wooden rail to admire the view. It's beyond words. The city of Seoul is a breathtaking view, all lit up like a poster. It seems like a dark velvet rug covered with diamonds of different colors, sparkling all around us. That's when I hear the raspy, beautiful voice I adore so much behind me.

"Fans come here every day and put their locks with my name on it, hoping for an everlasting love with me. So sorry to disappoint them, but I've brought my own padlock with the name of *my only one*."

Turning around surprised, I discover Lukas standing several feet away from me. All smiles, he's doing his tongue thing, which drives me nuts, with his hands in his pockets. Dressed in a black turtleneck shirt, a long coat, and a beanie, he's gazing adoringly at me. The mere sight of this man is enough to melt my insides.

I glance at Marc who's walking toward Lola, approaching to grab his hand. I cover my mouth overcome with emotion, seeing Ty walking toward us too. They're all smiles, admiring my face in complicity.

They'd planned this. That's why I don't see other people. They've closed the deck for us. I can't contain myself and run to jump, grabbing Lukas's neck, grinning happily, holding him tight. He presses me in his embrace.

"Gaby. Finally in my arms, baby."

He steps back to capture my lips in a steamy kiss, full of longing and repressed desire. God, how this man shakes my world.

We're both aware the others are watching us, so we step back, smiling. Releasing Lukas, I run to hug Lola first.

"*Lolita de mi corazón.*" I shout while hugging her tightly, laughing aloud. "You made it. You're in South Korea, girl. I'm so happy you're here."

We're giggling, jumping all around like little girls. The guys laugh at us.

"It's crazy, right? *Estos locos* planned everything, and in one day, I'm on a plane crossing the ocean to be with my best friend. In Seoul. You know… Hellooo! I'm in Seoul."

We giggle again, raising our arms in victory signal.

"The reason I'm here is because these Korean men need a Latina beside them to keep them in line. And to control these *locas* who follow them. Keeping them at bay, you know me."

Marc's laugh is loud. He grabs her by the waist.

"That's right, baby girl. I need you to keep me in line always." Bending down, he quickly kisses her.

It's the first time I've seen them kissing. I blush watching something so intimate between them. I go to hug Ty.

"Hey, Ty. Congrats on your success in New York. The charts don't lie. Lukas kept me posted on everything. I confess I'm enjoying our encounters."

He grins, amused.

"Thanks for your words; the hard work paid off. Lukas's writing talent did the rest. Life made us know each other in a special way, Gaby. I enjoy our encounters too. So happy you're well."

Lukas stands beside me. Putting his hand inside his coat

pocket, he pulls a purple heart-shape padlock with our names written and today's date. Below he's written the phrase *Nothing can top this.* I raise my eyes full of love, touched by this gesture and completely overwhelmed.

"You're right. Nothing can top this now."

Taking my hand, we walk together, gazing into each other's eyes. I leave everyone behind. Everything around us disappears from our view. This instant, we're alone, just him and me. We stand in front of the rail with the city of Seoul as our witness of what we're about to do.

This is our own ceremony, our promise to each other, for whatever time we have together. No rings, no papers, just our pure love. Our own promises from the heart. He opens the lock with a key and puts the lock in my hand.

"Please, do the honors for us."

"No, baby. This is something we do together. How it should be done."

We hang it beside a green lock on the fence, pushing it down together to close it. An electric charge prickles our hands. We see a faint silver lighting on the tips of our fingers. It's like the fence is electrified, and we're receiving the energy.

We gaze into each other's eyes in amazement. It's our signal this is beyond us. There's going to be opposition. But this is a higher bond that can't be broken. Pretty potent stuff, unreal I would say. The enchantment of this instant is sealed with the most tender and heartfelt kiss. *Our wedding…*

Electric Hearts…

Chapter Eighteen

Gabriella

As we open his bedroom door, we're dropping coats and clothes to the floor, while we kiss hungrily. I'm filled with wanting, with a desperation to be joined with him. My heart is hammering hard in my chest, overcome by the profound love flowing between us. We're kissing in sweet agony, surrendering ourselves freely to this consuming fire. We undress each other in an instant, covering our bodies with lustful caresses. He eases me down on his bed, and his hand slides down my belly until finding my pleasurable bud between my legs, massaging it.

"I can't get enough of this… of you," he mumbles in my ear.

"I love the way you touch me."

Softly growling, he grins against my cheek while I gasp, heated by his strokes.

"I see…or should say, feel it." Lukas glides his fingers through my wetness.

I arch against his hand, gasping loudly.

"Ahh… Don't stop, *papi.*"

He chuckles sensuously. "You know I won't."

Breathing raggedly, he barely contains himself. He immediately thrusts into me desperately. Rolling my eyes, I feel every inch of him buried deep inside me in blissful lust.

"God, you are amazing. Aaahh."

"Jesus, woman. I love you."

I'm matching his thrust with the same vehemence, in the same state. But something different happens. Staring into his eyes, I grasp the intensity of his feelings. Our hearts connected. I swear I can hear him speaking without uttering a word. He's moaning loud in the throes of passion. Grabbing his face to brush my lips to his, answering him.

"Yes, my heart is yours. I'll never get tired of you."

Slowing his thrust, he stops, perplexed, breathing shakily.

"Wait. *What?* How… How did you know was thinking that?"

"I saw it in your eyes. I just…answered your question."

Troubled eyes look back at me, startled by our connection.

"Lukas, what's wrong?"

"Nothing. I'm not upset; I'm envious. I want to be able to read you as clearly you read me." Pausing he caresses my face and confesses, "Yes, I fear one day you'll get tired of me, of dealing with my crazy life. At the end, you will want a peaceful, more mature relationship. I'm aware of how unique you are, Gabriella. I'm lucky you let me in your life. But I understand you may want someone better than me."

Did I just hear him think he's lesser than me? I'm the lucky one to be deemed worthy of his love.

"I don't think so, sweetie. I already told you nothing can top this." I gift him my most reassuring smile.

His relieved grin blinds me. Lukas slowly lowers his mouth to take mine. Breathing lightly, I'm purring against his lips and inflamed beyond reason. His tongue continues to explore my mouth while his hands grab my waist to thrust frantically, making me mindless. Our love drunken moans fill the air, flying again in a celestial race to ecstasy, reaching heaven itself with him.

You can show me how it feels... Heaven...

Seoul presents a magnificent sight, this morning, from Lukas's bedroom. Bright blue skies and white cotton clouds frame the cityscape. I turn to see him sleeping soundly, his arm covering his eyes. The heat from his naked body is so delicious I can't resist my urge to cuddle up against him. Lowering his arm, he pulls me into his embrace, brushing his lips to my forehead.

"Mmm... Morning, love."

Only Lukas Lee can murmur those words and turn me on with them. Grinning, I kiss his chest softly. His long fingers caress my naked back playfully up and down, giving me goosebumps. My hard nipples poke him, and he lets out a soft chuckle, enjoying this little play.

"So you're awake. Are you going to talk?"

I shake my head in denial without uttering a single word, eyes closed and grinning wickedly.

"Wow. Now I'm worried. Well the truth is, someone told me if my *Boricua* woman is silent I should worry. There must be trouble brewing in her mind. It usually goes to her crazy side, you know, and I should run for my life."

Now I'm laughing aloud.

"Who told you that? That's a vile lie."

My hands slap at his chest. He grabs my wrists to stop me, both of us laughing.

Moving on top, he pins me down to the bed.

"I must have hit some nerve to have you flustered like this. I like it when you're flustered."

His lips leave a trail of fire going down my neck. Half-closing my eyes, a lazy moan escapes my lips. His mouth makes me weak, vulnerable. I want him to know I belong to him, utterly and completely.

"Fuck, woman. You make me lose control."

With him already inside, pounding slowly, I'll do whatever he asks of me. Gazing languidly into my eyes, he's reading mine. I open myself completely for him. His groaning breath answers my concerns.

"No… I'll never get bored with you. Until you walk away or ask me to go, I'll be here."

I smirk back, in the throes of passion, adoring him more.

"I needed to hear that."

No more words. Our moans speak of demanding desires, of fierce love that needs attention. The ripples of my release begin to crawl up my body. I'm blinded by this ecstasy. Love is overflowing without control. Grabbing his arms to raise my hips, I meet his thrusts in desperation. Louder, frantic, and holding each other like life itself, I explode first, followed shortly by him. Screams of passion slowly fade until we're drained. Both slowly coming down, embracing each other lovingly.

I want nothing on me but you…

I assume Lukas is taking me back to my hotel. Tomorrow afternoon, Lola and I reconvey to California. He'll return after several meetings with his record company, regarding the launch of his solo album, but in the car, he tells me where he's really taking me.

"I'd like you to meet my family, Gabriella. They live in a district nearby. I told my parents we're going to visit so they can meet you."

I'm disconcerted by this sudden news. My anxiety advises this is wrong. I have to convince him not to. Maybe speak some sense into him.

"Lukas, I don't know if this is a good idea. Your culture is very traditional in this sort of thing, like mine. In fact, yours is stricter. Are you sure you want to do this? We might get the same reaction we did from Xavier or worse."

His peaceful expression tells me he's decided.

"I'm so sure of what I'm feeling that no one can change it, not even my parents. I'm being honest with them, as is custom in my family, no secrets. I want them to know you, meet the woman I'm in love with."

I sigh, troubled. This can go the wrong way so quickly. I don't want to be the cause of a dispute between him and his family. I'm not supposed to even exist in his life. Seeing my worried face, he tries to soothe me.

"Can you please calm down? Everything is going to be all right. Trust me."

For me, it's a long, stressful drive, seems like an hour to get where they live. My nerves are a wreck. I'm apprehensive about this conjecture, thinking about their reactions when they meet me. *His Mom,* Jesus. What will she think of me? Oh God, I'm so distressed.

We finally arrived at a beautiful house near the top of a mountain, surrounded by a big, crude, concrete fence. Lukas presses the keypad, and the gates open. I see a very minimalist two-story home, with walls in glass, dark wood, and crude concrete but has a lot of modern features around it. It's breathtaking. I imagine he'd bought it or built it to their liking.

I love the gardens and greenery surrounding the structure, giving this sense of peace, their own perfect, private world.

A big, wooden double door opens, and a little boy comes out, around three or four years old, running to Lukas with his arms open, smiling, and shouting in Korean.

"Uncle Lu, uncle Lu."

I'd completely forgotten he's an uncle. I know he's mentioned it once in our intimate conversations about our families. I'd read on the internet that his older sister is married. The men of SMX18 are very private about their families and personal life. You can't find anything about them anywhere; their identities are protected. They wish to remain anonymous from all the madness with their fame. It's a smart and safe move.

I'm certain bringing me to meet them is a huge step in our relationship. The truth is, I don't want to be exposed to any rejection on their part, and it makes me nervous. I'm realizing this is real. First the love lock on the Namsan Tower deck and now this. And I'm the one having conflicting thoughts about it.

Lukas catches his nephew, lifting him in the air.

"Oh, my goodness. You're so big. You've grown so much since the last time I saw you." He hugs him tightly, kissing his cheek lovingly. The child's musical giggle floats through the air.

Watching this scene from a distance, his eyes glow with a joy he can't hide, holding his niece so lovingly. It strikes me in that moment this is an experience I can't deprive him of it, and I'll never be able to give him. Even if he told me it's okay and doesn't realize it right now, he needs to be a father. Understanding this, my insides twist painfully. With this first profound cut in my heart, I gaze to the floor, trying to hide the sorrow prickling in my chest.

"Gaby. Are you okay?"

Raising my face, I smile. "Yeah, I'm good."

He isn't satisfied with my response. Carrying his nephew in his arms, they continue to talk like old friends walking in front of me.

Coming out the door is a beautiful young woman with perfect, white skin, red lips, and long, black hair. She has some resemblance to Lukas. I figure she must be his older sister. She grabs the child from Lukas's arms while greeting him in Korean, kissing his cheeks. He beckons to me. Complying with my hands in my pockets, I'm nervous for her reaction.

I approach slowly, mostly in ignorance of how to behave. Bowing before her in respect to their custom, I salute her. She gives me the friendliest smile.

"No need to bow before me. Leave it to Dad and Mom. It's a pleasure to finally meet you. Lukas talks so much about you, how in love he is with you. Frankly I'm glad you can take charge of this nuisance from us."

I can't help but let out a chuckle. I instantly adore her.

"It's a pleasure to meet you too." I extend my hand in greeting.

"I'm Ji-Yeon, and this is my son, Jun-Seo. Jun, say hi to Gabriella."

He extends his chubby, little hand toward me, grinning shyly.

"Welcome, Gabyela."

He melts my heart with his cuteness, and I instantly fall in love with him. Taking his tiny hand in mine, I squeeze it gently.

"Hi, Jun-Seo. It's so nice to meet you."

Lukas stares at us adoringly. He seems complete, a satisfied grin on his face.

Ji-Yeon turns to speak to me. "Mom and Dad are waiting. Don't worry, they know about you."

I turn to look at Lukas, scared.

"I spoke with them yesterday, Gaby. This is simply a formality for them to meet you in person."

My chest turns cold, a knot forming in my stomach in apprehension. This can go either way for me. He grips my hand to help me calm down.

"Hey. We do this together, remember? Breathe."

"Easy for you to say. You're not the older, evil woman seducing an only, young, male son."

Letting out a chuckle, he pulls me to walk inside the house, following his sister. It's a beautiful home, simple but elegant. Now I recognize where Lukas's minimalist style comes from. Every decoration is just perfect where it is.

We enter a big living room. On a huge white sofa in the center, sits a gorgeous woman. She looks a little bit older than me, with shoulder-length, black hair surrounding her beautiful face. This is where Lukas got his good looks and great body from. Beside her sits a handsome gentleman in his early sixties, hints of gray throughout his black hair. His face shows a strong personality. Like father, like son. This is how I envision Lukas will look several years from now.

My anxiety takes over, and I'm panicking. I'm an intruder, invading an intimate family moment. I shouldn't be here. Lukas notices I'm terrified. Tightening my grip on his hand without noticing, he murmurs in my ear.

"Gaby, relax. You're crushing my hand."

"Sorry." I release it completely.

His father is the first to stand up, staring at us seriously, bowing his head to welcome us.

"Welcome to our home."

Lukas bows, walking to embrace his dad first, speaking in Korean, and his dad strongly pats his back. Then he greets his mom, embracing her, kissing both her cheeks. I'm observing all this from a distance, unable to move. The three of them stare back, waiting for me to snap out of my frozen trance. Reacting I bow before them saying the only Korean words I've learned.

"*Annyeong haseyo.*"

I'm trying to impress my mom- and dad-in-law with this. It's kind of hilarious. I can't even call them Mom or Dad as is their custom. It would sound ridiculous if I refer to them like that, being around the same age.

His mother comes forward to embrace me.

"You don't have to be so formal. Call me Sook. Welcome to our home."

I nervously smile.

"It's a huge honor to finally meet you, Sook."

Her honest smile eases my tension. I exhale in relief. Turning to extend my hand to Lukas's dad, I bow again while lowering my eyes.

"It's an honor to meet you, Sir. You're so gracious for receiving me in your home."

His earnest expression is unreadable, extending his hand to shake mine.

"Pleasure is mine. Hyun-Woo." His greeting is short and formal, forcing a polite smile. I'm pretty sure he doesn't share his wife's view of me.

Sook intervenes. "We're more than happy to receive you both. I hope you're hungry. I prepared a feast, and lunch is already waiting. Let's go."

Little Jun-Seo jumps up and down beside his grandma, informing her, "I want to sit beside Uncle Lu."

Lukas picks him up again.

"Of course you will."

We sit down at a long, rustic wooden table, where our places are already set with beautiful place settings. This lunch is superb. We eat like royalty, and every dish is delicious. We maintain a cordial conversation during lunch, and I notice both parents watching us closely. Evaluating every gesture I make interacting with Lukas. In several instances, he takes my hand to kiss it in front of his parents, not caring about what he's doing.

They gaze closely at us. Sook stares with loving eyes, grinning pleased. Mr. Lee, on the other hand, gives me hard, judgmental glares as if he doesn't trust me. It seems I'm in some kind of test I have to pass, not knowing the correct answers.

After lunch, we sit outside on several big, brightly colored wooden chairs placed around their breathtaking backyard garden. The afternoon is beautiful and sunny with a light breeze blowing. Lukas lies on the grass with his nephew sitting beside him, talking like two little boys. His sister sits beside them, laughing at their conversation. Sook and I sit together, away from them, while Mr. Lee is taking a call inside the house.

We're smiling, seeing Lukas playing carefree with his nephew. Sook turns to ask.

"So you truly love my son?"

She looks directly into my eyes. I'm shaken. I wasn't expecting this so soon. The best course of action is to tell the truth.

"Yes. I love him with every fiber of my being."

"This is the first time he has brought a girl to us. Well, in your case, a woman. I know you love him. I see it in your eyes. *The eyes never lie.* But I also see you're struggling with this, am I right?"

I'm amazed she reads me. I'm kind of relieved she does. I have the urge to speak to another woman who understands me, and we have almost the same mindset, experience, and age.

"Yes, I know this is unusual. I can't shake the inadequacy I feel about this. But a friend has told me life is a tiny speck in time, and I should grab happiness while I can. That's what I did with Lukas. I'm happy when he's near me. You know? He fills my days with joy and hope. I'm finally alive and happy after feeling alone for so, so long."

I'm getting emotional. She puts her hand on top of mine, patting it.

"What I'm going to tell you might be a shock to you, but I'm glad he found you. Please, I beg you never tell Lukas nor my husband I said this. They won't understand. For a mother, there's nothing more important than to be certain her children are truly, completely loved and happy. I don't recall a moment I've seen him this happy and carefree. He's usually like his dad, a perfectionist and control freak. Since he was a child, he's acted like a little old man. Seeing him this playful and loose, smiling so much, I know without a doubt you're the reason for this improvement."

I beam at her in gratitude. Those words mean the world to me.

"I was so anxious you might be offended by my presence. It's not my intention to disrespect either of you in any way with my appearance here. I'm a mom too, and my son is the same age as Lukas…" My words trail away, utterly ashamed to admit this in front of her.

She sweetly smiles, observing Lukas playing with his grandson.

"Never be ashamed for what you feel for my son. True love, the genuine pure kind, has no age or boundaries. Seeing you both, the way you stare at each other…the way my son smiles when he's around you. I'm reliving and remembering those feelings. That kind of love only needs two souls connecting the way you both do. That's why it's my duty to inform you what you may face from now on. I'm just saying this as friendly advice. Knowing you love him deeply, you'll understand and make the best choice on which path you should follow."

This is my moment to receive some uncomfortable truths.

"Please, enlighten me."

"Our family holds an extremely strict set of traditions. Lukas was raised to keep those rules in mind as part of his upbringing. His exposure to the world of entertainment and fame have changed many of the perceptions he'd previously had. Let's say he saw another side of the world we usually don't want our children to see. He's been exposed to some ugly truths in this industry without us knowing exactly what he's faced alone. He's one of the survivors in this music business. And I mean he hasn't been corrupted by the things he has to faced, maintaining his true self. Lukas is much more mature than his age, even if the record company insists on giving him this youthful image for the world to see. That's what makes money. Everyone knows how talented he is."

She sits straight, lowering her voice, while checking no one is near to hear us.

"Lukas let us know very clearly how in love he is with you and how set his mind is in this matter. So eventually, the rest of the world is going to know. That's huge. It might bring you some pain for quite some time, if you're willing to endure it. First, his fans. At his age, society expects him to have a girlfriend, but an older woman will not be well received. You both could be brutally judged. In your case, it will be harsher. Fans can be mean, making your life miserable. You'll turn into the evil witch in the story. You may not even be able to go outside without the threat of being attacked by one of them here in Korea if you decided to live here. Not to mention the possible consequences for Lukas. The biggest market for his music is this side of the world. If his fans decided to reject him for you, he'll be devastated by it, even if he doesn't realize it now, and the career part is the least of the concerns."

"There's more?"

"Oh, yes. The family part. Lukas is our only male son. By tradition, he is expected to marry a Korean woman who can give him offspring to continue his bloodline. I think it's safe to assume that you having another child is not possible at this point. His father wasn't thrilled when he learned of Lukas's decision. He raised him and respects his choices, even if he disagrees with them sometimes. But knowing my husband, he's not going to let this one go. I'm sure he's planning something to persuade you both to desist this craziness, as he calls it. You'll have to be on guard and not let my husband make your decision for you."

She's been so painfully honest, so truthful with me. I want to reciprocate her honesty.

"Sook, I understand everything you've told me, and I appreciate your insight. I know it's going to be a difficult road for me, and that's the ongoing debate in my mind. I don't know what's going to happen nor can I guarantee which decision I'll make. But there's one promise I can make to you, and I'll fulfill it until my last breath. I'll protect him at all cost, even with my life if necessary. I will never, ever let any harm come to him or his career."

Her hand on mine is a sign of love and gratitude.

"Thanks. That's all a mother needs to hear to be at peace. I know he's in good hands with you."

Tears of gratitude burst with her approval and confidence in me.

"What did I miss? What happened here?"

Lukas approaches us, staring and clearly confused about why his mom is holding my hand, and I'm teary.

"That's between us. You know, girl stuff."

Sook smiles in complicity.

The next hours pass more smoothly. I'm more relaxed, but I've barely spoken to or interacted with Mr. Lee. I'm sure he's avoiding me. He's kept a cordial distance the whole time. Knowing what I know now, I understand. But just as we are about to leave, he approaches me.

Lukas talks to his sister and mom near the car while I walk toward them after using the bathroom before we leave. That's when I hear Mr. Lee's voice behind me, calling my name.

"Ms. Morales, I'd like to speak to you for a minute in private." I turn, panicked, seeing his stone face.

The intimidating man stands straight before me. Putting his hand inside his jacket, he pulls out a white envelope. It seems full. Handing the envelope to me, his face turns menacing, staring me down.

"Here's $25,000 in cash and a check for $20,000 more. All yours to release Lukas from your grip. If this isn't enough, I can give you more but leave my family alone. You know this relationship of yours is nonsense. I've seen your type, and you're always after the fame and money. You could be his mother."

Glaring at me, upset and lips tight, he doesn't say anything else. I'm aware he's taking a big risk doing this with his son nearby.

I watch in disbelief, my face feels slapped with his offer and words. I'm so deeply hurt. I want him to like me as Sook does. Why can't he see how happy Lukas is? What a better man his son is?

Enough. I'm not going to let him stomp on me like this. I stand tall, proud of myself. My body's blocking the view from outside, so Lukas is unable to see what's going on.

"It wounds me deeply you got the wrong impression of me, Mr. Lee. I came here today, terrified, wishing with all my heart you'd like me for who I am. I'm well aware I am old enough to be his mother, don't need to remind me. I'm sorry I'm not the woman you want for your son. I genuinely love Lukas. I tried not to fall in love with him. But your son can be convincing and tenacious when he sets his mind on something. You must know that. You raised him that way. There's nothing in this world I wouldn't do for him, like you're doing right now. That's why I'm going to let this rude, insulting behavior pass by me, out of respect for you and him. I'm aware you love your son dearly. But I regret to inform you there's not enough money in this goddamn world to buy what I feel for him. It doesn't have a price, and it's not for sale. I can't comply with your wishes. I don't want nor need your money. Thanks for the lovely lunch. Goodbye, Mr. Lee, *Annyeong Haseyo.*" I push the envelope back in his hands while stepping away from him, upset and annoyed.

His dumbfounded face tells me he wasn't expecting this response from me. With a final bow before him, I compose myself to hide my humiliation and walk away. Lukas stares at me, serious. Arriving at his side, he asks, "What happened? Is everything okay?" He's upset, exchanging looks from me to his dad. I force a smile.

"Yep, everything is okay. Just saying my thanks for everything and goodbye to your dad."

Sook shows me she already knows, grinning sadly. Now she's sure I'll protect Lukas without causing any disputes between his dad and him, even at the cost of my own pain and humiliation.

You got your mother's eyes... and your daddy's temper...

The whole ride back to my hotel, I'm quiet, thinking about what is branded in my memory so vividly. Lukas pulls me out of my thoughts with a question.

"You've been awfully quiet since we left my parents' home. What's troubling you? Did dad say something to upset you?"

He's trying to find out what we discussed. I limit my response.

"No, nothing is troubling me. He had a minor misconception, and I clarified it, that's all. Everything's okay, sweetie. Don't worry about it."

Raising my hand, beaming, I caress his face lovingly. He seems satisfied with my response, and that's the end of it for him but not for me. My mind is returning to a dark place I left a long time ago. Sometimes love isn't meant to be. Like Xavier said, maybe this is an illusion, a fantasy. Maybe I don't deserve this.

Chapter Nineteen

Gabriella

I'd thought this day would never end. I'm exhausted. After a long day of meetings, presenting reports of everything that had gone on at the festival, I've finally arrived at home. I'm drained, still feeling the jet lag. Thank God Lola had been my companion on the flight back, keeping me entertained. We'd talked about the details of the planning of the surprise in Namsan Tower. How Lukas had coordinated our encounter. Hearing Lola tell the story makes me fall in love with him even more. Lukas has informed me he's managed to catch a flight to arrive home tomorrow, but I probably won't see him until Wednesday.

Taking a long, hot shower to help my muscles relax, I'm eager to be tucked in early. As soon my head touches the pillow, I'm knocked out. I start to dream crazy stuff, my dream about Seoul turning into an incoherent nightmare.

Kim locks me up in a small, glass room with a door made of thick iron bars that I can't open. I can see what's going on outside, and I'm yelling, asking anyone I see to open the door and let me out.

Lukas appears with an angry look and starts to fight with Kim. Extending my arm through the bars of the door, I finally reach the key to open the door and free myself. But when I step outside, I fall to the floor. My legs won't work. While struggling to stand up, a shadow wraps around my legs from behind me. I keep fighting but can't get free.

That's when a hand tightens its grip on my neck, choking me. I wake up from my nightmare to see a man on top of me. With one hand, he grabs my neck, using the other to cover my mouth, muffling my screams. The darkness in my room doesn't let me see his face, but my wide eyes plead in panic anyway. Who is this? How did he get inside my apartment? I'm going to die, and no one will know. No, please no. Don't let my life end this way.

I'm struggling for air while he continues to choke me. Grabbing his hand with all my strength, I try to unclasp it from my neck, but he's too strong.

Panic explodes, activating my survival instinct. I don't know where the impulse or strength comes from, but I've taken him by surprise. With both hands, I push him hard enough to lose balance, slipping his grip on my neck and falling from the bed, hitting hard the floor.

"Fucking bitch!" A deep voice sounds enraged.

He coughs, gasping, and a painful moan leaves his lungs.

It gives me enough time to get out of the bedroom, running to the front door. The sting of a cut on my arm slows me down. Glancing quickly, I see blood.

I feel another stinging cut on my back when I'm reaching the kitchen to the entrance. I stop, screaming in pain. My attacker grabs my arm, pulling me back to punch my face with his closed fist. I fall on the floor. My nightshirt feels wet and sticky as my own blood soaks through the fabric. This is the end for me. All I can think of is Lukas and Xavier as the pain of the punch has me beginning to lose consciousness.

I see him, blurry and kneeling before me. Both of his hands grab my neck again, and through my half-closed eyes, I see a tall, dark shadow behind him. The shadow grabs my assailant by the neck, strangling him with a second shadow joining the fight. Both are brutally punching my assailant without mercy. I hear their grunts, the fighting, and a loud crash, followed by glass breaking, vibrates in the air. A voice that sounds like Lukas calls my name before everything goes black.

The strong smell of ammonia wakes me up accompanied by a pounding headache. My face hurts like crazy, and I raise my hand to touch it. I don't think there are any bones broken, just soreness. What hurts even more is my neck, where his hands were strangling me. I wipe my neck, trying to erase the memory of his hands squeezing.

I touch my arm to find the cut is already wrapped in a bandage. With my eyes closed, I slowly begin to sit up straight, touching my chest to feel if I'm naked or dressed.

A hand grabs mine, and I instinctively pull away, opening my eyes in terror to see who it is.

"Easy, easy. Please, Ms. Morales. Calm down, be still. You're safe, and you'll be all right. We're taking you to the ER...."

A police officer stands near me, watching the two paramedics tending to me. He starts to leave while informing.

"I'm going to tell Morrison she's awake."

I jump to stop them from moving me.

"No, I don't want to go to the ER, please. I feel fine now, just soreness. Please, no ER for me." I know I'm acting illogically, but right now, I'm in denial, terrified. I don't want to leave my apartment. I'm aware they can't force me to go to ER if I decline it.

Raising my eyes, I see Lukas and Marc entering my apartment with desperation. Their anguished eyes now relieved seeing me alert.

"Gabriella, you're awake." Lukas exclaims first.

Their shirts are stained with blood. They're acting so courteous and formal. Lukas is extremely polite with me, which confuses me until I finally grasp what's going on. The situation with their fame prevents any type of familiarity. So I have to go with it. This is so hard and cruel. My face must present an unpleasant sight from the attack, so I lower my head, overwhelmed.

"What happened? Was the guy captured?"

I raised my head to observe him, my eyes conveying the fear inside me. I'm dying to be in his arms. I wish the world already knew about us, instead of acting like we barely know each other, like he's doing right now. So he still has his reservations about us. Ouch.

"We were arriving from the airport when I heard your scream from the hallway. We ran to your apartment only to find your door broken. We feared the worst. I entered right as the coward knocked you out. I was the first to grab the bastard, and between us, we struck him down."

Glancing at his hands, I discover his knuckles swollen and some clean bandages wrapping his hands. My heart constricts. I don't know whose blood is covering their clothes—theirs, mine, or the assailant's.

Another police officer enters, accompanying a man in a suit who identified himself as Detective Morrison. He begins to ask questions about what I remember, and I tell him the whole truth.

He's the one to inform me the guy was apprehended and turned in for questioning, thanks to the timely intervention of Lukas and Marc. He leans in to tell me privately that the man who broke in has a criminal record including previous kidnappings, arson, and other related criminal activities in the past. He belongs to a gang known to be hired for these types of jobs. They explain they're going to investigate who possibly hired him.

Lukas and Marc stand behind the detective, trying to overhear everything. The officer asks me if I suspect anyone who would want to do me harm. I respond no. I won't tell of the two I suspect could be behind this: Vivian and Lukas's dad. I'm going to find out myself which of those two would go to such lengths for his or her purpose.

They finish their questions, collect my statement, and take everything they believe is evidence from my apartment. Even my doorknob is replaced so they can take the original.

Exhausted and overwhelmed, it's already morning with rays of sunshine peek through the curtains of the sliding door. Marc and Lukas leave to talk to the police in their apartment. After signing their waiver, refusing to go to ER, the paramedics are the next to leave after covering my cuts, with my promise I'll visit the ER in less than 24 hours to make sure nothing is broken.

My emotions are too unstable to deal with more questions or people nosing around. My body and soul are bruised just the same. The last ones here are the building's maintenance guys, installing my new doorknob.

When the maintenance crew is finally done and leaves my apartment, I quickly close my door, leaning against it. The faint sting of the cut on my back reminds me it's there. All the events of this night roll like a movie in my head. I stop being strong, letting myself sob uncontrollably.

A knock on the door halts my cry. Staring through the peephole, I see Lukas standing there in jeans and a clean shirt, already changed after the police collected our bloody clothes. Opening the door, I throw myself into his arms. He's surprised by my outburst and pushes me inside so our curious neighbors standing nearby don't see me in this state, closing the door behind him. I continue crying, soaking his shirt.

"I was so scared, Lukas. That monster was going to kill me. I still feel his hands on my neck…"

I'm sobbing without restraint, distressed with a trembling voice. I understand what real panic tastes like. Hushing me while hugging tightly, Lukas tries to calm me.

"Shh, calm down. It's okay, Gaby. I know, baby, I'm here. You're safe now." He kisses my forehead, comforting me, while I plead with him hysterically, crushing his t-shirt with my hands.

"Please, stay with me. Don't leave me. I don't want to be by myself. I'm so tired, Lukas. I don't want to sleep here alone. Please, please stay with me."

His face constricts seeing me this emotional. His glistening eyes show me he understands how shaken and hurt I am.

"Don't worry, Gaby. I'm not going anywhere. I'm staying with you, calm down. Come."

Taking my hand, he leads me to the bathroom, turning on the faucet to fill the bathtub with hot water. Meanwhile he tries to help me get undressed, but I flinch in terror when he touches me from behind. His eyes show concern from my reaction.

"Gaby, it's me. I won't hurt you. Let me get that night-gown off to clean you, love."

He tries again to carefully touch me. I let him undress me.

Gently, Lukas helps me enter the bathtub and sit down. He sits on the floor beside the bathtub and searches for my washcloth. I lower my face, ashamed and hurt, crossing my arms around my knees in surrender. I'm in pain and sore from the struggling. I can barely raise my arms. He pours water over of my head to wash traces of dry blood stuck in my hair. Tears are mixed with the droplets of water falling on my face. He bathes me with such tenderness, taking his time to cause the minimum discomfort. His pain is etched in his tears when he sees the cut on my back and the purple bruises on my neck. He's beyond upset.

He helps me out of the bathtub, dries me carefully, and brings my bathrobe to cover my nakedness. Tucking me into bed carefully, he starts to walk toward the door. I pull my hand out from under the covers, grabbing his to stop him.

"Please, don't go. Lie with me until I'm asleep."

My heart is heavy with an indescribable sadness, knowing someone wants me dead. And I'm sure it's all about him, for loving him. Without saying a word, he lies beside me, enclosing me in his strong arms. I take his hand to kiss it, inhaling his scent that's so soothing to my senses. Closing my eyes, so tired, exhausted, and broken, I fall asleep nestled in his arms.

This is the only place in this world I feel secure and at peace right now.

Another nightmare. *I'm reliving the attack, but this time, I see Lukas's face clearly when he grabs my assailant by the neck. The hate in his eyes scares me more. His face distorted, hating everything that's happening. Staring at me in disgust, yelling, accusing me.*

"Because of you, I'll never have peace. Why am I with you? You can't even give me children."

The pain those words inflict in me is so overwhelming I

fall on my knees, covering my face with my hands and yelling, "No, Lukas, no. Don't say that."

Now his voice sounds distant, calling me.

"Gaby, Gaby, wake up. You're dreaming…"

His scared face is the first thing I see when I open my eyes.

"I'm here. Marc is here too. You're safe. It's just a dream, okay?" His hand caressing my face soothes and calms me.

It takes me several seconds to realize he's the one talking. I feel the thundering rhythm of my heart pounding against my ribcage. Overwhelmed by the dream, the emotional wreckage I'm in, and what occurred these past few weeks in my life, I finally snap. Something triggers inside me. My anxiety attack is full blown.

"Lukas, I can't deal with this anymore. I can't. I thought I was strong enough to overcome this, but I'm not. I need a break from you. I want my peace back. All these events…Vivian…Kim…that monster… They're all because of you," I yell at him. I don't mention his dad.

He's wounded by my words. I've been unjust, putting the blame on him, but deep inside, I see it as a way to protect us both. By going our separate ways, I'll protect him too. I am the target not him.

"That's not fair, Gaby. I'm not responsible for these situations. Why are you trying to put the blame on me?"

I'm going to save him, as I promised his mother. I'll always be the target of hate.

"I'm not putting blame on anyone. I'm just stating the facts. I can't deal with the stress being in a relationship with you brings. My nerves can't take it anymore. I'm asking for a time out between us, that's all. To organize our minds, think clearly."

The words are coming out of my mouth, but they're tearing me apart more than him. The honest truth is I need him by my side, but I want to run away instead of fighting for us. He's taken aback by my request.

"Is that what you really want from me, Gabriella? To stay away from you?"

His gaze speaks of sorrow, of disappointment, and it breaks my heart. There's still some resistance, believing what I'm saying. I harden my heart and my attitude to respond.

"Yes. For our emotional health, we need it. We need to be at peace in our lives and our careers. We don't have to worry about each other, okay? You can rest from me."

"Why are you talking like I'm tired of you? What's going on? What are you not telling me?" Out of control, he's yelling back at me.

He's hurting badly. I use his yelling to fuel my own anger.

"I'm not hiding anything. Isn't it obvious, or do I need to explain it to you like a little boy? I'm fed up with people attacking me because I'm with you. I want my peace back."

That's the final blow he needs, looking heartbroken, beaten, and disappointed in me. Standing up from the bed, he observes my face while walking backward. I'm seeing the pain my words have caused him. It's tearing my insides out, the disdain building in his eyes. *Don't break down, Gaby, be strong for him.*

"Fine. You wanna take a break from me? If those are your wishes, Gabriella... I'll take my leave now. Like we promised each other."

He turns around, passing Marc, upset. I hadn't been aware he is standing at my bedroom door, hearing our discussion. Lukas leaves, and I flinch hearing the front door slam.

Marc is glancing at me seriously from the bedroom door,

arms crossed over his chest.

"Do you want me to go too?"

I lower my face. With him, it's different. He reads me easily. I can't hide anything from Marc.

"No."

Entering my room without taking his eyes off of me, he sits down on the bed, with an admonishing look.

"Gaby, maybe Lukas is so confused right now he swallowed that sorry-excuse of a story you just gave him, but I didn't, okay? I see you both from afar. I know the way you love Lukas is so strong you would do anything for him, even sacrificing yourself if necessary. Am I right? I'm pretty sure that's what you're doing right now, and please don't insult my intelligence denying it."

It's unnerving how he always knows exactly what my thoughts are.

"I'm not denying anything. But you'll understand my reasons. You'd do the same if you could. I'm the target Marc not him. Someone wants me dead or at least out of his life. Keeping him far from any danger that might lurk around me is the best course of action. You know how hot-headed Lukas can be. He'll insist on being by my side, and I would never forgive myself if something bad happens to him. I can't even imagine… He has to be far from me with nothing connecting us to stay safe."

I'm barely controlling the sorrow that threatens to overtake me. His gaze pierces my soul, knowing I haven't confessed the whole truth. Damn him. Exhaling in defeat, I finally admit to him.

"I need him to be disappointed in me. The disappointment will turn into disgust, and he'll go away. His life and everyone in it will be just fine." He rolls his eyes at me, annoyed.

"Gaby, are you hearing yourself? You're talking nonsense. This is insane. Don't do this. You need friends nearby. Besides what you did to him right now, that's a low blow, and it's hurting Lukas deeply. You gave him a burden he doesn't deserve."

"I prefer to hurt him now rather than later. You both are young and have your whole lives ahead of you. He'll eventually heal from me, find a young Korean woman to marry, and have children. Like it's supposed to be. Please, Marc, try to understand me. I know your loyalty is with him, but you're also my friend."

I grab Marc's hands, and with my broken voice, I continue, "This is tearing my heart into a million pieces. But I'm going to confess something to you, and it's going to stay between us, okay? When you love someone the way I love him, you'll do anything. Because of it, I'm willing to sacrifice my own happiness so he can obtain his. It's not selfless; it's logical. I'm older, Marc, and I can't give him everything he wants out of life. Besides he should be with someone who's more suited for him, someone the public will accept. Please, give me this, and keep my secret. I know I can trust you, and you won't tell him."

With pleading eyes, I've made my honest request. His expression becomes pained, upset he can't talk about it with Lukas. He seems to understands my motives but doesn't agree with them.

"Gaby, why do you have to be the one to sacrifice everything?" is his final question. We understand each other so well. I grasp the meaning of his question.

"Because he has a better opportunity to change the world in a profound way. The world needs him more than me."

It's All for Love... It's All for Love...

Chapter Twenty

Gabriella

I'm not myself anymore. My emotions are a mess. I'm trying to regain a tiny bit of my old life, but it's useless. I'm scarred and wounded, and the worst part is that I don't have him by my side to comfort me. He's done as I'd asked and disappeared from my life.

Around a month has passed since he'd stormed out of my apartment when I'd asked for a break. I haven't seen him, not even in the hallways of our building. He must be deeply upset with me. I know it's for the best, but it doesn't help. I'm so heartbroken without him. In my fragile, emotional state, I can't deny it. My heart and body ache for his company, his touch, how safe he makes me feel. But I try to convince myself he's out of my life, forcing my mind to accept it.

After the attack, I'd decided to take self-defense classes and resume my shooting lessons from years ago. It's time to overcome the crippling fear haunting me by learning to better protect myself. I'm taking these classes without anyone knowing. I've even bought a gun I carry with me in case I'm attacked again.

I've always been a strong woman, and this is not the time to be paralyzed by all these events. I use my shooting classes to take out the rage I've kept inside me for so long, poisoning me. I've empowered myself to be more resilient and fearless than ever before, and I'm proud to be able to heal myself without my son being at my side like in the past. I'm gaining my courage and strength from within rather than letting the sadness consume me. And I'm doing it all by myself.

I've learned through Lola that Lukas is working hard to finish his album, putting all his time and attention into it, and is almost completed. He's working on tweaking small musical arrangements to his liking. Lola tells me he thinks it should be finished with the mixing in couple of days. Then he'll go back to South Korea for the presentation of the album and concert tour all throughout Asia. Japan, China, Thailand, Indonesia, Taiwan, South Korea…all of the major cities in those countries are part of it. They'll be touring for around three or four months. Once it's over, they'll return to LA for a major concert. I'm confident this time apart will help him heal and eventually get over me.

The bruises on my face and neck have almost disappeared completely. Only the scars of the cuts on my arm and back remain. Detective Morrison calls me to keep me updated about the investigation. The guy hasn't confessed anything yet, and an anonymous person has appeared to pay for his legal defense. We're both sure the mastermind who'd plotted my attack is paying for all this, but lawyer-client confidentiality forbids from revealing whom is. Morrison even tells me he's tried to bargain a reduced sentence for a name, but he refuses. The guy is confident he'll get out of the charges even though the evidence is damning. The detectives have asked me several more times why someone might want me dead. I always answer the same way: no idea why, no enemies I can think of or any reason whatsoever for attacking me. I know the reason, but his name would never come out of my mouth.

I've been working nonstop from the office to avoid being alone in my apartment. Obviously Harrison is thrilled, since he now has me nearby to nag whenever he would like. All the bosses are joyous about all the new books and projects the company has acquired thanks to my brilliant idea with the K-pop history book. The idea has turned into my first solo project as an author. Harrison wants me to write it quickly, but I ignore him as always and work at my own pace.

In my apartment, memories of what Lukas and I'd shared are still there, haunting me every day. Sometimes at night, my hand searches for his body, forgetting he's not in my bed. I need to keep my mind busy to avoid thinking of him, so I become a workaholic, distracting myself. My last project with the new author is finished, and we have a big cocktail party to present the book tomorrow in LA. The party is mostly just a gathering for the press, but I will, of course, be there as well.

Arriving home from work, I see Lukas for the first time in a while, standing in front of his door, ready to enter. I freeze, seeing him, and my heart skips a beat. In silence, my longing screams his name. As if he hears it, he turns to stare at me, disdain in his eyes. Swallowing hard, I look down and walk to my door. I feel his eyes on me the whole time, burning.

At my door, I dare to glance at him once more. He's watching me, sad. I enter my apartment quickly so he doesn't see my reaction. I can't bear to see him. Tears are sliding down my face, and I can't stop them. I'm miserable with this situation.

I'm emotionally snapping again, hyperventilating. I need to get away. I'm desperate and not thinking straight. Opening my agenda on my laptop, I look for what I can work on to escape reality so I don't think of him. I'm just seconds away from running out of my apartment, knocking on his door, and throwing myself into his arms as soon as he opens it.

In my pending assignments, I find I need to schedule a meeting with one of the best photographers in China named Shiu Man, who's taken photos of various artists in the fashion and various entertainment industries. She has an impressive portfolio, including the first generation of K-pop idols and the very beginning of the movement. Her base is in Beijing, and her schedule shows she'll be there next week. Perfect. Away from both South Korea and California.

I immediately email her secretary, confirming the appointment for next week, and I ask Harrison to book a flight for next Monday, if not sooner. I even suggest spending a week in Beijing after the meeting with Ms. Man. I know he'll book it quickly since he's been nagging me constantly to finish this project. My book project is the main event the company wants done quickly, and the press has continuously asked for it. My main goal is to be out of California as soon as possible. Lola has assured me that once I return, he should be gone to Seoul to launch his album and tour.

Hoping to calm my unstable emotions, I take a hot bath, put on my pajamas, and try to eat, but I can't swallow anything. I'm a caged lioness waiting for the moment my cage is opened to run away as far as possible. Away from this pain. The truth I refuse to accept is that I can't. The pain goes with me wherever I go.

I need to breathe fresh air to soothe my mind. Opening the sliding door to stand by the railing, I take deep breaths, but the tears still fall. Closing my eyes, I let the breeze caress my face the same way he has caressed me.

A sound startles me. I open my eyes, discovering Lukas appearing at the railing of his balcony. I hide behind the wall that divides our apartments, But I think he saw me.

"Gaby? Are you there?"

I inhale sharply, covering my mouth to hold back the sob trying to escape from hearing his voice.

"Gaby, I know you're there. I saw you hiding. Please, let's talk. We need to talk, baby. Please. Don't shut me out, I miss you."

My chest is tight in pain, hearing those words. I can barely breathe. The sob is choking me. Walking backward, I slowly open my sliding door to enter my apartment, closing it quietly to avoid making noise so he wouldn't know. I slip into my bedroom and turn off all the lights.

Sitting in my bed, I grab my pillow against my mouth to silence the cries of pain rushing out of my chest. My heart is breaking again, but I still feel strongly even though it's destroying us in the end, it's the best for him long term. And that's all that matters.

Softly killing me, I can feel it in my bones...

There had been one moment I'd thought I wouldn't arrive on time, but I did. The PR department had told me this book launch is going to be a social event, due to the author's family fame in Asia. "*Entering the elevator at Skyview Plaza*", I send a text to Harrison to let him know I'm here. As I'd expected, he's booked my flight to Beijing tomorrow. I had to add winter clothes at a last-minute change of plans following the weather reports; that's why I'm late.

Looking at myself in the elevator mirror, my black bustier

and pencil skirt look perfect with my matching suede pumps. I decided to give my hair a hint of color, so I asked for purple highlights.

Tonight I feel confident. I've learned to see beyond what other people see or think apart from Lukas. I see my own worth and beauty. I am grateful for the lessons I've learned.

Walking through the crowd gathered at the entrance of the lounge, I see the place is packed. I'm waving to some people I know along the way, with my eyes searching for Tania Kwon. She's one of the new authors I acquired during my trip to Seoul, who wrote the book we're presenting tonight. I finally spot her standing beside Harrison and Lola chatting amicably. Moving through the people to reach them, a hand grabs my arm. I'm startled and turn to see who it was, and I don't know why I'm surprised to see Shayan standing beside me, smiling.

"Hi, Gaby. Was hoping to see you tonight."

He sounds so cheerful it makes me suspicious.

"Can we talk just for a moment? It won't be long, promise."

"Eh… Sure, Shayan." I point him to one of the empty tables at the end of the cocktail lounge.

I search for Lola's face. She's already surveilling us in case I need assistance. I nod to tell her everything is fine, and there's nothing to worry about. We sit down, looking at each other.

"You're the only person I wanted to say goodbye to."

I widen my eyes in surprise, not understanding why he's telling me this.

"What? Goodbye, why? I don't understand."

"I've been offered a position in one of the channel's stations in New York. The pay is higher, and I was promised more opportunities to grow and develop some of my ideas.

I'm leaving Monday and officially becoming a New Yorker." He pauses, staring directly into my eyes.

"Gaby, I apologize. I behaved badly. There's no excuse for my conduct, the way I treated you. You definitely deserve better. After our last talk, I did some inner thinking on my part. I messed up big time with you. But I confess I still have feelings for you. I'm aware I'm the only one to blame for pushing you away. Like you said, I'm paying for my bad decisions. But because of you, I want to be better." Lukas's and Marc's exact words. He moves my heart.

He takes my hands in his. It's weird feeling his hands under mine. Vague memories creep back to when we loved each other, and this simple gesture means the world to me.

Staring into his eyes, I see truth behind them for the first time. In the past, not once has he been vulnerable in this way.

"If I stay, I'll start chasing you again. I want you for myself so badly I'll pressure you into it, like I did in the past, and that isn't how I want things between us. We will never have the same relationship, but I do want to achieve a new and better beginning. I need to deal with myself first and make some adjustments, but after a while, I'll be back to make sure you're okay. If not, I'll stay. That's my promise to you."

Raising my hands to his lips, watery eyes gazing into mine, he kisses them. My heart is touched by his confession. My hand caresses his face, understanding.

"It's going to be okay for both of us, Shayan. You'll see. You're on the right track. I'm so proud of you right now. Telling me this shows me how committed and strong you are. When we recognize our failures and mistakes, our weaknesses, it's the first step to growth. And it takes lots of courage to do so."

I inhale, then add, "Remember… *Cante Tinza,* brave heart

warrior." His eyes widen, seeming amazed I still remember our secret words.

The rest of the night, we talk like two old friends, free from any pressure. Lola passes by like five times, staring dumbfounded about what the hell is going on since we're treating each other like best buddies. I see her talking on her cellphone while looking at me. I'm hoping she's not giving any information to Marc. It's the same as giving it to Lukas. I don't want my friendliness toward Shayan being misinterpreted into something it's not.

Pulling Shayan by the arm to accompany me, "Come. I want you to meet our new author. That's why you're supposed to be here tonight, not talking to me."

He grins back. We walk over to where Ms. Kwon is standing.

"Shayan, this is Ms. Tania Kwon, our new star author at Longest Quill Editorial. She's a very promising talent. We are blessed to have acquired her during the Seoul Book Festival. You should watch her closely from now on. Maybe her name is familiar. She's the sister of one of the most prominent K-pop singers, who's considered a pioneer in the movement. His stage name is DD. Did I explain it correctly, Ms. Kwon?"

She bows modestly. "I prefer to be recognized by my own talent instead of my brother's international fame," she replies, smiling timidly. *Fuck me and my big mouth.*

"My apologies, Ms. Kwon. Of course you stand alone with your incredible talent. That's why we're all here tonight."

Instantly she bursts into laughter, looking at my face.

"Come on, Gabriella. I'm joking. Of course I don't mind if people know me as the sister of *D-Dragon.* I'm okay, really, I don't mind."

She takes my hand and shakes it, so I know she's not mad

at me. I grin at her ingenuity, feeling outsmarted.

"The pleasure is all mine, Ms. Kwon," Shayan interjects, extending his hand to shake hers.

Tonight I've laughed so much with Shayan. I've needed so badly to laugh. Without Lukas, these past weeks have been pure misery and despair for me. I think I'm going insane without him.

We dance and enjoy ourselves like two school kids just having a good clean time, that's all.

Shayan offers to take me home when he learns I didn't bring my car. Arriving at the leasing office's parking lot at almost midnight, he exits the car to open my door. We've been joking, so we get out giggling in complicity. It's pretty late. I shush him and lower my voice.

"Shh… Let's not wake the neighborhood. I'm really thankful for all we talked about tonight, Shayan. I needed to laugh. I hope everything goes well in New York, and you find yourself there. I'm sure you will."

"It was like old times. Yeah, I enjoyed it too. I also needed to laugh. Thanks for understanding."

We hug each other briefly, and I start to walk away. He grabs my wrist to pull me in his embrace, softly kissing me. I widen my eyes in disbelief at this sudden move. I quickly step back.

"Thanks again for your words tonight. I'm hoping this guy makes you as happy as you deserve."

Those were his final words before getting into his car, driving away. Hope you find happiness, Shayan, you deserve it too.

I take the elevator, lost in my thoughts. The door opens to reveal Lukas standing dressed in a black tuxedo. He has a pissed-off expression, eyes full of fury, staring straight at me.

"Lukas, what…what's going on?" I'm scared of his facial expression.

"What the fuck was that, Gabriella? Letting the guy kiss you? That's why you want me far from you? To have this time with him?" he shouts at me.

"You were spying on me?" I demand, outraged.

It's the first time he's cursed without apologizing. I don't want to deal with him like this.

"I saw everything from my balcony, Gabriella." he yells, enraged. "I was on my way to deal with him."

Stepping out of the elevator, I glare defiantly.

"You don't need to deal with anyone. Neither do I have to explain myself to you. I haven't done anything wrong. Besides I don't want to listen to your rambling or jealous outburst, Lukas. Good night. Cool down first, we'll talk when you're calmer."

I pass beside him to walk through the parking garage to the hallway entrance. The sound of his steps striding fast, following me, is intimidating.

"Gabriella, stop there. We need to talk now. I can't wait any longer. I SAID STOP THERE." he roars behind me.

I turn to face him shocked, my eyes wide, enraged.

"Lower your goddamned voice. People are sleeping. I already said don't want to listen to you. Can't you understand?" I glared at him in defiance.

That's when he does something I wasn't expecting at all. Lukas bends down to grabs my legs and throws me over his shoulder, hanging me upside down over his back. I'm instantly furious, so enraged I forgot to speak English.

"*Lukas, carajo, sueltame ahora.*

He chuckles sarcastically, which makes me angrier.

"If you insist on behaving like a little girl defying me, so be it. I don't understand your Spanish. Have no idea what you just said. But because you don't want to listen willingly, I'll make you listen."

Striding through the hallway, he walks directly to his apartment, while carrying me. I change my strategy, softening my voice and start pleading with him.

"Lukas, please, I said let me down. I don't want to talk now."

The truth is I want to avoid this conversation not postpone it. But he's making it inevitable.

"No, if this the only way I can make you listen, so be it."

He puts me down in front of his apartment door, grabbing my wrist firmly. He shoves the door open, pushing me inside and locking the door behind us.

He stands tall, impressive, and intimidating in front of me, blocking any possible escape route to the door. His imposing gaze is a mixture of rage and primal desire. My legs turn to jelly just watching him.

I'm paralyzed but so turned on. He looks so fucking hot in his tuxedo. The fire in my belly ignites just seeing him. I want him so badly it's insane. All the longing hits me like a train, making me weak. I'm heaving raggedly, holding myself up at the kitchen counter for strength.

"I can't live another day without you." He gasps for air saying this, voice anguished.

"This Monday, I'll go back to Seoul. I'll be away three months, Gaby. Maybe more. This is tearing me apart, don't you see? I know you love me and how strong our love is. Why can't you understand and accept it as it is? Yes, my life is full of craziness. I can't offer you the peace you desire. I recognize that. What I can promise is I'll protect you, no matter what. But you have to let me do it, Gaby. And to be able to do it, you can't push me out of your life."

"So what you want me to do, huh? You want me to renounce to my own life and goals? Sacrifice myself to follow you around the world, is this what you're implying? To be your hidden lover waiting backstage for a glimpse of your time? For what, Lukas Lee? To satisfy you?"

His somber face is taken aback by my words. He opens his mouth but can't speak. Anguished eyes are trying to express what his lips are unable to do. His glistening, pleading eyes appeal to my heart.

"Do you still love me, Gabriella? Tell the truth."

He's trying to trick me into being blinded by my love for him. I'm infuriated by this.

"Don't try to manipulate me, Lukas. Loving you has nothing to do with this. You're being selfish."

The silence between us is making me nervous and my tongue loose. I'm trying with my words to put some sense in him.

"I love you in a way that not only aches in my body but my heart. I can barely breathe without you. I don't know what more you want from me. I don't even know myself anymore. You infuriate me. Sometimes I just want to strangle you for driving me crazy like this."

He's observing my face, desperate. His eyes darken with the lust growing inside him, same as me. Having him standing so close, his masculine scent drugging my senses, looking so disturbingly hot makes me ache all over. Even when we're enraged at each other, the profound love and longing we feel is bigger than us. *That's it for me.*

We jumped to devour each other with kisses.

"Lukas… Oh, Lukas, baby."

His hands move up and down all over my body, caressing

desperately. I moan aloud, feverish, while he devours me with kisses over my chin, trailing down my neck.

Trembling fingers raise my pencil skirt, searching the rim of my panties. He kneels down to take them off my legs. Grabbing my waist, he places me on the kitchen counter. Spreading my legs, he opens his zipper to let his hard arousal free and thrusts into me right there, on the kitchen counter, still dressed.

"Fuck, woman, I don't recognize myself. Don't you see you own me? I'm a slave to you." He exhales, his lust full blown.

He's basking in the moment, taking his time with his thrusts, sliding deliciously inside me. My arms wrap around his neck, and I arch backward while breathing raggedly.

He grabs my thighs to thrusts deeper, clawing his fingers into my skin. Slamming hard, fast. We're both mindless. I let out a scream of lust and pleasure.

"Ahh! Deeper, *Papi.* Like that."

With each thrust, I moan louder. He knows what I want and is eager to deliver. The rawness of the emotions we're experiencing is so intense and primal that tears falls while in the throes of passion.

"I'm yours. Keep going. Take me deep. Brand me with your love."

Crushing his face against my breasts, I hang on to him like life itself. He is about to get his release and gazes into my eyes, love drunk, gasping.

"You're mine, Gaby. Do you hear me? You belong to me. I don't want anyone touching you but me."

Frantic, thrusting faster and faster until he's gasping for air.

"Come on, finish for me."

Closing his eyes, he lets out his scream of pleasure, jerking inside of me. Mine is about to explode.

"Don't stop. Almost there." I plead, out of air.

He complies fiercely, and I shatter in his arms, following him to heaven itself. I gasp for air, unable to speak.

My fingers softly caress his hair, embracing him, kissing his forehead tenderly. I'm sobbing, the sorrow crushing me inside. The sadness of knowing what's about to come is ripping me to shreds. I finally confess to him, staring into his eyes.

"You have to let me go, Lukas. I need you to be strong. You have to help me let you go. I need you to do it for me. Please… I'm no good for you."

Taking my face in his big hands, full of pain, he admonishes me.

"Don't say that. Don't even think that. You gave me new purpose and make me a better version of myself. How can you say you're no good for me?"

All his fears coming to the surface. But it's time for the harsh truth.

"Because a life together is impossible for us, Lukas. Wake up. We can't be together without being attacked for it. It's even worse for you than me. I know your dad doesn't want me with you. You're expected to marry a Korean woman. I can't give you babies. Even if you said is not important to you, I'm sure you want them. If people knew about my existence in your life, your career could be ruined in an instant. At least that's what the internet and everyone reminds me constantly. Your company forbids our relationship to be known. You're having your doubts of letting the world know about me, and you can't deny it. Should I continue, Lukas?"

My eyes pierce the very core of his soul, to make him

understand this can't continue.

"Be honest, Lukas. This is the moment of telling the truth. Are you ready to give it all up? Your family, your career, everything you have worked so hard for over these years? Throw it all away, renounce this instant... *for me*? You want me to believe that?"

He gazes with hurt eyes. He knows I'm telling a raw, disgusting truth we have been ignoring since the beginning of our relationship. This decision he has to make for himself, what his heart desires.

He tries to come up with an answer, but words fail to come out. There's no argument whatsoever to what I stated. His silence is his answer. And it hurts like crazy. Inhaling for strength, I continue stating the facts.

"That's what I thought. Too much sacrifice and too high of a price. I don't judge you, Lukas. I understand perfectly. I saw it with my own eyes. So much work, so many tears, all of the sleepless nights and sacrifices you've made over the years. That weighs when you think about it."

Pulling out of me, closing his pants. He steps back defeated, ashamed, not been able to respond. Jumping down from counter, I pick my panties from the floor and hide them in my purse, lowering my skirt. I look at his face one last time.

"Now do you understand? There are too many obstacles standing between us, Lukas, too many. It's unjust to put this burden on me, pretending we're nothing to protect your career. Right now, I can't handle any more than I already am. I have my own stuff to deal with, just like you. The attack has left me shaken. That's why I told you we should take a time out in our relationship. It was my hope that during this time, you'd understand this. Now you do."

We both stare at each other in agony. He has a petrified,

guilty look on his face. I walk slowly to his door, opening it with reluctance to leave, my heart twisting painfully.

Once I walk through this door, it's over for us. Before I leave, I turn one last time to look at him with the love consuming inside me, speaking between sobs.

"If this can console you… I'm heartbroken too. I'll love you forever, Lukas. No matter what… 'Til eternity, my heart will always be yours."

I turn my back to run to my door. Entering my apartment quickly, slamming the door behind me, I put a definitive end to it. My heart is bleeding again in what I had been avoiding.

Baby, tell me to convince myself… It's all for love…

Chapter Twenty-One

Gabriella

Me and my compulsive need to arrive early to everything. Why do I always overdo it? Now I'm sitting in Shiu Man's office lobby way too early because I was trying to avoid traffic jams. I hadn't known how the traffic behaves here in Beijing, so to compensate, I'd left the hotel two hours before my appointment.

My charcoal gray, wool, sweater dress and dark gray knee-high boots make me look more mature in contrast with the purple highlights in my hair. I touch my hair, remembering him. *Fuck it.* I have to stop this pity party.

The truth is everything reminds me of him, and he doesn't give me a break. He still calls and texts me, asking for a chance to talk. I'd blocked Marc's and his number this morning. Lowering my eyes, I'm overwhelmed thinking about him.

A handsome, young Asian man appears from nowhere and sits next to me, startling me. He notices I've jumped and apologizes.

"Sorry, I didn't mean to scare you."

"It's nothing," I respond while taking a good look at him. His soft black hair is a little bit longer than most Asian guys wear it. Handsome and tall can barely describe him. He seems a couple of years older than Lukas, with mesmerizing, honest olive green eyes and pouty deep-rose lips. The shadow of a beard against impeccable skin gives him a rogue look. He has this vibe of *Bad Boy* all girls crave and desire once in a lifetime. You know…play with fire.

His face seems familiar, but I can't recall from where. We stare at each other curiously. It's a little bit weird.

"Do we know each other from somewhere? I can swear we do, but I can't figure out from where," he blurts first, smiling. I chuckle. It's really funny.

"I thought the same but can't recall from where either."

I pause to extend my hand to greet him.

"Let's do this the proper way. Hi, I'm Gabriella. And you are?"

He reaches for my hand, smirking amused, and shakes it. He has big strong hands.

"My friends call me Shotaro," he answers, smiling with his eyes in the same way Lukas does.

Wait, he said Shotaro? That name… I've heard it before. I've read it somewhere. And then it hits me. He's one of Lukas's bandmates from one of his previous groups. He notices my shocked expression.

"You remembered. Tell me, where do we know each other from?" He watches me curiously with the widest and sexiest smile. Those mesmerizing green eyes, I can't stop looking at them.

"Well… I know who you are, but we've never met in person. I know some of your old bandmates. Marc, Ty, and…" I pause for a second. "…Lukas," I finally add, dreading to say his name, like he may appear suddenly.

Surprised eyes stare into mine, realizing where he's seen me before.

"The lady in the news. The K-pop history book, of course." He shakes my hand with enthusiasm.

"It's truly an honor to meet you. You look younger in person. The photo in the news don't do you justice."

I'm taken aback and touched by his words. His smile brings a softening to his features.

"The honor should be mine, to meet someone as talented and hardworking as yourself." My answer heartfelt, I return his handshake. He stares mesmerized. I blush and lower my eyes. He smiles seductively at me.

"What time is your appointment with Ms. Man? I imagine that's what you're here for. Her portfolio is impressive. You're in for a treat," he informs me, knowing why I'm here. I'm impressed.

"Ten am, I've arrived too early, but it's okay."

I'm puzzled with the way he keeps staring at me. He's studying me, and I don't understand why. And then he asks the oddest question in the most casual way.

"Do you model for photos, Gabriella?"

I burst into laughter, thinking he's joking, wondering why he's asking. Now I'm curious.

"Well not professionally. The occasional news photo, that's all. No nudes or bikini photos," I respond jokingly. His serious gaze with a timid grin shows he's not teasing me.

"If I led you to think I'm joking, my apologies. What I'm saying is, I would like very much, if you have the time, for you model with me in my photo shoot tomorrow. It would mean the world to me. Everyone is talking about your book. You've been mentioned on the entertainment news. To do a promotional photo together would benefit both our careers. Think about it. For your book and my singing career. Please, will you be able to do it?" he pleads, almost laughing now.

I'm in the news here, whoa. That's a first. I grin, understanding what he's implying. As an advertisement expert, it's good publicity to promote together.

"It would be interesting to explore the concept. I'm no Adriana Lima, you know, but I think can manage it."

Ms. Shiu Man exits her office to find us laughing in complicity, smiling at our good mood.

"Hey, let me in on the joke so I can laugh too."

We look at her, grinning silly. Shotaro speaks first.

"I just asked her to be my model for the Bazaar photo shoot tomorrow. It will be amazing to do the photo session together. Think about it. The newest solo singer and the author of the history of K-pop book together, breaking barriers. Don't you think?"

Okay, he can be dramatic and funny to sell his point.

Now she looks at us differently, understanding what he's proposing and maybe seeing the potential in it.

"Yes, I see where you're going.... Yes, We can do it. We're going to get the vibe of *East meet West.* I've got the perfect dress for her to match your outfit, Shotaro. Front page material. If that's okay with you, Gabriella."

Now I'm serious. Is this for real? They're seriously talking about it.

"Are you sure you want me?"

"Why not?" is Shiu's response. "I already have envisioned those pictures, so there's not much planning to do. Shotaro is here to coordinate it. After our meeting, if you have time, we can do the fitting. It's going to look amazing on you. I even have the props necessary to set the mood. Sometimes these last minute ideas turn out to be my best work all the time."

I let out a laugh, raising my hands in surrender.

"Okay, I'm here all week. Why not?"

Shotaro's expression is so trustworthy it's impossible not to agree to his request. He seems honest. I'm the one watching him, puzzled. He utters shyly.

"Would you like to have a cup of coffee with me? If you don't have any other appointments afterward, just to talk."

Direct approach, I respect it. Besides, he seems nice.

"Sure, if you can wait until I'm finished." I smile kindly at him.

"Great. I'll wait for you," he answers cheerfully.

Ms. Man grabs him by his arm.

"Come on, lover boy. You have plenty of time to engage in your flirting later. Let's do this first."

She pulls him toward her office. Giggling, he winks at me. He has sincere eyes—that's a plus for me. And doesn't mind being around me. *Besides those green eyes.*

They both emerge from the office an hour later, his cheerful mood greeting me.

"Your turn. I'll wait here, enjoy." He winks at me while taking a seat.

Once we're behind closed doors, we discuss plans to pick from the archives Shiu possesses. We look at album after album. The photos are all breathtaking, and she explains her vision and the stories behind the pictures of each artist, concert, and promotion. As our fascinating conversation continues, she suggests the ones I should use. It's as Shotaro told me. I'm mesmerized by them, discovering a history of a movement I didn't know existed a year ago. She brings the last portfolio to the meeting table.

"This is my most recent work. These photos are from several K-pop singers launching their solo albums soon. I love the overall vibe of this one in particular. We shot it in Thailand. This is Lukas Lee's album cover for his first solo project. The pose he makes, like aiming to the sky, gives the vibe there's no limit for him. He's truly talented and one of the most handsome guys in the industry right now. He also models for designers like Gucci and Mulberry."

I place my hands on the photo of Lukas's album cover.

This is like rubbing salt on a wound. *Even here in Beijing, far from you, you're still tormenting me, sweetie.*

It's an enthralling picture, Lukas standing with his back to the camera in the middle of an empty street of an old town. Dressed all in black, tight leather fringe jacket hugging his muscles deliciously. He's walking to a red MV Agusta F4 with his arms raised in victory. The album title is written above him: *Unlimited.* I wish that for him, to be unlimited, without boundaries, not caring what others think.

We select some more photos. Synchronizing our agendas, we make several appointments to contact each other though Zoom meetings, in addition to several trips to Beijing to select the best ones. Shiu even helps me by contacting other photographers to share their work and meet with me to amplify my research. I've taken the liberty to ask her to be an advisor, helping me select those who follow the storyline. It feels weird. After correcting everyone's books, now it's my turn to write my first one, and I'm giddy about this project.

Shotaro still waits for me while texting on his cellphone. I feel bad he has to wait for me to finish the fitting of the dress too. Once I'm out of Shiu's office, it's so late we decided to have lunch instead.

In the hour we spend eating lunch, I learn he's single and an only son. *First negative checkmark on the list*, I chuckle inside. But instantly he informs me he's only focused on his career right now. He talks about the time Marc and Lukas were in a group with him. Lots of funny stories of pranks, jokes, and unique memories between them. His cheerful conversation makes me forget my sorrow, for a moment, enjoying his amenable company.

On the subject of music, he mentions he's free from his previous company, the one Lukas belongs to. A Chinese based company has signed him for his first solo record. He's thrilled to be able to record the music the way he's always wanted to. The last company wouldn't allow it.

For his rebellious nature, he's gained the title of K-pop's Bad Boy. I already knew this, but I laugh, nodding my head. He's actually a gentle soul with a soft heart. Another thing I appreciate is the way he stares at me every time I laugh, as if he's fascinated by it.

"Gabriella, has anyone ever told you your entire face lights up when you laugh? Those dimples are enchanting. You should laugh more often. It's breathtaking."

I'm without words. My mood changes to sorrowful, remembering those words from Lukas at Disneyland.

Lukas... Back in my mind, always lurking around. I lower my eyes, deep in thought.

"Did I say something wrong?" He watches me, worried.

"No, I'm sorry. I just remembered someone once said those words to me." A certain sadness trails my voice.

"Boyfriend? Husband?"

"Ex-boyfriend. I'm still struggling. It's recent."

I shrug my shoulders in surrender. Maybe this explanation would push him away. But I don't want to hide the truth nor talk about it. His reaction to my words is the opposite. I'm pleasantly surprised.

"If he told you that, he's wise. But letting you go is the dumbest thing he's done. I'm sure he's already regretting it," he replies, beaming bashfully. I grin back, flattered by his words.

After lunch, we walk around a park near my hotel. The conversation is entertaining. Shotaro knows so much about everything. He's showing off the beautiful cherry blossom tree with tiny buds about to bloom, describing their breathtaking beauty. I mostly laugh at his jokes. He's funny and a proper gentleman. Several fans approach us during our walk to take pictures with him or ask for his autograph. I'm impressed by his humbleness and commitment to treat them with courtesy.

The sky is getting dark, and it's a windy afternoon. Even though we're wearing coats and gloves, it's still really cold, but I'm kept warm from the inside, relaxed to be walking beside him. I don't pretend to be anything I'm not. And he accepts me just as I am.

He insists on accompanying me to the lobby of my hotel. When we arrive, I face him, smiling, truly grateful for the time we've spent together this afternoon.

"Thanks, Shotaro. I enjoyed myself today. I'm so glad we bumped into each other in that lobby."

He grins at my words, pleased.

"I'll pick you here at seven tomorrow morning to be there on time. You don't have to take a taxi. Rest well, Gabriella." He winks at me, caressing my arm casually, making a funny face that causes me to burst into laughter before he turns around and leaves the hotel. I stand there, exhaling a breath I didn't realize I had held. Wow, this guy is so interesting. Is he for real?

I can't help to chuckle to myself, covering my eyes. This is insane. Another young Asian man smitten. Gabriella, girl, you're a threat to the Asian male community, especially the young artistic kind.

The next day at 7:30 am, we arrive at Shiu Man's studio to start on makeup and wardrobe. I receive celebrity treatment for the first time, and I'm enjoying all the pampering. My hair and nails are done first, then makeup and the final fitting of the dress.

They allow me to get a glimpse in the mirror before leaving the dressing room, and I don't recognize myself. *Who the fuck is this woman?* I gasp in amazement. Never in my life have I looked as jaw-dropping gorgeous as I do right now.

My short hair is combed in casual spikes, making me look disheveled and younger. The makeup accentuates my Latin attributes, and the dress hugs my curves nicely. It's ankle length with a sweetheart neckline and long, see-through sleeves. The deep burgundy-violet fabric has sewn golden ribbons on the corset, giving me a Greek-goddess vibe. Matching rhinestone ear cuffs, like leaves rising toward my hair, creates a royalty-crown-type impression to complete the look.

Three assistants escort me to the studio, and I'm blown away by the amazing set prepared for us. It's designed to look like a jungle at the base of a volcano that's about to erupt. That's what we're about to do with these photos.

A door opens, and Shotaro enters, dressed in a black tuxedo with satin lapels, and a white shirt, unbuttoned at the collar, with no tie. He wears several silver chains, and a tattoo of a small, red dragon on his chest peeks out of his open shirt. The makeup artists have painted his neck, knuckles, and hands with black fake tattoos he didn't have yesterday. His hair is combed sideways with a lock of hair falling casually over his forehead. Some smoky eye makeup accentuates his hypnotic green eyes. He looks picture-perfect to me, dare I say kind of sexy. Noticing the intensity of my gawking, he beams back devilishly. Halting to study me from head to toe with admiring eyes.

"Wow." He puts his hand over his mouth before adding, "You don't look anything like yesterday. Where has this goddess come from? And you say can't pull an *Adriana Lima?* Gabriella, right now, you look better than her, seriously. Simply ravishing." he expresses excitedly.

His words make me blush, pleasing the woman inside me. Hey, who wouldn't like to receive a compliment from a hot, young male K-pop idol dressed in sharp tuxedo?

Shiu enters through another door, and bright spotlights turn on, illuminating the background. She stops in her tracks, observing me with wide eyes. Shotaro is adjusting his cufflinks.

"Wow, Gabriella, you look so different. This is way closer to how I'd envisioned you'd look. Makeup team, you've outdone yourself," she exclaims upon seeing me. The makeup team in the corner grins proud, a faint happy shriek escaping from someone.

"Same. I told her she's stunning. This is going to be a hit. I know it," Shotaro comments, pleased.

Behind us is a long, red and gold Victorian sofa placed in the middle of the jungle, for us to sit on I presume. She starts giving instructions to everyone around.

"Well, people, let's get started. B team, please finish setting up the second set. The people for the second shoot are already in makeup. They're coming shortly and have to leave this afternoon, so we're busy today. Please remember everyone, stay as quiet at possible inside the studio. Understood?"

Everyone responds with affirmations. Working for her, they already know what to do. Everyone immediately falls silent.

"Shotaro, sit on the sofa casually, one foot on it, knee bent…. Yes, like that. Gabriella, come," she calls to me.

"Recline on Shotaro's chest, sitting sideways between his legs, like he's pulling you to him. A little higher, yes, that's better. This is the vibe: He found his muse, and he's embracing it, understood? Your face must show his touch makes you tremble; you belong with him. Okay?"

That sounds rather intimate for two strangers. But in advertising this type of thing sells. Doing as instructed, my back against Shotaro's chest, my head rests on his shoulder. Faces touching, his hands hold my bodice. I feel the heat of his fingers on my torso. The sultriness of his touch startles me.

I put my hands to rest on his arms in an intimate way. The heat of his body and his breath on my face push my heart to pump fiercely in my chest. He chuckles, noticing how jumpy I am.

"Relax, Gabriella. Everything will be just fine. Don't be nervous. I'll lead you. You look enticing."

Having a gorgeous man whispering in your ear while his hands hold your body is enough to distress any female in the same situation.

An assistant comes to spread my long skirt all over the sofa, letting just one bare leg out with my deep purple stiletto sandal in a sexy pose. A group of people enter one of the doors of the studio, but we're unable to see them. The lights pointing at us blind us, and everything behind them is utterly black from our point of view. I have to trust Shotaro and follow instructions. I feel so awkward right now.

Lukas

Ty, Marc, and I will only be here for a short time, but it should be long enough to find her. We only have three hours to complete this for the visual introduction at our concerts, then we leave for Seoul at late afternoon. A last-minute change of plans that had been decided by Jong. We're told Ms. Man has commenced another shoot and to keep it quiet. We walk in the dark room to where the assistants point us to sit.

We're dressed for our shoot in early-'70s clothing, all three of us in different dark suits. We sit in a corner where we see Shiu working but not who she's working with. As soon as we sit down, I take out my cellphone to see if I have any missed messages.

I've been texting her, and she's ignoring me. I need to speak to Gabriella, knowing my silence hurt her so badly. I feel awful for letting her down. I want to apologize, to tell her I plan to show off our love to the world once my contract ends and finally start my own record company. We don't have to renounce this love. I need to convince her to be patient and wait just a little bit longer, that's all. I'm still hoping she answers, and I can find her here in Beijing, to talk.

"I wish I knew where she was, to ask her forgiveness. It's hard not be able speak with her," I comment casually.

"Maybe you should ask Shiu. Lola told me that's who she came to Beijing to meet with. Maybe you can figure out what day the meeting is scheduled for," Marc responds me.

Suddenly Marc turns away, feeling Ty's hand slapping his thigh insistently. Ty covers his mouth, eyes in shock, looking to where Ms. Man is working. Following Ty's gaze, Marc gasps loudly.

"What the actual fuck?" he remarks aloud in disbelief.

I raise my eyes to observe where everyone is staring. My jaw drops when I discover the most ravishing woman who looks exactly like Gabriella. All my muscles tense instantly as I narrow my sight to watch her closely, devouring her unmistakable, long legs. Those delicious legs have been wrapped around my waist many times when I'm buried deep inside her. It's her.

What the hell is she doing? My God, she looks bewitching and seductive as hell. Why is she hanging out with Shotaro of all people? How does she know him? These questions emerge in my mind as I watch her. Standing hostilely, I'm ready to rush to where they are.

Marc notices me, grabbing my arm to pull me back.

"Oh, no you don't, Lukas. Chill out, this is a photo shoot, remember? Don't make a scene."

Ty stands beside me. I know it's in case I decide to do something impulsive. Right now, jealousy seethes through my veins. This is my goddess, and I'm the only one allowed to touch her.

We watch Shotaro and Gabriella with incredulity. With this makeover, she's a different woman. There's some darkness I didn't notice before, some wickedness still to explore with her. Her image brings to mind the Greek goddess of love. She's desirable and hypnotic. I'm enthralled with what I'm seeing.

I start to fume inside, seeing Shotaro's hands holding Gabriella's bodice. It's clearly a sensual touch. His face shows it, and I'm losing it. Why can't I control this rage, this uneasiness inside me? This maddening jealousy is eating me up. Her hands rest on his arms like they're a couple.

Shiu is shouting instructions to Shotaro.

"Now turn around and casually kiss her temple. Gabriella, when he does it, close your eyes, like you're enjoying it."

Shotaro leans toward her ear to whisper some words, wearing a wide grin. I can't hear them, but I see her scared expression, cheeks flushed, her breasts rising and falling with her breaths. She's affected by him, partially closing her eyes when his lips touch her temple so tenderly. Enough.

"Okay, that's it." I shout, my voice vibrating through the studio.

Marc gasps when I yank my arm from his grasp and move forward.

"Lukas, stop. Calm down and lower your voice."

Marc and Ty try to get ahold of me to calm me, but I twist and turn to get free from their hold, forcing my way to Gabriella and Shotaro's set. I'm out of control.

Gabriella

Am I losing my mind? I hear their voices. Marc's and Ty's voices arguing with Lukas shouting. *Lukas is here?* I stand instantly, eyes wide open, pulling myself from Shotaro's embrace. Raising my hand to my forehead, I shield my eyes from the brightness of the lights, looking everywhere.

"What the hell is going on? Who's shouting?" Shiu Man spins around to see who's yelling.

That's when we all see *him* walking toward the light. His enraged expression could be mistaken for fury, but I know it's jealousy. He pushes his way toward me while Marc and Ty try to hold him back.

"Lukas," I blurt out, exhaling ashamed.

I blush deeply, feeling guilty. It feels like I've been caught cheating. Shotaro stands behind me, watching Lukas's face over my shoulder. Seeing Lukas's expression and my reaction, he stares at me, realizing something. Speaking low for me to hear.

"So, he's the ex?"

I turn to stare, terrorized, shocked he's read us so easily. There's some disappointment in his eyes.

"Shotaro, please let me explain…"

"It's not necessary. You can explain to me later."

He turns to speak loudly enough for everyone to hear.

"Let's all take five, okay? I'll be in my dressing room." Ambling away, I extend my hand to grab his.

"Please, don't go; let's talk."

He offers me a sad smile. "Let's talk later, Gabriella. No rush. You've got your hands full right now. Look behind you. You have unfinished business to deal with." He points his eyes to where Lukas is standing. Shotaro turns away to leave and exits the studio.

Facing Lukas, I'm enraged at this intrusion. Everyone in the studio stares at us stunned, murmuring amongst themselves. If every public encounter between us is going to be like this after this breakup, it's going to be a problem. He has to learn to control himself.

So here we go again, establishing these boundaries between us. I stride fast to him, irritated. Lukas watches me with hungry, furious eyes. Stopping in front of him as close I dare, I pierce into his eyes. Marc and Ty stand behind him. *He always smells so good.* Focus, Gaby. I speak in whisper for only him to hear me.

"What the hell are you thinking, Lukas? What's wrong with you, barging in like this? You have no reason whatsoever to do this to me. Nothing is supposed to be going on between us, remember?"

I'm whispering, but I'm so enraged with the fact he doesn't even realize what he's done. Watching me the way a lion watches prey about to be devoured, he whispers back.

"What the hell is this, Gaby? How the hell do you know him? How did you meet?"

My rage is about to get out of control hearing his questions.

"I don't have to explain myself every time you demand it, Lukas Lee. I'm not your fucking property whatsoever," I answer in defiance.

I'm so hysterically furious at him. I want to strangle him this moment. The lustful way he looks at me, his angry eyes revealing my rage and defiance excites him in a potent way. Seeing him inflamed excites me more.

Our eyes speak their own language without saying a word. Without stopping to think, Lukas seizes my wrist and drags me past everyone until we're outside the studio.

In the hallway, I try to cool him down.

"Lukas, what the hell are you doing? Slow down. Where are you taking me? Release me."

He doesn't say a word or look at me, just pulls me down a long corridor. Arriving at a black door, he opens it, pushing me inside then locking it. The raging fire of desire shows defiance in his caramel eyes. He's locked us in his dressing room.

"What the hell do you want from me? Are you insane?"

He doesn't answer. I shut my mouth and step backward slowly, at the sight he's presenting. He's transformed. Before me is a giant ferocious lion, ravenous, intimidating, and majestic, about to jump me, a cat prowling. This is the man I belong to, no doubt about it. Seeing him like this, untamed and demanding, I crave him more than ever. The lion jumps on me.

Wrapping me desperately in his arms, moving his mouth over mine hungry and eager. Shoves me backward until I trip onto a black leather sofa nearby. He drops on top consuming me with kisses, gasping like he's run a thousand miles. Hands desperately fondle my breasts, claiming them, and I let out a big gasp, inflamed. I want him like this.

Our moans intensify as he kisses my neck, driving me insane. Reaching down, Lukas pulls up my skirt. Desperately he finds the rim of my panties, yanking them off. Staring at my face with the most desperate expression I've seen on him, he pulls his pants and underwear down and bends, grabbing his arousal to thrust deep into me, making me scream. There's rage in his passion. It's angry lovemaking.

Thrusting fast and deep, he gazes into my eyes, speaking through fiery moans.

"You want me like this, don't you? You want me nuts for you? I'm going to satisfy you, like I know you crave. No one else can give you this, only me."

He kisses me like I'm the best thing he's encountered in his life. His lips worship me, every inch of my skin. My body is squirming beneath him feverishly. He grasps my hips to push harder, making me scream louder, a mixture of delightful pleasure and exquisite pain.

"Right there. You can take it. You want it,"

"Fuck, Lukas."

Those words send me toppling over the edge. As I moan aloud, Lukas covers my mouth with his to receive them. The blissful instant arrives, falling into pieces, seeing stars in the sky bursting before my eyes, jerking my release. He works himself in and out until he finds his own release, screaming his passion in my neck, huffing in agony. Now we know for a fact this burning love is inevitable every time we're alone with each other. This is too strong, too big to be contained. Our raging fires and wants match perfectly. He knows what I want and enjoys giving it to me. It's too insane to explain.

Still gasping for air, he caresses my thigh, recovering, he whispers, his lips on my neck. His arousal jerking inside of me, just like I love.

"I'm scared to lose you, Gaby. And I know each day you become more distant. I'm scared of what I saw in your face back there. When he kissed your temple, it wasn't fake. You liked it. I want that look only for me, no one else. With you, Gaby, I'm selfish." He dips his head to kiss my temple.

With my eyelids lowered, I glance at him love-drunk, unable to speak. This orgasm was so intense I can't utter a word yet. Gazing with lust for several seconds, caressing my body, he seems to have decided this is the moment to make sure he brands me as his.

"You look so beautiful right now, Gaby. Flustered by our lovemaking, eyes half-closed, your cheeks blushing, and I'm the one who did that. Can you see how perfect we are together?"

I understand he's asking to be reassured even if we can't be together. For me, there's no point to it.

"This is insane, Lukas. We can't keep doing this. I'm a hazard to your life. Why don't you understand that?" I blurt through ragged breaths. His jaw clenched. His eyes slightly narrow at my words.

"You honestly believe that? That you're a hazard? You're the only woman I want in my life. You're a blessing for me not a burden. We can make this work out. I love you so much, Gaby. We belong to each other. Don't push me out of your life." Raw hurt glitters in those dark eyes.

He seals his emotional confession with a tender kiss. He kisses me with a passion that takes my breath away. Enough to revive my lust once more. His pulsing arousal grows inside of me, stretching me completely. A delightful shiver of wanting runs through me. I'm already lost again.

He starts to pound with the same desperation as when we arrived. Our moans escalate again.

"Ah, Ah, Ah, you feel so good, baby."

I hear voices afar outside the hallway.

"Shhh! Be quiet for me," he mutters breathlessly in my ear, hearing the noise too. The unmistakable sound of Marc's voice instructing someone outside the dressing room.

"It's okay, let's go back. Give them time, they're resolving their issues right now. Let's give them some privacy."

He must have heard us. What must he be thinking that this is our way to resolve our issues.

Once our steamy encounter ends, I clean myself to avoid staining my dress. I pull up my panties, walk to the mirror in the dressing room, making sure my makeup isn't too smudged by our lovemaking. Lukas finishes dressing himself and comes to stand behind me. Putting his hands on my shoulders to kiss them, we stare at each other in front of the mirror, expressions earnest.

"I need to speak with Shotaro."

I can't stop thinking about how he must be feeling, right now, because of me.

Lifting his lips from my shoulder, he glances, upset at me.

"Why? Why do you need to speak with him?"

There's some anger in his tone. I face him.

"Why? You're really asking me? Because he didn't deserve what you did to him, Lukas. You ruined his photo shoot with your outburst of jealousy."

I'm about to raise my voice in anger but decide to shut my mouth, closing my eyes. Inhaling for calmness, I explain, "I met Shotaro yesterday at Ms. Man's office. It was their idea to include me in this photo shoot for the cover of China Bazaar Magazine. To help promote my book and his solo record, that's all."

I understand he can't help these outbursts, but he has to learn to control himself. He can't go through life like this.

"You know I love you, but I don't have to prove my love every second. Now not at all because we've broken up. Do you understand what breaking up means? This lovemaking shouldn't have happened. I try very hard to avoid you, but you always appear in the most unexpected way. I'm weak and can't help it with you. Now we have to mend what everybody saw out there. You dragging me all the way to your dressing room, and some of them may have heard us making love in here. We're usually pretty damn loud about it."

His hands release my shoulders. He doesn't seem to consider the consequences of his actions. Now he's grasping the possible damage he's done to himself. He can't afford people linking us emotionally, for his career. And his reaction to my words confirm it. Our passion has overtaken us this time. Reason finally returns.

"You're driving me insane, Gaby. I can't stand another man touching you. You turned my goddamn world upside down. Seeing you the way you look right now, you're exquisite. I'm usually controlled in my reactions. And this isn't me."

He's annoyed with himself, trying to justify his outburst. I don't remark on it because I can relate to what he feels. I'd be just as jealous if I were to see him with other women. Thank God it hasn't been the other way around. I know I'll be torn apart if a see him with another woman by his side.

Touching his face gently with my finger, I softly turn it so he can see my eyes, hoping to make him finally understand me. I'm not asking; I'm ordering him.

"This cannot happen again. Do you understand? I'll help you out. Let me speak on behalf of us, and I'll talk with Shotaro in private after. You'll follow my lead and don't screw up. I already told you I'm not going to be your hidden lover. It's emotionally exhausting for me, okay? This stops now, Lukas. Do you hear me?"

I stare directly at him to make sure we're in agreement. He nods his head in affirmation.

We go outside to the studio. I notice the hem of my dress dangerously close to making me trip with my heels. Picking it up, I sense Lukas walking closely behind me, observing me without saying a word.

Once we enter the studio, I go directly to Shiu, my face truly ashamed.

"Shiu, I apologize for the outburst of Mr. Lee. It's all a misunderstanding, a silly one. He thought I was stealing some of his ideas we discussed for another photo shoot for the book. But as I already clarified for him, this idea was yours, so no one is stealing ideas from anyone. Everything has been cleared up just fine. I need to speak with Shotaro. Where is his dressing room?" I blurt quickly to make sure no one suspects.

"The left door beside yours," she answers with a dumbfounded look, staring at me confused by my senseless explanation.

"I'll let you go about your other photo shoot with the guys while Shotaro and I have a chat. We'll be back shortly."

The intensity of my stare yells at him to be calm and not to do anything stupid. His agonized face lets me know he doesn't want me going to Shotaro.

I walk down another hallway to find Shotaro's dressing room. I knock on his door.

"Shotaro? It's me, Gabriella."

The door opens.

"Hi." He smiles casually.

"Hi, can I come in?"

He moves aside to let me pass, closing the door behind me. Gesturing for me to sit, I decline.

"Did Lukas calm down? I'm not judging him. If I were him, I'd react the same way if I saw you with him in that pose." He chuckles sadly.

His gaze is tender, making me feel guilty, and I haven't done anything wrong. Maybe I'm guilty of encouraging him without knowing. His words move me. It deserves an honest answer.

"Shotaro, I love Lukas with all my heart. But I'm not the right choice for any of you, that's the plain truth. Sadly many things have happened between us that make any relationship between us difficult, not to say impossible. Love isn't enough for us. You know Lukas, his career is too important to renounce it for love. And I understand. I'm conscious there's so much sacrifice you all have gone through and the cost is too high."

I pause to inhale and observe him. Lukas has awakened the woman in me. That's an undeniable truth. My inner goddess is restless. And she's flattered by the attention received. It has nothing to do with feelings. This is honest pride. But I can't let pride take over.

"Knowing you, Shotaro, I confess it's been different. I don't have to hide nor pretend to be different. You accept me, without feeling shame being associated with a *ajumeoni*, knowing you'll be judged for it. You'd invited me to this photo shoot, understanding the world would see us together, and you don't mind the outcome. I'm at ease around you, but I want to be honest with you. I can only offer you my friendship, nothing more."

Slowly standing before me, his deep soul-searching stare studies me, his emerald gaze burning. Holding my chin, he leans in to kiss my cheek softly.

Pulling away, he smiles with a sad smirk on his face.

"Thanks for your honesty. I know where I stand with you. You're an incredible woman, and it's so easy to fall for you. You don't realize it, Gabriella, but you're bewitching as hell. I'll take your friendship, and let's see where it goes from here."

I press my lips in a polite grin to his confession. We leave the dressing room to the studio. We walk in silence, side by side, but I sense his intense gaze upon me.

We enter and everyone stares at us in surprise. Shotaro and Lukas glare at each other. I give him a serious stare to control himself. Lukas inhales sharply seeing us, understanding what we had discussed previously.

"Well, once I finish with these guys, I can start again with you both. Take this time for makeup retouching. I hope we don't lose more time. I'm squeezing you in before my next appointment. Okay?" Shiu speaks loud enough for everyone to hear.

Stealing one last look at Lukas, I'm at ease. He finally understands why. It's painful for us, but this is the best course of action. I feel Shotaro's hand grabbing mine to pull me away to the makeup room. There's pain in Lukas's eyes. Maybe this will be the last time we see each other for a long time. I know it's for the best for him.

Chapter Twenty-Two

Gabriella

Okay, I admit. It's been an agonizing torture. This is the reason I had avoided getting into another relationship, of falling in love again. The longing, the pain. I'm trying to keep my mind occupied, my usual way to cope with heartache.

More than a month and a half has passed since our impulsive encounter. I reflect on that day constantly, with a longing to see him so passionate and ravenous again. Well at least a couple of times a day. In the tiny daily details, something always reminds me of him. I miss my lion so much. It's torture not knowing where he is or what he's doing.

We've agreed to have separate lives. A real break-up, no connections whatsoever besides being neighbors in California. I've internalized that life without him is a reality for me. So life must continue. We've been summoned for the trial of the assailant who broke into my apartment in two weeks as witnesses for the prosecution. I'll see him for a brief moment in court. I just want to be done with it. Close this chapter of my life, try to heal and move on.

Shotaro and I have cultivated our friendship, talking occasionally. I fly to Beijing frequently for reunions with other photographers coordinated by Shiu Man, for additional material to pick from. My book it's almost finished. We go out to eat every time I'm there and enjoy an occasional event together. We have no romantic relationship whatsoever—he's tenacious—I still won't allow it. Other than the unexpected embraces I let him steal, there's nothing more.

The press follows us, and we've been the entertainment news of the week, not to mention the month. The *China Bazaar Magazine* cover of Shotaro kissing my temple, *east meets west,* is an instant hit. It had been so beautifully taken, portraying honesty in our faces. That's why people are fascinated with us, believing there's something between us. We always answer we're good friends, nothing more.

Surprisingly people don't judge for the age difference. We're breaking cultural stigmas. In China, people see us with respect. Through the way we treat each other, we're teaching everyone age doesn't matter when you spend time together. People admire our courage for not caring about the opinions of others. I'm well aware Lukas knows, through the news, we're spending time together.

Lukas's career skyrockets with the launch of his album. As predicted, he's a sure hit. *Our* song, "I Surrender My All", is in the top five of the music charts across Asia in his English and Korean versions. He's been on tour for more than a month, and right now, he's touring in Japan with Marc and Ty.

Ty's album also quickly climbs the charts in the States, giving Lukas a new standing in the music business as a composer and producer of his own full solo album as well as Ty's record. His tour includes several TV presentations and some award shows. I still search for news of him on the internet, just to get a glimpse of him now and then.

Back in California, my bosses are thrilled with all the unexpected mayhem in Asia, regarding my first book and my so-called relationship with Shotaro. The free publicity I'm receiving is resulting in more new authors submitting their works, as well as new business connections in China, Japan, and South Korea. Advertisement and sales are going up.

My friendship with Shotaro turns out to be great for him too. His first solo record has also risen to the top five in China after only a week, and it's huge for him. Fans think our "friendship" is part of his rebellious persona.

The way we relate to each other is open and honest, like friends should be. He's aware of my feelings for Lukas but hopes I'll change my mind and choose him. Yep, he confess he's fallen for me. He's willing to go against the opinions of others to prove how important I am.

But he doesn't deserve lies or false hopes. My heart belongs to only Lukas. I've made peace with the fact he will be the wound that never heals until my last breath on this earth. I don't want to love anyone else. In my core, I know he's the one I'll carry in my heart.

I felt the blooming future... Feel it... Throw it,
because I can catch it...

Shotaro asks me to accompany him to an awards ceremony I happened to be in town for. I was going to stay in my hotel room to organize the final touches for my book, but I decide to go with him, pulling an elegant, ruby red strapless dress, that I bought yesterday, out of my suitcase. Tomorrow, Monday, I'll return to California to arrive early for the trial.

When the limousine arrives at the venue, my anxiety

crawls up my spine, seeing a multitude of people gathering at the entrance.

"You didn't tell me it was going to be packed like this. You know I don't like big crowds."

"C'mon, Gaby. You're an expert at this sort of thing. Besides it's by invitation only, so it's not as crowded inside, you'll see."

I watch Shotaro with suspicious eyes, exhaling, annoyed I have to do this. But he's right.

"Are you ready?" He gives me a wicked smile.

He's incorrigible. He enjoys misleading the press and his fandom with our relationship. He finds delight in provoking them. The paparazzi's flashes will explode as soon we step out of the car.

I glance at him, resigned.

"Okay, let's do it. Please, guide me as always, sweetie." is my heartfelt answer, grinning back.

Opening the limo door, the frenzy of flashing lights blind me. Shotaro offers me his hand to help me get out.

With his hand on my waist, standing still, we wait for the blast of photos and shouts all around us to calm slightly. Grabbing my hand, he leads me down a red carpet. Shouts ask us to pose, some volley indiscreet questions and comments. I let him deal with everyone, ignoring them as much as I can.

Whispering jokes into my ear, he provokes me to laugh in front of the press. It's enough for them take the bait, asking about our relationship. He's vague in his responses, letting them guess or come to their own conclusions about the truth. We agree on this: mystery sells.

Glancing ahead of us, I recognize Marc, Ty, and Lukas dressed in black suits and ties. A lump forms in my throat. I didn't know they'd be here. If I'd have known, I wouldn't have come.

My heart thunders in my chest at the sight of him. Collecting myself, I lower my gaze. Shotaro notices my reaction. Squeezing my hand in reassurance, he bends to whisper in my ear.

"It's okay, Gaby. You're not alone; you've got me."

I stare surprised. The exact words Lukas had told me in Puerto Rico. Adoring green eyes reassure me once more. I grin sadly.

"I know."

We walk toward them, the press still taking photos of everyone on the carpet. All three stand beside each other, posing together. Lukas is the first to see us approaching, and surprised eyes show it's still a shock for him to see us together. Staring hungrily with curiosity, he reveals a longing still burning bright inside. I can't avoid gazing at him the same way. *The love is still there…*

When Marc sees me, his face lights up, and he rushes over to hug me tight.

"Gaby, it's been so long, baby girl. So good to see you. You look gorgeous."

I hug him back, kissing his cheek, honestly delighted to see him again.

"Sweetie, you don't know how much I miss being around you. How're you doing? It's being so long since we last talked. Lola told me you're officially going steady. Congratulations." He chuckles, amused.

"That girl is handful, and I adore her. We're doing good so far. It's not easy, a long-distance relationship in this business."

After stealing one more glance at Lukas, I ask, "How's everything going?"

"We're doing okay, under the circumstances," he tries to inform me, casually extending his hand to greet Shotaro.

"Sho, man. So happy your career is taking off. Keep taking good care of our girl here."

The press continues to take photos of us.

"Marc, believe me, I treat her like the queen she is."

Lukas flinches, hearing him, trying hard to smile, but utterly failing.

"Ty, Lukas…how're you doing?" Shotaro extends his hand to whoever shakes it first.

Ty grabs it to greet him.

"Good to see you and glad you're doing great, Sho. Let's see if we can partner to do something together."

"Sounds like a plan. I'll tell my manager to contact your label."

Ty approaches me to kiss my cheek. His face looks different, seeming more unfettered. A pleasant change in him. He appears happier and more playful. Kind of loose. I'm curious what has caused this change in him. It comes across as maybe he's in love.

"Hi, Gaby. It's exhilarating to see you. I always enjoy these encounters with you, since they usually end in an unexpected adventure with all of us involved in some sort of shameful dispute." He grins, whispering so casually.

I couldn't hold my laugh in, hugging him. I'm astonished to hear him joking like this. It suits him.

"Don't hex it. Let's hope nothing happens tonight, and we finally avoid it."

Then my eyes settle on Lukas. His face is full of hurt, but he finally shakes Shotaro's hand.

"I'm really glad you're doing so well, Sho."

Observing me, he adds, "Take good care of her. You've got a priceless treasure in your hands, but I'm sure you already know."

His words twist my heart, shredding it. A sob creeps up my throat, tears threatening to spill. I swallow hard to control myself. *It could be you holding my hand, but…*

"You know I will," is Shotaro's serious answer.

A host signals us to face the press so they may take photos of us together. I wind up between Shotaro and Lukas. Shotaro holds my hand while Lukas's hand rests on the small of my back. I've never felt as anxious as I do with both of their hands on me. It's so hard to fake a smile like everything is okay.

We split apart to different tables once we enter the building. They seat us near the front of the stage, and behind our table is a double crystal door showing some breathtaking gardens at the back.

The show goes smoothly, a very structured program. Shotaro performs his hit song "Show Me". Seeing and hearing him perform on stage makes me giddy, like a groupie. He plays a masterful electric guitar, and the sensuality of his performance is intense. He's raw, passionate, and so fucking hot in his overall presentation. I'm aware why they call him the *Bad Boy of K-pop*.

Tonight he wins Album of the Year. When his name is called, he stands up, bowing to everyone. The audience is clapping, and he bends to softly kiss my cheek, for everyone to see. I blush like I always do when he pulls these stunts in public without warning.

He goes up to accept his award, giving his speech in Mandarin. He's talking about, or at least mentioning, me. His eyes are fixed on me while he speaks. Other guests exchange looks between us, watching our reactions. I dare to glance at Lukas. His intense lion's eyes observe me without flinching, lips parted. I lick my own lips at the sight of him.

After Shotaro's speech, the host announces one last performance. I'm surprised to see Lukas going onstage as two stagehands wheel out a piano. My heartbeat echoes louder in my ears as my breath fails me. I'm uncomfortable every time I hear the song. I know what he's about to do. He uses the song to speak to my soul, to keep me hanging on, and it's not fair.

He sits at the piano and starts to play. As he sings, he watches me the whole time. He's pouring his heart in to this interpretation. I even see one tear roll down his cheek. He's letting everyone see his pain while he sings. The raw emotion he's putting in this has everyone teary-eyed. Shotaro studies me, watching my reaction. He knows Lukas sings for me. I shamefully stare at him, overwhelmed.

"I need fresh air. I feel dizzy."

"Shall we go outside?"

I pat his hand to calm him, forcing a smile, reassuring him.

"It's okay. I just need time for myself. You're the star of the night, stay. Just five minutes, I'll be back shortly." I get up while people applaud Lukas's performance.

Turning my back to everyone, I go out through the crystal doors behind us to the gardens. Outside I inhale deeply, the nighttime breeze cooling my heated face. I walk quickly through the grass to reach the farthest end of the gardens.

Discovering a secluded fenced-off area several feet away, I pick my long skirt to walk even faster, almost running until I reach it. I'm hidden here. No one can see me here while I regain control of all the emotions strangling me. I've been suffocating since I left the banquet hall. My necklace is choking me, so I yank it off in a panic attack, holding it in my hand while stroking my neck with the other. I gasp for air to alleviate the shortness of breath I'm having.

Tears flow without being able to hold them. I'm overwhelmed and confused when a warm hand touches my bare shoulder. I turn to find Lukas standing behind me, his anguished stare watching me empathically. With his knuckles, he gently wipes the tears from my face. He lifts his hand to hold the back of my head, drawing me in to kiss me with all the love he bears for me. I respond by parting my lips to deepen our kiss.

I want to drown in his kiss, forget everything, and make love to him, right here. But the reality of our relationship creeps back in my mind. Bracing my hands against his chest, I push him away.

"No, you've got to stop this. You're torturing me. Stop toying with my emotions. I'm trying to move on, don't you see? Haven't you had enough of this obsession?"

"This is not an obsession. Don't speak of my feelings like they aren't real."

"This is insane, Lukas. Why don't you understand I'm trying to save your career, your future?" I raise my voice at him. We're both enraged at each other.

"I don't need you to save me. I need you to love me."

In an instant, my headache flare comes in the worst moment possible with gruesome fury. My legs buckle; I almost fall. I grab my head to let out a small shriek of pain, uttering, "Fuck."

Lukas catches me in midair, scared and staring at me.

"Gaby, are you having these headaches more often?"

He steadies me, to pull me back up, with a worried expression.

"I haven't thought about them. I don't know," I respond honestly while recovering.

From the shadows, Shotaro jumps to grab Lukas by his shoulder, yanking him away from me, shouting, "Don't you dare touch her. Leave her alone."

Shotaro's arm wraps around my waist to draw me into his embrace, facing Lukas, incensed, maybe thinking he'd done something to upset me.

"She's in pain, *Babo*. Do you know about her headaches? I'm only assisting her," Lukas shouts back in defiance.

"Yeah, right. You're here assisting her. Bullshit, I know what you want. You want her to still cling to you. How easy. Toy with her emotions a little bit for your amusement to keep her there, still hanging. But you don't have the balls to go out there and tell the world you love her. Help me understand. You want her to sacrifice for you, but you're not willing to do the same for her? Is this how it works for you, bro? This is how you love her? How convenient," Shotaro barks out.

He shoves me behind him, without giving me time to react. Striding to face Lukas, he stares in defiance. With an undertone full of rage, Shotaro declares in Korean.

"*You'd choose money and fame over love? You are a coward.*"

That's enough for Lukas to lose it and jump to fight. The crunching sound of fists hitting flesh is terrifying as they each land punches. I try to intervene, calling their names, not accomplishing anything. I don't possess the strength to split them apart. They're rolling in the grass, hitting each other with rage.

Luckily, Marc and Ty appear, running to us, probably suspecting this would happen. Marc takes hold of Lukas while Ty grabs Shotaro, finally stopping the fight.

"Guys, come on. Control yourselves. Remember where we are. The press is nearby." Marc's tries to speak some sense in them.

Both men resist the holds that Marc and Ty have, still

ready to rip each other's heads off and growling. Lukas bleeds from the corner of his mouth while Shotaro bleeds from his nose and a small cut next to his eye.

"Coward." Shotaro shouts, enraged.

Anger starts bubbling in my chest. I'm fed up with all of this, and shout, "Enough, both of you. I'm sick and tired of all this. Stop this moronic behavior. You're two grown men, not teenagers in a school fight. I'm not a fucking plaything or trophy to fight over. Get it into your heads. I only belong to myself, neither of you."

Both stared in shock at my outburst, not expecting this.

"You're bandmates, for the love of God. This is exhausting with you two."

I inhale sharply, shutting my eyes in fury. I open them. Yeap, I'm fed up. Raising my hands in surrender, I let my Boricua rage out of control.

"You know what? I'm going back to my hotel this instant, alone. Fuck you all. Do you hear me? *Vayanse al carajo.* You included, Ty, for jinxing this night."

Ty's eyes widen in disbelief at my harsh words. "Did you just tell me to go to hell?"

"Kill each other if you want to. Really, I don't care. I can't take this shit anymore. Fuck you all."

The four of them stand there, eyes and mouths wide open, watching my *loca* outburst. With one last deadly glare at each one, I grab my skirt to head back to the entrance, leaving them behind without looking back. A hand grabs my arm to stop me.

"Gaby, stop, stop. Please let me take you to your hotel. Just to be sure you arrive okay."

The voice of Marc halts me on my tracks. I turn around to face him, furious.

"I don't need any fucking help from any of you. You can stay with them." His hand strongly holds me, not letting me move.

"Gabriella, it's me, okay? Take a deep breath and cool down. I'm just making sure you arrive safe, that's all. Don't be so stubborn and let me take you back. It'll be only you and me, okay?"

Livid, I wipe the tears from my face. Inhaling deeply to lower my rage, I close my eyes in frustration. I open them to observe him, upset before answering, still feisty, but complying.

"Okay, okay."

We turn around and continue to walk together to the entrance, away from them. I can't deal with this rollercoaster of emotions anymore. Fuck them.

Who do you love? It is him or me?

I'm still bothered, arriving at my room, upset from everything that has occurred tonight. Marc had asked for another car to bring us back here. We'd both been silent the whole drive to the hotel, with occasional stares at each other. I'm just waiting for his speech on behalf of Lukas.

He insists on accompanying me to my room. We both enter while I take off my earrings and fling them onto the table with the necklace. That's when he speaks.

"Did you cool down? Wanna talk about it?" His questioning eyes search for mine. I turn my back to him in disdain, to not answer.

"C'mon, Gabriella. Really? You can be silent all you want, but I'm going to say something you won't like, even if you send me straight to hell. Part of what happened tonight is kind of your fault."

I turn around with wide eyes to face him, indignant. He crosses his arms, his eyes sharp and assessing. *Did he say it's my fault?* I couldn't hold my tongue.

"Excuse me? What the hell you mean by that?"

"You know damn well what I mean. What's the real deal between you and Shotaro? I know the press comes up with wild stories about you two, feeding on false gossip. We've been reading about it. But tonight, I saw Shotaro so into you. He seems to think he's entitled with you. Have you been feeding his hopes?"

His reasoning feels like a slap to my face, making me aware. The truth is, even though I told Shotaro once about my feelings, I allowed him certain attributions, almost letting him believe there could be a chance for us.

He's right. Now that I realized it, Shotaro's behavior shows he must believe there is a possibility. It just dawns on me now. I try to justify myself.

"Of course not. I told him where my true feelings are."

"But have you told him explicitly you don't love him like he wants?"

An uncomfortable silence spreads between us while I try to come up with an answer. But I'm unable to. He watches me, shakes his head, rolling his eyes, and walks toward me to grab my hands in his. His soothing tone just tries to put some logic in me.

"Gaby, I'm your friend too, I'm not here to make you feel bad. You're the only one who knows what you want. But I'm positive there's no possibility of a relationship between you two, because you still love Lukas, no matter how much you deny it. But you have to tell Shotaro the truth, plain and simple. He doesn't deserve any false hope. And I suggest you do it soon."

I'm unable to hide the conflicting emotions swirling in my heart and the guilt his words cause me. I've been kind of selfish, using our *friendship* to soothe my loneliness. To hide the true pain I've been carrying inside me all these months. I lowered my face, profoundly ashamed, realizing this.

"I didn't intend to encourage him. I don't want to hurt him."

With his finger, he raises my face to look at him.

"I know you don't. It's time to tell him where he stands with you, Gaby. See that I'm not excusing Lukas's behavior nor talking on his behalf. Right now, I'm only worried about Shotaro and you, baby girl." We observe each other in silence. Barely audible from my shame, I answered.

"I'll talk to him as soon as I can."

Marc leans to kiss my cheek sweetly. "I know you'll do the right thing. I'll leave you now to rest. We'll see each other soon."

I assent with a timid grin. He raises my hand a kiss my knuckles, smiling. Releasing my hand, he turns to walk out my room, with me following to close the door.

I'm about to take my dress off when a soft knocking stops me. Marc must have forgotten to say something. "What did you forgot, Marc?"

I open the door to encounter Shotaro. His eye is swollen from the cut over his eyebrow, and some bruises show over his nose.

"I don't want to talk to you." And try to close the door, but his hand stops me.

"Gabriella, please, hear me out. I'm so sorry for what happened tonight. I came to apologize for my conduct. Can I come in?"

There's shame in his voice, his puppy eyes imploring. Oh,

those eyes. Your eyes have always hypnotized me, Shotaro. The guilt of being half responsible for what had occurred tonight starts to take a grip of me.

"Come inside."

Once I close the door, we watch each other kind of awkward. I examine his bruises. My fingers touch the cut.

"How's your face?"

He flinches, shutting his eyes in pain.

"Easy. I think I'll survive another day as long as you don't press like that."

"Sorry. Let me clean and tend those wounds for you. Sit here."

I always carry a small emergency kit on trips, and this is the occasion to use it. He sits on the chair, loosening his tie, unbuttoning his shirt while I open the kit. Cleaning his cut and nose, I close it with butterfly strips. I tend to him in silence. He's silent too, watching me with the saddest eyes. I know the time has come. The conversation pending between us, and it seems it can't wait any longer. Shotaro takes my hand to kiss my knuckles.

"I'm sorry you had to witness our outburst. It was childish and shameful. I thought he was harming you. But I'm not sorry to tell him the truth you don't want to express, Gaby. It's easy for him to keep you waiting for whenever he feels the need for you. It's not fair the world doesn't know who you are to him. You're not something to be ashamed of or hide."

His truth hurts me. Still I don't want to acknowledge it. I gaze down in pain.

"Okay, you're right. But still…I can't help it, Shotaro. I love him. I can't control what I feel. Believe me, I've tried hard. I wish I could push these feelings far away from me, but that isn't how it works."

I look into his eyes with tears, my fingers slowing combing through his fine, long hair.

"You deserve so much better, Shotaro. You deserve a world of happiness, to be loved passionately and unconditionally. But the truth is I can't give you the love you crave from me."

There's a painful silence between us.

He stands, his face full of emotions. Strong hands hold my hips, and he pulls me to him with a hungry expression. Clutching his arms for balance, I stare at his lustful eyes. He knows he can turn me on right now, *but…it's not enough.* He wants more. He wants me all for himself, body and heart. He sees the lust in my eyes, nothing more. The lust is nothing but an instant if the heart isn't in it.

Now he has my full attention, holding my face, leaning down slowly to kiss me. I want so badly to reciprocate. The fire may burns in my body but not in my heart. I can have sex with Shotaro, but I can't *make love* to him, and he doesn't deserve half of me.

Marc's right. It's cruel to continue misleading him. He doesn't deserve it. Neither can I lie to please him. It would just feel wrong after seeing, hearing, and tasting Lukas tonight. Lukas is still a disease in my blood that I can't get rid of. He's the thorn in my heart. The one I will always belong to.

Noticing my unresponsiveness, Shotaro slowly retreats. Tears roll down his cheeks while he speaks, sniffing and forcing a smile.

"I know. I think I've known it since the beginning." He pauses to sniffle again. Nothing is more heartbreaking to see than a man you adore crying because of you. I cry seeing him like this.

"I took a risk falling in love with you, even knowing you'd

never love me the same way you love him. Since the moment I saw you in that lobby, I knew I had to be beside you. You're extraordinary, Gabriella. I'd assumed, no, hoped, in time, I could achieve some spark of love from you. I've always dreaded this moment. I knew it would come eventually, but I wasn't expecting it to be this soon."

I'm torn apart by his confession. I adore Shotaro, and the last thing I want is to hurt him. But we don't choose who we love; it just happens. Knowing I'm the cause of his pain is crushing me.

"Shotaro, I'm sorry. I'm so sorry." I cry, holding his face. "The last thing I want is to wound you. I love you. I truly do. But not in the way you want, need, or deserve, my friend."

His thumbs softly wipe the tears from my face. He gazes at me with affection.

"It's best this happened now. We need to move on with our lives, I know."

He raises my hands to his lips and kisses them adoringly, offering a faint smile to give me courage.

"I love you, Gaby. You're a stunning, attractive, brilliant woman, and the world deserves to know how amazing you are. We helped each other doing that. I'm forever grateful for the time we've spent together. Truly, Gaby, nothing can top this."

How can repeated words inflict so much pain? I want to erase the agony I see in his eyes, even for a second. I can't stand it. I kiss his cheek tenderly. He steps back as if my lips pain him. Another forced smile tries to lessen our sorrow.

"Call me whenever you're in the neighborhood. I'll be waiting to hear from you." He walks to the door, turning around one last time, finally adding, "Adriana Lima better watch herself. There's a *sexy ajumeoni* in town. See ya,

Gaby." Winking his eye at me, he leaves, and the door closes softly behind him.

My heart crumbles in despair. I'm aware a magnificent man is walking away from me. An uncontrollable sob escapes my lips. My hand covers my mouth while I cry. I'm crying for the both of us.

I can't stand the rain anymore...

Lukas

The doors of the elevator open, and Shotaro steps out. I'd followed him to find the hotel where Gabriella is staying. He glances around the lobby when he spots me. His eyes are filled with tears, and I'm scared, thinking something bad happened to Gaby. Trudging to where I'm standing, he stares into my eyes and show me his pain. He stops in front of me, inserting his hands in his pockets.

"Lukas... She's an extraordinary woman. A true and rare diamond, bro. We are so lucky to have encountered her in our lives. She let us discover her inner beauty, and she has one of the biggest and most honest hearts I've ever known. Don't lose her, man. But don't make her lose time. Every time you're near, she suffers. I've been there to witness it. She has tried to forget you, you know...really hard, and I think she's suffered enough. Respect her, man, respect her feelings. My advice to you: *myeongseong-gwa donboda salang-eun seontaeghae. Igos-eun jinjeonghan bomul-eul chajeulsu itda."*

I'm surprised by the words he said. *Choose love over fame and money. That's where you can find your true treasure.*

He puts his hand on my shoulder, gently squeezing like we always do.

"You're lucky, Lukas. You always have been, and you don't even realize it. You are blessed to have her love... Go and fix things with her. Don't let fear of what could happen make you lose what's really valuable."

Shotaro grins, heartbroken, sniffing and wiping tears off his face. Patting my back, he moves out of my way, shuffling out of the hotel and into the night.

I stare at the elevators, reflecting on his words and debating if I should go up to Gabriella right now. His spoken, undeniable truth compresses my chest and hammers my head. He's absolutely right. The realization of the hard truth makes me emotional.

She doesn't deserve the pain I've been causing her. I've behaved so selfishly lately, and I've never stopped to think about how she feels, all she's sacrificed for us, for me. I am tortured by my guilt for not seeing it before.

I don't have the courage to face her. What can I offer? Another empty promise? To wait for me hidden? I'm still trapped by my fears. The fear of failure, to contradict my company's instructions, and facing rejection in my career for my personal choices. I truly am a coward while she has been nothing but brave. I lower my head, defeated by my own ambitions. Ashamed of my own cowardice and with heavy heart, I turn back the same way I'd come. I'm not worthy of her. I don't deserve her. *I don't deserve her love.*

If you love her... If you need her... Tell her without holding back...

Chapter Twenty-Three

Gabriella

A couple more hours to California, then I'll be free of these two exasperating men. Of all the coincidences I've suffered, being on the same flight as Lukas and Marc is the most annoying of all. I thought they would fly private. It's the earliest flight available to be on time before Thursday, the day of the trial. They're sitting in first class while I'm peacefully in economy, glad to be far from them. Twice during the flight, I've received invitations from Marc to join them. I've declined—twice—telling them to stop it. It hasn't kept them from sending martinis and dinner to my seat, irritating me.

Arriving at LAX, I just run ahead of them, and we separate at the airport. I walk to the parking garage to pick up my ruby baby. It's a bit chilly today, so the roof stays on. Throwing my bags into the backseat, I notice someone on a motorcycle at the end of floor, helmet on, with the headlight on in my direction. I'm getting this weird vibe from it. Entering the car, I turn it on quickly, the biker advancing toward me.

There's nothing to think about. I step on the gas, driving as fast as I can in the cramped space to get away from him, but the driver of the motorcycle stays close, chasing me. *Mierda.* This has to be another assassin. The trial is near, and I'm the biggest thing standing between jail and freedom for that guy.

I connect my phone to my car's bluetooth, and I call Lola but don't let her speak.

"Lola, shut up and listen carefully. I'm being chased by a guy on a motorcycle, and I think my life is in danger. I'm leaving the airport parking garage. I can't stop, and he's gaining on me. So, please, follow my instructions, track my location on your phone as we've practiced before and call the police. Now, Lola. Do you understand? I need you to track me. This is a real emergency."

My plan is simple. I want him to follow me away from Lukas. I'm shouting instructions while driving as fast I can. I spot Lukas at the pick up area, getting inside an Escalade while I'm exiting the main lot. The good thing is, this assassin is following me outside.

I break through the exit barricade, sending pieces of wood flying in the air. I reach the road, drifting and almost hitting another car. Smoke from burned rubber trails behind me as I drift again to get on the onramp of the highway. I press the gas further, not minding if a police car appears to chase us. The motorcycle is making an effort to gain on me, to pull by my side.

I'm hyperventilating, knowing I can't let him get next to me. I try zigzagging the car so he wipes out, and I change lanes rapidly, but he dodges my maneuvers.

Lola's voice sounds through my speakers, startling me.

"Gaby, we are now in a three-way with Marc. They can hear you."

Lukas's voice sounds first, upset.

"Gaby, what's happening? Where are you?"

I can't believe it. I don't have time for this shit.

"*Pero, Lola,* told you to call the police. *Coño.*"

I wipe my face in frustration.

"You all listen to me. I'm only saying this once. I think another assassin is following me. The trial is near, and if I disappear, a lot of charges will be dropped."

I exhale, finally making my confession.

"I have a gun with me in the car."

I haven't told any of them I had bought one, but I consider myself a fairly good shot, or that's what my instructor tells me. The day has come to use my skills.

Gasps of shock could be heard, but it's Lukas who speaks.

"Gabriella, listen to me. Don't do this. Let me know where you are. We should be right behind you. We can—"

"She's not going to tell us where she is, man. I know her. She's so stubborn." Marc's annoyed voice states the obvious. He's right.

"Lukas, please hear me. I'm the target, not you. I know how to defend myself. After the attack in the apartment, I began making sure I'm trained for this. I have my gun with me, which I have a license for. Right now, I'm purposefully going far away from you to keep you safe, so obviously I'm not going to tell you where I am. Lola, please hang up the call, track me as I asked you, and call the fucking police, NOW," I yell, pissed I have to deal with Lukas this instant.

"Lola, don't hang up. Gaby, please let me help you." Lukas's voice is desperate, anguished.

The motorcycle driver gains on me and draws a gun.

"Oh, shit, he's pulling a gun."

Flooring the gas, the sound of a bullet breaking the rear

driver's window behind me scares me. Where are the fucking police cars when you need one? Now I'm terrified and furious.

"Lola, *Carajo*, for the love of God, hang up the call now. I swear to you we're having a hell of a fight if I survive this."

Lola's alarmed voice informs them.

"Sorry, guys." She's finally doing what I'd asked her.

"What the hell were you thinking, calling them? You're supposed to track me thru the app and call the police."

"I thought they could help you…"

"We need to seriously talk about the importance of following instructions. I need you to stay on the call with me until the police answer. You'll know where to find me through the app."

"Why can't they track you?"

"I blocked their numbers. Don't you remember? When I left for Beijing."

"Where are you headed?"

"I'm on the 91 headed to Lake Elsinore, maybe San Diego. I'm just leading him away from Lukas. I'm not reading the signs. Did you call the police?"

"It's already ringing."

"As soon they answer give them my location and explain what's going on. Tell them you're tracking me on the phone."

I open my glove compartment to take my gun, sliding it under my thigh.

My cellphone rings, I see a number I don't recognize. It start with an eighty-two, the area code of Seoul showing on the screen. They must be calling from another of the two cellphones they usually carry. I ignore it. I look for the first exit to Lake Elsinore while the motorcycle keeps pursuing me closely. Seeing I'm taking the exit, he points his gun at my tires. A bullet blows one, causing my car to veer out of control.

My screams of terror increase as the car spins out while I grip the wheel. The car rotates several times until it slams into a concrete barrier along the highway. I'm dizzy from all the spinning. I take a couple of seconds to see the motorcycle driver parking several yards behind the car, getting off the bike. He walks toward me with the gun in his hand. Still dizzy, I reach for mine, releasing the safety. Watching through the corner of my eye, I hold the gun waiting for the moment he comes near. I have to be steady, precise. Blood pumps in my temples. I'm panting hard, trembling. So scared.

While starting to raise his gun to point at me, I turn and fire two shots aimed at his clavicle area. The impact makes him shoot the floor, the gun falling from his hand as he falls back on the pavement. I get out of my car quickly to kick his gun far away from him. Aiming my gun at him, I grip the handle with trembling hands and yell, "Who do you work for? Who's paying you to kill me?"

"I'm not paying anyone, anymore. You're supposed to be dead already."

I'm shocked to hear a woman's voice behind the helmet. She sounds familiar. I tuck my gun into the back of my jeans, kneeling down. Pulling the helmet off of the woman's head, a braid of red hair springs out with the face of Vivian Orly, distorted by the pain of the wound. I'm stunned.

"What the hell? Why? Why go through all this?"

Taking off my blazer, I press it against her wound. She's bleeding profusely, my shots hitting their mark, per usual. Several cars park behind us, and I finally see the lights of two police cruisers in the distance, approaching our direction.

I stare down at her. She's glaring at me with hateful, crazy eyes, hissing through her pain, while I press her wound.

"Lukas was mine. You stole him from me. Once you appeared, he changed. You bewitched him. You're the problem. I just have to get rid of you. He used to worship me, you know. Being worshipped by Lukas is the ultimate heaven. But then you appeared and ruined everything."

She starts coughing blood. Alarmed I try to clean her face with my hand in my nervous state. Glancing up, I see the police officers running toward us and an ambulance in the distance. Looking at her, my compassionate heart can't avoid reassuring her.

"Hold on, the ambulance is arriving just now."

The fear of knowing there's not much time left to tell your thoughts is reflected in her eyes, knowing what's happening. With a disgusted mock, she smirks with a sick certainty.

"You'll never be happy with him." are her last words before closing her eyes, exhaling her last breath.

Blood continues to spread in a puddle over the pavement around her body. I am horrified by it, walking backward, realizing what I've just done. Staring at my hands, covered with her blood, I'm appalled. I've never taken a life before. My strength leaves me, and I fall to my knees on the road beside Vivian's body, broken by this conclusion.

Head Games... I can't take it anymore...

After more than four hours of interrogations, signing statements, and Vivian's body being collected by the forensic division, I'm numb and tired. There's no more strength in me. *I'm done.* Staring vaguely at the floor, reclined on a chair, I'm waiting for Lola to pick me up.

She had cried when I called her. Lola had explained she'd heard my screams over the phone plus the gunshots. Then there had been silence and the call cut. She'd thought I had been killed. She hasn't stopped repeating how relieved she is, knowing I'm okay.

My tired gaze watches the entrance of the station and sees Lola arriving with Marc and Lukas looking at me with distressed stares. I watch them, numb, overwhelmed, and ashamed. I bow my head in defeat, to not watch them anymore.

All I want is to be in Lukas's arms. And I'm so miserable because I can't be. This is wrong. I'm wrong for him. *Collateral damage.* I swallow hard as I see the press starting to flood the entrance of the police station.

Daring one more glance at him, he's walking past the reception desk, striding fast toward me. Pulling me by my arms to stand up, he crushes me against his chest.

"Gabriella. My God, I thought I'd lost you."

The warmth of his lips on my forehead and his arms embracing me answers my deepest wish.

I'm still in shock, unable to move or comprehend. I stand there frozen while he rubs my back, hoping I react. Relaxing into the warmth of his body, something snaps, and I start to cry hysterically.

"Oh, my God, Lukas. Oh, my God. What have I done? I killed Vivian. I killed her. I didn't want to. I didn't know it was her. I killed her." I crush the fabric of his shirt in my fists, burying my face in his chest. My chest is so tight from the fear exploding in my heart.

"Shhh… it's okay, baby. Breathe. I'm here. I know you're scared but breathe. You didn't know… No one knew… You defended yourself." He comforts me, cleaning my tear-streak face.

A police officer approaches us.

"Sorry. Are you related to her?"

"I'm *her boyfriend.*"

Shocked, I stare at him, panicked by his words.

"Lukas, what the hell are you doing?"

"I'm doing what I should've done a long time ago. Speaking the truth. *I love you.*"

He turns to the police officer to ask, "Is it okay for her to leave now? Or is there anything else you need from her?"

"No, I got her statement, and forensics collected her DNA and fingerprints with the gun. She's good to go."

Without saying another word, Lukas gently takes my hand and raises it to kiss it quickly before pulling me to walk beside him toward the growing crowd outside. The press starts snapping photos of us from the entrance. I'm scared as hell, feeling a knot in my stomach as I walk with him.

I understand what this means, to be open about our relationship. It's his scream of freedom aimed at his record company, society, and everyone else who's prevented us from proclaiming our relationship. He has finally developed the courage to tell the world he loves me, potentially sacrificing everything.

I hope he's ready for any backlash that comes with this news. Lola and Marc watch us in astonishment. No more hiding, no more denying anything.

The press jumps on us like vultures once we pass the police barricade. A black SUV is waiting outside, a couple of feet away from the station entrance, with the doors open. Marc and Lola are walking fast getting inside the car with several reporters following after them. We pass through their flashes and questions while Lukas encircles my shoulder to pull me closer, opening the way for us. Rude reporters stick their microphones in our faces, trying to get any reaction from us. We arrive at the car and hop into it.

Once inside the SUV, the chauffer pulls a U-turn to get us

out of there in seconds, aware of two or three cars following us. Once we arrive at the apartment building, security guards at the entrance don't let any of them enter.

In the hallway, two tall men in black suits stand at each side of my front door. Alarmed, I step back. Lukas grabs my shoulders to whisper calmly into my ear.

"It's okay, Gaby. They're private security hired by the record company to avoid any unpleasant events. They were informed about what Vivian did to you. You're safe now." He takes the key from my hand and helps me get inside.

"I'll stay with her tonight. Take my keys. See you in the morning. Rest well," he says in farewell to Marc and Lola.

I still haven't grasped I'm inside my apartment. In the silence of my home, reality hits me painfully. I'm consternated how destiny continues to push my boundaries. Falling on my knees to the floor, I start to sob uncontrollably. I can't talk, just cry. Releasing all of the panic and strain of taking a life.

He kneels beside me on the floor, embracing me while murmuring soothing words to calm me. I rest my head on his shoulder, crying without stopping. The pressure I've felt these past months, ensuring nothing harms him, is let loose too. I stop being strong, and I can finally be at peace, rest. Curling up in his arms, I sit on his lap as he holds me close, cuddling me, his lips brushing my temple.

"Don't let guilt torment you, Gaby. You didn't know. No one knew how deranged she really was. This isn't your fault. You only defended yourself. Don't take on guilt that isn't yours."

Tiny, adoring kisses cover my temple and my forehead, soothing my unstable emotions.

"I'll never let you be away from me, ever again. I don't care anymore. I'm shouting I love you, and I want to spend the rest of our lives together, however long that may be."

His eyes find mine, full of affection, his finger caressing the frame of my face. Tears run down my cheeks, my heart filling with tenderness hearing his words. Shutting my eyes, I doze off in his arms, pushing this horrible ordeal I've gone through today to the back of my mind. He's my safe space, and I feel secure. That's all I need to be at peace. In my weakness, he's my strength. I drift into a deep sleep.

I wake up to see the clock on the microwave says it's 8:30 am. Looking around, I realize we'd slept all night on the carpeted floor, me in Lukas's lap while he holds me against his chest. He didn't move all night for me. My God, he'll not be able to move his legs.

Everything that had occurred yesterday crawls back into my mind. Adrenaline starts to rush in my bloodstream with those thoughts, making me relive every second of it. It's surreal, like a horror movie, but Lukas's words echo louder than anything, soothing my troubled soul.

"I'm doing what I should've done a long time ago. Speaking the truth. I love you."

I observe him sleeping soundlessly, sitting against the kitchen wall. Can't resist the temptation to kiss him, to feel his skin on my lips. Covering his jawline with slow, tiny kisses, lips trailing till I reach his neck, I taste him. I'm getting lost in the knowledge he belongs to me. He said so, and I belong to him. No more debating it. A purring murmur escapes from his lips.

"Mmmm...I like the way you're waking me up. Don't stop." With his eyes still closed, he grins, pleased.

My lips continue to trail his skin, getting lost under my growing, feverish lust. He lets out an occasional soft moan, so I move to straddle his lap. My fingers slowly trail his face, enjoying the softness. My whole being seems to be filled with unbridled wanting.

I can love him freely, openly—without reservation. The weight of this realization overwhelms me. I lower my mouth to kiss him with raw passion. This fire is a full-blown blaze. There is a murmur on his lips while I'm kissing him.

"I love you, Lukas. More than words can express. I want to show you the depth of my love. It's intense."

He inhales sharply, drawing in the promise in my words. My kisses are intended to arouse the lion I miss so much to ravish me. A sense of urgency is driving my actions. He tightens his embrace, his moans increasing, enjoying what I'm doing to him. We've waited far too long for this.

I stop to stare into his eyes, lovestruck, while taking my shirt off. I unclasp my brassiere and drop it on the floor while he takes off his shirt. The desperate kissing continues. Skin against skin, my body aching for this. We are famished for each other. I'm not holding back anything from him. My desire is blown, seeking to burn together.

"I love you so much, *papi.*"

"I love you more."

He rolls me over, desperate hands unbuttoning my jeans to pull them off. I'm fully naked, and he discards his pants and boxers in an instant. I climb back on his lap, his throbbing arousal begging, sensing the heat of my sex. I can't help but to grind against him. He groans in desperation, seeming pleasantly surprised.

"Fuck, Gaby. I love how you tempt me. You match my hunger… Ahhh! You're as desperate as me, aren't you?"

He slides into me easily, joining in our blissful love dance.

"God, yes. That's it, baby. You know how exactly to get me like this."

The sound of hips slamming in a frenzy of echoes in the air. He's deep inside, and I'm slowly rotating my hips. His strong hands hold my hips to stop me.

"Stay still, don't move..." He's gasping for air to hold his release. My hands grab his face, watching his expression. I'm so turned on by how lost in desire he is.

"Please..." I hiss, pleading desperately.

"Oh, God, baby."

He starts to pound frantically again, and every thrust feels so intense I'm losing my ability to reason. I'm his slave. Slave to this lovemaking, feeling him so ardent. I implore him with my eyes.

"I want more. Please, give me more."

"Fuck, woman, take it. That's it, baby. I'm gonna make you come so hard..."

He increases the speed of his thrust as I rest my forehead on his shoulder, feverish with the desire. Pulling me closer into his arms, he tightens his grip.

"Your thighs are shaking. Are you with me?" he asks, smirking lustfully, knowing full well what he's doing.

What's happening? I'm reaching another level with him. Love burns me like it's possible to actually die of pleasure. Oh, God, I'm at the edge like I'm going to faint. I murmur drunk on him.

"Lukas, I don't think I can take any more."

"Yes, you can. I know you can." He's pounding hard inside.

"It's too much. The pleasure is too much."

I've never thought it possible I'd say those words, to be drugged by love and pleasure. He knows it. He's teaching me.

"No." He moans. "This love is more. You can take it. You've done it before." He's breathing harshly in my ear.

"Ahhh!" I scream, losing myself in him.

"See? Take it all. Uhum… That's it, scream for me."

An agonizingly loud scream lets him know I'm at my limit. I wrap my arms around his neck while my hips meet his frenzied thrusts. We're both out of control, our releases coming at any moment.

"Keep your eyes open for me, baby," he hisses breathlessly.

With our love overflowing, we stare at each other the precise moment we explode simultaneously, rattling our cores. My scream of pleasure resounds with his. He buries his face between my breasts, quieting his screams.

"I love you, woman. I'm completely yours."

"I love you too, Lukas. You make me feel so alive," I respond, short of breath.

His fingers dig into my back. He's still convulsing his release, huffing for air aloud into my neck as fire consumes us. This is fucking glorious. The most satisfying sex I've had. Nothing can top this. At least that's what I thought.

My love goes deep, deep, deep... Your ocean got deeper...

If the expert chef I took classes with back in Puerto Rico could see the sloppy job I just did making this lunch, he would probably flunk me. But everyone seems to like it, all agreeing it smells delicious. We're watching the entertainment news to measure the damage caused by Lukas's "secret" now being public. Over the news, we see all types of gossip about our relationship and Vivian's death. This morning has been a mayhem of calls and texts to our cellphones.

Xavier is the first I speak with this morning. He calls early in a panic, having seen the news. I explain everything, calming him. Rey and Rene do the same. Harrison calls, making sure I am okay and to give me their full support on behalf of the company. I've even received a text from Shayan, checking on me, finally learning who my mysterious guy is.

Vivian's death, following her attempt to murder me, is all over the local news, but the entertainment news also reports the identity of Lukas Lee's girlfriend. The new K-pop sensation is in love with a woman too old for him.

We receive calls from our companies telling us several news outlets and reporters have contacted them, asking for interviews. We decide to make a single press statement through them, asking for privacy and respect. As always when this type of news appears, vultures pop up to gain notoriety with theories of why I deserve to die. Or what a creepy, opportunistic, sick person I am.

I am forced to close all my social media accounts to avoid reading hateful comments and threats. I'd expected this and had decided to avoid the backlash, that would inevitably come, a long time ago. My focus is on Lukas's career—the possible damage to his projects and his musical future.

"I understand, Jong. But this was inevitable."

He's speaking with his record company. His voice is firm, decided.

"No, no more hiding or covering up. Fans don't decide what goes on in my private life. Sorry, but this is not negotiable."

I hear him being firm about our relationship. I can't hear them, but I'm pretty sure they're trying to convince him to stop seeing me.

"I'm confident this is going to work on my behalf, Jong. People these days are more open about this type of relationship, and the public will embrace it, you'll see."

He's adamant in his decision. I wish I could be as hopeful as he is. The news is still spreading, and we don't know what the full impact of his declaration of love will be.

Some entertainment morning programs make hurtful jokes and disrespectful references about me. The word *cougar* has been mentioned several times, and the host had laughed, making jokes at my expense. Their mocking our relationship is hurtful, but I immediately discard their words from my mind, not giving them space.

In general, the foul comments aren't as bad as we had expected. I've been linked to Shotaro in past weeks. Today it's Lukas. I hadn't known the number of women who would relate to my story, but I've received hundreds of messages sent to my company from women in solidarity, many of them having also been judged for loving someone much younger.

I don't mind the opinions of others anymore. That's something Lukas has taught me well, and I'm grateful for it.

Thankfully news about Vivian's attempts to murder me spreads faster and farther than my relationship with Lukas does. Her actions leading to her death present a big blow for the record company.

I've been overwhelmed all day long, and now I'm exhausted. I don't feel like myself.

"I need to make a phone call," I inform them before closing my bedroom door under suspicious stares. I sit on my bed to call Rene.

"Rene, hi. No, I'm okay. I'm fine now. I just called to ask to run new tests. I haven't been giving them the necessary attention, but the headaches are a little more constant. I don't know if the meds are actually causing them. I want to make sure.... When? Okay, I'll be there tomorrow afternoon. Thanks."

I don't want Lukas to worry over something minor when there are more important things to focus on. I come out of my room to find all of their demanding eyes, expecting an explanation.

"What? Why are you looking at me like that?"

"You tell us, Gaby," Lukas answers earnestly.

"Nothing. It's nothing. I just called to verify an appointment I have tomorrow, that's all," trying to sound casual, changing the subject. "The trial is scheduled this Thursday. How quick before you have to return?"

Marc answers while Lukas gives me a scrutinizing look.

"We have several days off here before continuing the tour."

Lukas's gaze is unwavering. He suspects there's more that I'm not telling him, so I try to distract him further by asking something else.

"Have you received any negative news from your fanbase in Seoul about this? How are they behaving?"

Marc answers me again, "The damage has been minimal. Some deep-rooted fans are upset, protesting. But in general, the majority doesn't seem to mind our surprise. We'd feared the backlash, but it isn't the case."

Lukas stands up to walk to me. Seizing my arm, he pushes me in the direction of the bedroom.

"Can we speak in private?" Closing the door behind us, he turns to face me.

"Can you please tell me what you're avoiding saying? I'm not naïve, Gaby. Something's troubling you, and it has nothing to do with us, Vivian, fans, or the press. There's something else." He holds my face gently.

"No more secrets, remember?"

My troubled heart doesn't want to worry him, but he's

going to anyway.

"You made me think about Beijing, the night of the awards. My headaches have been frequent, but the truth is I don't remember how often they've come. I don't recall. That kind of worries me, so I made an appointment for a checkup to be sure everything is okay, that's all. I didn't want to worry you. It's a simple checkup, nothing to be alarmed about."

"Okay. Whatever you say."

He embraces me while exhaling, kind of relieved. He seems satisfied I've explained what's going on, but I can still feel the tension of worry he's holding.

"It's good you're checking that everything is okay. I'm always going to worry about you. It's inevitable and comes with loving you, you know? Making sure you're okay."

He caresses my face before his lips come down to capture mine in a tender kiss. He forces my lips open to his curious tongue. I quiver at his sweet tenderness. The fire in my belly flares up, ready to give myself to him. My hand greedily caresses his hard, pulsing arousal through his pants, stroking it. A guttural moan escapes his lips, making us giggle.

Stepping back from my touch, he groans sensuously, we regain control of ourselves.

"Stop that. Let's cool down. Even behind doors, you're right. We're pretty damn loud. And I want to take you again to hear you scream like this morning. So, later on?"

Adjusting himself, he gives me one last suggestive look. He opens the door, my face full of protest, staring back. He cracks in laughter, doing the thing with the tip of his tongue that turns me on so much.

Baby, don't play with me... What privacy do we need between us?

Chapter Twenty-Four

Gabriella

The trial ends with the guilty verdict. The judge takes into consideration the evidence for past felony convictions, plus he had confessed Vivian hired him, accepting a late deal from the prosecutors in exchange for a guilty plea. I'm so thankful she'd never revealed her reason for wanting me dead to him. He didn't know why. As far as he was concerned, I had only been a job. Some witnesses from the night of the presentation had testified they saw Vivian and me arguing and that she had acted rude and disrespectful.

The press got ahold of the court story, and Marc and Lukas are portrayed as heroes in the articles. When fans learn about the trial through entertainment media, the internet buzzes about how Lukas and Marc faced an assailant to capture him, risking their lives and how incredibly romantic it was that Lukas had saved my life.

Leaving the courtroom, a small crowd waits for us outside. Lukas and Marc are caught up, signing autographs and receiving congratulations from press and fans. I distance myself from them, walking away, when a hand grabs my wrist. It's Lukas tugging me back toward them.

"Where do you think you're going? Stay by me."

I smile shyly, understanding that it's finally true; he doesn't care about the opinion of others.

The next evening, a close group of coworkers from both our companies decided to surprise us with a private dinner gathering at a restaurant in Garden Walks to celebrate everything turning out all right.

Lukas and I are officially a couple before the world. He receives news their concerts have sold out in China, Japan, and Taiwan even after the news reached the press back in Asia. People are now fascinated with us and want to know more.

Our closest co-workers and staff from both companies are accompanying us. Marc, Lola, and I are sitting near a band trio playing soft jazz music, just talking while Lukas seems deep in conversation other people in a far corner of the room. As we're talking about all these recent events, Marc seems happy we can finally hang out together without struggle.

"Girls, we'll send VIP passes for you to join us at one of our concerts when we're in China. It's going to be so much fun."

It feels great to be this free. I'm beyond excited, myself. I stand, searching for Lukas and see him talking with one of the executives from the record company. I'm observing from where I'm standing, studying him with a loving, curious vehemence.

I love you, Lukas Lee. My mind yells with the intensity my heart feels for him. As if he hears me, he turns to observe me with an affectionate smile.

He makes a funny gesture, raising his eyebrow and biting the tip of his tongue, signaling for us to leave discreetly. He's hungry, and I let out a chuckle.

Our cellphones ring at the same time. We stare at each other, startled by it. Beaming, we show each other our cellphones ringing, proceeding to answer simultaneously.

"Hello?" I answer cheerfully without looking.

"Gaby, it's me. Sorry to bother at this hour. I have not so good news."

Hearing his sad voice, my heart freezes.

I turn to observe Lukas, with eyes full of fright and pain.

"Tell me everything."

I'm trying to hide my reaction but failing miserably.

Lukas

I'm more than happy when Jong calls.

"Lukas, my boy. How're you doing? I'm calling to give you the latest news we've just received. Besides the sold-out concerts in Japan and China, you been nominated for two Daesangs. Song of the Year and Album of the Year for Ty's production. Congratulations, my boy."

Daesangs are the biggest honor awarded to an artist in the Seoul Music Awards. Kind of the Asian Grammys.

"What? Is this true?"

"Yes, it's true. We just received the call. You did it."

"I can't believe it. Thanks, Baek. You're part of it." I blab, overcome with emotion, not knowing what to say. I'm blown away hearing I've achieved the goal I worked so hard to reach.

"Your hard work paid off. We're so proud of you. We'll plan a big celebration upon your return to Seoul."

Is this real? Is it possible to be this happy? My eyes fill with tears of joy that I'm getting the recognition I deserve. Everything is turning out so great, and it's surreal.

I search Gabriella's face, waiting to share the news with her. But when I look into her eyes, she frightens me. *Something is wrong*. She's sad, disturbed.

"Thanks, Jong. I'll get back to you." I end my call and stride to where she's standing. She lowers her face, hiding it from me. Gaby always does it when she's concealing something. I quicken my pace to grab her arms and chin, raising her face to mine.

"Gaby, what's wrong? Tell me the truth."

Her face looks awkward. She's choosing her words carefully. People nearby watch us.

"Rene just called. Studies show a small…growth in size. This isn't supposed to happen. The dosage has to be increased, and the pain flares might be constant. Because of it, I'll be tired often and even lose strength. Maybe… Sometimes I won't be able to function normally."

She stops talking, shaking her head in denial, her hand on my chest to push me away.

"I need to clear my head…need some time alone. I'll be back." She walks away, appearing numb.

Grabbing her arm, turning her back to me with imploring eyes.

"Let me go with you…" I plead.

I don't want to impose in this moment, knowing how shaken she must feel inside.

"Give me a couple of minutes by myself. Okay, sweetie? I'll be back shortly."

There's a deep sadness in her voice. She looks at me with resigned eyes, exiting the restaurant. My heart's torn, seeing her head down, carrying the weight of the world on her shoulders.

Marc watches us. As soon Gaby walks away, he approaches me.

"What's going on? What happened?"

I answer while watching her walk away, "Her mass grew. They will increase the dosage, resulting in more headaches. She will lose her strength."

The words fall from my mouth, hitting me hard as I realize their full meaning. I stare at Marc in pain. I'm lost over this news.

Squeezing my shoulders, he pulls me to a corner so no one can disturb us.

"It's okay, man. Breathe. Is not the end of the world, okay? You're not alone in this. You know I'm here for you. Gaby has shown us she's a strong, courageous woman. She'll overcome this too, you'll see."

I observe him with desperation. I want with every fiber of my being to believe it's true. Now that we've finally achieved some sense of normalcy together, this happens. It's like life continuously pulls pranks on us. Hurtful pranks.

Can't go living without you, girl...

Gabriella

Lola is exiting the restaurant, looking everywhere. I'm sure Lukas has sent her for me. But talking with Xavier comes first.

Turning my back, I know she's approaching the corner where I'm standing. So I try to end the call with him quickly.

"I know, I know. *Por favor, baja la histeria.* I'm keeping my word to tell you what's going on. Please, I need you to be calm, okay? I'll get more info and call you back, you have my promise. Love you too. *Dios te bendiga.*"

I turn to find Lola standing directly behind me.

"What's going on, Gaby?"

She sounds seriously scared and troubled. I explain what Rene told me about my mass, my voice breaking and tears falling down my face, the sorrow strangling my chest.

Embracing me with teary eyes, she cuddles me with tenderness.

"I'm so sorry, Gaby. I can only imagine how upset you must be right now. Is there anything I can do for you, *bonita*?"

She takes my hand to squeeze it in sympathy. That's all I need; it's enough. I wipe the tears off my cheeks with the back of my hand.

"Yes…I need to think. I need time to myself. I'll take a cab home, okay? I want to be alone for a little while. Please tell Lukas I'll see him there later. My head can't deal with anyone right now. Can you cover me on this?" I plead with my eyes.

Lola sniffles, drying her tears.

"Sure, Gaby. Take your time, I'll cover for you. I'll tell Lukas you need this time alone, don't you worry."

She hugs me tightly and pushes me to go. I walk away slowly, hugging myself, feeling lost and defeated. I don't want to think. I'm still processing all this. My sorrow spilling in tears, I'm unable to stop them. I walk numbly as people stare, seeing me cry as I pass by. I don't want to call a cab immediately. I need to walk off the desolation this news has caused me.

Lukas

What's taking her so long? I start to worry. Surveilling the entrance, I see Lola entering to approach me. As soon as she reaches me, gives me her message.

"Lukas, Gaby just left."

"What? Where?"

"She left. She'll meet you back at the apartment later on. She needed this time to think, you know. It's really hard for her to receive this kind of news at this moment."

"Where did she go?" I've decided to follow her.

"She went walking, mentioning she'll take a cab on route. She didn't want to deal with anyone. Give her this space, Lukas. Right now, she needs to be alone. I know her well. Be patient, you'll see her later."

I exhale in frustration. This is the moment she needs me at her side. I'm supposed to be comforting her. Can't we finally be happy? *I'm so messed up for you, Gaby.*

My Caribbean Queen...

Gabriella

I'm debating on what to do, for several seconds, I stand outside my apartment, staring at the door, afraid to enter. The problem is here, and I can't ignore it anymore. I have to deal with the situation and make the best of it. Finally I open the door and enter reluctantly.

I've fought every kind of battle in my life. It hasn't been easy, but the struggles I've endured have helped me discover strengths I didn't know existed in me. Those strengths have made me the woman I am now. I have to rely on those to make the best of these difficult times. Fighting isn't new for me, but I believe this is going to be the hardest of them all. *I'm tired of being strong.* Tonight I don't want to be strong anymore. I need him to be strong for me instead.

I hear the doorbell and peer to see Lukas standing outside. Opening the door, I encounter hurt eyes staring back at me.

"Hey. How are you coping with everything?"

He timidly reaches for my hand. I'm dying to be lost in his love. Embracing his waist, I hide my face on his chest, sobbing, without saying a word. I just need to be in his arms, hearing his heartbeat and inhaling his scent. Knowing I have him is the most precious gift life could grant me, and I'm so damn lucky for it.

Caressing my back gently, he soothes me and lovingly strokes my head, giving my forehead a soft kiss. His ragged breathing reveals how upset he is too.

"We'll overcome this, Gaby, you'll see. We've made it through so much. We'll do it again. Our love will always win."

I want so bad to believe him. Watching me with moist eyes, I'm aware he feels my pain.

Life is truly a tiny speck in time... in the universe... What you have is now, this moment... So I let love run free.

"Lukas, make love to me. Now. I need to feel you, to love you, baby. Make love like tomorrow isn't going to be here," I plead, my emotions swirling unrestrained.

Caramel eyes darken showing the lion stirring from his slumber, awakening at my request. His cheeks blush, heated by his desire. The raw emotions we're experiencing is so powerful it needs to be released, or we're going to explode.

He leads me to my bedroom. Closing the door, he stands before me, caressing my face lovingly, kissing my forehead again. His index finger trails to my cleavage and slowly unbuttons my shirt. There's no rush, no desperation.

Tears flowing, he takes my shirt off, kissing each shoulder softly. Unclasping my brassiere, he pulls the straps down my shoulders. The warmth of his long, sleek fingers on my skin is so delicious. Facing him, I succumb to the luscious demand of his lips. He tugs me against him. The kiss grows too passionate and intense.

Gasping for air, I unbutton his shirt slowly, taking time to caress his chest. My lips trail kisses down his pecs, pressing my hands against his hard abs. He lets out a sharp moan of pleasure, letting me know he's as famished as I am.

He wipes the tears from my cheeks, murmuring in his ragged voice, "I love you, Gaby. I'll be beside you until our last breaths. I can't imagine a world without you."

We gaze at each other tearfully, exposing our emotions for the other to see. I want to become one with him. I want us so connected our bodies and souls fuse into one.

He covers my face with delicate, tender kisses, and I close my eyes, receiving, feeling, enjoying this blissful whirlwind. We step back from our embrace to finish undressing.

Fully naked, we explore each other with our hands. Gasps of delight cut the silence when his touch triggers my senses. I see my sweet, protective lion staring back at me. He traces my neck with his tongue. He dips his head down to lick and hungrily suck my breast, driving me insane. I moan, holding his head, enjoying his pleasant, warm tongue encircling my nipples. He moves down through my cleavage to my belly, licking it greedily.

"Oh, Lukas…baby. I'm so lucky to be with you." I moan, trembling.

His mouth continues across my body sucking, licking, and kissing all over me while kneeling before me. He pauses to look up in adoration.

"You're part of my existence, part of me. I will never get enough of you, Gaby." He gasps aloud.

His hands caress my thighs, sliding up to grab my hips while standing.

"You're so exquisite, love. I yearn for more from you. I wanna be so far in you our souls join. I'm all yours."

Sitting on the bed, he takes my hand to guide me sit astride his lap, gazing feverishly into my eyes. The hardness of his thick arousal slides deliciously inside until it fills me, making me gasp, inflamed for more. His tongue licks my lips, mimicking his thrusts.

I have never felt him so unrestrained and passionate like this. His thrusts are unrushed, steady. He's truly making love to me like there's no tomorrow. Tasting, relishing, enjoying every inch of our bodies.

What we're feeling isn't meant to be analyzed. Like a massive wave about to crush us, we dive in. Gazing through half-closed eyes, gasping.

"That's it, love. I want you to feel me."

His words boil my blood. His sweet, passionate thrusting is drenching me. *This is heaven.* I match his urgency, pounding my hips against his.

"Lukas," I cry.

"Yes," he groans into my neck. "I feel you, love. I want more."

I'm riding him, relishing his exquisite thrusts, while his

hands holding my waist firmly. Louder, faster, deeper, the intensity increases with each plunge. He's close to obtaining his release.

"Come, baby…*now.* Let me feel you coming," he commands.

I climax, screaming his name, arching backward, collapsing. He holds my exhausted body until he finds his own release with a half-scream, gasping for air. His fingers dig into the skin of my waist with one last push deep inside, riding down our orgasms together.

Eyes closed, we struggle for air. I recover, opening my eyes to see tears in his and a grief-stricken face.

He chokes up. "I don't want to lose you. I'm scared for the first time in my life."

He clutches me tightly. It pains me to hear the dread in his voice. The vulnerability he's showing me. He loves deeper than I can comprehend. For him it's raw, profound, agonizing. I want to give some peace to his troubled soul.

"I'm not going anywhere. This is just a minor setback. We will overcome this, just like you said."

While holding his face, my mouth swoops down to capture his lips in reassurance. He drops me onto the bed while kissing me. We lay down in the aftermath, staring at the ceiling. I want his fear to go away.

"Let's live life to fullest, not waste time worrying. It's not worth it." I want to sound optimistic, trying to give him reassurance that everything will be all right. He turns to gaze at me with lazy, adoring eyes. A slow, sad grin grows to show me he understands what I just said.

"Okay then. Let's live life to fullest."

The truth is, we don't want to acknowledge the possibility of another outcome. Caressing his chest, my lips brush his warm skin, trailing kisses down his abs. He purrs what sounds like a faint moan, delighted with my teasing. An idea pops into my mind, wheels in my head turn, planning instantly, convincing myself to do it. I raise myself to lay beside him, combing his hair with my fingers.

"When you have to go back to Tokyo?"

He turns to gaze at me, his expression puzzled by my question.

"In nine days. Why?"

I beam at him. My voice sounds cheerful. He smirks, curious to my sudden good mood. Life should be cheerful, even in these unexpected moments. And I intend it to be that way.

"Let's take these next days before you go to escape just the two of us. No one has to know where we're going. A road trip. Taking the five to the 101 wherever the road takes us. Sleep wherever we encounter a place."

His grin tells me he approves of the idea. I knew he would.

"Lukas, we love each other so deeply we don't need anyone to confirm it. No ceremony or papers to prove it. We already said our own vows the day Xavier found about us. We had our ceremony at the Namsan Tower with the love padlock. Now give me my honeymoon. Before you go back to the tour, and I do to the media tour of my book. We deserve this time for ourselves after everything we've been through. Do you think you can do it for me?"

I already know the answer. I'm letting him understand every moment together is precious. We shouldn't waste it.

"You know I'll never say no. I love to be with you all the time. I'll inform Jong and the record company. When do you want to leave?"

"As soon as we can. Tomorrow. Can we do that?"

The happiest smile beams at me adoringly.

"Okay, Gaby. Let's do this. I'll give you your honeymoon."

I grin, immensely pleased. His arms squeeze me tight, capturing my mouth in a steamy kiss, rousing my passion, his own growing stronger. I smile against his lips, drugged by him. He'll never understand the indescribable joy I experience just by being in his arms.

Gripping my knee to position himself, he presses me in his embrace, trembling while thrusting deep inside of me. Rolling my eyes, I taste sweet agony as his thrust provokes me on.

"Ahhh, it feels so good. You feel so amazing, sweetie."

Huffing in my ear, his whispers are full of lust.

"You boil my blood in a way I can't explain, love. Ahh, don't you feel it? I'm trembling inside you, fighting to hold myself. I'm so turned on."

His arousal buries deeper inside me, letting me know I'm his. Our anguished moans keep escalating with each pound of his hips.

"Fuck, love."

Once again, we achieve ecstasy, soaring new heights of pleasure and passion. We burn ourselves, almost touching the sun. I give everything, and he takes everything, leaving me satiated and fulfilled. Every cell in my body screams I'm worthy, loved. I'm complete.

He's been true to his words, loving me in a way words cannot describe and can only be felt. Now in his arms, I'm flying with him. And he's doing what he always does, taking me to heaven again and again.

I selfishly want only myself to be living in this fairytale called you.

Chapter Twenty-Five

Gabriella

I'm trying to remember the last time I've been this giddy. After picking up my Mustang from the shop—thank God it's fixed—we load our luggage in the backseat. We've contacted our bosses, informing them of this time-off for us. I've also texted our friends that we'll be unavailable the following days. Don't call or text, we won't answer.

We're both so cheerful about taking this time for ourselves, that we can barely contain our joy. Lukas is beyond himself, euphoric about this. After we make sure we have everything packed in the car, I stare at him, grinning. Pulling the keys from my pocket, I throw them. He catches them, surprised.

"It's time *my husband* drives our car."

Giggling, watching his shocked face, he freezes, staring at the keys with a dumb grin. It's mesmerizing to watch when he smiles from his heart.

"Just take the I-5 north. It connects with the 101, and we'll see what surprises await us down the road," I instruct, winking at him. Opening the passenger door, I sit down on the front seat.

God, this man can illuminate the world with his beautiful smile. Grinning, he enters the driver's seat, admiring the car with his hands on the wheel. I laugh at his jubilant expression.

"Come on, Lukas. It's just a car. Let's go."

"Where do you want to go first?" he asks while turning the car on.

With my arms around his neck, I kiss him adoringly, staring into his eyes.

"Wherever the road takes us, baby. Wherever we can be happy. Let's just enjoy being happy, Lukas."

"I couldn't agree more," he answers, putting on his sunglasses with a smirk. We start our trip, leaving the building, making sure no one is following.

It's a breathtaking, sunny day. I love the intensity of the blue plastered above us. The skies are clear, and it's a perfect day to drive a convertible. As we merge onto the highway, I decide to put on some music from my cellphone. I find one of his songs he performed years ago. I think it's perfect to describe this moment. When the first strings of the song sound through the speakers, I start to sing, mimicking the language. He glances at me surprised, almost choking a laugh.

"How'd you know about this song?"

My proud stare says it all.

"Now I know almost every song you've sung. I know about your music, sweetie. I particularly love this one."

With the volume up, I genuinely sing, carefree, not minding the judgement of the crazy stares we're receiving from the cars passing us by. Today this song belongs to us.

"...We'll ride our highway to heaven

Near the 101, love bloom fierce for sure..."

I must sound awful, but I don't care. The immense joy I'm feeling is indescribable. My inner goddess is awake and proud. Life has granted me another opportunity I didn't expect. In this moment, I have it all.

Raising my arms up in the air, closing my eyes, I feel the breeze brush against my face. If I could mark an instant in my life when I'm utterly happy, fulfilled, and complete, I guarantee you this is it. Life runs potent through my blood with him beside me. I want everyone to know how much I love this man. So I just shout for anyone to hear me.

"I LOVE YOU, LUKAS LEE."

He lets out a laugh, delighted seeing me behaving like this. I kiss his cheek in adoration.

"I truly, deeply love you," my lips murmur on his cheek.

He turns to capture my lips briefly, returning his gaze on the road. *He is my highway to heaven, always.*

We drive along Interstate 5 until we find the exit for Route 101 to Santa Barbara, bordering the coast.

We have lunch in a little restaurant, which had caught my eye near the beach. We sit down, feeding each other, giggling silly. We're behaving like honeymooners. For our first night, we rent a small motel room beside the beach with a beautiful view of the ocean from our room. We ardently make love, giving everything. Our souls, our hearts, our true selves belong to each other. Our love is free to overflow as it pleases with no restraints, not caring what others think. Our only focus is how deep we can go in our own love and how profound it will be when we reach its depths.

We're taking our time during these days, no rush to reach anywhere. We park along the seashore, sitting in the car, just staring at the horizon and enjoying the sunset together while he holds my hand. Every second by his side is priceless. Gazing adoringly at him, I can say I'm a fortunate woman.

We stop multiple times along the route to stare at nature, and like young lovers, we find a hidden place where we discreetly quench the thirst that is now constant between us.

On the third night, we find a beautiful, cozy, small restaurant in the middle of nowhere. It's all lit up like a party inside. It's surrounded by the most breathtaking gardens with lots of pink and white flowers all around us. The place looks magical. I ask Lukas to stop, finding it so heavenly.

The nice weather allows us to wear some light clothes. A white cotton dress with long, see-through sleeves, a round cleavage window, and a knee-length skirt with a rugged jean jacket and flat white sandals is my attire. Lukas is dressed in dark jeans, a light blue, long-sleeve shirt, and gray sneakers.

We go inside, and the atmosphere is as cheerful as it had looked from afar. Loud music mixes with the laughter of the people. Lots of tiny, blinking, white lights hang from the ceiling, giving the place a charming look. Potted palm trees and flowers are beside each column. It looks surreal, magical.

Couples dance around us while others chat cheerfully. A sweet older lady, maybe around seventy, approaches us.

"You're new around here. Are you visiting or moving nearby?"

"Just passing through," Lukas answers. "*My wife* and I would like to dine, but I think we've interrupted a private party, so we'll be off—"

She interrupts him, "Nonsense. Where do you think you're going? You're already in, so you're part of our celebration. Come have a seat and dine with us."

She grabs Lukas's hand like he's family, pulling him to follow her. Twisting his mouth, he makes that funny face when he encounters something shocking. I giggle, watching him, following closely. We learn the sweet lady is the owner's wife, and she seats us at her table.

"Please, sit down. It's a pleasure to have you dine with us. My name is Jessy. That handsome guy over there is my husband, Earl."

She's pointing to a tall, skinny, wrinkled, white guy older than her, serving drinks at the bar.

"This is our restaurant, but today we're celebrating our birthdays. We share the same birth date. So it's a family-and-friends celebration. Now you're part of it. How long have you been married?" she asks, curious, looking mesmerized by us.

"It's our *honeymoon*," I respond shyly to her.

"*Newlyweds*? Oh, my goodness. This is a pleasant surprise and blessing."

She shouts to her husband, "Earl, Earl. Come, come here. Bring a bottle of champagne and four glasses. I want you to meet my new friends."

Earl stares at us, clueless, but complies with his wife's instructions.

"Coming."

He arrives at the table, carrying a tin bucket with a bottle of champagne and four ordinary glasses.

"Honey, I want to you to meet…" She stops, looking at us. She hasn't asked our names yet.

"Gabriella and Lukas. It's a pleasure to make your acquaintance, sir," I blurt out, extending my hand to greet him.

He takes my hand, then salutes Lukas with an honest smile.

"Welcome to our home away from home. That is one mile from here."

"They're newlyweds, Earl. It's their honeymoon. And

we're now part of their memories. Isn't that romantic?" Jessy gushes to her husband while pouring champagne into the four glasses.

"Well, I'll be damned. Let me give a toast for the newlyweds."

Turning around, Earl urges everyone to shut up. The music and all sound halts. I'm blushing crimson red with embarrassment at being the center of attention.

"People, silence. We've got a newlywed couple with us tonight. They're on their honeymoon, and tonight we're part of their honeymoon memories. Let's toast to a long and prosperous marriage for Lukas and Gabriella," Earl shouts for everyone to hear.

In an uproar, everyone raises their glasses, cheering, shouting, and laughing, complying with Earl's toast. We cheer along with everyone else, laughing too.

"Put on some music, Will," he instructs someone, who may to be his son, if resemblance is anything to go by.

I find out that Will is the DJ for the night, with a computer and two very high-quality speakers. For a moment, though, there's a group playing live, and it sounds so good.

Jessy brings out two monstrous plates full of food and sets them in front of us. One plate would have been plenty for Lukas and me. Everything is exquisite, a mix of mediterranean and Mexican flavors, very original. Lukas immediately asks for recipes for those dishes, and they pack the remaining food for us to take. Now that our bellies are full, we're urged to dance.

"Every newlywed couple appreciates a dance. Go and enjoy yourselves. My son can find any song you like. He has a massive library of music."

My flirty stare at my *husband* lets him know I'm asking

what song he wants.

"Go, pick one for us. I want that one to be our song. We haven't picked one yet. I gave you one; we need another."

With one eyebrow raised and a sexy smirk, he lets me know I'll be teased while dancing. He's smiling devilishly and doing the tongue-biting thing he knows drives me nuts. I'm flustered, craving him, deliciously ashamed of all the naughty things we haven't done yet that my mind is showing me.

I walk to Will, who shows me the playlist of love songs on his screen. Scrolling down a huge list, I decide to find one specific piece of music. And there it is. The perfect song to describe this moment. I stand in the middle of the dance floor, smiling at him. My fingers lock my hands together in front of me like a nervous school girl. Because tonight, my inner groupie girl is fulfilling her fantasy. I'm in love with my music idol. And he loves me back.

I think I saw this moment in a dream. Everything seems so familiar. Talk about déjà vu. He stands up, observing me with adoring eyes.

Seeing this man walk toward me, I'm consumed by emotions swirling in my chest. I never thought it possible to love someone as fiercely as I love him. If I could give every ounce of life in my body for his happiness, I would without hesitation. Body and soul. I beam, starstruck, watching him.

Strong hands grab my waist, pulling me closer to dance. The speakers blast with Nick Jonas's song *This Is Heaven*. We dance to the rhythm of the music, chuckling. I trip, sometimes, while he swirls me around, giggling. Some applaud us while others just watch. The smile doesn't leave my face. We haven't danced since our first time out. This is our first dance as husband and wife.

Gazing up, I notice a glass skylight in the ceiling. Night

has fallen, and stars can be seen, giving this moment an ineffable vibe. I see two shooting stars crossing overhead beside each other. That's a good omen. I make my wish to get lost in Lukas's gaze. He slows his pace, looking intrigued.

"Gaby, what is it? Tell me, babe."

Overwhelmed, words flow, and my emotions roll through me freely, full of gratefulness. With the biggest smile, I respond, "Just thinking how lucky I am to have this handsome, young Korean man, who loves me and adores me with the same intensity I have for him, in my arms and in my life. I have to pinch myself every day to believe this is real. How blessed I am to live this instance, this moment, with you. Right now, I'm the luckiest woman in the world to have you. If this was my last night, I'm grateful to God and life for you, sweetie. You make me feel complete."

With his thumb, he wipes away my tears. I close my eyes, receiving his loving caress on my face.

"I'm damn lucky to have this gorgeous, breathtaking, sensuous Boricua woman in my arms and in my life. I can't believe this goddess chose me. A woman who possesses the same fire and intensity equal to mine. I'm the luckiest man to have you in my arms tonight, Gaby. I'm grateful to life for encountering you, just when I'd needed someone. I'm a better man. Now I'm complete."

Blinded by the love consuming us, he lowers his mouth to capture my lips in one of the most passionate kisses he's given me. I'm dizzy from the intensity, feeling breathless. I tighten my grip around his neck to crush him against me.

Our wake-up call is someone shouting, "Get a room, you lovebirds," and lots of laughter after.

We step back with crimson faces, embarrassed by the whistles and jokes about how ardently we kissed.

The hardness of his arousal jerks against my thigh. I chuckle to myself. It's time to leave, so he doesn't become the prey for *stiff* jokes.

"Walk behind me. I'll cover for you." I giggle while staring seductively.

He smirks, seeming to be annoyed by his arousal.

"This is your fault, okay? This is how I react every time I feel you against my body. I can't help it," he murmurs into my ear while walking behind me.

I have to bite my lips to avoid laughing out loud. I'm a little tipsy from the champagne our gracious hosts keep pushing us to drink.

I inform Lukas there's a motel an hour ahead of us, so we should go now to arrive at a proper hour. Earl approaches us to show us an instant photo.

"I took the liberty of taking this photo of you guys. We have a wall here we call Guest Wall over that corner where we post photos of guests who visit us. If you allow it, I want it to be part of our special place."

I'm moved by this request. I take the photo from his hands to observe and show it to Lukas. It's a beautiful snapshot. We're laughing, carefree, starting to dance. I murmur in Lukas's ear what I want him to remember with me.

"See that smile on my face? You're the reason for it," and quickly smooch his cheek. He blushes bashfully at my affectionate outburst.

After our farewell with everyone and the promise to return to celebrate our first anniversary, we finally exit to our car. My mind is scheming with the help of the alcohol flowing in my blood. My inner goddess is ready to be playful with him.

Lukas opens the passenger door to help me get in, but I grab him by the shirt, encircling his waist to pull him close, whispering, "Let's make love in the backseat of the car, Lukas. I have this… *fantasy* of having sex in the back of the Mustang. Let's do it here, now. I want you right now. Please. *Dale, Papi.*"

My lips trail his jawline with soft kisses, using my seductive tricks to convince him to do my bidding. I close my eyes, breathing heavily. Feeling my voraciousness, he starts to breathe raggedly.

"Gaby, this is crazy. Someone could see us. We're in a parking lot. Anybody could walk up to us."

He gasps through half-closed eyes, with my lips on him. I stop my kissing to glance at his face, protesting, "Everyone is dancing inside. We're at the end of the parking lot; it's dark. Who would walk all the way out here? Come on, baby."

I'm so determined to get my way that I raise my dress to take off my panties, laughing. Lukas watches in shock, mouth open. Once I take them off, I put my white lace panties in his pocket, like it's a handkerchief. Giggling devilishly, I enter the back seat and, while reclining, make myself ready for him.

"Come inside and close the door, baby. Take me now, I'm ready. Make love to me, *Papi.*"

I don't have to plead any more. He jumps on me in the backseat, closing the door. He encircles me in his arms, kissing in desperation. Through moans and kisses, we roar in laughter at this craziness. He licks and sucks my lips in a lustful onslaught, our desire full blown.

I whimper with my arousal unfurling. His hand slides down my belly until reaches the hem of my dress to pull it up. His hand slips between my legs, finding my swollen bud, rubbing it slowly with his fingers. A loud, sharp cry of pure pleasure breaks the silence as I enjoy his touch.

"Fuck, woman, you're so wet."

He raises himself to open his belt and zipper when a flashlight is pointed at us. We feel like two teenagers caught red-handed, making out.

Lukas's expression is hilarious. Panicked eyes, mouth wide open, red face with one hand on his zipper and the other trying to block the light from his eyes.

"Oh, Earl. It's just the kids. Turn that thing off, you're embarrassing them."

I hear Jessy admonishing her husband for discovering us in this compromising position. Lukas gets out of the car, apologizing for us, scared. I bite my lips to not explode in laughter inside the car, because I caused all this.

"I'm so sorry..." Lukas blurts in shame.

"Someone came inside telling us coyotes are prowling the parking lot. He swore he heard one howling back here."

That's it for me. I crack up, laughing out loud, rolling onto my side in the backseat. My stomach hurts from the intensity of my laughter. Lukas hears me and can't contain himself either. He's trying to be serious, but he chuckles, hearing me.

"I apologize for interrupting you two lovebirds on your honeymoon. You carry on. I'll make sure no one disturbs you or comes through this area."

Hearing him is my cue to get out and rescue the situation. I grab Lukas's wrist to help me up, chuckling while getting out of the backseat.

"No need to worry. We should be on our way to arrive at our destination on time. We'll go and take *the coyotes* with us." I wink at them, smirking.

Jessy chuckles wickedly with me. Earl's face turns red, realizing what I said. Lukas is tucking his shirt inside his jeans, my panties hanging from his pocket. Buckling his belt with an ashamed expression, he walks to the driver's door.

This is a hysterically funny moment I'm definitely going to remember always.

On our way to the motel, we're laughing, discussing what just happened. When we're halfway from there in the darkness of the night on this country road, Lukas takes a dirt trail. He drives farther in until he parks the car behind a big, spiky bush. Getting out, he lowers the rooftop. The only light around us are the stars in the sky. Everything is utterly dark.

"Lukas, what's going on with you? What you're doing?"

"Don't think I'm not going to fulfill your fantasy to have sex in the backseat of the Mustang. I want to take time for you to enjoy me, to give you the best orgasm under the desert sky where you can cry as loud as you want." His voice trembles with excitement, informing me his plans. He helps me out of the car.

Way to go, Lukas. Don't be afraid to be spontaneous. His behavior leaves me pleasantly speechless. Pulling me toward him to embrace me, he kisses me deeply, slowly, and sensuously like we have all the time in the world. His tongue circles in my mouth, enticing me. His hand slowly grabs the hem of my dress, reaching between my legs to my sweet bud to rub it, to see how ready I am. I flinch when his fingers stroke slowly on me. I let out my first loud scream in the middle of the night. He chuckles, the sound vibrating against my core, then moans.

"You think you're the only one teasing here? Ahh, baby! Oh, you're so ready for me. It inflames me to feel you this wet. Let me love you here, drive you insane." He smiles wickedly.

Settling into the backseat, while lowering his pants and underwear, his marble-like arousal pulses free, inviting me. He extends his hand to help me get inside, sitting astride him. I slide slowly until he sinks deep inside of me. I'm enjoying the wickedness of doing this. The adrenaline rushing through our veins, the danger of getting caught.

Oh God, this is crazy. I'm so fucking crazy for convincing him to do this. But this is so wickedly delicious.

He's gasping aloud, his eyes half-closed, enjoying this immensely. He unbuttons the front of my dress to pull my brassiere down, exposing my breasts. He leans to devours them with his mouth, sucking and licking hungrily. I can't contain the screams of pleasure. This is fucking wild. We're out of our minds. He continues with his steady thrusts, grabbing my waist while the tip of his tongue licks across my skin.

"Scream, baby. Scream like you want."

I want this. He's staring, love drugged as he pleases me, so turned on under my spell. The fullness of him stretching me as he pounds faster, building a delicious ache. I lose all restraint. I'm intoxicated by him. Now I'm screaming pretty loud and carefree.

"Ahh, Ahh, You're killing me."

"That's it, baby. You can take more…You want more. Enjoy it… Scream your pleasure for me." He moans aloud against my neck feverishly, grabbing my buttocks to push frantic, making me howl for him.

"Don't stop, baby. Yes, yes… Give me more, I want more," I plead, shouting as he presses his face against my breasts.

My hips meet his thrusts with the same urgency to the point I'm squirming with anticipation, about to explode. He notices I'm quivering in the throes of passion, so he quickens the pace, increasing the intensity of my release.

I'm pretty sure the scream I let out was heard miles

around. I'm still screaming my release and shaking when he finds his. He screams like nothing before, inhibitions completely gone. We stare at each other, gasping for air, still love drunk from our orgasms. We try to catch our breaths, giggling at this delightful madness. Screaming your lungs out in the middle of the desert night is a pure adrenaline rush, priceless.

Still short of breath, I dare say to him, "I'm madly in love with you. I can't ever, ever, get enough of you. Do you hear me? I didn't fall in love because I need someone to love or to make me happy, I swear. I fell in love with you because you showed me how to feel valued. You make reality feel like a fairy tale. I'm so lucky to have you, baby, so lucky."

His fingers caress my back, holding me up, while he pants for air.

"Gaby, I adore you. There's nothing I wouldn't do for you, even this." He lets out a soft chuckle, grinning lovingly. Holding my face with his hands, he explains, full of emotion, "I adore your spontaneity and need it in my life. Your spark, your optimism, all of you. I need the calmness and craziness you give me. I want you all for myself."

The emotion of those words vibrates in his voice. We stare at each other, lovestruck.

"We're perfect for each other, are we?" I ask, smiling.

"No doubt whatsoever," he grins lovingly.

His arousal slowly grows, filling me again, as he seizes my lips unhurried once more. Wrapping my arms around his neck, I return his kisses with aching need.

And under this magical, starry night, our howls of pleasure begin again. We may be mistaken for the mating howls of the coyotes in the wilderness of the western desert—Who cares? The night is ours to scream our love freely, unrestrained. We only need each other to achieve paradise, to create our own heaven on earth.

Chapter Twenty-Six

Lukas

Already five days have gone by? I can't believe it. It feels like just yesterday we were leaving the parking lot to start this adventure. It's insane how quickly time flies by when you want it to be eternal. One day with her seems like an instant; it's never enough.

We're close, bordering the beach of San Jose. We continue to visit every little town along the way, long hours of making love in more hidden places and enjoying our time together.

With each day, I'm falling more in love with her. Her gestures hypnotize me. I adore when she bites her lower lip, when she's turned on, without realizing it. I'm spellbound, looking into her eyes in the throes of passion, laughing at my jokes or just reclining on my shoulder. Sitting in the Mustang together, we watch the sun set along the way in silence. Finding every spot available for us to make love is pure joy. Never in my life had I imagined the kind of love I'm experiencing with her, this intimacy existing. I'm not talking about the physical part but our heart, our soul, sharing time is pure gold. Finding a woman who understands me the way she does is remarkable. I'm in awe that I am lucky enough to have her.

We decide to stop in a small town nearby the beach to eat lunch and explore the area. As we walk through several small stores and boutiques, Gabriella asks if she can buy something in one of them. We enter a store, and while she speaks with one of the employees, I browse around. That's when I see a small Death Star from *Star Wars*.

I ask another employee and buy it for her as a surprise. I watch her from afar picking a silver chain with some type of crystal pendant. I'm intrigued to see her happy face as she buys it. She comes over to me.

"It's a gift you'll receive, but not now." There's some sadness in her voice telling me this.

"Are you okay?"

"Yep, feel fine. Just thinking…these days have been the most happy, intense, and magical of my life. What we're living is unrepeatable. I never dreamed I'd experience this love we have, Lukas. For me, it's surreal. After so much wreckage in my life, I thought and believed happiness wasn't meant for me. But you prove me wrong. You've made me believe in love again. Believe I'm worthy, and for that, I'll love you forever."

She pulls my shirt to seize my lips with hers in a famished kiss, to let me know how serious she is. I put my hands on her bodice to deepen the kiss. This woman stirs my very core.

"It's mutual, Gabriella. I'm madly in love with you." Her perfect smile brightens my day.

After shopping, we visit some local museums and stop to eat ice cream. She insists on poking my nose with the ice cream cone to wickedly lick it, well aware how aroused I am with her licking me like this. She matches my lustfulness and hunger like no other. It was as if she was made for me.

We stop by at a local market to buy some fruits, ham, cheese, bread, and couple of bottles of wine to take with us. I notice, as we walked by, no one cares about us or glances at us in judgment. Good. I want her to be happy with me, only me.

Late afternoon, we find a secluded spot on the seashore. We bring our own wool blankets, a picnic basket with food, and a small cooler with a bottle of Chardonnay. The place looks enchanting hidden between two big rock formations, giving us privacy. Putting my military expertise to good use, I build a fire for us with dry branches and logs I've found near the ocean shore. We spend the afternoon and night talking, kissing, and joking. I dare to gaze at her. She looks like a dream, wearing a deep pink cotton dress with an orange cardigan.

We sit on the wool blanket with her wrapped in another blanket, resting between my legs, head reclined against my chest. My arms are around her waist while we watch the sea at night, my lips pressed to her temple. I shut my eyes and inhale her scent. That mix of gardenia with her own smell is a drug for me. I can't get enough. My chest constricts, realizing how deeply I need and love her. This is deeper than the deepest ocean.

"What're you thinking, Gaby?" I dare to ask, breaking the silence between us. She's being unusually quiet. Inhaling slowly, she drops the blanket from her shoulders.

"I wish we could be like this, together, forever. To capture this moment in time and never, ever have to go back to reality."

A sob sounds, taking me by surprise. I sit up straight, watching her cry.

"Hey. Why are you upset?"

She blurts out her response, "I'm selfish, Lukas. Now that I know this love, I want you for myself. I'm jealous of the whole world. I don't want to share you with anyone, and it pains me that I have no choice. The world needs you, Lukas. You have a blessed opportunity to change lives in such a profound way through your music, your songs, and your talent. People listen to you; they see you. I'm aware you've become a better man. Now show the world what you've learned. Show them how to become better like you did. The world truly needs you, baby. And I can't be selfish about that."

The intensity in her words is heart-shattering. I lift my hand to caress her face and wipe the tears from her cheeks, with eyes full of adoration for this woman who deliciously came to turn my world upside down in a wonderful and unexpected way.

I gently kiss her cheeks, trailing where her tears fall. I want my lips to wipe any fear or sadness she may feel. Pressing her close, our kiss sings through my veins. The tip of my tongue wets her lips, and I suck them softly. She tastes like strawberries and wine. I deepen the kiss with an aching need as lust takes ahold of me.

I kneel before her to take off her cardigan and toss it aside. I pull off my own shirt to drop it where the cardigan is. She's watching me, mesmerized, as I stand up to let my belt loose, opening the zipper of my jeans and getting naked in front of her. I adore her expressive, curious eyes watching me in desire, gazing hungrily as I get undressed. She stands to unbutton her pink dress, dropping it to her feet, only wearing her pink underwear. She's a goddess, and I yearn to worship her.

I turn her to take off her bra, then kneel again to pull down her pink lace panties while trailing them with my mouth and tongue down her legs. Her lazy moans welcome me, caressing my hair with her hands. I suck and lick her inner thighs, driving her mad with passion. When I pull her down to lie beside me on the wool blanket, she complies eagerly. I cover us with the other blanket.

I must have done something right in my life to be able to have her. I've found a rare gem, a loving soul that equals mine. Gabriella has a flame as fierce as my own, synchronizing our hearts and bodies so perfectly. Right now, she's the goddess of love I saw in Beijing. That day is still etched clearly in my memory. The raw hunger in her look and the lust we had for each other had been so insanely intense.

"Maybe the world needs me, but I need you more, Gabriella. This… I need this more. I daresay forever."

My hand trembles with eagerness down her body from her neck to her belly. She arches, whimpering while shutting her eyes in surrender, gasping at my touch. Trailing my fingers down between her legs, I rub her sweet swollen bud, my lips tracing kisses along her jawline. Capturing her earlobe with my tongue, I suck it playfully before whispering lustful words to inflame her.

"Ahh, I can't get enough of your sweetness, baby. You like that, don't you?"

She starts to grind against my hand, moaning and inflaming me more. My arousal throbs painfully, seeing her free, showing me how she likes it.

"You're a naughty woman, Ms. Lee. You want to come on my hand, huh? I think I can help you with that. I love to hear you cry your pleasure."

I quicken the flicking of my fingers, sliding in her wetness.

She's contorting her hips against my hand. I'm almost on top of her, pleasuring her with my fingers. The fire inside of me is getting uncontrollable, seeing her in the throes of passion like this. I crave seeing her out of control.

She moans louder, about to get her release with only my fingers touching her. My arousal pulses, begging to be buried deep inside her. It takes an incredible amount of willpower not to take her this instant. She lets out her scream of release, pressing her hips against my hand.

The little moan escaping her lips as she comes down from the high of her orgasm breaks the end of my control. I can't hold it in anymore. I groan, quickly positioning myself between her legs and thrust desperately. The lust in me is unrestrained. My only focus is feeling her warmth on me as I slide in and out. I close my eyes, savoring the feeling of her skin against mine, of being inside her. She's my addiction, and I need my fix now.

"Fuck, Gaby, Ahh."

I crush her in my embrace, murmuring my heated words to her. My mouth on her neck trails kisses on her skin as I inhale more of her scent of lust and gardenia that's driving me mad.

I raise my face to watch her. This woman is so breathtakingly beautiful, even in the throes of passion with her heavy eyelids, cheeks blushed, and her plump lips swollen from my kissing, parted and moaning for me. How can I be this blessed?

I can't stop staring at her face while I make love to her. It's like my mind instructs me:

Keep this image, Lukas. Treasure this moment. This is all yours. Look at her. See the way she stares back at you? See her surrender herself to you like this? This is unrepeatable; it's magic. This is pure heaven, man.

I'm overwhelmed by emotions, catching her lips. She

screams in my mouth, climaxing again, shuddering under me. A moment later, I'm gasping my scream of raw passion into the night.

A lion's roar rips the silence, claiming this woman for myself, letting the universe know she's mine, body and soul. I'm branding her for me.

Girl you're just mine, mine...

I realize this morning how short this time together has been. On the road, on our last day before returning home, she sleeps the entire drive. This morning, she suffered one of those headaches the doctors warned about. Her strength is low. I suggest we return a day early, but she refuses, saying she'll recover with a nap. It pains me to see her tired, knowing how active she normally is.

Several times, I gaze at her. She sleeps peacefully reclined on my shoulder, grinning in her sleep. She must be having good dreams. She looks so lovely. I understand what she means when she says she doesn't want to go back to reality. I don't either. Now that I've discovered how happy and complete we are together, I don't need anything else. What had been important before seems meaningless now.

I'm not thrilled to go back to my famous singer life, realizing the happiness in the simplicity of having her feels enough. Even mundane, daily things are new and spectacular with her. I'm at the point if she asks me to renounce everything for her, I'll do it without hesitation. My love for this amazing woman by my side is strong. Never in my life would I have thought I'd end up believing the way I do now.

She stirs slowly, taking me out of my thoughts. With her eyes half-closed, she murmurs a question, "Did we arrive yet?"

I glance down at her.

"We'll be there in couple of minutes."

"Good. I'm feeling much better. I needed the nap."

She sits straight and turns to press her lips against my neck.

"I think it's more exhaustion from the energetic activities we've been doing together. It's not easy for me to keep up with your… *stamina, papi.*"

I giggle at her remark.

"Well, some of it is your fault. You told me it's not easy to keep a Boricua woman satisfied, so there's more to come still."

We both laugh out loud. I adore her laugh. We've been exerting ourselves more than usual these past few days. But I can't help it with her. I crave the way she makes me feel. The more I taste her, the more I hunger for her. She's addictive and makes me feel invincible, like I can accomplish anything. The happiness of finally having everything I've dreamed of is overwhelming.

I've planned a special surprise for her. I've bought a ring, and saved it inside the small Death Star ring case I bought. I've made reservations at one of the restaurants in the hotel's lobby, planning to propose to her after dinner. I know she doesn't need another ceremony, but for me, it's important the world recognize her as my wife. An official wedding ceremony before our families and friends. I want to be the first thing she sees in the morning and the last at night. To be by my side everywhere I go without anyone questioning it. It's my way of letting her know she deserves a new happy chapter in her life.

The hotel lobby is busy. Unexpectedly two fans recognize me, approaching for photos, which Gabriella is more than happy to take for them. What moves her are the fans' words when they say goodbye.

"Keep showing the world true love has no boundaries."

I see her become teary while I thank them for their kind words. The front desk agent immediately checks us in and hands us our keys, escorting us to our room.

I tell Gaby we have dinner reservations, so our attire should be more formal. She decides to soak in the bathtub while I make some phone calls informing everyone that we're doing okay, and we'll be back home tomorrow. I call Marc first to let him know what I plan to do, of course.

"Marc, how are you doing?" I almost shout, happy and excited to share the news.

"Hey, man. You sound pretty upbeat. I can only imagine how it's going with you two lovebirds. How's Gaby doing?"

"She's okay, taking a bath. This morning, she had the first of those headaches they warned us about. If you had seen her…man, it broke my heart seeing her so tired. She slept the entire drive today. Well…we've also been extremely physical these days, so maybe she's just exhausted."

"How's it feel, Lukas? I've never heard you so happy. Your tone of voice has changed. Tell me, man."

"It's like… Every morning waking up, seeing her beside me sleeping, the happiness is indescribable. I want it every day. It's like a guarantee the day is going to be okay just because she's in it. Having her in my arms, I can conquer anything. There's no obstacle I cannot overcome. Pure heaven, Marc, nothing less. I wish this time together wouldn't end. The word to describe it is surreal," is my heartfelt answer.

There's a short silence on the line.

"Now, this is you man. I finally got my brother back, and it makes me so fucking happy. I'm overjoyed for you."

"That's not all, Marc." I pause to sit on the bed and lower

my voice so she doesn't hear me.

"I bought a ring. Tonight after dinner, I'm going to ask her to marry me. I know she doesn't need it, but I want to make it official. So naturally, I'm asking you to be my best man."

I hear a roar of laughter, celebrating the news. Clapping and shouting in Korean. I chuckle hearing him.

"Oh, wow, man. This is really unexpected. This is going to blow everyone's minds. Congratulations, bro. I'm so happy for you both. I've witnessed everything you've both been through. So this is great news. Of course it's an honor to be your best man. Count me in."

Hearing his answer fills me with emotion. I'm truly blessed.

"I'll let you know how it goes, as always."

"Remember I got "the other part" who wants to know everything about what's going on with you two," he replies, inhaling sharply, resignation in his tone. I laugh, knowing how Lola can be.

A loud hollow thump from the bathroom followed by Gabriella's pained scream frightens me. I stand up in panic.

"Gaby."

I drop the phone on the bed, running to open the bathroom door, shouting, "Gaby, are you okay?"

Scared as hell, I search for where she is, finding her lying naked on the floor beside the bathtub all wet, her legs wrapped around a white towel. She looks identical to a little girl who's been caught doing something wrong. My eyes widen in disbelief, reaching to scoop her up, carrying in my arms.

"Sorry. I slipped on the wet floor, getting out of the bathtub to grab the towel. I know. Sometimes I'm so clumsy. I think I twisted my ankle. It hurts like crazy," she explains with puppy eyes, embarrassed.

I can't avoid chuckling, watching how adorable she looks.

"You scared the hell out of me," I confess while kissing her forehead.

I place her gently onto the bed, and she pulls up the towel to cover her nakedness. She's so enchanting wet with only a towel covering her. This hunger has to wait, though, and I grab the phone from the bed to inform Marc.

"Gaby fell. Nothing serious. Call you later."

I sit down on the bed beside her to check her over.

"Let me see your ankle. I used to tend to the guys' injuries sometimes back home."

Her ankle is instantly red and swollen.

"Yep, you got a sprained ankle. I'll call front desk to ask for ice and see if they have first aid kit with compression bandages available. I'll immobilize it for you, okay?" I raise my eyes to observe her as she shows me a pained expression. So my plans for dinner aren't going to happen today. *Fuck.*

Naturally the management pulls out all the stops for us, because of me. Not only to bring us ice but a doctor as well to check on Gaby, confirming my diagnosis. The doctor immobilizes her ankle with elastic bandages and prescribes acetaminophen with codeine tablets for the pain, which are brought in a short time from a local pharmacy nearby. He recommends that she sees her doctor once we get back home.

The hotel also sends dinner to our room since we aren't able to make it downstairs for our reservations. The doctor advises her to stay in and rest. We dine next to each other on the bed. Once we finish, she takes the tablets plus her own medications while I clear up the trays. We talk, and I explain my concert schedule to her.

"Come with me on the tour, Gaby. You can work from anywhere in the world. I want you to be with me." I gaze deep in to her eyes to let her know how serious I am.

She becomes somber and replies gloomily, "Lukas, I can't. I just finished my book, and it's time to present it. Like you, I'm doing a media tour for it. I can't go, sweetie. I need to stay here."

Her tender caress makes me forget my frustration. Her fingers touch my lips. I exhale, feeling her, kissing the tip of her fingers.

"I love you so much, Lukas. You don't have any idea how much."

While combing my hair with her fingers, I close my eyes, enjoying the heavenly sensation.

"There's nothing I wouldn't do for you, babe," she blurts.

Hearing those words, I gain my courage to pop the question. *It's now or never.*

"Gaby… There's something I would like to ask you."

I inhale nervously while she examines me with a confused look. From my jacket's pocket, I pull out the ring box. I show her a small round Death Star. She smiles with curiosity. I open the small Death Star, and her face shows shock at the ring I've been hiding for days. My heart is hammering in my ribcage. This is scarier than standing in front of millions of fans screaming your name. I speak with a bit of apprehension.

"I know you told me you don't need papers or ceremonies for us. But this is important to me, it would make me very happy if you agreed to become my wife officially before the world. I've never felt surer of what I feel right now. You're the person I want to have millions of adventures with, dancing in the kitchen or under the rain. Cook all the recipes with. I want to cry, laugh, and fall in love with you all over again, Gabriella. Would you agree to be my partner, share this adventure called life and be my soulmate for the rest of our days?"

Bursting into tears, she covers her lips, overcome with emotion. I see a certain sadness in her eyes, which constricts my heart somewhat. Her smile spreads wide, nodding her head in approval.

"Of course, I'll say yes to you, Lukas. A thousand times, yes."

She grabs my face with her hands and kisses me, then pulls back to add, "I have only one request. Let's get married after your tour and awards are over, ok? When you're back in California."

Taking her hand, I slide the ring onto her finger and lift her knuckles to kiss them.

"Deal, Ms. Lee. It has a nice ring to it," I comment, just to provoke her.

She looks at me sassy, chuckling, with tears in her eyes.

"You know Boricuas usually don't take their husband's names, don't you? Or are you teasing me? Provoking my Boricua wrath from hell?" She raises her eyebrow in a funny expression. I know she's teasing me.

I crack, laughing out loud. I lean in to seize her lips in a kiss full of love and promises, thrilled she said yes.

I murmur against her lips, "Something like that. I like how feisty you turn when teased."

Deepening the kiss, my craving starts to get out of control. I'm moving on top, encircling her in my arms, when my foot touches her swollen ankle. Her small cry of pain stops me. Hearing her has cooled down my passion, thinking of her injury first.

"I'm sorry, Gaby. I'll calm down. I forgot for a moment…you know."

She stares with half-closed eyes, talking slowly but grinning. I think the meds are kicking in.

"I'm sleepy, sweetie. Give me rain check for tomorrow. I prefer to be alert when you're all over my body, you know…touching those enjoyable places. Let's wait. Okay, Lukas?" she babbles at the end trying to be funny, before succumbing to a deep sleep. I smile, staring at her sleeping comfortably in my arms.

My wife… I slowly lower her head onto the pillow with care. Leaning in to steal a kiss from her lips, unable to resist.

I accommodate my sleeping beauty the best I can, and raising her injured leg, I put a pillow under her foot to help the swelling go down. She flinches, pain etched on her face when I move it. Damn, I don't want to cause her any pain. So clumsy of me. I cover her with the comforter and turn off the lights except for the one atop my nightstand.

Standing beside the bed, I watch her sleep soundly, my goddess at rest. Fuck yes, I could do this every night, not minding it at all. I enjoy taking care of her like this.

I put on my pajama pants to slip under the covers as close as possible to her without jarring her leg. Her scent and her body's warmth have turned into a necessity at night. In her sleep, she grabs my hand firmly, placing it on her chest. My heart swells at this gesture. I don't doubt that's where she keeps me, where I live. I'm pulled by my heartstrings, knowing she loves me with the same intensity I love her. I'm truly a lucky bastard.

From now on we want to be one… I hope we will be one…

Gabriella

The sun's rays peek through a tiny crack of the close curtains, filling the room with soft light. Pain wakes me as I move my leg. Stirring, my eyelids open to find Lukas's arms wrapped around me. His breath on my neck tells me he's in deep sleep. I'm kind of dizzy from the meds. Trying to get out of his grip without waking him, I find it impossible.

"Lukas, baby. I need to go to the bathroom. Let me loose, sweetie."

Tightening his grip, he chuckles playfully.

"No. I don't want to."

"Well…it's either that or I'll pee myself here, on the bed."

He lets out a laugh, releasing me and helping me sit up.

"Do you need help getting there?"

"Nope."

I limp to the bathroom, closing the door. Sitting on the toilet, relieving myself, a big headache flare strikes unexpectedly. Breathing raggedly and terrified by the pain, I recline backward while losing my strength, avoiding a fall on the floor. *Like yesterday.*

Staring at the door, I debate with myself whether I should call him. No, I don't want to worry him. So I stay there, eyes closed, breathing deeply, focusing on regaining my strength as quickly as my body allows it. A single tear rolls down my cheek. Squeezing my eyes shut, I feel the pain subside until it disappears, my strength slowly returning.

Once I'm able to stand up, I limp to the vanity to turn on the faucet. Splashing some water on my face, I grip the counter while my strength continues to return. I gaze at the ring on my finger.

I'm engaged to be married. I stare at myself in the mirror, sorrowful eyes watching me back. I shut them once more, inhaling deeply. *You're stronger than you thought you were, Gabriella.*

I come out of the bathroom, several minutes later, limping to drop myself on the bed, smiling. He watches me the whole time.

"How's your ankle feeling?"

"Still hurts, but I can manage."

"I just received a call from the front desk. The fans we encountered yesterday posted their photos on social media, so there's a healthy group of paparazzi outside the hotel, waiting for us to appear. We've been warned. What a way to spend our last day."

Turning sideways, I glance at him seductively.

"We don't have to check out until one pm, and we can stay inside. You know, doing stuff… Even breakfast in bed."

Darkened eyes smile with the promise I've given him. He lowers himself sideways to observe me, his hand pulling my waist to him.

"And what do you have in mind, *future Ms. Lee*?" He kisses the tip of my nose.

I smirk at his *Ms. Lee* comment. It sounds full of promise in his voice. I sigh.

"There's a matter of the pending celebration that had been postponed last night because of my clumsy fall. Let's ask for mimosas with our breakfast," I answer, wickedly playful. He chuckles.

"I was thinking another type of activity." Lukas smirks, raising his eyebrow and doing his tongue-biting thing. I lick my lips in hunger, watching him.

"I wanna see what you have in mind. *Enseñame…*" I can tell he wants to show me.

I half close my eyes, teasing him while lying on my back, my body language yelling for him to take me.

He doesn't wait long, jumping on top of me as we both giggle.

"It would be my pleasure to show you. Be a good girl and spread your legs for me, will you?"

He bends to take my lips, giving himself freely to the passionate kiss.

We make sweet, slow, tender love once more before packing to leave. We call the front desk for assistance, avoiding incidents with the paparazzi. They're more than eager to help. It's free advertisement for them, showing they are capable of hosting high-profile guests.

Walking, guarded by two employees as bodyguards, between flashes of photographers lined up in the hotel lobby, we make our way home. Some of them follow us onto the highway, but Lukas's fast driving outdistances us from our unwanted followers. We're both giddy at the success of losing all of them, and we arrive at our apartment building with no further incidents.

Standing at my door feels so awkward. I'm scared to go inside. Scared of facing myself and the truth, to be apart from him, when we've spent every waking moment together for the past few days is shredding me. I hadn't thought it would feel like this. I turn to look at him.

"I don't know how to enter." A sob chokes my throat. "*I don't know…*"

Dropping the bags, he hugs me. I shut my eyes, letting emotional tears roll, finding comfort in his arms.

"When we're married, we'll be together always," is his

response to console me. Hearing those words is my wake-up call.

Gabriella, compose yourself. This is not you. You're a strong woman. Show him how strong. Be strong for him.

Straightening myself, I sniffle though my tears.

"You're right. It's just a matter of time." I force a smile.

He steps back to caress my face, making sure I'm okay.

"If you want, I can stay here tonight, or you can stay with me, your choice," he offers.

Even though I'm dying inside to ask him stay with me, I suggest the opposite.

"No, it's okay. I'm okay now, don't worry. Tomorrow we both have early meetings to attend. We need to be our best selves, properly rested. Tomorrow night, I'll stay with you," I reply, trying to sound casual.

"Okay. Remember, I'm just a door away if you need me." Lukas stares with serious expression, trying to see I'm really fine. My mind divagates, memorizing his face.

I'll need you forever, Lukas. *And forever isn't enough for me.*

I pull him down to peck his lips quickly and pick up my bag to enter my apartment, turning to say goodbye.

"See you tomorrow. Love you."

I put my back against the closed door, like so many times before, but this time, I slide down to sit on the floor, covering my face while crying silently. I don't know how to cope with his absence, with being apart, these difficult days ahead about to come. And I need him. I really need him. Be strong. *Sé fuerte por él.*

I become stronger thanks to you...

Chapter Twenty-Seven

Lukas

Five more cities added to the tour. Why am I'm not surprised? This is getting insane like it usually does. It's typical of the company to squeeze dates in between to increase gain. This means the tour will be extended, and I'll be away from Gaby longer.

"What's wrong?" Marc asks, whispering when he notices my face.

"They're extending the tour again."

Puzzled, Marc answers in a mocking tone, "And that's bad? Bro, sometimes you confuse me."

I can't avoid chuckling at his comment; it's true. It doesn't make sense for me to be distressed by it. It's what we all want.

"I don't want to be away from Gabriella so long, that's all."

"Did you ask her to come with us?"

"Yes, but she said she can't. The book launch, remember? She has her own media tour to attend."

We continue to pay attention to the executives speaking. After multiple meetings planning the details of our American tour, I'm ready to spend the rest of the day with Gaby. Marc and I leave tomorrow for Tokyo to resume our tour, and Ty will meet us there. I call her to find out where she is.

"Gabriella?"

"Hello? Lukas?"

Her upset voice tells me she's not okay. She's sniffling.

"What's wrong?"

"It's just…I finished my meeting with Harrison and the board. They're assigning someone else to help me with the media tour. Because of my condition. You know… It sucks when a health issue limits your performance. It's my first personal big project and to not be able to attend it properly…" Her words trail off.

I feel awful for her. I can relate to her frustration, the rage against something you have no control over.

"You know what? Let me take care of you for the day. I'll bring food. We'll meet at my apartment, spend the rest of the day together."

"That would be awesome for me right now. I need you, Lukas. Really need you, now."

Hearing her pleading tone in her words melts my heart and ignites my blood instantly. My groin pulsing painfully from the yearning.

"I'll be back in an hour, waiting for you."

"See you then."

We arrive at the parking lot at the same time. I put the bag of food on the trunk of her car while I pull her in my embrace to kiss her adoringly. Pleasantly surprised, she wraps her arms around me. Her mouth invites me to deepen the kiss, and as her passion grows, my own grows stronger.

"Gaby." I gasp for air. "Let's get to the apartment, baby. I'm ready to have you now, but this is not the place. Even for your unusual sexual fantasies." I chuckle at her.

She giggles at my words. That's right, my love, laugh. I want you to smile. *I love to see you smile.* Grabbing the food bag and her hand, we to walk to my apartment. Once we're inside, I put the bag of food on the counter and lead her to my bedroom.

Seizing her face, I muster the profound love I have in my honest hungry voice. I want to worship her with my love. To brand this day on her skin like a memorable scar.

"Now let me fulfill your wishes, your desires. Tell me what you want me to do to you. I want to fulfill all of them now."

"You have given me more than I've dreamed of, my love. What more can there be?" she whispers, an expression of satisfaction showing in her eyes.

I rejoice in the knowledge her confession gives me. Leaning in close, I drop soft kisses all over her face. Today I want to memorize how she smells, tastes, sounds, feels, and looks. We're going to be apart for a long time, too long for me. I need to overdose on her. Even one day away from her constricts my chest. She's the air I need to breathe. Three months will be an eternity for me.

"Unleash me. Unleash my lust, Lukas. You know what I like and what I don't. Tease me. Make me lose control." She gazes at me, ready to comply. "I'm completely yours. Show me how I can make you remember this moment forever."

Her eyes reflect her complete and total surrender to me, to please me and my desires. My chest is about to explode. She's truly mine. No one can take her from me.

My thumb brushes her wet lips, staring in hunger. To my

surprise, she takes my thumb in her mouth to sucks it lustfully. Her warm tongue circling around it has the power to lick my groin as well. Letting out a moan of pleasure, caressing her neck while watching her suck my thumb greedily is driving me crazy. If it wasn't enough…

"I want to taste you, Lukas. Please, let me worship you with everything I've got."

I want it all. She unbuttons my shirt with calmness, taking her time. Her mouth captures my nipples to suck them. I've never seen her this unashamed, carefree, or ravenous. She's blowing my mind.

Her mouth and tongue trail down my belly, until she kneels before me. I'm paralyzed, gazing down at her. Hurriedly unfastening my belt and pants, she takes them down, while my arousal bounces free. She gently pushes me to sit on the bed, finally tugging my clothes off to drop them on the floor.

"I'm dying to taste you once more."

She's a lioness on the prowl with hunger in her eyes. Bending her head, she takes my arousal in her mouth, sucking it. My eyes shut in utter bliss. God, this is unreal. She's going to kill me with pleasure.

Grabbing her head, my fingers caress her hair while she sucks and licks my hardness all over, showing how voracious she is. Feeling her warm tongue, her desire, I'm becoming insane. I throw my head back, gasping for air.

"Gaby… Gaby, baby… *aaargh*… You undo me."

The pleasure she's giving me is intense and so raw. I'm at her mercy, but I don't want to spill my seed yet. I'm dying to be inside her.

"Baby, let me have you. Slow down. I need to be inside you, feel you," I plead.

With a feral look, she stops. She has the eyes of a hungry

lioness staring at her mate, ready to surrender. Teasingly she releases me from her mouth, slowly licking me. Gaby stands to undress herself, taking her time for me to watch her and enjoy.

I sit up straight, keeping my eyes on her, turned on beyond reason. Seeing her take her clothes off is one of the most breathtaking spectacles I've ever had the privilege to watch. The lioness lies face down beside me, surrendering herself for her mate to take her. I'm her mate. I'm her lion.

I grab her waist while she's kneeling to slowly thrust, sheathing my arousal fully inside her from behind. This is pure, raw, untamed lust fueled by our love. We're burning so fiercely the whole room could light up in flames from our combustion.

She's screaming and moaning, enjoying every movement. The pace of my thrusts is hasty, my hands fondling her breasts, my mouth on her neck kissing, softly nibbling, and my breath ragged. If I could, I would fuse with her like this. The first waves of my release are rippling through me. She feels so good that I can't hold it back anymore. I'm surrendering to it.

"I'm coming, Lukas. I'm coming, baby."

Her loud scream confirms she's getting her release with me. I'm in a trance, frozen in time, with her in my arms, groaning at the sensation of being joined together. Her hips convulse against mine; her inner walls clamp around me, making me gasp as I scream my own release with her, grabbing her hips roughly.

"Gabriella," is my shout of release. My thrusts getting choppier as I empty myself into her. With a last pound, I drop on the bed embracing her, gasping for air.

My whole body trembles with the pleasure she gives me. I crave this woman, and I don't know how the hell we're going to be apart for so long. I know we both feel the same.

I lie with her in my arms, not saying a word, while I recover my strength, inhaling her scent that soothes me.

"Gaby, baby…if this is heaven, I want to dive into eternity with you this way. Every single time reaching this."

Eyes shut, still gasping while my arousal jerks slowly inside her, enjoying every delicious bit of her.

After several minutes, she rolls over me. She straddles me, looking down, love-drunk, announcing, "Then let's dive together."

She kisses me with famishment, waking my arousal again. We're caught in a tornado of desire, pulling us without control, over and over.

We're kissing, sucking, licking, and tasting each other with an ardor touchingly unrestrained. Today feels different. We're giving each other everything, joining in heavenly bliss.

We fall asleep for several hours, waking around seven pm to heat and eat the food I'd brought home. We're exhausted. Around three am, a sniffling sound wakes me to find her staring at me in silence with a tear-streaked face. Alarmed, thinking she's suffering another headache, I ask worried, "Hey, are you in pain?"

Her response moves me.

"Yes. Yes, I am. I'm in pain. But not the pain you think. The pain is inside my heart, my soul. It pains me to know in a couple of hours, you'll be gone, and we'll be apart. It pains me in a way that tightens my chest and is breaking me inside. I never thought I would love someone the way I love you, Lukas. It's so much it hurts. Letting you go now is one of the hardest things I've ever done in my life."

She stops to lower her head, wiping her tears with the back of her hand. Gaby lifts her eyes again to watch me lovingly.

"Seeing you happy is everything for me, sweetie. True love entails sacrifice. This time apart, even it's hard, is going to be for the greater good, for both of us."

Her hand caresses my face. Tenderness and love gape back at me. Something inside my chest breaks, seeing her like this. Sadness crawls in my heart, recognizing what she's saying. Pulling her by her neck to kiss her softly, I let her know I understand.

"Gaby, knowing we'll be apart is killing me too, but you taught me to be strong, to wait. Three months will pass quickly, you'll see. Then we'll be together always."

"Yes, always."

She smiles, staring into my soul while saying, "For eternity, my heart will always be yours."

She inclines to gift me one of her most heartfelt kisses. Deepening the kiss, I push her to lie back. My hands grab her thighs positioning myself between her legs to start our lovemaking again. This time, I take it slow, savoring her lips, her skin. Feeling myself slide in and out of her blissfully. Branding her to remember this night, my body pressed to hers.

Again we reach peak bliss, almost burning like the sun. We make love until the first rays of daylight filter through the bedroom window.

She's sleeping on top of my chest, exhausted and satiated. The tips of my fingers caress her back down to the beginning of her buttocks.

I'm memorizing this, her naked body over mine. Her musky smell mixed with sweet gardenia brand my memory. The pressure of her breast crushes against my chest. The steady beats of her heart after being properly satisfied. The softness of her skin under my touch. Her long legs wrapped around mine so casually. *The body of a real woman.*

This memory might help me endure this time apart from her. A single tear rolls down my face, realizing how much I love her and how hard it's going to be. I have to be strong for her. Finally I close my tired eyes, enjoying having her in my arms. No exhilaration or joy in life could compare to this. Nothing.

Until the dawn where the light has fallen
asleep...
We can fly tonight...

Chapter Twenty-Eight

Gabriella

We arrive at the John Wayne Airport Tack area in an Escalade the record company sent us. I had decided at the last minute to accompany Lukas and Marc, and I have been promised to be returned to my apartment upon Lukas's request.

It's his moment to shine and achieve those goals he's worked so hard for. I'm positive about it. In my heart, I know he's going to win those awards. It will help him in his journey to accomplish the projects he has in mind. I want so badly for him to succeed. He wants to help others achieve their dreams in entertainment, creating his own company. The heavens will reward his selfless wish.

The attendants from the record company unload the luggage from the trunk, taking it to the jet already preparing to take off. Lukas exits the car first and helps me out.

"Wait for me here."

He walks away to speak to the captain of the plane. Marc approaches from the other side of the car. Dropping his duffle bag to pick me up, hugging me tightly and swirling me around.

"Come on, Gaby, you should come with us. He's going to be whining about you on that plane, you know. Last chance to change your mind."

I chuckle at his funny face and adorable dimples.

"Stop it, you know I have to stay for my book tour. Besides I'll just be in the way of you guys doing your famous-star-shit thing there. I'll be okay." I wave my hand in the air, joking about it.

Fuck, Marc, I love you so much, but I'm not letting you in today. Sorry, buddy, I know you'll be pissed off with me. Raising my hand to touch his face, I kiss his cheek.

"Love you, Marc, thanks for being such a good friend to me. Remember that."

I hug him so tight I could break him.

"Take care of Lukas for me, will you?"

My eyes fill with tears, the pain in my chest threatening to choke me. *Let's keep it together, girl.* A couple more minutes.

"I will, sweetheart. You take care for us. And take care of my girl, Lola, too. You know, don't let her get into trouble," he replies calmly, making a funny face.

I giggle. Holding my chin with two fingers, he kisses my cheek tenderly. I'm aware he's got teary eyes too. Shaking himself, he smiles wide again.

"We'll see each other soon. Three months will pass quickly."

Marc winks at me before turning around to pick up his duffle bag and walking to the plane. He turns one last time to wave at me. I blow him a kiss. Love you so much, Marc. I'll miss you too.

Lukas walks toward me. This is it. The moment I've

dreaded, but I've decided to be strong. My strength will give him security.

"Are you sure don't want to come with us? You don't need luggage, just say so," he whispers, rubbing my arms, kissing my forehead.

"Marc already made that offer, and I declined," I answer, putting my arms around his waist. I bury my face in his chest, dreading to look him.

God, help me. A bit more strength to endure this. His scent, let me memorize it.

"You always smell so good," I whisper while he lets out a soft chuckle.

I raise my eyes to meet his. Too late. His are filled with tears, and I can't help it. I sob on him.

"I love you, Lukas. With every cell, every fiber of my being, I love you. I want you to understand it. My heart and soul belong with you. I believe in you. Conquer the world for me, promise me." I try to speak between sobs.

Taking my face between his big hands, he reassures me.

"I promise, love." Sealing it with a kiss that escalates. There's no tomorrow, only now. We're fused in our souls. He breaks the kiss to plead into my eyes.

"Give me your word you'll take care of yourself. I'll be back as soon the concerts and the awards are over. Please, let me know if there's any change. I'll be back immediately."

"I will. If something changes, I'll let you know."

I hold the lapels of his suit. He looks amazing in this dark gray suit with the dark purple satin tie I bought him during our week together. My kiss gives every ounce of love I have inside. This time, I'm the one who breaks the kiss.

"I'll wait for you. That's my promise." And I mean it honestly.

He plants kisses all over my face. His lips burn my skin, leaving his mark. It took a lot of willpower to push him gently.

"Go on, sweetie. It's late. I'll be okay. Remember these words, baby. You're braver than you believe. You're stronger than you think. You're already a winner to me."

Wiping the tears off my face with my sleeve, I wipe his too. Stepping back, putting on my best face, he holds my hand tightly one last time.

"I love you, Gabriella. I can't hardly wait to make you my wife. You're the best thing that has ever happened to me." Stepping back, he's still holding my hand.

We keep twining our fingers until he lets go of me to walk to the plane. Reclining against the car, the pain is overwhelming. I'm not sure if I can hold it together any longer. Wearing my best face, I stay there watching the plane's door close, and through windows, Lukas and Marc wave at me.

God, how much I love these two. I wave back, grinning at them, focusing my gaze on Lukas.

His sad eyes observe me broken. Giving him my most reassuring smile, I blow a kiss and even stick out my tongue at him, making a funny face. He laughs.

That's right, my love, laugh. You need to laugh more often. I adore your smile.

The plane taxis to the runway, while the chauffer opens the door for me. I open the window to watch them go. The plane accelerates on the runway, taking off to the skies. Taking my life with it. I give the signal to the chauffer to take me home.

Opening the door to my apartment, the loneliness hiding behind the door welcomes me like an old friend who waited too long. I put the keys on the counter and sit on the sofa. I'm numb, disoriented. Something breaks inside my heart, and I can't hold it in any longer.

I drop on my knees on the floor in defeat, losing all composure and cry uncontrollably, almost hysterically. Gasping for air, covering my face while talking to myself, trying to ease my conscience, I pray for the first time in a long while.

"I'm sorry, sweetie. I'm so sorry. God, help me. Give me strength. Please, forgive me, Lord. Ease his pain, please."

And there in my living room, on my knees face down on the floor, I pour out and surrender to the pain I've held inside for so long.

Gotta end it tonight, to start again...

It's four in the morning, and I haven't slept well. Ultimately, I don't sleep much. Only tiny bits during the day or night. Pain flares keep me awake most of the time now. I hear Xavier in the kitchen, maybe preparing some food for me to eat, even though he knows I eat less with each passing day. The truth is I'm not hungry. But he keeps trying, and I appreciate his efforts. I'm glad Lola has stayed with us since yesterday, keeping me company. I hear the knock at my bedroom door and Xavier's voice from the other side.

"Hello? I'm coming in."

The door opens while Lola sits beside me. I don't open my eyes, but I hear them. I also know I don't look good. I've heard from one of the nurses I'm getting paler, and the dark circles around my eyes confirm it. Lola speaks in whispers with Xavier.

"She didn't sleep well. The pain flares... She only fell asleep a couple of hours ago."

There's this silence, and I'm sure they're both staring at me.

"Do we have to wake her up?" she asks.

"We have to. She'll not forgive us if we don't. All she

talks about is this award show, and she wants to see him. We can't take this away from her. That's what's pushing her."

Lola grunts, protesting in a low tone.

"I don't understand why she insists on us keeping our mouths shut. He should know. I feel awful lying to Marc, to both of them."

I decide it's time to let them know I'm awake already.

"Can you two lower your voices? You both know I'm here, right? That I can hear you?" I murmur, my eyes still closed.

"Gaby, please let me call him; he deserves to know," Lola begs in an anguished tone.

I open my eyes slowly. Today I'm tired.

"Help me sit up, please," I request, ignoring Lola's suggestion.

Xavier puts the tray on my desk and helps Lola sit me on bed. Lola piles the pillows at my back to make me comfortable. My breathing is ragged. I fully open my eyes to inform him.

"I will comply with you, Xavier. With both of you. After the award show is over, you can call him. I'll not mind at all."

They stare at each other dumbfounded. Lola's teary eyes observe me with a shy smile.

"Really, *bonita*? You'll let us tell him?"

"Yes. Please turn on the TV and search for the app where the show is streaming. I told Lukas I'd watch it, so he's expecting it."

Their anguished eyes confirm how fragile I look. I don't want to pretend anymore. Xavier brings a tray of food to offer.

"*Mami, hice crema de arroz que a ti te gusta. Come un poco por favor.*"

Placing the tray of my favorite rice cream over my lap,

Xavier's begging me to eat. I shake my head. "I'm not hungry," I protest, shutting my eyes. It's the truth.

"Gaby, you need to eat something to take your medicine."

"I don't want more medicine, please. Today I don't want them." I protest, feistily.

"Mom, at least drink the hot tea."

Frowning, I observe his annoyance. I know he means well and answer, "Okay, okay, I'll drink it."

Giving the cup to Lola to help me drink it, he removes the tray from my lap. He turns on the TV, searching for Seoul Music Awards in the app as I'd instructed. The show has already started. In Seoul, it's around eight pm.

I'm overcome with this sense of love and gratitude seeing them worried about me, taking care of me. I watch my son with love, patting the bed for him to sit next to me.

"Come sit beside me, Xavier. Let's watch it together."

Eyes glistening, he agrees lovingly.

"Sure, Mom. Anything you say."

The three of us sit together.

My gaze shifts from him to Lola, and for the first time in weeks, my smile widens. I grab each hand to kiss before adding, "I'm so happy you are here with me. I'm grateful to God to have you both in my life. Please, remember this always. I love you with all my heart."

Lola's sobs escape, crying heartbroken, same as me.

"I love you too, Gaby. You're the best friend life could give me."

She lifts my hand to kiss it. Xavier imitates her.

"*Te amo mucho, Mami.*" He stares with tears in his eyes.

"*Yo te amo más, mi amor.*" I caress his face.

We watch the award show in silence and barely understand anything they're saying. The moment comes for the Daesang award for Album of the Year. The presenter lists the nominees, and we hear Ty's name and Lukas as composer/producer. They announce the winner. Ty's record *Transcend* wins. I clap, excited for the first time in weeks.

"Oh my God. They won. Ty won." I grin at Lola, who smiles back with teary eyes.

The next award is Song of the Year. Lukas is nominated for our song. Xavier stares at me. My eyes are fixed on the screen, waiting for the announcement. My hands clasp together in silent prayer for him.

Please God... He's a noble heart. He deserves to fulfill his dreams. He too has suffered enough. Make his goals come true. Give him the love he deserves, the family he needs...

Like in slow motion, I hear Lukas's name called as the winner. I let out a small scream of joy.

"He won, he won!"

Xavier's expression is filled with emotion, seeing me this happy. Cameras follow Lukas standing up, hand covering his mouth to hug Marc who is sitting at the same table. Eyes glistening, overwhelmed, while bowing to everyone and walking to the stage.

"He looks so handsome in his tuxedo. Look, Lola, he's crying. He seems so happy."

Lola exchanges anguished glances with Xavier. I'm breathing with some difficulty.

"Gaby, take it easy with your emotions, don't overdo it."

I recline against the pillows behind me. I'm exhausted.

We all watch Lukas standing at the podium, holding and observing in his hand the award he's just won. He starts to speak in Korean, giving thanks to everyone, all choked up. Then he speaks in English, staring at the camera, knowing I see him.

"I want everyone to know my soon-to-be-wife, Gabriella Morales, is the inspiration for the song 'I Surrender My All'."

Everyone claps at his words, some shocked faces. He wipes the tears in his eyes and adds, "Gaby, I know you're watching. You have been so faithful, supporting me in every step since we met. I wish you could be here with me. I wouldn't be standing here if you hadn't come into my life and shown me what's really important. You're my muse, my inspiration to be better. I love you so much, and this award is yours too, baby. I couldn't have done it without you."

Takes a lot of courage to say what he just did. Everyone stands, clapping in an uproar, giving him a standing ovation. Many of them have teary eyes like him, including Marc. We are all crying at his speech. Even Xavier.

Xavier turns to look at me. My hand is over my mouth and tears fall, listening to his words. I rest my hand on my lap and contentedly say, "He did it. He really did it. Now the world belongs to him."

Lola cries in silence. I smile, overjoyed, at Xavier. Feeling weary, I need to rest. Everything I've prayed for is done. Closing my eyes, I inhale deeply and feel this overwhelming joy and peace that everything has turned out good for him.

My mind flies through the memories of our time together. White clouds and satin sheets floating in the air, caressing our skin. How I wish he could be here, holding me in his arms.

My only regret is not telling him the truth. But he's a bright man, he'll understand. I'm falling on a comfortable cloud hugging me, making me happier, satisfied. I don't feel pain anymore. I hear a distant voice. Far away, Xavier's voice calls me. I grin full of joy.

"Mom? *Mami? MAMI.*"

Lukas

Seoul nights have been crazier recently. I never understood this insanity of partying or staying up until early morning. I'm not a morning person, but I was dying to be back home. For me, 2 am is late enough.

Today's been great. I won the two main Daesangs, for Christ's sake. I think I'm the youngest one in the industry to achieve it. I open the door of my apartment, leaving it ajar so Marc can enter.

I'm unbuttoning my jacket while ogling the two Daesang Awards on my entrance table. It's insane. I still can't believe it. This stupid grin hasn't left my face all night. I walk into the living room, loosening my bow tie. The view of Seoul from here is impressive tonight. I'm tired. It's been an intense, emotional night for me.

Winning these awards means opportunities will now be available to work as I wanted. My dream of creating my own company will be a piece of cake now.

The only regret is Gabriella wasn't here with me. Revealing her name and our-soon-to-be marriage during my acceptance speech was a bold move, but I don't mind acknowledging her before the world anymore. Being apart these past months has made me irritated. She told me she'd watch the show on TV when we spoke this morning. She sounded tired but confident I'd win. Something has been off with her lately, and it makes me uneasy. After the press conference tomorrow, I'll take the first plane to California to be with her.

"Want another glass of champagne?" Marc shouts, entering the apartment, also dressed in his tuxedo. Closing the door behind him, he walks into the kitchen.

"That's a major win tonight, Lukas. You know doors are going to fly open for you. It's so sweet."

He rubs his hands together, smiling in a playful way, then pours champagne in two glass flutes.

Walking over to me, he gives me one glass flute, and we clink our them together.

"Cheers, man. I'm so proud of you. You're officially the *GOAT* now."

Marc's cellphone starts to buzz and rings on the kitchen counter. He runs to pick it up. After looking at the screen, informs me jokingly, "It's Gabriella. Let me answer." He's smirking playfully, about to do one of his jokes.

"Hi, Gaby, your real boyfriend speak—"

His speech got cut. Sipping my champagne, I stare at Marc, loosening the top button of my shirt.

"*Who?* Slow down, man. I don't understand. What did you say?"

Hearing Marc's upset voice, panic rises in my chest. I sprint to the kitchen, and he looks up, staring at me with wide eyes, full of tears. His pale face is distorted, lips almost white, all the color drained from them. I freeze.

No, no, please, God, I don't want to hear it…

It only becomes real after it's spoken. Shaking my head at Marc, wanting the nightmare to be over, my eyes beg him. *Please, please, don't tell me….*

"Hey, man…"

He tries to speak, but his voice keeps breaking up. Lowering his cellphone, the words won't come out. And then finally, he spit her name in a heartbreaking sob.

"*Gabriella….*"

That's the only thing he says. Choking up, a gasp escapes his lips. He brings his hand up to cover his mouth, crying.

My world crumbles under my feet instantly. My nightmare becomes a reality. What happened these past months now makes sense. Every piece of the puzzle fits.

She knew it. That's why she stayed behind. She didn't want me to be there when it happened. She was protecting me again.

An invisible knife cuts my chest wide open, and the pain is so unbearable I can't breathe. Burning tears run down my face. They're mixed with rage and pain overflowing from my heart, leaving me gasping for air.

Realizing I'm going to live in a world where Gabriella isn't anymore makes everything meaningless. The glass flute drops from my hand, shattering in pieces. My legs can't hold me, and I fall on the floor, trying to assimilate this.

Marc drops his cell on the counter to catch me but arrives too late. He sits beside me, embracing my shoulders, crying with me.

This is not happening. Not now. Tomorrow I'll wake up to go back and find her waiting for me. Yes, she's waiting. She promised me. This isn't real. But the cruel voice of truth shouts at my face, mocking my pain.

She's gone… Gone forever. Finally I let out the most heart-wrenching scream anyone heard from me, releasing the sorrow strangling me. I cry in anger, for her to hear me.

"GABRIELLA!"

Chapter Twenty-Nine

Lukas

Xavier opens the door, moving aside to let me enter first. I walk inside, face distorted by the tidal wave of emotions drowning me.

"It's just a couple of minutes, won't take long," Xavier informs me while closing the door.

The memories this apartment holds hit me hard. I walk over to sit on the sofa. My strength left me days ago. We're dressed in black suits, white shirts, and black ties. My eyes sting. They're red from all the crying these last few days.

Today was Gabriella's memorial. It was a beautiful ceremony honoring her life, exactly the way she would have wanted. Everyone who knew her closely was there. Xavier gifted me a crystal pendant holding a small portion of her ashes to keep.

Together we scattered the rest over the ocean at the end of Santa Monica pier, one of her favorite places, as she requested. I'm so heartbroken right now. The pain makes me numb, lifeless.

A knock at the door interrupts us. Xavier opens it to find Marc, Lola, Shotaro, and Ty standing there.

"Sorry to interrupt, guys. Just wanted to let Lukas know we'll be waiting in the apartment. Take the time you both need, no rush. The jet leaves in five hours, and we're near the airport, so we still plenty of time, okay?" Marc says before walking away. Xavier closes the door again to regain privacy for what he's about to tell me.

"I want to start by apologizing to you, Lukas." Xavier's voice trembles. Hearing him, I raise my face to stare.

"The first time we met, I was so rude to you and Mom. I was so enraged with her, fueled by my dad's gossip when he called me after he found out you were together. I was ashamed of her for sleeping with someone younger. I was beyond reason."

He pauses for strength, then continues, "I didn't have any right to be mad at you guys. To be honest, I was madder at you than her. I thought you were taking advantage of her, of her heart. She was a kind woman, you know… I was wrong."

He lowers his eyes, catching his breath. Tears and sadness are strangling him too. Looking straight into my eyes, he emphasizes his words.

"Lukas, I want you to know what you two had was *so fucking special.*"

His voice is full of emotion, choked by pain.

"I love *Mami* with all my heart. To hear her explain in her last days how happy, loved, and complete you made her feel. She showed me the ring, the one you gave her. She was so grateful and blessed you chose her and for the time you spent together. She said she felt more alive, young, and loved as a woman with you than with anyone else, not even Dad. And for her to admit it to me was a big deal. Now she's gone. This is so unfair. I had no right to yell at her or at you." He stops talking as a sob breaks from his mouth.

Standing quickly, I squeeze his shoulder in reassurance.

"You don't have to apologize. She knew you cared for her more than anything. Believe me, she did. She knew you were only guided by love, to protect her."

"Man, I miss her so much."

Xavier finally breaks down crying, lowering his head. I realize the strength of his resemblance to Gabriella, and I'm overcome by a wave of love and sorrow.

It's her blood living through him. I can hug her one more time. I pulled Xavier in to embrace him, and we hug each other tightly for the first time, like brothers, tears wetting our faces, sharing our pain. He's the closest thing to Gabriella I have left.

"I know, I know, man. I understand. I miss her too," I confess, crying while stepping back.

We wipe our tears with the backs of our hands, composing ourselves the best we can. Xavier starts to tell me the part I was unaware of, the one she'd hidden from me.

"She called me before you guys left for the concerts. The same night Rene called her, she called me to tell me everything. She knew she was dying and time was short. She asked me to be with her once you left and not tell anyone. Made me promise I wouldn't tell you until now. No one knew exactly how much time she had left. The doctor gave her around two or three weeks at the rate the mass was growing. She lasted more than three months. Her doctors were amazed that she lasted so long and how strong her willpower was. She told them you were the reason, pushing her to fight."

He exhales his despair to continue, "Apparently the meds

she was taking stopped working for her. The mass grew more aggressively than before. Everything happened so fast, and her organs started to shut down, losing her normal bodily functions. First she lost movement of her legs and was confined to a wheelchair. Next, her kidneys went, and she was forced to start dialysis. I swear to you I tried to convince her to call you, to tell you the truth. But every time, she refused, making me promise not to tell you again. Her pride wouldn't allow you to run back, just to see her sick, and she didn't want you missing the awards and presentations. You know how stubborn and hot-headed she can be sometimes," Xavier adds, speaking of her like she's still here.

He describes, in detail, the conditions of her passing. Everything that had happened that morning. Learning about it crushes my heart even more, understanding the depth of her love for me. Needing me to be close but not wanting to be a burden. *Selfless and caring.*

I'm truly heartbroken and hollow knowing all this. To encounter in my life such a magnificent love like the one she'd gifted me, what we'd had, is priceless. This was once in a life time experience. Breathing deeply, I try to stay focused despite this whirlwind of despair threatening to choke me. I must be strong, like she would have wanted.

"One last thing," Xavier informs me while sniffling. "Mom left you this."

He pulls from his pocket an envelope with Gabriella's handwriting and a set of keys.

"I think she wrote this letter right after you left for the concerts. She made me promise to give it to you with the Mustang. You're the owner now. She did all the paperwork." I'm shocked.

"What? Why?"

He chuckles sadly. “The truth is, I don’t like old cars. She said you’d appreciated it more than me because of some backseat story.”

I force a sad grin. Taking the envelope and keys with trembling hands, I’m barely holding myself together, dreading what’s written in it. Finally we shake hands.

“Thanks. We’re family Xavier. You’re my brother. I’ll keep in touch, and if you ever need anything, please let me know. You have my direct phone number, so don’t hesitate to call.”

“Likewise to you. We’ll keep in touch,” Xavier answers and hugs me tight once more. “Thanks, Lukas. Thanks for giving her the happiness she deserved,” he adds as our final farewell.

I enter my apartment, numb. Everything is packed in boxes and ready to be moved. I ask everyone to give me some private time alone, so they go for a walk. I need to process all I learned.

The memories of our love had encountered in this apartment start to torment me. I remember the first time she told me she loved me, all drunk and flustered. And when we made love on the kitchen counter.

All those memories creep back. I smile sadly, remembering her, and immediately my heart constricts, painfully realizing we won’t have the chance to make more memories together.

Pain like a tsunami rises high above me, threatening to destroy me. I’m trying to breathe, and without her, I barely can. I don’t know what to do. For the first time in my life, I’m lost. And right then, I remember the letter.

Pulling it from my pocket, I read my name in her handwriting. With my index finger, I open the envelope and turn it upside down.

The first thing that falls is her ring. A sob stings my throat seeing it on my lap. Picking up the ring, I study it closely while remembering the day I put it on her finger.

Tears fall freely, unrestrained. She'd known she was going to die when she accepted it. A wave of rage and pain grows inside my chest. I can't hold it in anymore. *This is so fucking unfair.*

Losing composure, I start punching boxes, throwing things in rage, breaking vases. I'm in a desolate rampage. Crying out in anguish, almost screaming.

"You were supposed to wait for me. We were supposed to be married. I was going to give you your happy ending, Gaby."

Kicking one of the boxes, I trip, falling on the carpeted floor, in my tantrum, defeated, covering my face while crying for her like a lost child.

"I need you, Gaby. I miss you so much, baby. *Please... please... please...* please, come back, baby. I can't deal with this. I can't breathe without you." I sob aloud in denial, desperately looking everywhere, trying to make sense of this.

Taking my hands off my face, I see the ring on the carpet. I pick it up to kiss it like I did that day. Putting it in my pocket, shutting my eyes for an instant, I know this pain is going to cost me time and effort to overcome. If I'll ever overcome it.

I remember the letter. Turning, I see all of the papers scattered on the sofa. I reach to grab the pages, organize them, and read her final words. My heart pleads for an instant to tell her how much I love her. But reading this message, I'm positive she knows.

Sweetie:

I'm sorry for not telling the whole truth of what's happening with me. If you love me the same as I love you, you'll understand. I know if you were the sick one, you would do the same for me. That's how big your heart is. Time was too short to lament or dwell on it.

My intentions were that our last days together were the best, and for me, they were. The best days of my life. Plus I wanted you to remember me like the day we said goodbye at the airport, not seeing me sick. It isn't a pretty sight.

I'm heartbroken, knowing the pain I'll cause you when I'm gone. Life pulled this cruel joke on us. Especially on me, to find you at the end of my life. But I understand it was supposed to be this way.

Every single minute we spent together was worth it. You gave me the happiness I was searching for, abundantly and without limits. I discovered the extraordinary woman living in my skin because I saw her through your eyes.

I love the memories we created and treasured together, just the two of us. That's the biggest gift anyone can obtain in life, and I'll take them with me. The beauty of it is no one can steal it from us, baby. They're hidden where no one can reach them, inside our hearts.

Love is about finding a soulmate who fills in the missing pieces and makes you be a better person. I remember you told me this. We become better because we have each other. I learned through you love is limitless, it can't be contained. I rediscovered my strengths through you.

If I could leave you something, it would be the abil-

ity to see yourself through my eyes. Then you'd realize how extraordinary and amazing you are. Understand the power you carry inside to transform your destiny and others.

In the middle of my chaos, you became my peace. The best love story is when you fall in love with the most unexpected person at the most unexpected time. I was dead until we bumped into each other's lives, and you changed mine for the better. I love you so much, Papi.

I know in heaven we will meet again. But until then, LIVE, LUKAS. Live fully, passionately, and without reservations or limits. Promise you'll eventually heal and be ready to love again. Don't let happiness pass you by. When you see it, grab it with both hands and don't let go. That's what I did with you.

Give others what you carry inside your heart. It's too much to keep it to yourself, and the world needs it. The world needs your talent, your music, and your passion. It's there, ready for you to conquer, and you possess the ability to do it. Change it for the better.

I'm going ahead to wait for you at the pearly gates, baby. You'll be my highway to heaven, always. I promise to be the first in line, waiting. Yeah, the gorgeous Boricua girl dressed in white waiting there, you know, haciendo alboroto, making a fuss.

My love will cover and protect you. Love is the biggest, most powerful force in the universe. We've got this force inside, making us invincible.

Thanks for making me the happiest woman on earth by sharing your love with me. To live what I lived with you, sweetie, I can say for sure nothing can top that. For eternity, my heart will always be yours.

Te amo, mi vida. Sarang hae.

We are Unbreakable…

Eternally yours,
Gabriella

PS: Please, give Marc a chance to drive the Mustang, at least once. He wanted to, and given the circumstances, he's earned it.

Chapter Thirty

EPILOGUE

Lukas

Driving this dusty, desert road, it's inevitable I'll think about her. Memories of our last time together still haunt me. Images of her beauty and uniqueness pop in my mind from time to time. Her bubbly personality still makes me grin, recalling her. The familiar knot in my stomach starts to tighten, just with a glimpse of her memory. Thinking about her last night, during my concert in LA, I'd realized I have to do this. It's unavoidable. This is the closing we both deserve. You can't ignore the sting of the pain waiting for you, no matter how much you disregard it. The only way to get it over quickly is to go through it. Own it.

It's been two years since Gabriella passed away. Not a day goes by without remembering her. She's the type of woman who enters your life, transforming everything, even your way of thinking. Unrepeatable. She has affected me in ways I can't describe. Taught me there's more in life to aspire to. To love intensely, without reservations. It's taken this long to ease my pain, accepting I'll live with it.

Last night, I'd decided to drive back the same route we followed the glorious week we spent alone. I haven't been able to drive this road since then. I'm doing it in Gabriella's Mustang. Well my Mustang. After a fine tune-up, it was time to take this ruby baby out of storage for a ride. Time to gain closure to heal, grow, and move on. Still my heart aches for her. I miss her. Her smell, her body, her presence. The nourishment her soul had given me.

Driving by, I pass by a small restaurant, in the middle of nowhere, surrounded by pink and white flowers. It's the place we'd stopped to dine and got caught making love in the parking lot. I smirk, amused, remembering. I recall the owner taking a photo of us he put on his Guest Wall. An inner impulse tugs me to see if the photo is still there. Turning around, I park in front of the restaurant. I get out of the car, going inside like I'm a regular here.

What a difference from that night. The restaurant atmosphere is gloomy, almost empty. Besides three occupied tables, you'd never believe how alive and magical this place was last time. Taking off my sunglasses, I tuck them in my pocket to look around. Locating the Guest Wall, by the huge worn-out sign, I strut directly to it. As I approach, I recognize our yellowish photo, like we were. My heart constricts, staring at it.

That night, we were so happy. Her face glowing with joy, grinning widely. So full of life, laughing and dancing carelessly like a schoolgirl. I'm proud to be the reason for her smile, not thinking about tomorrow, only the now.

Fixing my eyes under the photo, I finally notice it. Hanging from the tack holding the photo is a silver chain bearing a piece of clear white crystal, similar to the kyber crystals we'd acquired at Disneyland. A dusty post it note under it makes my heart bleed, recognizing Gabriella's handwriting.

"The strongest stars have hearts of kyber."
– Rogue One
You'll be the brightest and strongest star.
And I'll be your kyber forever.
Welcome back.
Yours, Gabriella

I'm trying to breathe normally, but the sob rising in my throat is making it difficult. The wound in my heart bleeds again reading those words.

She'd known everything that would happen before it did, knew her time was short, and made the best of it. She'd known I would mourn her, and it would take time to heal but eventually I would. I'd come back to this place, seek our photo, and read this note. She'd known me so well. No one will know me like she had.

To experience love the way we had is a blessing. By divine grace our souls had connected as one. Our love surpasses everything, both body and soul. That's rare and special. I'm proud to be one of the lucky ones to experience this. I'm grateful.

Taking the chain from the tack, I pull it over my head to rest on my chest. I also grab the note, folding it to place it in my wallet.

Earl, the owner has been watching me since entering the restaurant. As I put my wallet in my back pocket, he proclaims aloud, "I remember you. *The coyote/honeymooners*. She came back a week later with another young man. She brought that chain. I remember because she found me to give me instructions. Feisty woman. Was very emphatic she leave it with the photo, sure you'll come back for it. Was wondering if you ever would. She was right."

He chuckles, amused. I glance at him, smiling with certain sadness.

"Yes, she was. She knew me well."

After a pause, I add, "Thanks."

Walking outside the restaurant, I put on my sunglasses. I gaze at the sky, mesmerized by the cotton-candy colors painting the clouds. It's a breathtaking California sunset. I watch it for a while, freezing this instant in my memory. Closing my eyes, filling my lungs with the healing this moment brings, this freedom she'd gifted me.

A soft breeze caresses my face. A hint of gardenia scent in the air fills my nostrils. My smile widens. It's her subtle way of letting me know she's here, and she's pleased. I lower my face, staring at the crystal in my hand.

"I'll live intensely for us, Gabriella. I understand I have the strength to do it. I'm ready for the next phase in my life. Thanks, my love. Until we meet again." Gently I kiss the crystal.

I enter the car, make a U-turn, and return to the same road I'd come from. There's no need to go further. The closure is done. I understand a life beyond her is possible. A good, fulfilling life. What she'd taught me will stay with me forever. I think I'm ready now for what the future holds for me. Grinning satisfied, I drive straight into the sunset, disappearing into the bright light. I'm ready to conquer the world as I'd promised her.

Every day I wait and wait…
For the day we meet again…
Promise you…

ABOUT THE AUTHOR

Gianna Maria was born in San Juan, Puerto Rico. She studied for twelve years of arts, including painting, drawing, sculpture, and piano in her younger years. After earning a bachelor's degree in advertising with a concentration in Public Relations and law studies, she worked with several advertising agencies in Puerto Rico and was a TV production assistant, where she studied video editing and TV production. Since her youth, she has written short stories, theater scripts, and poems, and drawn art for comic books. This is her first contemporary romance fiction novel. Has been a Star Wars fan since 1977. Now she's a full-time author located in Orange County, California.

For more information about the author, social media, and future books releases about the author you can scan the QR code bellow to visit her page at Linktree: linktr.ee/giannamaria author

Playlist of the music that inspired the book **HIGHWAY TO HEAVEN** available now on *Spotify* platform:

https://open.spotify.com/playlist/0waMlfsxNoWHT6MyBAgtY7?si=Of-MGIHDQc2aXclZMtF9lg

Don't forget to send your comments about the book to our email:

contact@giannamariaauthor.com

Made in the USA
Coppell, TX
14 June 2026

81528383R00246